Fortune's Sonata

EDWARD GLOVER

Published by Edward Glover

Cover photograph of the statue of Fortune on the Palace of Charlottenburg, Berlin © Frank Dinger

ISBN: 978-0-9929551-1-3

To Arabella, Countess von Deppe
A fictional life which inspired two books

Soave sia il vento
May the wind be gentle

Cosí fan tutti
Wolfgang Amadeus Mozart

CONTENTS

"True music is the language of the heart"

Jean-Philippe Rameau, Composer
1683–1764

"The greatest and noblest pleasure which we have in this world is to discover new truths, and the next is to shake off old prejudices"

Frederick the Great
1712–1786

FOREWORD

For a writer, memories, dreams and chance encounters may sometimes spark a work of fiction. But so, I believe, can pictures and relics of the past. Despite Berlin's recent architectural innovation and artistic renaissance, its troubled history still offers a rich source of the latter for stories. It has proved so for me.

As I described in the foreword to my previous novel, over twenty years ago in Berlin I acquired two eighteenth-century paintings. One was a portrait of Frederick the Great of Prussia, painted when he was comparatively young by a known artist. The other was a picture of an unknown, well-dressed, good-looking, middle-aged man, painted by an unnamed artist – apparently in 1765, according to a faded label on the reverse. Around the same time, in the city's well-known flea market, I found (amongst some 1938 German army call-up papers) an original British passport personally issued, in London on 3 October 1853, by the then Foreign Secretary, the Earl of Clarendon, to Robert Whitfield, his wife and son to travel on the European mainland. On the back are stamps of some of the German states the family visited.

Together, these three items persuaded me, much later, to write my first novel, *The Music Book*: the passport – a tangible, organic link to a real person in the past about whom I knew nothing but which provided a canvas on which to paint a fictional ancestor of the nineteenth-century Robert Whitfield; a portrait of an enlightened eighteenth-century king but who had an acknowledged dark side that could be exposed in fictional circumstances; and a painting of a man without a name, appealing for an identity. In the process of creating an imaginary identity for the unknown man, I was able to develop the primary female character, whose image is still only visible in my imagination but which I sought to describe in the book I had chosen to write. The result was the creation of two principal fictional figures – a young English woman, Arabella Whitfield, and a retired Prussian army officer, Carl Manfred von Deppe (based on the unknown man in the picture) – mingling with real historical personalities, such as Frederick the Great and King Louis of France, set in the period 1764–1766.

In *The Music Book*, Arabella, a passionate believer in a woman's right not to be treated as a chattel, runs away from home to avoid an arranged marriage. Accompanied by a mysterious stranger, von Deppe has undisclosed business in England on behalf of King Frederick. Arabella and von Deppe come face to face in London's demi-monde. Their fates become intertwined in a story of intrigue, revenge, death and redemption. The young woman's music book – one of her few treasured possessions and an accumulation not only of pieces of music but also of various writings and drawings, in the manner of a commonplace book – is the thread in the game of deception, which crosses to aristocratic Paris, continues in a bleak German winter landscape and plays out in the royal palace of Sanssouci in Potsdam. This was the story recounted in my first novel, published in May last year.

Though diplomats are used to solving difficult problems, despite many efforts over the years I had been unable to find out who the unidentified man in the picture really was. By writing *The Music Book* I finally unlocked both his identity and that of his painter.

The sitter was Wilhelm Rudolf Daniel Ludwig Philipp von Gall, a senior army officer who fought first in the Seven Years War and who later – from 1776 until 1781 – led his Hesse regiment, with various controversial ups and downs, alongside British forces in Canada and then during the American War of Independence. Subsequently, after time in prison for what appears to be alleged fraud, he became Chamberlain to the Duke of Sayn-Wittgenstein. Despite this discovery, I decided to leave *The Music Book* – and its principal male character, Carl Manfred von Deppe – unchanged.

As for the painter of the picture, a respected German art expert revealed it was most likely to be the Haina-born Anton Wilhelm Tischbein, the youngest of five sons of a master baker. Each son became a painter, including the most well-known, Johann Heinrich Tischbein the Elder. Anton Wilhelm eventually moved to Hanau where he remained until his death in 1804, as painter to the Court of Prince William; he painted not only the family members of his royal masters but also other wealthy patrons, in Frankfurt and elsewhere.

Once *The Music Book* was written, the principal characters began to press me to know what happened to them in later life. Where would the thread lead? So with pleasure I began during last year's brilliant Norfolk summer to write the sequel. As in my previous novel a musical theme is evident throughout the book.

I believe that fortune – whether good or ill – can play some part in our lives whether we wish it or not. The von Deppe and Whitfield families and the characters around them – some fictional and some historically real – were no exception to this rule of life. Above the Royal Palace of Charlottenburg in Berlin – built before Frederick the Great came to the throne but which he embellished, and which I often visited while living and working in Berlin in the late 1980s – there is a wind vane, cast in the figure of Fortune, or Fortuna as the original Roman goddess is better known. Like all weather vanes, in gusty wind it swivels to and fro, making a music of its own as it does so. This representation of Fortuna, believed in the classical world to be an arbiter of fate, led me to the title of this book – *Fortune's Sonata* – since the principal characters are buffeted by sudden winds beyond their control, yet together form a coherent whole, like the elements in a piece of music. At the same time, the book's protagonist, the independent, determined Arabella, strives to create something positive out of the hand Fortune deals her, with music itself often being the vehicle of her achievements.

* * * * *

I wish to draw the reader's attention to six facts about this book.

First, for ease of narrative, I have used the Gregorian calendar – the internationally accepted civil calendar – throughout, with no adjustment for local variation, either in the case of the French

Revolutionary calendar or of the Julian calendar, to which the Orthodox Church in Russia still adhered in the time of Catherine the Great. For that reason, in Chapter Three, I have exercised a writer's licence to state that in St Petersburg, in 1768, the celebration of the Feast of the Epiphany took place on the 6th of January as opposed to the later date, under the Julian calendar, of the 19th of January. Second, all the dates in the book correspond with the actual calendar for each year in which the action occurs. Third, again for ease of reading, I have used – with one exception – anglicised versions of European names throughout rather than different national language versions. Fourth, it has proved difficult to calculate precise journey times by coach or horse within different countries and across international borders. I have therefore simply guessed the length of time specific journeys might have taken. I do not think this approach detracts from the storyline. Fifth, the book spans a long period of time – from 1766 to 1816 – during which time the harpsichord lost ground to the pianoforte. More precisely, grands began to emerge during the 1770s, equalled harpsichords in the 1780s, and definitely overtook them in the 1790s. But the speed of replacement was not uniform; it varied from place to place, though in Germany it appears they came into use earlier than elsewhere. For the purposes of this story I have vaguely introduced a grand into Schloss Herzberg in the late 1780s, and accordingly references in the latter part of the book to keyboard playing suggest a pianoforte rather than a harpsichord. Last but not least, though the book refers to certain actual historical figures, I wish to emphasise that their dialogue is entirely fictional – my own invention. What you may assume, however, is that nearly all of the fictional conversations in the book would have been in French, which was the international language at that time.

* * * * *

I would not have completed this book without the help, support and advice of a circle of invaluable friends.

My first thanks go to Jenny Langford, my patient and tireless researcher who, despite other pressing preoccupations more deserving of her time, investigated various facts and suppositions, and read and corrected early drafts of the book as well as preparing the family trees for the von Deppe and Whitfield families. The book refers to a lawyer in Norfolk, Elisha De Hague, whom I have incorporated into the story. He actually existed. It was Jenny who found him and who discovered that in January 1776 he paid stamp duty for the recruitment of an apprentice (an articled clerk) called Edward Glover. Much-deserved gratitude goes to Niall Cook who, as with my first book, designed the artwork and in so many other ways prepared *Fortune's Sonata* for publication. Equally deserved thanks go to Sue Tyley, my highly professional and experienced copy-editor, who once again waved her magic wand to improve punctuation, grammar and style. Nothing missed her eagle eye, which is as it should be. I wish also to thank Julia Rafferty, a highly accomplished freelance photographer and photography tutor, for her contribution to the reproduction of the map in Appendix 2. Equal gratitude goes to Julia Bell, Senior Lecturer in Creative Writing and Convenor of the MA in Creative Writing at Birkbeck, University of London – my postgraduate alma mater – for her literary advice, technical assistance and encouragement. She and I share a profound love for the city of Berlin.

There are others who receive my gratitude.

First, I wish to thank Madame Odile Castro, my French friend and neighbour in Norfolk, who provided excellent advice on the French Revolution, the backdrop to my story, and who helped invent some fictional French names. Thanks also go to her sister, Marie-Claire, with her longer-distance advice from Paris. Second, I send my personal thanks to Eleanor Christian, a lawyer and close family friend, who provided much-needed advice on eighteenth-century English wills and property entailment. Third, my abundant thanks go to Katya Gladka in Ukraine, a colleague of my wife's, who most kindly helped me with Russian names and nomenclature to which I had need of recourse. Once again I send my warmest appreciation to Bianca and Jurgen Freymuth-Brumby for their invaluable research of German material for my book.

To switch from the art of diplomatic drafting to novel writing requires patience, determination and a different mental approach. I wish to thank Lady Fiona Fraser, a close and long-standing personal friend, who kindly helped to launch my first book in North Norfolk, and so enable me to begin to gain recognition as a writer, but who also encouraged me to write this sequel, and who kept an eye on me as I did. I convey equally warm thanks to Simon Rowland-Jones, violist, composer and founding violist of the Chilingirian Quartet, best known for his arrangement of the Bach Cello Suites for viola. Simon, together with his baroque-expert friend, Dr David Ledbetter, helped me with important eighteenth-century musical information. I thank too John Needham, a close neighbour and friend, who provided me with invaluable material relating to England in the late eighteenth and early nineteenth centuries and the importance of drawing at that time.

As for source material, I wish to acknowledge the deeply impressive exhibition *Catherine the Great: An Enlightened Empress* at the National Museum of Scotland in 2013. The exhibits and catalogue provided a valuable insight into the Empress, her rule and her approach to art and culture generally. I also acknowledge the equally impressive exhibition *The First Georgians: Art & Monarchy 1714–1760* at The Queen's Gallery, Buckingham Palace, last year, which provided a fascinating picture of this remarkable period in British history. Not least I wish to thank the BBC for their compelling television series, presented by Suzy Klein, exploring music, mischief and morals during the eighteenth century. The two exhibitions and the BBC series gave me excellent material to help validate some of what I have written. Another helpful exhibition I wish to acknowledge is *Germany: Memories of a Nation* at the British Museum. It – and Neil MacGregor's much-valued accompanying book – helped shine particular light on the essential backdrop to my book. I also wish to acknowledge Stephen Green's recent book about Germany, *Reluctant Meister*; Andrew Roberts's comprehensive biography, *Napoleon the Great*; and Jan Swafford's book *Beethoven: Anguish and Triumph*. All three were useful sources of background information, as was Faramerz Dabhoiwala's book *The Origins of Sex: A History of the First Sexual Revolution*.

I wish again to acknowledge Nancy Mitford's outstanding book on Frederick the Great, written so many years ago but as enjoyable and as enriching as ever; and Lady Antonia Fraser's fascinating and highly readable book *Marie Antoinette: The Journey*, which helped me to paint a vivid picture of life at the Palace of Versailles, so creating some fictional opportunities for me to develop. Sebastian Haffner's *The Rise and Fall of Prussia* was an equally invaluable source of background material. I also wish to acknowledge Classic FM's impressive *The Big Book of Classical Music*, which was a good source for key dates in the musical calendar and quotations; its publication last year was timely. Moreover, I thank Classic FM and BBC Radio 3 for providing countless hours of musical enjoyment from which I was able to choose orchestral pieces that I imagined the Camerata Herzberg might have played in their growing repertoire, as well as the arias that its founder and patron, the Countess von Deppe, might have sung over the years. Appendix 4 includes a selection of pieces that helped to inspire a few of the scenes in the book.

I wish to thank my wife, Audrey, for her continuing inspiration and for allowing me to spend longer than planned alone with my laptop to unfold the story I wished to tell; my daughter Caroline, who, assisted by her eldest daughter, Amelia, did valuable research into the short life of Luise von Mecklenburg-Strelitz, who aged only seventeen married Crown Prince Frederick William of Prussia, later King Frederick William III of Prussia; and my younger daughter, Charlie, and my two sons, Rupert and Crispin, for their regular encouragement of this project, despite leading busy lives of their own. And my thanks also go to my fitness trainer, Chris Langley-Waylen, for keeping me in good physical shape.

Last but not least, my thanks go to our many friends in Norfolk and London who, having read *The Music Book*, urged me to hurry along with the sequel. I hope that *Fortune's Sonata* will meet their and your expectations.

Edward Glover
North Norfolk
March 2015

DRAMATIS PERSONAE PRIMAE

Prussia

Countess Arabella Mariette von Deppe
Count Carl Manfred von Deppe, her husband
Frederick Daniel von Deppe, their son
Elise Catherine Hildegard von Deppe, their daughter
King Frederick II of Prussia, known as Frederick the Great
Waldemar Drescher, the man in the shadows
Countess Katherina von Schlegel, companion to King Frederick
Father Johann Schmidt, priest to the Countess von Deppe
Herr Albrecht Bamberger, leader of the Schloss Herzberger Camerata
Mr (later Sir) Charles Gray, visitor to Herzberg
Andrew Mitchell, British Ambassador to the Kingdom of Prussia
Viscount Dalrymple, British Ambassador to the Kingdom of Prussia
Lieutenant Joseph Lange von Schellenhorst, friend of Crown Prince Frederick William
Luise von Mecklenburg-Strelitz, future wife of Crown Prince Frederick William of Prussia
Crown Prince Frederick William of Prussia, later King Frederick William III of Prussia

Russia

The Empress Catherine, known as Catherine the Great
Count Nikolay Sokolov, suitor to the Empress
Countess Kseniya Sokolova, Count Sokolov's wife

France

Vicomte Etienne de Vervins, aide de camp to General de la Rivière and later to Louis XVI
Vicomtesse Maria Louisa de Vervins, his wife and sister to Count von Deppe
Marie-Aurore, Comtesse de Puyraveau, daughter of the Vicomte and Vicomtesse de Vervins
Armand, Comte de Puyraveau and husband of Marie-Aurore, the

Comtesse de Puyraveau
Louis XVI, King of France
Marie-Antoinette, Queen of France
The prisoner in the Bastille
Jacqueline d'Anville, daughter of the Comte and Comtesse d'Anville
Robert Trudaine, friend of Frederick Daniel von Deppe

England
Lady Thérèse Whitfield, mother of Arabella, Countess von Deppe
Sir Robert Whitfield, husband of Lady Whitfield
George Whitfield, their son, missing in France
Mr Elisha De Hague Snr, attorney in Norwich to the Whitfield family
Mr Elisha De Hague Jnr, successor to his father as attorney to the Whitfield family

PROLOGUE

After a week's stay in Paris, followed by a brief diversion to see Aachen Cathedral, Robert Whitfield, his wife, Emily, and their young son, Charles, arrived in Berlin on Monday the 14th of November 1853, four weeks after leaving Dover. They had been following the footsteps of a forebear, the young Arabella Whitfield, who had left the same port for Calais and beyond eighty-eight years before, in dire circumstances.

Full of manufacturing enterprises and innumerable small workshops and markets, the city of Berlin bustled and hummed – visibly bursting its medieval walls. Textile products, clothing, farm and railway equipment, chemicals and machinery were on sale everywhere. Steam engines pumping water were frequent and noisy. The streets were thronged with people, horses and carriages. The evident poor sanitary conditions – with waste water from houses collecting in the gutters, emitting a strong and unpleasant smell – were for the Whitfields one of the less attractive and most noticeable, indeed unavoidable, features of the city.

After making his family and himself comfortable in their hotel, Robert Whitfield, without further delay, wrote a note to the British Ambassador to Prussia, His Excellency Baron John Bloomfield, Envoy Extraordinary and Minister Plenipotentiary to the Kingdom of Prussia, asking if he might call on him at his earliest convenience to seek his assistance in tracing the descendants of his ancestor, who had married a retired senior Prussian military officer in 1766 and who had lived in Prussia for the rest of her life. He had with him a letter of introduction from the Earl of Clarendon, Secretary of State for Foreign Affairs, who had issued the Whitfields' passport in London on the 3rd of October. As the Foreign Secretary's letter recorded, the Ambassador's help was important to realising Robert Whitfield's desire to make contact with the Prussian family into which his forebear had married and, if possible, to establish a bond of friendship between the two families, a gesture that the Secretary of State warmly encouraged. The Ambassador replied promptly, inviting Robert Whitfield to call on him the next day at four o'clock in the afternoon. He pledged to do his best to help but, without more precise information, his assistance might be limited.

The Ambassador's residence was within walking distance from the hotel and close to the ancient, lime-tree-lined boulevard Unter den Linden. Robert Whitfield went alone, leaving his wife in the company of a guide to take their son to see one of the plentiful museums and yet more noisy steam engines belching out smoke and heat. The Ambassador's residence was large, attractive and well-furnished. Judging by the extent of his personal possessions it was evident that His Excellency had been resident in Berlin for several years. After an exchange of pleasantries and questions from the Ambassador about the latest London news, Foreign Office gossip (he was eager to make the most of the opportunity to quiz a fellow diplomat, Mr Whitfield's position having been revealed by the letter of introduction) and the state of the English autumn weather, the British representative to the Prussian kingdom invited Mr Whitfield to his library so he could explain in more detail the purpose of his journey to Berlin.

Robert Whitfield explained to the Ambassador that he had discovered from a long-hidden music book that his father's step-sister, Arabella Whitfield, had left the family home of Meltwater in North Norfolk suddenly in 1765; the details remained unclear, though her departure had apparently been a matter of intense gossip in Norfolk and London at the time. After some months in the capital (staying in Mayfair, in possibly insalubrious circumstances), Miss Whitfield had travelled to Paris in the company of a retired senior Prussian military officer, Colonel Carl Manfred von Deppe, and another person, whose identity had never been disclosed. Subsequently, in deep winter, she had travelled alone to Potsdam, where several months later she had married Colonel von Deppe. Robert Whitfield said he wished to find out what had happened to her thereafter.

He placed the music book in front of the Ambassador, explaining that it appeared to have been a gift to Arabella Whitfield from her mother, Lady Thérèse Whitfield. Judging by its condition and some of the sketches within, it seemed she had taken the book with her on her journey almost ninety years before. It had undoubtedly been a treasured possession. He had recently found it – locked away at Meltwater Hall in Norfolk – amongst the personal possessions of Lady Thérèse, who had died in 1773. The discovery had inspired him to find out more about his forebear. He hoped His Excellency might be able to help.

The Ambassador picked up the music book and leafed through its loose pages. Neither man spoke. The only sound came from a ticking clock. Though not an accomplished musician, Baron Bloomfield was instantly struck by some of the transcriptions of works by Johann Sebastian Bach and other famous composers. He noticed in particular some delicate pen-and-ink drawings – scarcely thumbnail size – of a large house framed by trees. One sketch had the name Herzberg beneath it and another portrayed two figures sitting on a bench beneath a tall tree with the house in the distance behind them. The Ambassador put the book down.

"Mr Whitfield," he said, "what a fascinating book you have shown me. It could be worth a significant amount of money. You might wish to take it to Mr Ascher's bookshop on the Unter den Linden. Sadly, Mr Ascher died earlier this year, in Venice, but his assistants are equally knowledgeable. They will surely be intrigued by the book and prepared to say how much it might be worth. They should know, after all, as they provide the British Museum with valuable historical manuscripts."

"But I do not wish to sell the music book," protested Robert Whitfield.

"I am not suggesting you should," countered His Excellency, "but it might nonetheless be desirable to have experienced bibliophiles look at the contents, particularly since they have clearly prompted you to come all the way to Berlin at this inclement time of the year."

"Of course, you are right," replied Mr Whitfield, somewhat defensively.

After pausing, the Ambassador continued.

"You refer to the von Deppe family. Their home is Schloss Herzberg, now in these modern times less than a day's journey from Berlin. It is a fine and imposing house, as I recall from a visit I made there some years ago. It is now in the possession of Count Joseph von Deppe and his wife, the Countess Beatrice. They share Herzberg with their family. Arabella, Countess von Deppe, the Arabella Whitfield to whom I think you are referring, was Count Joseph's great-grandmother. She is still a much-revered woman in Prussia. She was a great musician and singer, the founder of an orchestra, an acquirer of an impressive collection of paintings, an astute landowner, and a great friend of Queen Luise, wife of the late King Frederick William III, particularly during the difficult years of Napoleon's invasion of Prussia. Count Joseph is a senior official in the Prussian parliament and his brother-in-law has a position at the royal palace. Both families are gracious, open-minded and much-respected, with equally charming children. If it would help you I will write to Count Joseph immediately, to ask him if he would meet you while you are in Berlin."

"Your Excellency, I am deeply grateful to you for giving me your time and for shedding some light on the Countess Arabella and her life in Prussia after her marriage to Colonel von Deppe. I also thank you for kindly and generously offering to write to Count Joseph. I should find that most helpful."

"Very well," replied the Ambassador. "It will be done as soon as you have left. And do not forget Mr Ascher's bookshop. Their opinion of what you have shown me may be most useful. Of course, it will be for you to decide whether to disclose the existence of the music book to Count Joseph. I know that at Schloss Herzberg they have assembled a collection of personal items belonging to the Countess. I am sure they would like to have it. But you have already said you wish to keep it."

"Yes, I do," Robert Whitfield replied.

With that he took leave of the Ambassador to return to the hotel and recount to Emily, his wife, what he had learnt. Later that evening, he recorded his conversation with the Ambassador in his journal, which he intended to submit to the Earl of Clarendon on his return to London.

The next day Robert Whitfield took the music book to Mr

Ascher's shop on the Unter den Linden. It was a veritable cave of books and manuscripts collected over the years. But a great sadness had clearly enveloped the shop following the death two months before of the owner, Adolphus Ascher, at the comparatively young age of fifty-three. One of the assistants studied the music book closely, asking as he did so from where it had come. Robert Whitfield explained. After a long examination, the assistant pronounced the book to be a rare find, particularly since some of the musical transcriptions were originals. He asked if Mr Whitfield wished to sell it. He could offer a good price. Whitfield said he wished to keep the book. It belonged to his family in England and he was obliged to return it to their safekeeping. The bookseller was obviously disappointed by the reply. If Mr Whitfield should change his mind while he was in Berlin, Ascher's would be ready to propose a rewarding price.

The following day Robert Whitfield received a letter from Count Joseph von Deppe, suggesting that he come to the parliament building on Monday, the 21st of November. He replied immediately that he would be delighted to do so.

Joseph von Deppe received the Englishman in one of the imposing parliamentary state rooms. The Count was tall, straight-backed and elegantly dressed. He moved with ease and grace and, though appearing at first somewhat withdrawn in manner, he had a warming smile. He spoke excellent English.

"How can I help you, Mr Whitfield?" he asked.

"I have come to ask about one of my forebears, whom I believe was your great-grandmother, Arabella, Countess von Deppe. My father inherited Meltwater Hall in England, where she was born, and I recently found this music book amongst her mother's personal belongings."

He pulled the battered leather-bound music book from his satchel and handed it to Count Joseph. The Count began to turn the loose pages slowly, doing so with great care, often pausing to study particular sheets with rapt attention. From time to time he paused to look towards the window, apparently lost in thought.

"Thank you, Mr Whitfield, for coming to Berlin and showing me this book. I sincerely appreciate your most kind gesture. The book is an unexpected and poignant reminder of a truly beautiful woman, a tirelessly attentive wife and loving mother, a gifted musician and a most trusted servant of the kingdom. Both King Frederick and, subsequently, King Frederick William III greatly valued her talents and her loyalty. Even though many years have elapsed since her death she is still much missed by us all."

The Count turned and pulled from a large leather bag beside his chair a small elegantly framed portrait.

"This," he said, "is your forebear. It was painted in 1768, some months after the birth of her first child."

He held the picture towards Robert Whitfield.

The finely executed and nuanced pastel drawing – with its subtle colours and exquisite use of light and shade – showed a vivacious, confident and smiling young woman, looking directly at the viewer and wearing a revealing low-cut off-the-shoulder dress in the fashion of that time. Her complexion seemed almost translucent. Her dark hair was loosely tied back with a pink ribbon, one end of which ran down the side of her neck. Behind in the distance was the outline of a large house.

Robert Whitfield audibly gasped at the image before him.

"Thank you for showing me this. She was a most beautiful woman."

"Indeed, she was," replied the Count. "My great-grandfather thought so too, which is why he fell so quickly in love with her. Their love and respect for each other never waned throughout their married life. They brought a sad and forgotten family back to life – with love, music and art. We, their descendants, are deeply proud of them, as are so many others in the kingdom. But, Mr Whitfield, I will be blunt. Sir Robert Whitfield, her father, behaved unforgivably towards her. His cruelty, even deeper than the cruelty to his wife, caused the Countess immense pain, but, through her bravery, she was able to find a new life in Prussia at my great-grandfather's side. The radiance of this picture masks the lasting legacy of bitterness she felt towards her father. I am afraid your visit has disturbed what may best be forgotten."

The Count's reproof was palpable.

Robert Whitfield's mouth was dry. He found it difficult to express words after the censure he had just experienced.

"I apologise profoundly for what may have happened to the Countess in England – at the hands, moreover, of my namesake. I did not know of the conduct to which you have referred. So that I can understand better, it would help me greatly if you would be kind enough to tell me more of the Countess's life in Prussia after her marriage to Colonel von Deppe."

"Return tomorrow morning and I will tell you before I leave Berlin on pressing parliamentary business."

"I will gladly do so," replied Mr Whitfield. "If you agree, I should like to bring my wife, Emily, and son, Charles."

"Please do so," replied the Count. "I will ask my own wife to join us, so that in the – I venture to say, unlikely – event that your wife and son do not find Countess Arabella's story as compelling as I feel certain you yourself will, she may accompany them on a walk in the nearby park."

The next day, the 22nd of November, Robert Whitfield, this time with his wife and son, returned to the parliament building to hear more about Arabella, Countess von Deppe. Three days later the family left Berlin to begin their journey back to London, the much-travelled music book still in their possession. As the train left the Anhalter Bahnhof, they re-opened the music book and, as they leafed through it, reflected on what they had been told – a story of light and darkness.

PART ONE: ALLEGRO CON BRIO
SUNLIGHT AND SHADOWS 1766–1778

CHAPTER 1

Schloss Herzberg

It was Friday the 20th of June 1766.

The long drive from the main road, which went in one direction towards Potsdam and in the other towards Magdeburg, crossed a small river marking the western boundary of the Herzberg estate before leading eventually to the house itself. The estate through which the drive passed was largely open land, interspersed with small areas of woodland, each cluster of trees now an oasis of tranquillity and translucent sunlight, but in the winter dark and impenetrable places of stillness and lurking gloom. On that early summer's day a mist from the previous cold night was quickly evaporating in the warmth of the rising sun. The trees continued to cast the drive in shade. But as the morning advanced, ever stronger and higher beams of light penetrated each copse and bathed the road and the open farmland in rich, clear brightness. Further along the drive Schloss Herzberg suddenly emerged from behind a last bastion of woodland.

The foundations and original, small fabric of the house dated back to the early sixteenth century, but over the past 150 years it had grown in size and elegance. Square in design and surrounded by an expansive garden below a broad patio, the red, brick house had large downstairs windows while those on the floor above were smaller, yet their proportions still fitted perfectly with the architectural symmetry of the entire building. To the front of the house a somewhat Palladian-style portico had been added, which brought distinction and depth to what had originally been a modest structure. Against the now cloudless sky, the white colonnades of the portico helped to reflect the glare of the sun onto the surrounding lawns. The overall effect was of understated wealth and Prussian stability. This had long been the home of the von Deppe family, the owners of a large estate that had steadily increased in size, wealth and influence.

Any visitor would have been struck by the singular, almost breathtaking beauty of Schloss Herzberg. Previously known simply as Herzberg, the estate had, since the beginning of the year, acquired its new prefix on the insistence of one particular visitor, due to return again to the estate on that June day.

There was much coming and going within and around the house during the long, warm day. In the evening there was to be a *fête champêtre*. Though it would bear little comparison to the extravagant garden entertainment at the French court, where areas of Versailles were landscaped with *folies*, pavilions and temples, the event at Herzberg would nonetheless be tasteful and elegant. The limpid, lazy river near the road meandered slowly on its way as each hour of preparation passed. By the evening the sun sat heavy and low in the sky, casting shafts of soft but still-defined light across the house and its gardens. With each remaining hour the warmth of the day sank ever closer to the ground; the temperature was still comfortable but with a touch of moisture on the grass, and the air was filled with the scent of roses and honeysuckle. Birds chirruped and lanterns were being prepared for when the sun would finally disappear behind the trees in the west. Candlelight began to appear in the windows of the house. Strains of music began to float on the evening air, as the first of a long line of carriages followed the driveway towards the house. Ladies – suitably powdered and coiffed – emerged from their coaches in fine dresses inspired by the pastoral scene to take the arm of men in well-cut frock coats and wigs. Finally a larger carriage arrived – deep cream with the emblem of the black Prussian eagle on its sides. The guests parted to pay deference to its royal occupant. With his arrival, the evening celebration of summer had begun.

The great and the good, the rich and the powerful, and the titled and untitled of Prussia were present at Schloss Herzberg, together with ambassadors and ministers plenipotentiary. All had accepted the invitation with alacrity. The presence of the King apart, many came out of curiosity to witness a new era at this large and impressive estate, and of course to take a closer look at the much talked about new Countess von Deppe. Men in white breeches, patterned waistcoats and knee-length coats constantly doffed their hats to acquaintances more and less familiar while the ladies on their arms, wearing elegant dresses (hooped and unhooped) and sheltering under broad-brimmed hats or lace parasols, bobbed up and down. Seated close to the trees, an orchestra played discreetly. Whether the guests were attached or unattached, it was – though unspoken – a joyous celebration of friendship; and naturally, barely hidden beneath the surface were whims of flirtation, courtship and requited and unrequited love. This rural and somewhat baroque idyll had the air of a garden of unalloyed pleasure to which the master painter Peter Paul Rubens would have done justice with his palette of paints and the stylish and dazzling strokes of his brush.

At the centre of this pastoral tableau of colour, deference and good taste was His Majesty King Frederick of Prussia in his customary simple blue uniform, together with the Count and Countess von Schlegel and their hosts, the Count and Countess von Deppe. Though the King had visibly aged to those who had not seen him in recent years and was still deeply preoccupied with advancing Prussia's expansion, he was in good spirits that evening as he sat on a high-backed, red-velvet armchair at the top of the steps leading from the patio to the garden below, observing the guests who had gathered for the occasion. He had been to Herzberg before to enjoy the tranquillity of the estate and to admire the application of new farming techniques he had long advocated. Now he had another reason for coming.

To his right sat Count Ernst von Schlegel, now elderly, and beside him his much younger second and exceptionally striking wife, Katherina, in a low-necked dark-blue flowing satin dress and wearing a large diamond necklace. With dark hair, high cheekbones and flashing blue eyes, inherited from her mother, she had long been regarded as one of the beauties of the King's court. She was rarely absent from court events, ready to offer discreet advice and opinions in such matters as the King's sometimes tempestuous relations with the Russian Empress Catherine, his wily opponent in the game of territorial ambition. To the King's left was Count Carl Manfred von Deppe, owner of Herzberg and formerly a senior officer in the King's bodyguard. The Count had been one of the most trusted and loyal of the monarch's officers, and the year before, at the King's command, he had been on a secret mission to England to discharge a deeply unpleasant order. As a result of his reconfirmed loyalty, King Frederick had appointed him Count and drawn him back into his diminishing circle of advisers on other secret business, together with the man in the shadows who had accompanied him to London. The last person in this vignette was the English-born Arabella Whitfield, now, since her marriage to Carl Manfred in Berlin earlier in the year, Countess von Deppe.

Arabella, a Catholic, who had just celebrated her twenty-third birthday, wore a yellow satin dress with a low bodice, revealing even more of her breasts than the Countess Katherina. Unhooped, the dress followed more closely the contours of her slim and willowy body. Arabella was vivacious, flirtatious and provocatively attractive. Her almond-shaped face was open; she had large green luminous eyes, and lips that were an accurate representation of Cupid's bow; and she possessed long naturally dark hair, which on this occasion (contrary to her usual style) was pinned up, though without additional adornment. Born in England at Meltwater Hall in Norfolk, she was the daughter of Sir Robert Whitfield, a wealthy landowner, while her French mother, Thérèse de Miron, came from a well-known and prosperous family south of Paris. Many who had watched Arabella grow up considered her even more beautiful than her mother, particularly as she had consistently eschewed the rouge and heavy make-up that other young women of her age tended to apply to the detriment of their complexion.

Arabella was strong-willed, well-read, a gifted harpsichordist and an equally fine soprano. Her music teacher at Meltwater, Herr Kunzl, had given her the title of *Kapellmeisterin*, the family's court musician. She had left home suddenly, rather than surrender to her father's choice of husband. After several painful, dark and distraught months in London, about which she had divulged no detail but others speculated readily, Arabella met her future husband at the establishment where she was staying in hiding. Their hurried departure from England was succeeded by several weeks in Paris, which included a musical encounter with King Louis of France and came to an end when she followed Colonel von Deppe (as he then was) to Prussia; there they had professed their deep love for one another and married in the chapel of the Royal Palace in Berlin. That June evening Arabella was blissfully happy at her husband's side.

With the sun finally below the horizon, the King turned to his host.

"Count, let's have less of this tiresome *Tafelmusik*. We need more lively notes to raise our spirits at the end of this day of warmth."

"Of course, Your Majesty. I will arrange it instantly," responded Carl Manfred von Deppe.

"No, you will not," interjected the King. "Your charming wife, who played for me so expertly at the beginning of the year, is better suited to the task. Come, Countess, what can you offer to cheer an old man?"

Arabella rose and curtsied before him.

"What are your wishes, Your Majesty?" she said, smiling.

"I leave that to you. Something lively and beguiling, like you, and as quickly as you can," he replied.

Arabella blushed.

"So be it," she said.

Arabella left the patio and quickly approached the orchestra. She spoke to the young conductor, Herr Bamberger, whom she had recently recruited to assist with collecting a musical repertoire to add to the handsome leather-bound music book the King had graciously given her some months before. With shared musical enthusiasms and Arabella's encouragement, Herr Bamberger had brought together a group of talented young musicians, including young women, who, Arabella thought – rather ambitiously – might one day form the heart of a respected orchestra at Herzberg. Though Herr Bamberger looked even younger than his age of twenty, he had already proved to be an accomplished conductor, harpsichordist and violinist. For his part, he was already hopelessly in love with his young patron. He dared not disclose or even hint that she had captured his heart so spectacularly. But Arabella knew his secret – a woman's intuition, you might say. She was amused and from time to time flirted with him in order to see his blushes, and his further embarrassment when he knew she had noticed his red cheeks.

"Herr Bamberger, the King has asked for livelier music," Arabella whispered in his ear. "Whether this might lead to a royal jig I do not know," she added, giggling behind her hand. "What do you suggest?"

The young man reflected, but his suggestions did not seem suited to what Arabella thought was required.

"Do you remember those minuets, jigs and gavottes by Agostino Steffani that we played some weeks ago? Play the lively ones and see what happens."

"Countess, your choice is inspired."

"Thank you, Herr Bamberger. What would I do without you?" she said, her hand touching his arm.

Blushing, he turned to the orchestra and, once they had found the music, began to conduct. The change of tempo had an instant effect as people looked up at the louder, faster beat and then, with encouragement from one another, began to dance. The stately tableau at Herzberg suddenly sprang into life, accompanied by the noise of laughter. And there was a new frisson in the air.

Arabella returned to her husband's side.

"At last," said the King, "the Countess returns and with her the sun. You are a young woman of many parts and skills. Your husband has more than met his equal." The monarch paused in thought, then continued: "I must leave soon to return to Berlin, but before I do so I should like to dance."

Those around him looked in astonishment. The Countess von Schlegel stepped forward immediately. The King offered her his arm and they walked down the patio steps as the music increased in tempo. Arabella accepted the arm of her husband, who squeezed her hand tightly and whispered, "My dearest Arabella, it appears you have worked a miracle. I am amazed how you mould your musician friends in your own tastes. And Bamberger has fallen hopelessly for you – not without some flirtation on your part, I might add."

"I know," said Arabella, giggling. "How irresponsible of me."

They joined the King and the Countess von Schlegel in some gavottes.

As Arabella danced a minuet Herr Bamberger turned and

caught her eye. She mouthed the word "faster". At the end of the minuet he raised his baton to signal an even quicker pace and the orchestra began to play the overture to Agostino Steffani's *Il trionfo del fato.*

On hearing the roll of the drums the King suddenly turned to Arabella.

"My dear Countess, I wish to have the last dance with you."

Taking his leave of Katherina von Schlegel, he offered Arabella his arm and to the driving drum beat of the overture the two began to dance. The other dancers fell back to watch, with the Countess von Schlegel standing beside Carl Manfred von Deppe.

Whether the notoriously wily King's gesture at the beginning of a martial overture was spontaneous exuberance or premeditated plan, its significance was not lost on those who made it their business to observe the conduct of the affairs of state. The Prussian King, unknown for open demonstrations of this nature, was dancing with the English countess, as she had rapidly become known. Was this a deliberate but nonetheless subtle public declaration of his wish for an alliance with England against Russia and Austria? Or was it the result of a bold and calculated move by the English countess to advocate an English alliance? The prevailing view that evening was that the answer lay with the King, since the young Arabella von Deppe was too new to the court scene to be an accomplished schemer.

As the dance ended, the King remarked to Arabella, "Your dancing is as exquisite as your musical talent. You must come and play for us later in the year at Charlottenburg. I insist on that. Count von Deppe, I expect you to see that it happens."

Carl Manfred nodded.

With that the King departed. The guests continued to dance until midnight and then they too left, still speculating about the King's sudden change of dance partner – from the Countess Katherina, so often in close and almost inseparable proximity to the monarch, to the English-born Countess Arabella.

Nor did the royal gesture towards Arabella escape the attention of the British, Austrian and Russian ambassadors, well used to fathoming the significance of unspoken signs and actions. There were already rumours of the prospect of renewed war. The Empress Catherine of Russia well knew that further territorial expansion was still on King Frederick's agenda of unfulfilled tasks, and that he favoured an alliance with England, while she saw King Louis of France as a potential ally to thwart the Prussian king. For its part, Austria remained determined to reclaim lands already lost to Prussia. In the endless diplomatic manoeuvring every gesture and every utterance – whether intentional or not – was observed, reported and weighed in the balance. It was certainly the case that evening.

The event was not overlooked either by the man in the shadows. He would have to be ever more vigilant in his constant surveillance of the King's enemies. It was now urgent that he should warn the English countess – to whom he had owed his life only months before – that she stood on the edge of a pit of vipers towards which she had been unwittingly drawn that evening. This innocent young woman, now under greater scrutiny, should be warned to be most careful in what she said and did.

* * * * *

It proved to be an industrious summer at Herzberg. Carl Manfred was often away in Berlin on undisclosed royal business, often much to his irritation and indeed Arabella's. With his encouragement, she began to study the estate accounts, assisted by the elderly land agent, Maximilian, and before long began to ask penetrating questions about income and expenditure, recalling – unwillingly – as she did so similar questions she had heard her father put to his staff about the prosperity and stability of the Meltwater estate. She compiled a fresh inventory of the paintings and furnishings at Herzberg and arranged for up-to-date valuations. With the assistance of her new young personal maid, Hanne, Arabella began to learn German. Her rapid progress impressed all the staff, helping significantly to warm them to their new mistress, and was of course well received in nearby villages and estates where King Frederick's lifelong preference for daily use of the French language was not replicated.

In between all these activities, Arabella would ride. Rather than wear a woman's riding habit and sit side-saddle, she had the young man's boots, breeches, waistcoat and jacket in which she had escaped from England the year before tailored so that they fitted her tightly, thus emphasising (perhaps deliberately) her attractiveness to the men around her and scandalising some older women of her acquaintance, not least by her encouragement – whether intentionally or unintentionally – of a sense of ambiguity about her sexual identity. Frankly, no one had ever seen such abandon before. Thus attired, Arabella often galloped across the Herzberg estate, jumping streams and log piles without fear, just as she had once ridden fast over the sands and creeks on the North Norfolk beaches. To all who saw her at Herzberg this was no ordinary lady of the house. The English countess was different and refreshing – and to the local men she cut a dashing and flamboyant figure in her tight-fitting riding clothes.

If there were evenings when Carl Manfred was not with her, Arabella often discussed and played music with Herr Bamberger and his musicians, who welcomed the frequent opportunity to be at Herzberg in the company of an accomplished lover of music always ready to experiment.

Arabella's arrival at Herzberg, her marriage, social gatherings and even more so the *fête champêtre* in June had given the estate a renewed reputation as a place of activity, style, virtue and informed debate reminiscent of what had taken place at the King's court in earlier years. Accordingly, there were increasing numbers of visitors to the house keen to make closer acquaintance of the English countess over coffee in the morning and tea in the early afternoon. As not everyone spoke French, Arabella's linguistic skill in German was often put to the test, frequently causing peals of laughter. Her charm, humour, musical prowess, elegance and natural beauty, unenhanced by powder, rouge or wigs, captivated everyone. Carl Manfred, ever more in love with his wife as each day passed, sat back full of pleasure at the admiration she so easily earned. She was a free spirit whose brilliance and intellectual reach were formidable. He knew, as the clouds of war over Prussia darkened, that he would have to do whatever was necessary to protect his wife from the dangers that might ensue.

* * * * *

Autumn came early to the Prussian plain. Fewer people visited Herzberg, as landowners concentrated on bringing in the remaining harvest and preparing for the rigours of winter. Carl Manfred persuaded Arabella to accompany him several times to Berlin, where life was more formal. They were able to secure a small house for a while, not far from the Unter den Linden, to avoid frequent travel back and forth to Herzberg.

In October Arabella was presented to the King's sister, Wilhelmine, at Schloss Charlottenburg. She was charming and vivacious, unlike her brother. Their conversation lasted twice the allotted time. Later that month Arabella paid her first visit to the Berlin opera. It was an impressive evening. Though the etiquette of the city's social life was simpler than that which Arabella had briefly experienced in Paris, it was still stiff and somewhat unrefreshing in content. She curtsied, smiled and engaged in the small talk at which her mother had been so adept. But it was always with relief that Arabella returned to the freedom, privacy and informality of Schloss Herzberg – and of course to Herr Bamberger and his musicians.

Throughout the autumn the Countess Katherina von Schlegel was an attentive and enjoyable companion to Arabella, frequently inviting her to her home at Schloss Richemont. In her thirties, the Countess was an imposing and physically attractive woman, full of self-confidence, joie de vivre and purpose. Afternoons at Richemont were often amusing. Countess Katherina was frequently indiscreet in her disclosures to Arabella. Whether this was by design or simply her natural exuberance was unclear. After a while, Arabella began to suspect it was the former – to demonstrate, perhaps as a subtle warning to her, that the Countess von Schlegel's close proximity to the King was special, thus making her one of the most informed people as to the possible motivations for the actions he took; and that in such a role there was no room for another. Arabella recalled what the man in the shadows had whispered to her at the Palace of Sanssouci after her first audience with King Frederick at the start of the year: she should be careful about placing trust in Katherina von Schlegel.

*****

It was towards the end of October 1766 that two people requested permission to call on Arabella in private at Herzberg in her husband's absence. The first was His Excellency Mr Andrew Mitchell, Envoy Extraordinary and Minister Plenipotentiary to the Kingdom of Prussia. The second was the man in the shadows.

The British Ambassador had asked if he might call on her on Monday the 27th of October since he would be passing close to Herzberg on his way to England for a short visit. He arrived by arrangement shortly before ten o'clock. Though it had been cold for some days the windows of the library were open to let in the shallow warmth of the sun. Here they sat face to face, divided by a shaft of sunlight, sipping coffee.

A tall and immaculately dressed man, Andrew Mitchell was softly spoken and elegantly mannered, as befitted an English diplomat. He had arrived in Berlin in the earlier part of the year and by all accounts had been assiduous in establishing a good rapport with the King's officials.

"Countess, it is most kind and generous of you to receive me at this early hour so that we can become better acquainted."

"I am pleased to oblige," replied Arabella. "I wish you a safe onward journey."

"I hope to reach Magdeburg by nightfall," the Ambassador said. "My intention is to complete my visit to England as quickly as possible in order to return to Berlin, with Mrs Mitchell, by the beginning of December."

"I wish your plans well," replied Arabella, recalling as she spoke the long, arduous and at times frightening journey she had made from Paris to Potsdam at the start of the year.

"I thank you again," continued the Ambassador, "for the delightful *fête champêtre* you and Count von Deppe hosted in June. It was a truly splendid evening and it was reassuring to see His Majesty the King in such good humour – indeed, dancing to the music of the orchestra you appear to have formed with such great success. Have you made any plans to play for him again as I believe he may have asked you to do?"

"Excellency, thank you for your kind remarks about our summer festivities. I am deeply touched and I will convey your sentiments to the Count on his return from Berlin. As for the King's musical wishes, I have as yet received no specific instructions."

"How often is your husband absent from Herzberg?" asked the Ambassador.

"Too often for both his and my liking," responded Arabella quickly. "But it is on the King's business, so neither of us must complain. And there is more than enough to occupy me in my husband's absence."

"Including music?" interjected the Ambassador.

"Indeed, Excellency, including music."

"And do you intend to play again for the King, if he does indeed ask?" enquired the Ambassador, recalling his earlier question.

"As I said, Ambassador, I am at the King's disposal," countered Arabella, becoming aware that the Ambassador's questions were beginning to suggest his call on her that morning was possibly more than social. He was clearly probing.

There was a pause in the conversation.

"Do you miss England, Countess?" asked Mr Mitchell.

"Why do you ask, Excellency?"

"Prussia is a long way from England, as the journey on which I am about to embark will remind me only too well. I wondered if there might be some aspects of English life you miss, such as your family. I had the great honour of meeting your mother shortly after your wedding in Berlin earlier this year. She was most charming. And I met your father, briefly, one evening in London, at his club, shortly before my departure for Prussia."

Arabella bristled at the reference to her father.

"Ambassador, let me be frank, if that is possible in the world of diplomacy – of which, of course, I as a woman have no experience. I greatly miss my mother, Lady Whitfield, whom I love deeply for all that she taught me. But I have no wish to discuss my father. I have no interest in his affairs, for reasons I do not want to talk about. He has always insisted on doing what he believes he has to do. For my part, I too insist on doing what I have to do. That is the only similarity between us. Other than that, our paths have parted and there is an end to the matter."

The Ambassador did not respond to Arabella's mild rebuke, one that indicated he had strayed into a matter of personal sensitivity – as he had deliberately intended to do.

"You have been absent from England for a year," he continued. "May I ask you how you perceive England's fortunes from the library here at Herzberg?" He gestured towards the garden and beyond. "Despite your many preoccupations as the mistress of the estate and patron of your orchestra, do you still take an interest in English affairs? Do your friends and acquaintances seek your views on matters that concern us all?"

"Excellency, I wish to assure you that no affairs of state, let alone English affairs of state, are the subject of discussion at Herzberg. My country of birth is, as you have pointed out, far from here and few visitors from there come to this house. You are amongst the first to do so. For these reasons, I am afraid I am uninformed about what happens in London. Moreover, Count von Deppe and I have many matters of a domestic nature to discuss whenever he returns from settling those of the King. Naturally, my friends and acquaintances often debate subjects of social and literary interest but the affairs of Europe are best left to others in Berlin. That is not surprising since, as you will know as an experienced practitioner of the art of diplomacy, a woman's opinion is rarely sought. That being so, as you have rightly observed, I occupy myself with my interest in music and, of course, the affairs of the estate."

"But surely the rumours of renewed war are of interest to you?" responded the Ambassador.

Arabella interjected.

"Let me be clear, Excellency. My personal bond with the country of my birth is enduring and unbreakable. I will never be disloyal. But my beloved husband has captured my heart and so my life henceforward will be at his side in Prussia. That prospect fills me with profound pleasure and on that account I will not be disloyal to him or to his King. Whatever secrets I may learn in due course about England, or whatever opinions I may have about it, I will not share with another. By the same token, whatever secrets may be divulged to me about Prussia I will not break. I have learnt during my life so far that trust is a rare and precious commodity. That is why I will keep my own counsel."

"Thank you for being so explicit, Countess. I agree with your sentiments entirely. But I do hope that we can keep in touch in the months ahead, even if affairs of state do not feature in our conversations."

"Of course," responded Arabella, reassured that the Ambassador had understood she would not reveal to him – even in the strictest confidence – whatever might pass between her and her husband concerning the King and matters of state.

Before taking his leave of Arabella – whom he now regarded as a worthy conversational opponent and who, he conceded, at least for the moment, was highly unlikely to divulge to him any information she might glean from court or in her husband's bed – the Ambassador asked one more question, so as not to leave their conversation on a disappointing note.

"Countess, is there anything I may do for you in London?"

Arabella thought for a moment.

"Excellency, there is perhaps one favour I might ask. If indeed there proves to be a concert for His Majesty in Berlin before the end of the year – and, if that were to happen, I hope that you and Mrs Mitchell would be able to attend, provided, of course, you have returned from England in time – I would very much like the audience to hear a suitable piece of English music. It would please me greatly if you were able to bring back some of Mr William Boyce's music, such as one of his symphonies or a similar piece. I would need several copies, of course. I would quite understand if it were not possible for you to do so. And so you see, Ambassador, perhaps there is something I miss about England after all – its music."

"Countess, it will be a pleasure to see what I can do. I agree that it would be a good thing to hear more English music played in Berlin."

"Thank you so much," replied Arabella. "I will look forward to your return with keen anticipation."

As the Ambassador sped on his way to Magdeburg, he reflected on his conversation with the Countess. She would not spy, so to speak, for the country of her birth, but it was her wish for him to purchase some English music. Was this a coded message from her to him that she intended to do what she could to advance the values and interests of England through the medium of music? If that were the case, the beautiful young countess might after all prove to be a subtle and worthy player on the diplomatic chessboard. Securing Mr Boyce's music for her was therefore highly desirable – a first step in winning her to his point of view.

Arabella also reflected on their conversation. She had soon become aware that the Ambassador was exploring her possible willingness to be a source of information and opinion. There had indeed been private moments in the past months when she had thought of England, of Meltwater, of her mother and the happy times they had enjoyed together at the keyboard and trying on bonnets in Norwich. Adjusting to her new life in Prussia had not been easy and there had been times when she felt lonely and vulnerable. But she had made a choice and it was necessary to prove her steadfastness. She loved her husband deeply and she admired the King he served, cynical and difficult though he might be. She would do nothing to cause either to doubt her. But a plan was beginning to evolve in her mind as to how she might survive in a country so different in many ways from her country of birth, and, moreover, how she might promote greater respect for her husband's name and for Herzberg. If the advancement of English music could help to do that, she would promote its cause with subtlety and determination. And if that were to increase respect for England in other ways, so be it. But she recognised this could be dangerous in a kingdom so distant from England and one that she did not yet fully understand.

As she reflected further a note arrived from the man in the shadows, asking if he might call on her as soon as she had time – perhaps in the absence of her husband – to discuss some musical matters. Arabella responded immediately.

> *My dear friend,*
>
> *I was deeply touched to receive your note about your wish to come to Herzberg on Tuesday the 4th of November to tell me more of the King's love of music. I would of course be greatly honoured by your visit. Regrettably, Count von Deppe will be attending His Majesty and therefore unable to join us.*
>
> *I propose you come on the morning of Tuesday the 4th, as later that day Herr Bamberger and my small group of musicians will meet. It would be beneficial for us to be informed of what is intended.*
>
> *With my warmest best wishes,*
> *Arabella, Countess von Deppe*
> *Monday the 27th of October at Schloss Herzberg*

She received a prompt reply, agreeing to the time, but was

unaware that music would not be the principal matter for discussion.

*****

Count Carl Manfred von Deppe deeply regretted receipt of the King's summons to see him so soon after his marriage to Arabella. He had duly called upon the King as requested. In the audience at Sanssouci the monarch had spoken of the need for trust and vigilance during the events that would inevitably unfold. He wanted Carl Manfred by his side as there were now few people in whom he could place that trust, whereas his faith in Carl Manfred had been renewed following the demonstration of the Count's loyalty in England the year before. But after many months of waiting it remained unclear what the King wished him to do. Each day he attended on the monarch no disclosure or instructions came. As he twiddled his thumbs in Berlin or Potsdam, Arabella for whom he longed tended to the needs of the estate without him at her side. In the previous week he had seen her only once – on Friday the 31st of October at the opera in Berlin. He had wanted her to stay longer in the city but she insisted on returning to Herzberg on the Sunday, to prepare for a call two days later by the man in the shadows and a musical session that afternoon with the young Herr Bamberger and his players.

As Carl Manfred strolled in the garden of the Neues Palais, waiting for the King to make another inspection of the building still under construction, the elusive man in the shadows approached him.

"I intend to call on the Countess tomorrow, as she may have told you, to discuss the King's growing interest in her musical skills."

"Yes, she has told me," replied Carl Manfred. "And may I ask what the King's growing musical interest is, precisely?"

"He wishes me to encourage her and her musicians to perform for him before the end of the year," replied the man in the shadows, whose real name was Waldemar Drescher. He was the King's most secret spymaster, known by a handful as the thresher of men – the despatcher of the King's enemies. Few people knew of his existence; he was rarely seen at court, and operated in deep shadows. It was said by the few who did that what the King proposed to him in private, he disposed without any risk of Royal incrimination.

"I could tell her that," replied Carl Manfred testily.

"It is better from me," said Drescher.

"There is another reason for your visit, is there not? A man of your dark talents would not concern himself with the King's musical wishes. What is your real motive? Come, man, speak up. She is my wife. I should know."

"Music, and to warn her of the pit of vipers on the edge of which we all stand, her included," replied Drescher calmly.

"Your mind comprises wheels and cogs forever turning, grinding the grain of fact and fiction." Carl Manfred almost spat out the words.

"Just like the King's enemies," responded Drescher with some impatience of his own.

"Do not involve the Countess in your games," warned Carl Manfred.

"She is involved whether you wish it or not, Count von Deppe," replied Drescher irritably. "My task is to protect the King, you and all who serve him well. But I must also protect her. You may not like it but that is how it must be. She is English, a beautiful young woman. She has met and sung for the King of France and, surprisingly, has found a place in the heart of our King. There are people who are already becoming jealous of your love for her – and, I might say, jealous of her. And there are many who would like to bed her. If that were not enough, our King is plotting again to extend still further the boundaries and influence of our kingdom. I believe there is fear in St Petersburg and Paris of an alliance between our King and England. The King's decision to dispense with the Countess Katherina and to dance with your wife at Herzberg set tongues wagging. Why else would the British Ambassador go to the trouble of calling on your wife on his way to London? He no doubt wished to explore the extent to which she might be a source of information to him, become a British pawn in the game of alliances. So, as I am sure you will understand, an English-born and highly intelligent young woman, recently arrived in Prussia and now with the rank of countess, could be perceived by some to be an asset to their plans or an obstacle to be removed.

It is my task, unmentionable though it may be, to use any method – dark or foul – to scatter the King's enemies. I do not use the honourable ways of life and death that you deploy on the battlefield. The Countess has to be part of my device. And that being the case I will protect her from the malevolence of others."

"If she is harmed, I will kill you," replied Carl Manfred angrily.

"I cannot tell you how many people have threatened me with death."

"I mean it," said the Count.

"I am sure you do," replied Drescher. "Your wife is already exposed to danger simply by being at Herzberg and dancing with the King, but I will protect her life whatever the personal cost to me, just as she protected me earlier this year."

"Are you going to tell her of what is afoot?" asked Carl Manfred.

"No," replied Drescher. "But I will ask her to be vigilant, to take simple precautions."

"I warn you again. Be careful."

"Let me be precise, Count von Deppe. There is a traitor amongst us – one of a number. My job is to find them and pick them off one by one. In the present case I intend to set a trap in order to catch and destroy my quarry. The Countess will be the bait. I will ensure no harm befalls her. But she must not know, even from you, the game that is about to be played. If you tell her, there is a risk she may get caught in the snare set for another."

"Who is your quarry?" Carl Manfred asked sharply.

"I cannot say."

"So be it, but I warn you a third time," said Carl Manfred.

"Yes, yes, yes. I know that. And you should know that I hold you responsible for playing my game. Your wife's life is as much in your hands as mine. Now be gone. The King's coach is arriving."

With that Waldemar Drescher slipped away.

* * * * *

The next morning Arabella greeted Drescher at Herzberg.

"It is such a pleasure to see you again. I have not seen you since my marriage to the Count in March earlier this year. I had hoped you would come to the *fête champêtre.*"

"I was there, Countess – in the shadows where I prefer to be, as you know."

They sat in the library. He asked about the progress of the autumn harvest at Herzberg and her musical evenings with Herr Bamberger. Arabella responded to his questions with enthusiasm.

"Herr Drescher, you are remarkably well informed. But I should not be surprised, as you have a finger in many pies. I know you and my husband do not always see eye to eye. But you demonstrated to me earlier this year not only the depth of your loyalty to the King and to Prussia but also your care and protection for me. I will never be able to repay the profound kindness you showed me."

"And I, Madame, will never be able to repay you for saving my life from an enemy of the state. So we are in equal debt." Coming quickly to the point of his call Drescher continued: "I believe the British Ambassador came to see you last week."

"Yes, he did," replied Arabella.

"May I ask the purpose?" asked Drescher

"I think his purpose was to explore my loyalty to my country of birth. I told him that, while I would never be disloyal to England, equally I would not be disloyal to my husband, to Prussia or to His Majesty the King. And that what secrets I might hear would remain locked within me, as would my opinions. I wish to add now that my loyalty extends to you, Herr Drescher, for whom I have great respect."

"Thank you, Countess." He paused and then spoke again. "Winter approaches and with winter will come plotting and scheming. It's that time of the year, as they say."

"Or you say," interjected Arabella with a smile.

Drescher smiled too.

"It will be difficult in the months – perhaps even years – ahead to detect friend from foe. I say to you, Countess, as your friend, that you are right to be careful. You are young, beautiful and the possessor of great talents. Your husband is of great comfort to the King as his circle of friends and advisers continues to diminish. But you, not just your husband, will attract increasing attention. So I urge you to be vigilant for the vipers. Trust no one."

"Herr Drescher, thank you for your warning. Though I am still inexperienced in the ways of the world and have much to learn about Prussia, I have already concluded that in life people often profess friendship and pledge confidentiality, but what they proffer is shallow and frequently corrupted by private opinions and desires of their own. I consider trust in humankind to be the rarest of commodities. Accordingly, I have vowed that I will not be corrupted by any manner of gift or promise, and that I will be faithful to my husband and the King to whom he and you are most loyal. I will do my best never to break this vow. As for my personal trust, I assure you it will extend to fewer in number than the five fingers on my right hand."

"Countess, what you have vowed greatly warms my heart. Whatever may happen, you should know that I will do all that is required to protect you from any harm and vilification that may befall you. I live in the shadows but I will watch for you every day, every minute. Now, let us talk about music. The King is mindful that he said at the *fête champêtre* he wishes you to play for him again. I recommend that you write to him immediately, offering to perform with your musicians on the 1st of December, to mark the beginning of Advent."

"I will do so tomorrow morning, after I have spoken to Herr Bamberger later today," replied Arabella.

"Good," replied Drescher. "I am sure you will receive an early reply."

Drescher rose to leave. As he did so, Arabella said she wished to seek his advice on a sensitive personal matter.

"I do not wish to draw notice to my religion but I would like to have the private services of a Catholic priest who would come discreetly to Herzberg from time to time. I have discussed this with Count von Deppe and he has no objection. I have no intention to cause embarrassment to His Majesty but it would ease my heart if a trusted priest could be found without fuss or attention. I know other matters preoccupy you but I would greatly welcome your advice."

"My dear Countess, the King has often said that all religions must be tolerated, for every man must get to his heaven his own way. What he remarked applies to everyone, man and woman alike. What you have requested will be done with speed and care. Please leave the matter in my hands."

So saying Herr Drescher took his leave to return to the shadows.

*****

The next morning Arabella wrote to the King, in French, as Drescher had recommended.

To His Majesty,

Forgive me for any impression of impertinence this letter may mistakenly convey.

Last December at your Palace of Sanssouci, when you graciously received me on my arrival from France, and more recently when you were our much-honoured guest at Schloss Herzberg, you asked me to play for you. I wish you to know that I am ready to discharge the obligation you placed upon me, if it remains your intention that I should do so.

As Monday the 1st of December is the first day of Advent, my musicians and I stand prepared to perform for you to mark this significant event in the Church's liturgical calendar.

I am your most humble and obedient subject,
Arabella
Countess von Deppe
Schloss Herzberg, Wednesday the 5th of November, 1766

A week later she received the King's reply in his neat handwriting and exquisite French, delivered to her by Carl Manfred.

My dear Countess,

As I advance in years I may forget and overlook what I have said. But your graceful keyboard presentation at Sanssouci, your lively musical intervention at Herzberg in June and your charming personal disposition have left an indelible impression on my weary mind.

I have no intention of removing the obligation I placed upon you. I therefore expect you to play for me. I wish it were possible to do so at Sanssouci, but as it is likely to be too cold there at this time of the year I ask you and your players to perform for me in the chapel of my Palace of Charlottenburg. I do not often go there, but your presence will cheer the building and my heart.

I have asked Count von Deppe to make the necessary

arrangements to enable you to attend. The choice of musical programme I place entirely in your hands. Remember in your selection to warm my spirits as you did a year ago.
Frederick
Berlin, Tuesday the 11th of November, 1766

Arabella smiled and handed the letter to her husband to read.

"My dearest Arabella, you have moved the King's heart in such a way as to cause others to marvel. But please be careful. There are those at court who cherish their positions and who will respond adversely to any perceived threat to their influence. The King still has friends, but he has courtiers around him whose loyalty is questionable. Herr Drescher will watch over you as indeed will I. Please, Arabella, take care."

"I will, my sweet husband. I promise you I will." She kissed him. "And you too must be vigilant."

A few days later, after further practice with Herr Bamberger and his players, Arabella wrote again to the King.

To His Majesty,

I have prepared with my group of musicians to play for you in the chapel of Schloss Charlottenburg at five o'clock on Monday the 1st of December.

I enclose with great pleasure a list of our musical intentions for your approval.

Arabella
Countess von Doppe
Schloss Herzberg, Thursday the 20th of November, 1766

Arabella received no reply but her husband assured her, as did Herr Drescher, that the King had read her letter and perused the enclosed list but without comment. Given his preoccupation with other pressing matters, his silence was, in their opinion, tantamount to approval.

It was at this time that Arabella received a private letter from Herr Drescher, advising that he had arranged for Father Johann Schmidt, a young Catholic priest, to visit her frequently so she could receive Communion. He vouched for Father Schmidt's discretion but urged her nonetheless to exercise caution in confession until his commitment and trust had been closely observed and proven. Almost immediately the young priest arrived, fresh from a seminary.

* * * * *

On Saturday the 29th of November Arabella and Carl Manfred left Herzberg for their house in Berlin. Following an hour or so behind were Herr Bamberger and his young musicians.

Arabella and her husband arrived at Schloss Charlottenburg at twelve o'clock on Monday the 1st of December to prepare for the concert. Advent had come. To their surprise, they were invited to stay at the Schloss until the next day, at the King's personal wish.

The palace was impressive. It comprised two grand wings and a central section capped by a copper-topped dome on the apex of which was a wind vane in the form of a golden statue representing Fortune. In answer to his wife's eager questions, Carl Manfred had explained to Arabella that the original, smaller palace had been commissioned at the end of the seventeenth century by Sophie Charlottenburg, the wife of Frederick III, Elector of Brandenburg. It had been expanded in the earlier part of the eighteenth century and King Frederick, on his accession to the Prussian throne in 1740, had further decorated the palace, with the intention that the ground floor would be for the use of his estranged wife, Elisabeth Christine, from whom he had been separated since their marriage. But she was only an occasional visitor, preferring to stay at another palace. The King had also redecorated the upper floor, including the White Hall, the Banqueting Hall, the Throne Room and the Golden Gallery, to which he had also added a separate second apartment at the distant end of the east wing.

The square-sided chapel, where the musicians were to perform, was lavishly decorated in the baroque style with elaborate pilasters and rich wall hangings. Though large and decorated with dozens of candles, it was still intimate in atmosphere and thus a suitable setting for a concert to entertain the King. Shortly before five o'clock the court was in attendance, and Herr Bamberger and his musicians assembled on the dais in front of the altar, with Arabella standing to one side, her fingers firmly locked to avoid any display of her anxiety. Her husband stood outside the chapel entrance. The

Countess Katherina von Schlegel stood beside him with her elderly husband. She wore a deep-blue high-throated velvet dress, laced on the bodice with diamonds. Her mane of black hair was tightly swept back. They waited as the minutes ticked by.

Then the assembled audience heard the distant sound of the King's voice – "Is the Countess there?" – as he strode along the corridor towards the chapel. "Will someone answer? Is the Countess there?"

As the King drew near, somewhat breathless, the Countess Katherina stepped forward and curtsied.

"Ah! I see the Countess von Schlegel, as charming as ever. But I meant the other Countess, the Countess von Deppe, the musical countess. Is she here?"

Carl Manfred stepped forward.

"My wife awaits you in the chapel."

"I am glad to hear it," said the King. "We could not begin without her."

The King entered the chapel. The audience rose to their feet. Gentlemen bowed and ladies curtsied.

"Please be seated," said the King. "Let us begin. I have other matters to attend to later."

The orchestra of young players took their seats. Arabella, in a white, almost off-the-shoulder sack-back dress, a matching shawl draped over the daringly low-cut bodice, her hair loosely tied back with a stream of pink ribbon, curtsied deeply to the King and took her place at the harpsichord. She nodded to Herr Bamberger. The concert began.

The first piece was the *Concerto for Harpsichord in D Minor* by Christoph Nichelmann, who had died four years before in Berlin. From 1744 until 1756 he had been the second harpsichordist of the royal operatic ensemble and the King had known him well. There was polite applause. The second piece in the programme was Johann Sebastian Bach's *Double Violin Concerto.* Herr Bamberger, first violin, led the orchestra. The young Herr Johann Schroeder from Potsdam, a recent addition to Arabella's group, joined him as the other soloist. Though nervous, the two young men played with skill and lightness, much to Arabella's great pleasure and relief.

Clasping the music book the King had presented to her as a gift earlier in the year, Arabella stepped forward.

"If His Majesty permits, I will sing one of Mr Handel's well-known arias, *Ombra mai fu*, from his opera *Xerxes*, composed in London in 1738. This aria is sung by the Persian King Xerxes, admiring the shade of a plane tree."

The King nodded.

Arabella sang. Her words floated up towards the chapel's painted ceiling.

Tender and beautiful fronds
of my beloved plane tree,
let Fate smile upon you.
May thunder, lightning, and storms
never disturb your dear peace,
nor may you by blowing winds be profaned.

Never was the shade
of a plant
dearer and more lovely,
or more sweet.

There was a momentary silence when she finished, so surprised were the King and his guests by the sweetness and clarity of her singing. The King leapt to his feet, leading the applause.

"Encore," he called out.

Arabella turned to Herr Bamberger and whispered, "*Castor and Pollux*." He nodded. She turned to the King and began to sing Télaïre's aria, *Tristes apprêts*, with great eloquence, her hands sometimes clasped tightly against her breast or held out in front of her as though in supplication.

Melancholy apparitions, pale torches,
Day more dreadful than darkness,
Mournful stars of the tombs,
No, never more shall I see anything but your funereal rays.

You who see my broken heart,
Father of daylight! Oh Sun! Oh my father!
I no longer want the gift that Castor has lost,
And I renounce your light.

Unencumbered by sheets of music, she sang the words with poignant intensity, sadness and emotion. Even the angels around the altar seemed to turn to look down with compassion on the source of the ethereal voice reaching the innermost recesses of the chapel. To Carl Manfred it seemed that Arabella was expressing through the aria her despair and grief of recent times, and seeking redemption. Her face and hair were bathed in the soft light of the candles around her. The King appeared lost in deep thought. Others were mesmerised by the pellucid notes seeming to hover in the air. Carl Manfred stood unable to move.

When the aria ended, the King slowly rose to his feet, visibly moved to tears. He beckoned Arabella to come forward, and taking her hands in his said, "My dear Countess, I have not heard such a beautiful voice in all my long life. It has pierced my heart. I will for ever have a lasting memory of what I have heard this evening. What is next?"

"I invite you to play with us your own composition, your flute sonata," said Arabella.

"Countess, you are so beguiling. Is there no end to the magic you weave?" The old warrior paused. "Tell me, Countess. You have in your short life witnessed three kings. Not the magi but George of Hanover, now the king of a united Britain, the land of your birth. King Louis of France, the land of your mother, for whom you sang at Versailles. And now me. How do these three monarchs each stand in your favour?"

There was silence. Everyone listened for Arabella's response. Carl Manfred thought the King's question unfair, but suspected he had been prompted to ask it. Had it been an enemy? Or had it been the man in the shadows, playing his devious game?

"Sire," responded Arabella. "King George rules the land of my birth and while there I was his subject. King Louis indeed rules the land of my mother's birth and while in France I was but a guest of his country's hospitality. You rule with great wisdom the land where I have willingly come to live for the rest of my life as the devoted wife of my dear husband, Count von Deppe. You are the king to whom I owe heartfelt allegiance."

The King looked at Arabella intently and then smiled.

"You speak with great sensitivity, eloquence and persuasion. I admire that."

The King stepped onto the platform. Arabella presented a flute to him. He smiled once more, took it, then moved to the music stand and began to play. The audience marvelled at what Arabella had achieved.

The King finished to warm applause and returned to his seat.

The penultimate item of music was played without prior indication of the composer. After a ripple of gentle applause, Herr Bamberger announced that the orchestra had just played the *Symphony No. 7* of the English composer William Boyce. Still living, he was Master of the King's Musick.

Arabella stepped forward for the last time. She curtsied again to King Frederick.

Herr Bamberger spoke.

"As today is the first day of Advent, the orchestra wishes to play Signor Arcangelo Corelli's *Concerto Grosso in G Minor*. We will then have played music from the lands of Germany, France, England and Italy. The Countess von Deppe will lead us from the harpsichord."

As his wife played, Carl Manfred gazed at her, so sensual, so exquisite, her face lightly dusted with crushed pearl. As she played the fourth, *Vivace* movement, her shawl slipped, revealing her almost bare shoulders and her half-exposed breasts above the low-cut bodice. The candlelight seemed to burnish her loosely tied dark hair, turning it rich auburn. Arabella's sensuality, her beauty, her untarnished complexion and her composure mesmerised him. He recalled the evening at his sister's house in Paris when she had played and looked fleetingly across the room at him. As she played now, she again stirred his physical longing for her. Carl Manfred turned to look at the King. He seemed equally enraptured.

At the end of the concerto's final movement, Herr Bamberger stepped forward, joined by Arabella. Facing the King, he bowed and she curtsied deeply.

"Your Majesty, our performance has ended," said the young orchestra leader. "We thank you for your gracious presence and for so generously performing your flute sonata. We are truly honoured."

Again he bowed and, with her hand in Herr Bamberger's, Arabella dropped a long, deep curtsy to the King.

He nodded.

"Countess, I congratulate you on your triumph – on your playing, singing and for bringing together such a talented group of young musicians. This evening you have been my worthy *Kapellmeisterin*. Now I must leave."

As he turned to go he looked back at Arabella and Herr Bamberger.

"I propose that henceforth you call your musicians the Schloss Herzberger Camerata. To preempt any hesitation on your part, Countess, that is by royal command."

"Sire, we are profoundly honoured. It will be done."

With that the King left the chapel, followed by the von Schlegels and other favoured courtiers and ambassadors. As he walked down the corridor to leave the palace, he confirmed in his mind the decision he had already taken: that the von Deppes should go to St Petersburg to promote the interests of Prussia. He would speak without delay to Drescher so that the necessary arrangements could be made.

For his part the British Ambassador smiled to himself. From what he had seen of the amicable exchanges between her and the King, the English countess could exercise significant influence at court if he could only persuade her to use her talents in the most suitable way. He decided he should call on her again.

Within a few minutes Arabella, her husband and the musicians were alone in the royal chapel.

"Herr Bamberger, I congratulate you and everyone in the Schloss Herzberger Camerata on your inspired achievement this evening," said Arabella, bursting with delight and pride. "Your triumph is unqualified. Do you not agree, Count von Deppe?"

"I do indeed," replied Carl Manfred. "The evening was intensely moving and a worthy celebration of the first day of Advent. Shall we go and find refreshment?"

Followed by the young musicians, as brimming with pleasure and satisfaction at their success as their patron, the Count and Countess walked arm in arm upstairs to the White Hall, where wine and meats awaited the happy players. As they ate and drank, Arabella and Carl Manfred circulated, laughing and teasing one another as they did so.

"Before we leave for our lodgings," said Herr Bamberger, "we ask you and the Count to dance for us. What music should we play?"

"Play another ayre or two from Signor Nicola Matteis," responded Arabella, giddy with joy. "To my mind your skills on the violin surpass even his, and so I offer to you the praise John Evelyn once wrote of him: 'I never heard mortal man exceed on that instrument. He had a stroak so sweete, and made it speake like ye voice of a man, and, when he pleas'd, like a consort of severall instruments. He did wonders upon a note, and was an excellent composer.' Come, Herr Bamberger, musicians, play him."

And so the Count and Countess danced. As they did so, the musicians danced in a circle around them in the candlelight. There were peals of laughter and much merriment. Almost an hour later, one of the palace servants came to announce that the musicians' carriages were waiting downstairs.

"I beg you play one last dance for us," said Arabella.

"What would you wish?" replied Herr Bamberger.

"Play Signor Matteis' chaconne."

"Yes, of course," said Herr Bamberger.

As the musicians played, Arabella, in coquettish mood, danced the lightest of steps, flicking the front of her skirt to reveal her delicate white-stockinged ankles and pumps beneath. Her eyes sparkled in the candlelight. She danced to within inches of her husband and as he reached to put his arm around her slender waist she teasingly pulled away. Again and again she provoked him, tracing the contour of her body and bust with her hands and then coming close to him, laughing.

"You are not trying hard enough to catch me, Count von Deppe! Come, try harder!"

Though Arabella continued to dance, the musicians began one by one to slip away, still playing as they descended the staircase. Then another new violin joined in, close by but out of sight.

"My darling Arabella, surely it is time to go to bed," said Carl Manfred.

She spun ever faster towards him, finally falling into his outstretched arms. They kissed.

"Take me to our bed. Possess me!" she whispered.

Together, arms linked and deep in thought, they walked along the corridor towards the royal apartment, the hidden violinist tracing their footsteps. They turned to look but the player was shrouded by darkness. They let him play and entered the royal apartment, where Hanne was waiting to help her mistress undress.

* * * * *

In the elegant bedchamber Arabella stood near the fire, its flames illuminating her slender body, covered only by a loose-fitting transparent shift tied loosely at the neck and waist. Her untied hair caressed her shoulders. Carl Manfred, undressed, kissed her, and again professed his love and admiration for her.

"My dearest Carl, your avowal of love is precious to me. I love you beyond any words that even the worthy Mr Shakespeare has written in his sonnets. But let us not seek to outdo each other with words. Let me feel instead your possession of my being – fingertip to fingertip, palm to palm, body to body. Touch me, hold me and penetrate me to such depth that you reach my soul. Carl, in the name of humanity I beg you to make love to me. I can wait no longer."

He undid the ribbons of her shift. It slipped effortlessly from her shoulders. He gathered Arabella in his arms and laid her on the bed against the pillows. He sat beside her. She took his fingers to caress the hardened nipples of her breasts and then her lips. Outside the wind blew; the fire crackled in the great hearth.

"Come, take me," she whispered.

Never before had she so moved him. Never had a woman given him such physical pleasure merely through the playing of a keyboard or through the sublime notes of her voice. His body had ached with lust for her as she sang in the chapel. Now he was at her side, gazing down at her. He kissed her – her lips, her slender neck, her breasts, and then down her body to the dark valley of her sweetness below. She closed her eyes as her body began to quiver in expectation. He delicately ran his finger upwards to her mouth and then once again his lips made their slow, meandering downward path to the softness between her legs, now parted to receive him. Arabella trembled more intensely, pleading with him to delay no longer, to enter her. As he did so, her arms encompassed him. She cried out, the pain of her pleasure deeper and longer than ever.

"Again, again and again," she called out.

An hour or so later she awoke in the arms of her sleeping

husband. She could still hear a distant violin playing Matteis' chaconne. Above the domed cupola of the palace, the spinning weather vane – the figure of Fortune, a lone minstrel – played her sonata of harmony and disharmony as she turned one way and then another in the swirling, bitter night wind. A year ago Arabella, friendless, had been fleeing from the demi-monde of London to France, a fugitive and in love. A year later, a countess, she was in the King's palace with her beloved husband, in Queen Elisabeth Christine's bed. Meltwater had become a distant memory. But where would she be in a further year's time? Though safe in her husband's arms, she still felt vulnerable. She heard the chime of a striking clock, marking yet another passing hour. Before long it would be dawn and it would be with great sorrow that she would say farewell to the night. She would pray for the winter sun to set quickly so that she could once again experience the night's sweetness. Taking her husband's hand to clasp it to her chest, her fingers intertwined with his, she fell asleep, resolved that when they awoke he should make love to her again before the shafts of sunlight pierced the window shutters, so bringing night to a final end.

As she and Carl Manfred slept, two people in the palace were still awake. The violinist, the man in the shadows, continued to play solitary ayres. He envied the physical love between Arabella and the Count. As a lover of men he could never enjoy the bed of the man he loved. His life would continue to be one of sorrow and regret. But from his sorrow came the strength to defend the man he could not hold in his arms. As he pondered the cruelty of unassuaged love, he saw in the darkness the other restless figure, pacing the corridors of the palace, plotting a fate for their quarry. A smile passed over Drescher's face; it was time to set the trap.

A week later, at Herzberg, Arabella received the following letter from the King.

To the Countess von Deppe,

God's patience with us mortals must be sorely tested in these troubled times. But I would like to think that your musical celebration of the Festival of Advent may have brought Him some crumb of comfort that the flame of the human spirit is not entirely extinguished. The flame of that spirit burns brightly in your heart.

Your voice still lingers in my thoughts, as does your eloquent expression of loyalty to my kingdom. I hope that before too long there will be another occasion when you and your musicians will divert me from the affairs of state.

To encourage further your love of music, which I share, and to underline that my recent words were no trifle, I command in writing that your young musicians, with your continued inspiration, be henceforth known as the Schloss Herzberger Camerata. With this title I trust they will flourish. I have warned my royal musicians that a new generation of players are hard on their heels.

Frederick

Berlin, Friday the 5th of December, 1766

Arabella placed the King's letter inside the leather-bound music book he had given her, after she had replied:

To His Majesty King Frederick,

I was deeply honoured to receive your most kind and generous letter.

Your command is my pleasurable obligation. The Schloss Herzberger Camerata will perform for the first time under its new title at the St Nicholas Church in Potsdam on Sunday the 18th of January at four o'clock, in the new year of 1767.

From your most obedient and loyal subject,

Arabella

Countess von Deppe

Schloss Herzberg, Monday the 8th of December, 1766

CHAPTER 2

From the Citadel to the Winter Palace

On Monday the 19th of January 1767 Arabella wrote in her music book:

Yesterday Herr Bamberger led our newly named Schloss Herzberger Camerata in its first public performance, at the St Nicholas Church in Potsdam. He was so nervous beforehand but he triumphed. Many people came – more out of curiosity, I dare say, than perhaps a genuine love of music. Congratulations to the Camerata.

We played much Bach – but not just old man Bach, as the King would say. Our players also performed – excellently – Johann Christian B's Second Wind Symphony, *during which there was quite some foot tapping. And Dorothea W, our flautist and harpsichordist and a good singer to boot, performed with passion and skill JCB's Keyboard Sonata in D Major.*

I sat throughout with CM, applauding at the end of each piece as enthusiastically as a lady's decorum permitted. At the finish came a request that I should sing. After thanking the audience in rather halting German for their great kindness and appreciation – my first public speech in this most difficult language – I sang Lascia ch'io pianga *from Mr Handel's*

> *opera* Rinaldo. *As I sang, it brought back memories of Paris and my inescapable realisation then how deeply in love I was with CM. After the concert ended it took over an hour for us to say farewell to our guests.*

The performance in the St Nicholas Church soon became the talk of Potsdam. Praise was widespread, but there was also a modicum of criticism – albeit muted – of the fact that the ensemble included three female violinists. As one elderly gentleman observed, it was becoming for a lady to play the harpsichord but less becoming for her to play the violin. Such an energetic task, he added, was surely for a man, in which case that musical and social convention should be left undisturbed. But the English countess was unrepentant – in accordance with her principle of equality between the sexes. After all, as she icily commented more than once, if a young woman's active fingers were sufficiently skilled to sew intricate patterns of embroidery for public admiration, they were also good enough to conjure musical melodies from the violin. And she took comfort from the fact that King Frederick had made no adverse comment when her protégées had played for him at the Palace of Charlottenburg.

* * * * *

A month later, on Friday the 13th of February, Carl Manfred returned from Berlin to Herzberg, now under deep snow. Arabella was playing the harpsichord in the library. She rose to greet him.

"My darling Carl, I am so pleased to see you back. His Majesty keeps you away from me too often. It is becoming most tiresome. But I should not complain as he has been so thoughtful to me in the past months. Sit down and warm yourself in front of the fire."

"The road was intolerable in all this snow."

"Never mind, you are home now," Arabella replied, putting her arm around his shoulders.

She went to pull the bell rope to summon hot chocolate for her husband.

"What were you playing when I came in?" he asked.

"It was a prelude and fugue by Bach."

"Old man Bach again," replied Carl Manfred.

"Yes," said Arabella, "old man Bach."

They both laughed.

"Please continue to play," he invited her.

He watched her fingers moving effortlessly across the keyboard; her hair, unusually, was pinned up, revealing her long slender neck. He ached to kiss her but he would not disturb her. After so many busy weeks and never-ending royal demands, he and Arabella were at last alone. He wanted this perfect moment of peace and privacy to last.

She finished playing and joined him by the fire.

Taking his hand, she said, "Carl there is something I must tell you."

"And what is that? Is it another Camerata performance you have planned?"

"No, Carl, it is not. I am expecting a child."

He looked at her, his eyes suddenly full of joy.

"My dearest and most precious Arabella, I am so happy – overjoyed. I hope you are happy, too?"

"I am, truly happy," she said. "The Queen's bed at Schloss Charlottenburg inspired our passion and our child's conception."

Carl Manfred smiled.

"It will be a new avenue in our lives," said Arabella, "and it will bring a child's voice into this house."

"Arabella, a year or so ago I thought I would finish my life alone and that Herzberg would have no heir. But the deepest of good fortune has given me you and now a child."

"Carl Manfred, it may be a girl."

"Dearest Arabella, whether the child is a girl or a boy it will be truly welcome and blessed in this house. He or she will bind together the fields of England and the plains of Prussia. May I kiss you, Countess von Deppe?"

"You may indeed, Count von Deppe."

"Tomorrow is the Feast of St Valentine," she reminded him.

"What a romantic gift you have given me," he said. He embraced and kissed her gently. "Arabella, my dearest Valentine, before we go to eat, please play Herr Bach again."

As she did so, both were pensive.

Arabella was full of joy at the prospect of impending motherhood and the pleasure this had given her husband, but apprehensive nonetheless at what lay ahead. If only her mother could be with her. Carl Manfred sat in a chair by the fire, gazing into the flames and lost in thought. How was he going to break to his wife the news that the King wished them to travel soon to St Petersburg? Should he travel alone, leaving Arabella at Herzberg, or ask her to accompany him – in the depth of a Russian winter in her new condition? He decided to reflect on the matter for a few more days before advising Arabella of the King's unavoidable instruction.

At supper Arabella said she would write to her mother in the morning to tell her of their news.

"You should indeed tell Lady Whitfield as soon as possible. She will be delighted. And you should also write to my sister, Maria Louisa. In fact, you might suggest that when the weather improves she comes to Herzberg – for a mother and a prospective mother to spend some time together in the spring. And it would be a joy to see little Marie-Aurore again."

As he uttered these words, he knew that he had already made up his mind. He would go to St Petersburg alone, hoping that his mission for the King would be completed in time for him to return to Herzberg to be with his wife at the end of her confinement.

The next morning, as yet more snow fell, Arabella wrote to her mother.

Dearest Mama,

So many months have elapsed since we were last together at Herzberg. I think of you often – of our times together at the keyboard and of the comical Monsieur Noverre in my dancing lessons.

The deep Prussian winter has us all in its icy grip. I am counting the weeks to the return of spring as I am sure you are too in Norfolk. How I remember those chilling winds across the marshes from the north. Those winds from the Russian steppes show little mercy at Herzberg. But within, the house is full of warmth and comfort.

You may recall that I wrote to you last year on your return to England to tell you that, with CM's encouragement, I had gathered together some young and talented musicians to join me in promoting the enjoyment of music. I was most fortunate to find an eager and gifted young man, Herr Albrecht Bamberger, to lead them. We played together for the first time in May and again at the fête champêtre *Carl Manfred and I hosted at Schloss Herzberg a month later. Their music was much appreciated. Indeed, it seemed to inspire His Majesty the King to dance, even asking me for the last dance before his departure. Much to my surprise and delight, His Majesty the King asked us to perform in his presence in the royal chapel at the Palace of Charlottenburg on the 1st of December, to mark the beginning of Advent. Afterwards, he wrote to me to say we had so impressed him that he commanded us to call ourselves the Schloss Herzberger Camerata. We now do so.*

Assembled, we are six violinists, of which three are women. Then we have one viola, one cello and one double bass, as well as a bassoon, a flute, an oboe and a bass viol. Everyone is under the age of twenty-one and each player is immensely talented and enthusiastic. We have such fun.

On the 18th of last month the Camerata gave its first public performance at the St Nicholas Church in Potsdam. We were received with great appreciation and I could not escape the demand to sing at the end. I sang Lascia ch'io pianga *from Mr Handel's opera* Rinaldo.

None of this would have been possible without the musical education you gave me at Meltwater. With your inspiration I am using the presence of women in the Camerata to persuade those who enjoy music of the right of women to be treated as equals in all social respects, including the playing of every musical instrument, not just the harpsichord. After all, it was music that helped me to find a loving husband, who I am pleased to say shares my opinion on this matter. It was Mr Rameau who once wrote: "True music is the language of the heart."

Most important of all, dearest Mama, I wish you to know that I am bearing CM's child. This news has given him and me great happiness and contentment. But I must confess that in my joy I am also somewhat apprehensive at the prospect of what may lie ahead. I hope that after the child is born you will once again return to Schloss Herzberg, to see your first grandchild. I will keep you informed of my progress in the months ahead.

With my love and fondest affection,
Your daughter,
Arabella
Schloss Herzberg, Saturday, the Feast of St Valentine, 1767
Is there any news of my brother George?

The same morning Arabella wrote to Carl Manfred's sister, Maria Louisa, in Paris.

Dearest Maria Louisa,

I am writing to tell you I am expecting a child.

Before I left England someone described to me the symptoms of pregnancy. I began to experience them early last month. I asked our nearby physician, dear Herr Brenner, to come to see me without delay. He confirmed my condition and calculated that the baby will come at the beginning of September.

What news I was able to give CM yesterday, on the eve of the Feast of St Valentine! Until then I had managed to keep my condition a secret from him. He is full of happiness and pride, as indeed am I. But you should be aware, as I know I can confide in you, that I do have considerable apprehension about the new experience that awaits me in the months ahead.

I very much hope that when this bitter Prussian winter turns its back on us – and, I must emphasise, only if your husband permits it – you will be able to come to Schloss Herzberg with little Marie-Aurore as soon as possible, to give me not only the pleasure of your and her company, which I greatly desire, but also much-needed advice on the experience of birth and motherhood.

With affection,
Arabella
Schloss Herzberg, this Saturday the Feast of St Valentine, 1767

Early the following week both letters were speedily despatched to their respective destinations and Carl Manfred prepared to break the news to Arabella of the King's irreversible decision that he should go with all haste to St Petersburg. At the same time, Waldemar Drescher made final preparations for an encounter at

Berlin's Spandau citadel. He was now ready to set his plan in motion – with dangerous consequences if it were to go wrong. The woman he had chosen as bait was unaware of her role. Though as active as ever, Arabella continued in her more private moments to contemplate with concern the prospect of giving birth in a land far away from her mother, about whom she thought often. Everything had been done during her time at Mrs Hallam's establishment in Chesterfield Street to avoid conception and she recalled with a shudder the monthly visits from the doctor to inspect her. His methods had been demeaning, railing as he did against the curse of pregnancy. But she did her best to brush her apprehension aside in her determination to do whatever was necessary to ensure that the Schloss Herzberger Camerata would continue to flourish during the wait for her child.

*****

Standing at the confluence of the Spree and Havel rivers, massive and visually uncompromising, the great citadel of Spandau, in the western part of Berlin, had been built in the second half of the sixteenth century. It comprised four immense bastions joined together by a large curtain wall, a formidable defensive structure that offered no blind spot for exploitation by an enemy. The citadel's interior was a garrison but also a dark place to imprison enemies of the state.

Three days after Arabella had written her letters, on Tuesday the 17th of February, 1767, the man from the shadows entered the citadel's inner courtyard. Waldemar Drescher was tall and thin. His drawn face was framed by loose shoulder-length hair. He wore a long, somewhat shabby coat. His appearance was transformed from the handsome man who had presented Arabella Whitfield at the altar during her marriage ceremony in the chapel of the Royal Palace in Berlin on the 18th of March the year before. Apart from that brief public attendance, Drescher lived out of sight, performing in the shadows his role of secret agent and ruthless killer in the King's pay. As the monarch's most clandestine spymaster he had created an intricate network of agents and informers across Europe, securing information he could put to use in the defence of the King's interests. He used whatever methods were necessary – however foul they might be – in his trade. His methods of interrogation were brutal. Those to be killed never saw him come; he struck with menace, in silence, and his aim was deadly. Moreover, he acted without royal restraint, though he knew that if he made a mistake his actions would be denied. A lover of men, his existence was lonely. He knew his physical love would never be reciprocated by the man he had loved since a boy – the King.

In the shadows he had complete trust in no one other than the King and the Countess von Deppe. He certainly did not trust her husband, though his justification for not doing so was hard to fathom. Drescher's confidence in his abilities as a supreme schemer had led him to choose this remarkable and beguiling young English woman – who had put her life at risk and had displayed great courage in her lonely and dangerous journey across Europe the previous year in pursuit of the man she loved – as the bait, without her knowledge, to catch another of the King's traitors. Drescher had triumphed over his previous adversary but only because the Countess had bravely saved his life in the final confrontation. She had subsequently beseeched him to keep secret her previous existence in London's demi-monde. He had gladly vowed to do so in return for her pledge not to disclose what had happened that dreadful dark night near Magdeburg. Thus they were linked together by a bond of mutual trust and respect. He would not see her harmed so long as he lived. But he had concluded that did not restrain him from using her again as a means to locate yet another traitor in the King's circle.

Drescher entered the Julius keep. Descending a twisting stone staircase and walking along a low dark corridor, he came to a thick wooden door reinforced with bands of iron. Before turning the large key in the lock, he felt for the blade in his left sleeve. It was there as it always was – long, sharp and merciless. After masking his face, he opened the door.

The room was dim, damp and cold. A vent high up in the wall – a mere slit rather than a window – cast a slim shaft of grey light across the floor and onto a wide wooden bench on which lay a figure wrapped in a thick musty blanket. Drescher shook the body.

"Get up."

The figure barely stirred.

"Get up, I said."

Still the figure on the bench failed to move.

Drescher pulled back the blanket and, grabbing the huddled figure by the scruff of the neck, dragged it across the room to a chair by a table. He took a candle from his pocket, lit it from the almost extinguished flare on the wall and, after tipping molten wax onto the table to secure it, put it in front of the hunched man. Sitting on the edge of the table and caressing his cherished blade in his long fingers, Drescher turned to the man.

"Sit up, you wretch. Sit up."

The man sat up. He appeared to be short and stocky. His hair was peppery grey and grizzled. His eyes were lifeless, their dullness far beyond that of the suddenly woken. His wrists were locked in handcuffs.

"Your name is Philippe Robinet, yet another agent of the French king."

"Prove it," a growled voice replied.

"I can," replied Drescher. "Your name was written on a scrap of paper found on the body of Auguste Gaillard. You and he were accomplices of the traitor John Bolton. All of you were in the pay of King Louis of France. After Gaillard's death you sought revenge by following a certain young woman to Potsdam and then to Herzberg, where you sought employment in the stable. I smelt your treachery long ago. It became as obvious as your forged papers. And that is how you come to be here, awaiting execution."

Drescher drew his knife across Robinet's neck.

Robinet's eyes suddenly focused.

"I did it for money. I had known Gaillard in London. I had run out of money and he gave me occasional sums to run clandestine errands for him. I did not ask any questions. I just did it for the money he paid me."

Drescher suddenly plunged the tip of his blade into the table, startling Robinet.

"You are lying. You did not do it solely for money. You did it out of conviction. You did it because of your loyalty to King Louis of France, just like Gaillard. No man with a name like yours is just in it for occasional payments. A petty messenger would not travel with his paymaster to France and then towards Prussia. You witnessed Gaillard's death and then you sought revenge."

Drescher could not be sure his theory of Robinet's presence near Magdeburg was correct, but he had decided to put it to the test nonetheless. He withdrew his knife from the table and with its tip slowly drew blood from just beneath Robinet's jaw.

"Which means of execution would you prefer – the axe or the garrotte?"

Robinet's eyes moistened, his face turned ashen. He realised he had no choice but to comply with his inquisitor if he were to save his neck.

"I confess. I will do anything to stay alive."

"You are scum, just like most foreign agents. No honour and no loyalty to your cause," replied Drescher.

Neither man spoke. Robinet clasped his manacled hands, his eyes turned downwards; mouthing what appeared to be a prayer. Drescher decided to roll the dice in the first move of his deadly game.

"What do you know about a young English woman called Arabella Whitfield?"

Robinet paused before answering.

"She was a whore who worked in London at the house where Bolton stayed. She went to Paris with an older man from Prussia – I think his name was Carl Manfred von Deppe – after he, Bolton and another man, whose identity was never disclosed, had done their business in England. After Paris she vanished but, though I cannot be sure, she reappeared at von Deppe's side in Prussia."

"You are remarkably well informed," said Drescher. "She is indeed in Prussia and now von Deppe's wife."

"What is that to me?" replied Robinet.

"The truth of the matter," Drescher responded quickly, "is that, while she may indeed have been a whore, she is also a spy in King Louis's pay, secretly cultivated by Bolton. And now she has the ear of my King."

"I don't believe you. Gaillard would have told me."

"Spies sometimes divulge only what another person needs to know."

"I still don't believe you."

"I think I am right and I want you to help me prove it," responded Drescher slowly.

"How can I do that locked up here?"

"Someone will come to see you soon. I want you to tell that nameless person that you have evidence to prove the Countess von Deppe is a French spy, cultivated during her time as a prostitute in Mayfair in London."

"But, Monsieur, I have no evidence to offer this person."

"I will give it to you, and you will write it down in your own handwriting and pass it on."

"But why cannot you do this?"

"Because, you see, it needs to come from you – a known French spy. It takes one French spy to identify and betray another French spy."

"And if I do not comply with your wishes?"

Drescher banged the palm of his hand on the table.

"You will die – by means of the garrotte. Do you understand?"

"I do."

"Good."

"Who are you?" asked Robinet.

The masked man leaned across the table and peered into Robinet's eyes.

"You will never know."

With that Drescher rose and left the cell. As he removed his mask and hid his knife, he smiled. Robinet had taken the bait. The first throw of the dice had fallen in his favour. Now it was time for the next more deadly throw. He emerged into daylight. He realised he had just compromised his professed loyalty to the young English countess. If she knew what he had done, she could justly claim he had betrayed her; and her husband would become his sworn enemy.

* * * * *

A day later, Carl Manfred von Deppe broke the news to his wife that the King had instructed him to go without delay to St Petersburg, as his personal emissary, to help bring all possible influence to bear in favour of Prussia at the court of the Empress Catherine. The prospects of war were increasing, he explained, and the King wanted to avoid Russian support for his adversaries the King of France and the Empress of Austria. Frederick had wanted Arabella to accompany him, in order to bring her musical skills to bear in the diplomatic mix. But the King had now reluctantly accepted that, with Arabella carrying a child, it would be safer for her to remain at Herzberg than risk her health in a long and arduous journey to Russia in the depth of winter.

Arabella took the news of her husband's impending absence with sorrow but forbearance. Her mother had taught her long ago that tears in such circumstances were a sign of weakness. Except in the most intimate affairs of the heart, where there was often less control over human emotions, she had insisted that young women should be brave and positive, not swoon. In the days leading up to Carl Manfred's departure they spent much time together at Schloss Herzberg, talking and planning for his return in time for the birth of their child. Much against her husband's advice, Arabella insisted that she would continue to oversee personally the work of his faithful land agent, Maximilian. With his departure imminent, he tried to persuade Arabella that such a task, combined with her musical activity, would be too much for her to bear.

"Dearest Carl, women are often portrayed as the weaker sex. And with this portrayal goes a loss of freedom – freedom of the spirit, freedom of the intellect, freedom of choice. That is not for me. That is why I took the decision to disobey my father and to seek an independent life whatever might be the personal cost. That decision brought us together. I once wrote, 'I will do what people want but only as I want it to be.' You, my dearest Carl, are the first person in my life to understand what I meant by those words. Please accept me for what I am and let me be free to do as I wish."

He attempted to interrupt her but she put her finger to his lips.

"I am now," she continued, "the happiest of women. I am your devoted wife. I am your lover. I am the bearer of your child and mistress of Herzberg. I come from strong Anglo-French stock and the tasks I propose to undertake in your absence will keep me active and committed to the cause of the estate. Allowing me to do what I wish to do will be a reflection of your love for me, your trust in me and your respect for me. I assure you I will do nothing to endanger my life or that of our child, or to compromise my profound love for you. What is equally important is that you take the greatest care on your journey and while you are at St Petersburg. Nothing must happen to you. Nor must you forget me, despite the King's business. I desire you back in our bed beside me with all speed. You are my guiding star. Without you I am a lesser woman."

He smiled and, realising that he had given the impression of possibly misjudging his wife, he capitulated.

"Do whatever you think is best. I will miss you. I will think of you every waking moment, regardless of the tasks the King has given me, and you will be with me even in my sleep. Without you I would be a lesser man. If I am your guiding star, so too are you mine. I assure you that I will be back beside you in our bed with all possible haste. Until then, I have something to give you."

He momentarily left the room, returning with a large package wrapped in brown cloth. He laid it on the table in front of Arabella. She slowly removed the wrapping to reveal an oil portrait of Pallas Athene, painted in the sixteenth-century Italian style. Instead of wearing armour, Athene's traditional attire, the figure was swathed in a dark-green gown with her hair partly loose, a strand of curls tracing the line of her slender neck. She was holding a small breastplate on which was a cameo bearing the word *Athene*, encompassed by a palm and olive branch.

Arabella gasped.

"My dearest Carl, this is truly beautiful. You are such a kind man."

She gazed at the picture, holding it up. Then putting it down, she turned and kissed him, her hands on his cheeks. Tears filled her eyes.

"I love you so much. It will be so painful to see you go."

Carl Manfred took her hands in his.

"Arabella, you are my Athene. Not only a true warrior but my goddess of wisdom. I hope this picture will be the beginning of a new and better collection of pictures at Herzberg, pictures chosen by you, a task I leave to you entirely. Will you do that for me?"

"I will," she replied.

They kissed again.

Two days later, on Saturday the 28th of February, 1767, Carl Manfred left Schloss Herzberg, which was still covered in deep snow. After he had gone, Arabella lay on their bed, wrapped in a fur shawl, with only the sound of the crackling fire and the low moan of the wind outside to disturb her private thoughts. She was alone – newly married, carrying a child and chatelaine of Herzberg

– without her husband. His departure and the responsibilities she had sought and would now bear alone preyed on her mind. If only her mother were here. But she chastised herself yet gain. Tears were of no use. She had to be strong and determined, at least in the sight of others, even though inwardly she feared she might not have the strength.

Two weeks later Arabella received a letter – dated the 5th of March – from Carl Manfred to say that he was about to cross the Russian border that day. The weather was wretched and might delay his progress. He would write to her immediately upon his arrival at St Petersburg.

Early the following week, Arabella received a letter from her sister-in-law, Maria Louisa de Vervins.

My dearest Arabella,

I was delighted to receive your letter and to hear of your excellent news. It has raised our spirits in this most miserable winter.

I have managed to persuade E to let me leave Paris before too long, which means that, weather permitting, I should be at Schloss Herzberg by the end of April. I will bring Marie-Aurore with me.

I hear rumours that CM has been sent on a mission to St Petersburg. While I will be sorry to miss him – unless of course he has returned to Herzberg by the time of our visit – it means we will have more time together to share gossip and to talk of the birth of your child.

With warmest felicitations,
Maria Louisa de Vervins
Paris, Saturday the 28th of February, 1767

* * * * *

In the weeks following Carl Manfred's departure for St Petersburg, Arabella made sure she was as busy as possible; not for her seclusion behind shuttered windows and locked doors.

Her beauty, understated elegance, gentleness of spirit and her deepening interest in Herzberg's well-being and those who served it, coupled with her already growing reputation as a gifted musician and a connoisseur of art, made her a growing topic of wider social conversation in Potsdam and Berlin. Those who called on her were impressed by her increasing knowledge of estate management, by her ease and flair in conversation – touching on matters of moral and intellectual substance – and by the evident equality in her relationship with her husband, whom, as was clear to all, she dearly loved and greatly missed.

As the spring sun gradually became stronger, Arabella found a sheltered spot on the patio where she sat from time to time, reflecting on the months past and contemplating those to come, not least the impending birth and her forthcoming role as a mother. Repeatedly her thoughts turned to her absent husband. Though she regularly received letters from him, to which she assiduously replied, assuring him that the estate and her health continued to flourish, Arabella missed him greatly – his embrace and gentleness in bed, walking with him arm in arm in the garden, and seeking his advice on her intentions for the orchestra, which he warmly supported. The Countess von Schlegel visited her occasionally, bringing news of the court, while the young and perhaps too attentive Father Johann Schmidt came regularly to hear her confession, which Arabella kept to the minimum, and to pray with her for the safe return of the Count and the health of the child in her womb.

Yet time for reflection and the slightest inclination to self-pity was limited. It was Arabella's wish – despite her condition – to continue to do all that was necessary to promote Herzberg's well-being and respect for her husband. On the latter, her maid, Hanne, told Arabella one day that since his marriage the master had become relaxed and spirited, barely recognisable from the man the household staff had known before. Apart from oversight of the estate, requests for performances by the Camerata increased. This prompted Arabella to intensify her search for new and less well known music to play – not just that of German composers but from elsewhere in Europe too. Herr Bamberger, proving to be a most knowledgeable young man, became a regular visitor to Herzberg to discuss new musical directions and experiments. Arabella welcomed his presence at the house. His enthusiasm and infectious laughter were an antidote to any tendency on her part to be introspective in her husband's absence. Ever mindful of Herr

Drescher's advice to be eternally vigilant, Arabella ensured as often as possible that she was not alone with him. This was not because she feared unbecoming behaviour on his part, but to avoid any possibility of misinformed gossip emanating from the servants at the house. She recalled from Meltwater and its surrounding communities the potential damage of such gossip and how quickly misconceptions and tittle-tattle could take root.

Though Arabella had chosen not to keep a diary, from time to time she recorded – sometimes in French, sometimes in English, in neat handwriting on loose sheets of paper – particular impressions or intentions, slipping what she wrote into the handsome blue leather-bound music book that the King had given her on the occasion of her marriage. This had replaced her earlier and much-treasured book, which she handed to her mother, Lady Whitfield, as a memento on her return to England following the wedding. Arabella kept the music book secure.

Maria Louisa and her daughter, Marie-Aurore, finally arrived at Schloss Herzberg at the end of April. For Arabella it was a time of much laughter, but underlying her outward happiness was sorrow at the prolonged absence of her husband. There was still no indication in his letters of his likely return from St Petersburg.

*****

During the remaining weeks of winter, Philippe Robinet, locked deep inside Spandau citadel, received three visits from a masked man. Unable to see his face, Robinet found it hard to judge his age, but he had a limp and a grey beard protruded from the bottom of the mask. The voice was deep and full of gravel. Sitting at the table in his cell, Robinet was obliged to write each part of a comprehensive confession. At the end of each visit the masked man put the sheets of completed paper into a leather satchel.

First he recorded how he had been recruited by Auguste Gaillard; revealed his knowledge of Gaillard's liaison with John Bolton; and provided information about the connections of all three in France. In the second visit, he documented, as instructed, that Arabella Whitfield, the young English woman, had been recruited to spy for France by John Bolton while working in a London brothel, and had now become acquainted with the

Prussian King. She had been involved in the mysterious disappearance of her brother, George, possibly murdered, and was aware of the killing of Gaillard. Having gained the ear of King Frederick, as a spy for the French King she had become even deadlier, though there was now possible evidence that she was no longer spying for France but for England. During the third visit, he wrote – again as directed – about the suspect allegiance of Carl Manfred von Deppe while in England. Robinet frequently challenged what he was told to say. Each time the masked man said that he should write as instructed if he wanted to save his neck.

A few days later the masked man returned a fourth time.

"I have checked your confession. Now sign it!"

"How can I sign it? The first part is an honest account of my work for Monsieur Gaillard. But the rest is untrue for all I'm concerned. How can I know about the Whitfield girl? If I'm to be tried, I want it to be on the basis of what I know to be true, not what I know nothing about. False testimony is not my business."

The masked man scoffed.

"What you have written is correct. I'm trying to help you. If you wish to receive leniency and your possible freedom, sign your confession now! If you don't, you will remain in this cell for the rest of your life. Now sign!"

Robinet took the proffered pen, dipped it in the ink well and signed.

The masked man took the confession, now more than a dozen pages long, and put it back into the leather satchel.

"In a few days' time you are likely to have a visitor. The visitor will ask you whether your confession is true. You will answer yes and add that you are ready to speak to your confession in court. On receiving that information the visitor will leave and in due course a trial will take place. If you have done everything as instructed it is likely that you will receive mercy and eventually you may expect to be returned to France. Do you understand what is required?"

"Yes," replied Robinet.

"Good," said the masked man.

With that the heavily disguised Drescher left the cell, already planning the next move in his game of chess.

* * * * *

It was in May, on Friday the 8th, that Arabella received the first of two unexpected visitors.

The King had been on one of his renowned inspection tours when he decided that he would call on the English countess at Schloss Herzberg. One of the royal guards arrived breathlessly at the house to announce that His Majesty was an hour away. This news put the household into a spin as everyone rushed around making sure that each of the main rooms was in good order. Arabella pondered what had prompted the King to make an unscheduled call. With only minutes to spare she stood at the bottom of the steps leading to the main entrance of the house as the dust of his carriage became visible beyond the nearest trees.

As the King stepped from his coach, dressed in his familiar public uniform, his often grave face broke into a gentle smile. Arabella stepped forward and began her curtsey but he took her hand firmly.

"I do not think that is necessary today."

"Sire, it is a great honour that you should visit us today. Sadly, my husband is not here to guide you around the estate, but I will gladly try to answer any questions you may have. The Count's sister is here but regrettably she is out riding. May I offer you some refreshment?"

They stood on the patio in the sunlight.

"Perhaps later," the King replied. "What I should like most is for you yourself to take me on a tour of the estate. I hear you have been doing good work in the Count's absence. Let me see what a woman can do. Let us go in my carriage."

A few minutes later the King, with Arabella at his side, rode around the nearer part of the Herzberg land. She earnestly described some of the improvements she and her husband had made. In the midst of her explanation, the King turned to her.

"Countess, I have missed seeing you in Potsdam and indeed in Berlin. More than that, I have missed hearing you sing, accompanied by that young and upcoming orchestra of yours, the Schloss Herzberger Camerata I think it is called. But I know you are expecting a child. When is it due?"

"It is due in the early part of September, Sire."

"Countess, let me be blunt. It is unlikely that Count von Deppe will be able to return to Herzberg soon. He is doing good work for me in St Petersburg – keeping an eye on the devious Empress Catherine. She is German by birth but has become entirely Russian and consequently tiresome in her attitude to Prussia. That is all the more reason for us to do what we can to persuade her not to interfere with Prussian interests. There is still much work outstanding to ensure this land has a safe future founded on sound alliances, and your husband can help us in that regard."

"When, Sire, might I expect my husband back?" asked Arabella nervously.

The King paused.

"Later this year, after the birth of your child, I wish you – and the child – to travel to St Petersburg to join the Count for a few months. I wish you to meet the Empress, to charm her with your singing, to talk to her woman to woman, to convince her that there is more to Prussia than a tiresome old king. Will you do that for me?"

"Yes, I will," Arabella replied apprehensively as the implication of what the King had just said became clear. Her husband would not be back soon.

"A loyal answer," responded the King. "Now show me some more of your good work. And, Countess, please say nothing about this matter until you receive further advice from Herr Drescher."

"My lips are sealed," replied Arabella, while quietly noting that this was only the second occasion on which she had heard the King utter the name of the man in the shadows, the other being their very first meeting, at Sanssouci.

"But not in St Petersburg, when you at last see your husband and you sing at the imperial court," interjected the King.

They both laughed.

An hour later Arabella and the King returned to Herzberg. After a brief conversation with Maria Louisa, he left for Potsdam.

"Arabella, did you know he was coming?"

"No, I did not. I had just one hour's notice."

"What did he want?" asked Maria Louisa inquisitively.

"He wished to see the estate and to ask if I was well in Carl Manfred's absence. I assured him I was and showed him some of our recent changes and innovations, which he approved. That was all," insisted Arabella.

"My dearest Arabella, that man is a wily old fox. He is up to something and you will surely be part of it, be certain of that."

True to her word, Arabella said nothing. Later that night, in her bed, she reminded herself of the need for constant vigilance. She felt deeply alone, longing to be with her husband.

*****

Almost a week later she received a note from the British Ambassador, Mr Mitchell, asking if he might call on her on his way back to Berlin from a provincial tour. He had some more manuscripts of English music she might wish to have for the Camerata. Arabella wrote immediately to say that he would be most welcome, though sadly Count von Deppe would not be present.

The Ambassador called at Herzberg on Thursday the 28th of May. Sensing that the Ambassador might ask her again about her thoughts on England, Arabella asked Herr Bamberger to be present, on the pretext that she and he had been discussing music. Over tea on the patio, the conversation was largely about the music of Thomas Arne – widely popular in England, particularly for his setting of James Thomson's poem *Rule, Britannia*, a transcript of which the Ambassador gave to Arabella – and of course the continuing respect for the late Mr Handel. Arabella again thanked His Excellency for the music of William Boyce he had provided earlier and which the orchestra had played with good effect in their Advent concert at Schloss Charlottenburg. After further pleasantries, the Ambassador rose to take his leave.

"Let me walk with you to your carriage," said Arabella.

"Countess, please stay."

"Your Excellency, a woman in my condition must have her exercise and that I should do daily if I am to be ready for what lies ahead."

"Of course, Countess, I understand."

As they walked across the driveway to the Ambassador's carriage, with Herr Bamberger following a discreet distance behind as earlier instructed, His Excellency turned to Arabella.

"I understand His Majesty the King called on you recently. You must have felt greatly flattered that he should do so. Did he have news of your husband in St Petersburg and when he might return?"

Arabella sensed Mr Mitchell was once again seeking to solicit possible information about the King's intentions.

"Ambassador, His Majesty called on me – as he was passing the estate – to ask about my condition and to request me to show him some of our recent land innovations here at Herzberg, some of which have implemented what the King advocated long ago as sound agricultural practice. We did not discuss affairs of state, as such matters are not worthy subjects for discussion with a mere woman, as you will recall I have said to you before."

"Madame," the Ambassador quickly responded, "that cannot be said to apply in your case. Your reputation for reasonable and indeed intellectual conversation goes before you."

"That may be so, Your Excellency, but military and strategic matters are not of that ilk."

Thus parried, the Ambassador took his final leave. As his carriage sped away, he speculated – as had the Countess's sister-in-law, and indeed others, earlier – that the old King would not have called on a lady awaiting her first child, her husband absent, without some specific purpose in mind. The Countess was an astute woman, who possibly knew more than many what was in the King's mind. He would attempt to probe again before long. Perhaps it was now time for Mrs Mitchell to intervene.

*****

Arabella continued her life as normally as she could, while becoming increasingly nervous about the impending birth – an event now only three months away. Regrettably, her mother would not be able to be with her as she was preoccupied with matters at Meltwater. But Maria Louisa had promised to return to Herzberg in August, to be present for the baby's arrival.

*****

It was late in June that Arabella received word the Count von Schlegel had died in his sleep at Schloss Richemont. She immediately sent her condolences to the Countess and apologised for her absence from the Count's funeral. On Wednesday the 8th of July the Countess called on Arabella. She was dressed in black and veiled, but her purposeful demeanour and occasional smiles were far from mournful.

"I wish to thank you for your most kind and thoughtful words of condolence on the death of my husband. Your letter and that from His Majesty gave me great comfort. The Count had been in pain for some time but I had not expected him to succumb to his latest illness so suddenly."

"I apologise that my condition prevented me from paying my husband's and my respects on the day of your husband's funeral at Schloss Richemont."

"I quite understand, my dear," said the Countess Katherina.

"Our thoughts continue to be with you," replied Arabella.

After further polite exchanges, the Countess asked Arabella for news of her husband.

"He remains on the King's business in St Petersburg, but it is my hope that he will return to Herzberg before the birth of our child. However, if that is not possible, his sister in Paris, Madame de Vervins, has promised to be here to assist me."

"And so will I," replied Katherina von Schlegel. "I have not yet had the blessing of bearing children but that will not stop me from helping you to ensure all runs smoothly."

"Thank you," said Arabella.

Preparing to take her leave, the Countess remarked to Arabella that she had heard the King had called on her. That was an unusual step for His Majesty to take. Had his visit carried any particular significance? Wary of the direction their conversation might now tend, and aware of the Countess's closeness to the King, Arabella knew she had to respond with great care.

"His Majesty's visit was most courteous but also most unexpected. He was passing by and wished me to show him some of the new methods of agriculture my husband and I introduced on advice the King first gave some years ago. He also asked after my health and hoped that before long my husband and I may be together again, though when that might be is unclear."

The Countess Katherina seemed reassured.

"I am sure your separation will not be prolonged any further than necessary and that on Count von Deppe's return, and following the birth of your child, we shall all be able to see more of you in Potsdam and Berlin."

"Countess, the affairs of court are not for me," replied Arabella. "What matters most to me is the safe return of my husband, the delivery of my child and the promotion of more opportunities for the Camerata to play in public. That is what is uppermost in my mind."

"I am sure that it is," said Katherina von Schlegel.

With that remark she took her leave. As the carriage hurriedly left, Arabella ruminated on the fact that the King's visit to Herzberg had indeed caused a stir. She sensed something was afoot but could not imagine what it was.

* * * * *

Philippe Robinet sat alone each day in his prison cell. No one came. He began to imagine that the masked man and his confession had been a trick of his mind. All he knew was that the seasons were changing. The daylight through the aperture in his cell had become stronger and the cell was less cold. He asked for a book to read but his request was repeatedly denied. All he could do was to read and reread his prayer book and plan and replan what he would do with the freedom he had been promised.

He had no idea which day it was when the cell door opened and a shrouded and masked figure entered. The mask covered the figure's entire face, distorting the voice it uttered so that Robinet had no idea whether the human being beneath the cloak was young or old, man or woman. But he felt the voice was perhaps being pitched deliberately low.

"You are Philippe Robinet, are you not?"

"Yes," he replied.

"You have confessed in writing to spying for a foreign power, have you not?"

"Yes," replied Robinet.

"Is this your writing?" the voice asked, with a gloved hand thrusting several pages of script under Robinet's nose.

"I cannot see properly," he said.

The other gloved hand thrust the candle towards Robinet.

The prisoner recognised his handwriting.

"Yes, it is."

"Are you ready to swear this is your testimony in court – all of it?"

Robinet hesitated.

"Yes," he replied.

"I am satisfied," replied the voice.

The figure in black stood up and walked towards the cell door.

"When might I be free in return for what I have written?" asked Robinet.

"That remains to be seen. Your life is in the hands of others."

"What day and what month is it, sir?" Robinet called out.

"It is Wednesday the 8th of July," replied the voice.

The cell door slammed shut. Robinet slumped back on his trestle bed in despair.

The figure in black quickly left the citadel to return the confession without delay to the place from which it had been illicitly removed. The document, which could easily be taken again, had become an irrefutable part of the gathering incrimination. The time to strike would come soon. Patience was required in the meantime.

* * * * *

In early August, following the return of Maria Louisa and Marie-Aurore, Arabella knew that, given the great distance between Herzberg and St Petersburg, Carl Manfred would not be back at Herzberg before the birth of their child. His letters home could barely conceal his increasing frustration with his instruction to remain in Russia. He repeatedly sought forgiveness for his absence. In her replies she urged him to be patient, to carry out his work diligently and to know that her love for him was even deeper than before.

Later in August she wrote a further letter to him.

> *My dearest loving Carl,*
>
> *I sense that the time for me to give birth is now not far away – possibly only two or three weeks are left. Maria Louisa is once again with me and gives me daily comfort that all will be well. She has made all the necessary arrangements with the physician. I trust in her judgement. But I must confess to you*

that I am filled with trepidation at what is to come. I have been praying daily to Our Lady for a safe delivery. I have tested God's patience often in my life, but I hope she may intercede on my behalf at this time. Should I not survive what is about to happen, I beg you to remember the words that follow.

You have during the short time of our acquaintance been the most loving, gentlest and kindest of men. As my husband, you have changed my life, wretched that it was, and by doing so have given me profound and constant happiness and satisfaction. As I said to you before your departure, you have been my guiding star, my source of wisdom and my voice of reason. Sharing my body – my inner temple – with you has been a noble and deeply physical pleasure. You have never abused my trust. If our child lives, despite what may happen to me, cherish him or her with all your heart and all your strength, and remember me always, whatever you may decide to do during the remainder of your life.

Lastly, if I do happen to die in childbirth, let us abide by what we agreed before you left Herzberg. If the child is a boy, he will be called Frederick Daniel von Deppe. If it is to be a girl, we resolved that she should be called Elise Catherine Hildegard von Deppe. May our child enjoy happiness and good fortune and may it be armed with an abundance of fortitude to overcome the perils of this life.

I must stop as a special messenger is here to take this letter with all speed to St Petersburg.

From your devoted and loving Arabella

Schloss Herzberg, Friday the 21st of August, 1767

* * * * *

The letter arrived at the beginning of September at Carl Manfred's house in Dvortsovaya Naberezhnaya – the Palace Embankment – in St Petersburg, a short distance from the Winter Palace. He read it, his eyes filling with tears. He rose from his desk, seizing a china ornament which he threw in rage across the room. He cursed the King for keeping him so long in Russia, far removed from the woman he loved. Much of his life had been loveless. Now he was being kept from his young and beautiful wife. Because of the King he would not be at Herzberg to see the birth of his child. What monarch served so loyally would permit such an injustice to happen? He sat back down at his desk and picked up a pen to write immediately to Arabella. But what was the point of doing so? He could not find the words to match hers and the letter would not reach her in time. He grabbed his coat and left the building to walk quickly to St Isaac's Cathedral.

He entered. The cathedral was almost empty. He had never worshipped regularly, despite the urging of his late father. But on the eve of battle he had often found a quiet place to pray for God's forgiveness and to ask to be spared death in combat. He lit two candles and sat in solitude, praying for his beloved wife and their child. As he was about to go, a priest asked him if he was well. Carl Manfred, explaining his presence in the church, asked him to pray for his wife. Father Pyotr led him to the icon of the Virgin Mary and together they offered prayers for Arabella's salvation and the safety of her baby.

On Wednesday the 9th of September, 1767, Arabella, Countess von Deppe, after protracted labour, gave birth at Schloss Herzberg to a son, Frederick Daniel von Deppe. The baby was small and the first days were difficult, but the child gradually gained strength in the arms of Frau Weiser, his wet nurse. Two days later Arabella was sufficiently recovered to sit by the window in her bedroom to write to her husband.

My dearest Carl,

It is with great pleasure that I write to tell you that you have a son bearing the name we agreed – Frederick Daniel. He is well, as am I. He will be a fine fellow.

Everyone is most kind. Maria Louisa has been of great support. She will stay at Herzberg until the end of the month, so that I can get as much rest as possible. ML has also kindly arranged for Frederick's baptism to take place here at Herzberg as soon as possible, in accordance with what we agreed earlier. Herr Drescher has arranged for the Catholic Bishop of Berlin to come in the next day or so for this purpose.

I have thanked Our Lady for her intercession. Now my prayers are directed to our coming together before long, so you can see your son and I can see my husband.

Your devoted and loving wife,
Arabella
Schloss Herzberg, Friday the 11th of September, 1767

Waldemar Drescher ensured that the letter was speedily delivered in St Petersburg on the 21st of September, quickly followed by a letter from the Countess to her mother. But for him, now that the Countess's baby was born, he could move to the next stage in his game.

On receiving the letter Carl Manfred returned that evening to St Isaac's Cathedral. He sought out Father Pyotr to tell him of the news of his wife and child. Together they lit candles in front of the icon of the Virgin Mary and prayed.

Later that night he wrote to his wife.

My dearest Arabella,

I received your most welcome letter today. I am overcome with joy and relief that you and our son, Frederick Daniel, are well and in good heart. I thank you profoundly for the priceless gift you have given me.

Your earlier letter greatly moved me. I tried to write but was consumed with rage that we were separated by a great distance when we should have been together at Herzberg. That was not a mood in which to respond to what you had written. Moreover, not even the fleetest of messengers would have delivered my words in time. I wish you to know that instead I went that very evening to St Isaac's Cathedral and prayed earnestly for your life and safety. A priest, Father Pyotr, and I lit candles before the icon of the Virgin Mary. I have since returned to the Cathedral and, with Father Pyotr, have given thanks for your well-being.

As I told you on our wedding night I do not have the same ease and eloquence with words as you. But I wish you to know that, if I am your guiding star, you personify to me the Sun and Moon – radiating brilliance and warmth during the day and silky softness and mystery at night. I love you so much.

I will continue to pray for you and our son and that before long we will be reunited. I cannot wait to take you in my arms.
From your loving and devoted husband,

Carl Manfred
St Petersburg, Tuesday the 22nd of September, 1767

*****

During the remainder of September a steady flow of well-wishers arrived at Herzberg to congratulate Arabella and to see her son. The Countess Katherina was amongst the first to call, followed shortly afterwards by Mrs Mitchell, wife of His Excellency the British Ambassador. Herr Bamberger was another prompt visitor and was surprised when, after the necessary pleasantries, Arabella plunged immediately into plans for future performances by the orchestra. A date was set for an early rehearsal at Herzberg, to be followed by at least one concert before the end of the year.

An even more immediate task for Arabella was to select a *Kinderfrau* to look after her baby. The nanny she chose – on the prior recommendation of Maria Louisa – was Frau Klein, a charming middle-aged widow from Potsdam with two grown-up children of her own. Her manners reminded Arabella of her own nanny and wet nurse in England, Sarah Bayley. As German was Frau Klein's only lingua franca, Arabella's German vocabulary had to expand rapidly to include the care of her child. With Frau Klein safely ensconced in the house and the wet nurse, Frau Weiser, nearby, Arabella was steadily able to become increasingly active, to the point that by the middle of October, to everyone's astonishment, she already rode astride her horse around the estate with Maximilian. By then also, Hanne was already lacing her back into her corset. Arabella was privately determined to be received into her husband's arms with unrestrained physical adoration. The mere thought of his touch aroused her.

With the congratulations came two further letters. The first letter was from the King.

Most Personal
My dear Countess,

I have heard from the Countess Katherina the excellent news of the birth of your son. I am honoured that you should wish to call him Frederick. I send to you, to him and to your husband my best wishes. Your plans to be reunited with the

Count will, I am sure, soon be clear.

I hope that before long it will be possible for the Camerata to play again. I am reliably informed they are much missed. Indeed, might they, with you, wish to consider performing in the Potsdam Garrison Church on the Feast Day of St Cecilia, the 22nd of November? That would be an excellent opportunity once again to hear your voice, of which we have all felt the lack over the past months.

Frederick

Sanssouci, the 29th of September, 1767

The King's oblique reference to her plans for seeing Carl Manfred she took to be a signal that the journey to St Petersburg to which he had referred now beckoned. She assumed that in due course she would receive further news of what was being arranged. Until then she would say nothing. She locked the letter away, together with those from her husband.

The second letter was from Lady Whitfield.

Ma chère Comtesse, ma chère fille,

I was overjoyed to receive your letter. My heart is full of happiness, though tinged with sadness that I cannot be with you and my grandson at this time. Sir Robert has asked me to convey his own best wishes, but I know his sentiments will be of no consequence to you – and rightly so. Sarah is beaming with pride, busy telling everyone how well she brought you up to be a mother. Everyone at Meltwater misses you keenly, though no one more so than me.

I will continue to pray daily to Our Lady for the health and well-being of you both. Please do take the greatest care in the cold winter months ahead; the two of you mean so much to me. And I do hope King F permits your husband to return home soon, to be where he should have been many weeks ago.

Another autumn has come to Meltwater and still no news of your brother, George. I am here alone most of the time as your father continues to spend ever more time with his London dalliance, Lady BW. I have no care for him or her. Ah! Les hommes . . .

But the pleasing consequence of Sir Robert's absence is that

I am able to do much as I please at Meltwater. Yet, Arabella, how much I miss our gossip, our journeys to Norwich, our music and dancing together! Perhaps next year we could arrange to meet in Paris. Before then, please do write as often as you can.
From your ever-loving Mama
Meltwater, Tuesday the 6th of October, 1767

* * * * *

Late on the afternoon of Wednesday the 14th of October, after arriving at different times, two people met discreetly in a house near the Alter Markt, the Old Market Square, not from the Stadtschloss, the King's winter palace. They were the Countess Katherina von Schlegel and Father Johann Schmidt. They entered a small dingy room at the back of the house. An elderly miserable-looking woman brought tea. Against the background of a ticking clock, the Countess and the priest, even though their paths had crossed at Schloss Herzberg, eyed one another with evident distrust, uttering no words, as though they were adversaries circling, waiting to pounce on the other's first move. Finally Father Johann broke the silence.

"Countess, please accept my condolences on the death of your husband. I met him only once but it was evident to me, as it was to others, that he was a kind and just man. His Majesty appreciated his advice."

"The late Count was indeed generous and fair, but also sometimes foolish, and the King mocked him for it," replied the Countess. "He found that ridicule hard to bear. But such is the nature of monarchs – to mock those who seek to be their trusted friends. Yet despite these painful slights I will not withdraw to seclusion at Richemont. Who knows? I might marry again some day – someone perhaps younger."

"You are an attractive woman, Countess, with a sharp mind and strong ambitions, which our ageing King still appreciates," replied the priest.

"We will see about that," said the Countess. "But chatter is not the reason we are here. We meet to discuss a matter of mutual interest."

"And pray, Countess, what is that?" asked the young priest.

"The Countess von Deppe is the reason I asked you to come," responded Katherina von Schlegel icily. "You are her confessor, are you not?"

"Yes, I am," he answered. "But how is that relevant to you?"

"The Countess von Deppe is an enemy," replied the Countess von Schlegel with venom.

"But I do not understand," said the priest. "Arabella von Deppe is young, highly attractive, brave. A skilled musician, a landowner's wife and now a mother. I can vouch for that as a regular visitor to Herzberg and her priest. She is rarely seen at court. Playing music, riding and estate matters are her preoccupations. How can she be an enemy?"

"Father Johann – if that is who you are – let me be frank," the Countess interjected. "Do not underestimate the arts of the devil. She may not be at court but the King still favours her. He danced with her at Herzberg last year. He called on her before the birth of her child, and he has written privately to her since. Moreover, it is also to be noted that the British Ambassador has visited her twice at Herzberg. As you see, there is much upon which to speculate. Is she cleverly advancing the interests of her country of birth, or is she – through trickery – advancing the strategies of France?"

"What do you mean?" asked the priest, suddenly taking greater notice of Katherina von Schlegel's words.

"I have read the confession of a certain Philippe Robinet, now imprisoned in Spandau citadel," said the Countess. "In it he has firmly stated that Arabella von Deppe was recruited as an agent for France while she was a whore in a London brothel. There she was introduced to Count von Deppe, who was on the King's secret business – the removal of a man who betrayed the King many years ago, when he was Crown Prince. If, as this confession attests, the Countess von Deppe is a foreign agent, whether it be for the French or the English, do we want such a morally corrupted young woman becoming a close confidante of the King? That is my role, not one for an upstart English girl, a common prostitute."

"How can you be sure this confession is genuine?" the priest asked.

"I have seen it and confronted in his cell the prisoner who made it. He swore to me that it was genuine."

"How were you able to see the confession?" he asked.

"I removed the confession from the jailer's office. The jailer revealed where it was kept. He relished the thought of an impending execution."

The priest paused.

"I agree with your sentiments. As a priest, I do not want a sinful British prostitute betraying our King in his advancing years. And you, Countess, what about you?"

The Countess von Schlegel was silent. Her eyes closed and her body stiffened. Then she leaned forward and, with a flushed face and eyes of fire, slowly replied, "I have my interests to advance and will not brook opposition from another of my sex, particularly a common whore. I want her removed. I trust I can look to you, Father, to help me find the means?"

Again the priest paused. Then he spoke with great precision.

"The whore, from what she told me in confession, intends to travel to St Petersburg before the end of the year, to be reunited with her husband. I propose that you and I should accompany her on her journey as her entourage, and that on arrival we expose her in the Czarina's court for what she is."

"Why not expose her now?" replied the Countess von Schlegel.

"Countess, we need time to plan – time to prepare the necessary documents to be found in her luggage as evidence of her background and perfidy. I will need a month to accomplish this. Once the deed is done, you will be able to tell His Majesty that you saved him from acute embarrassment, shaming Count von Deppe and reinforcing your position."

"And what is your personal gain from the matter?" asked the Countess.

"My motives shall remain private, but are of such gravity as to cause me to propose the course of action I have set before you."

"And what of Robinet?" asked Katherina von Schlegel.

"Surely that will be the business of the jailer. I'm certain a little money will grease the palm that holds the fateful axe."

Silence fell upon the room. Outside daylight was fading rapidly. The Countess Katherina liked Arabella von Deppe. The young woman reminded her of her own youth, and Count von Deppe of the husband she had never enjoyed. Now, growing older, a fact that soon no powder would disguise, she was consumed by jealousy. She perceived the young English countess as her cunning opponent, and opponents in such struggles had to be vanquished. Though fearful of the sin she was about to commit, she was compelled to turn to the priest.

"So be it. But if this plan goes wrong, I will drag you with me into hell."

"Thank you, Countess. You have made a sound decision. What I have said will come to pass."

As the two figures left the house, first the Countess, then shortly afterwards the priest, Waldemar Drescher, known as the thresher of men, smiled behind the spyhole. The trap was almost ready to spring. The following Monday, the 19th of October, Philippe Robinet was summarily tried in his cell for spying, as he had confessed, on behalf of a foreign power. The Catholic priest, Father Johann, was asked to administer the last rites and to witness the burial of the body in the prison yard. The jailer agreed to carry out the execution and promised to assist the priest later in the week to write an account of the recent events at the prison.

* * * * *

At the beginning of November Waldemar Drescher called unexpectedly at Herzberg in order, he said, to pay his respects to the new baby. But after a perfunctory view of Frederick, he turned to the obvious reason for his visit.

"Countess, the time is fast approaching for you to join your husband in St Petersburg. I am told that Christmas and the New Year are a good time to see the Russian court at its most pleasurable and magnificent. His Majesty has asked me to make the necessary arrangements for you to undertake the journey – once you have given a concert for him, to mark St Cecilia's Day. The journey will not be easy this time of the year, but I will ensure that all will be well."

"Herr Drescher," Arabella replied, "I have the utmost respect for you but I find it hard to understand why it should be so necessary for me to travel such a distance with a young child at the start of winter. If it were within my power, I would much prefer to greet my husband at Herzberg."

"Countess," Drescher answered, "let me quote the King, who is wise on so many matters. He once said, 'Diplomacy without arms is like music without instruments.' You see, Countess, in this instance you are our arms, even though your prowess is in the making of music."

"I am greatly flattered you should think so, but how can I, a young English woman, make a contribution to promoting good relations between Prussia and Russia when there is talk of so much at stake?"

"You underestimate your potential, Countess. In a game of chess it is sometimes the case that a lesser piece on the board can check an opponent. You are young, elegant and subtle and, dare I say it, a most attractive woman. You are well suited to achieving, with others, certain Prussian moves on the chess board at this time."

"Herr Drescher, again I am deeply flattered by your remarks. All I try to do is to be a loving wife, a good mother, a keen manager of the estate and a patron of fine music. But if it is truly the King's wish that I should travel to Russia because people of influence like you believe I can help, then I will go. Yet uppermost in my mind will be to reclaim my husband to my bed, from which he has been absent for too long."

Arabella blushed as she said the last words, not meaning to have uttered them. But Drescher had provoked her into doing so.

"Good, it is settled," he said. "You should be ready to leave on Monday the 7th of December. But in the meantime say nothing to anyone. Your intention to travel should be secret until just before you leave."

"And who is to keep me company on this journey, other than Frau Klein and Frau Weiser? Indeed, when I am allowed to tell them?"

"Countess, I suggest that you tell those two women at the beginning of December but not before. As for others to accompany you, I will choose a trusty coachman and two companions well known to you but whose names I cannot disclose at this time."

"Why should such secrecy surround my departure from Herzberg? I do not understand."

"My dear Countess von Deppe," Drescher replied, "please remember the experience of your journey from Paris to Potsdam last year. As always I urge you to be vigilant. Your reputation and perceived influence justifiably grow. Many around you observe closely what you do and some are minded towards malevolence. For that reason your vigilance must grow ever sharper. Let me quote His Majesty the King once more: 'Always presume that the enemy has dangerous designs and always be forehanded with the remedy. But do not let these calculations make you timid.'"

Arabella shuddered.

"I assure you, Countess, you will be safe on your journey. Once in St Petersburg, with your esteemed husband at your side, you may be able to ease Russian hearts in the interests of Prussia."

"I will do my best," replied Arabella.

As he rose to leave, Drescher asked one last question.

"Have you and the Count decided yet on the godparents for your child?"

"We are inclined towards certain people but our minds are not yet made up."

"Good," replied Drescher. "There is a certain person at the Palace of Sanssouci you may wish to consider."

Arabella looked hard at Drescher.

"Surely you do not mean His Majesty the King?"

"I do indeed. I believe he would be flattered if you asked him. Perhaps you should do so after you have sung for him on St Cecilia's Day? You and young Bamberger should concoct a persuasive programme of music to soothe him. But until then your lips on this matter, and indeed on the other matter of your travel, should remain sealed."

He bowed low and left.

As Drescher's coach disappeared into the distance, Arabella thought deeply about what he had said. If only she could have the comfort of her husband's support at this time.

* * * * *

On Sunday the 22nd of November the Schloss Herzberger Camerata took their places before the altar of the Garrison Church in Potsdam to perform in celebration of St Cecilia, the patron saint of music, keeper of the Pythagorean principle of *harmonia mundi*, which posited that music was a central force in Earth's creation.

For the previous three days the chamber orchestra and church choir had rehearsed regularly under the watchful eye of their patron, the Countess von Deppe, who was lodging in Potsdam. The choice of music in honour of the patron saint had been the subject of intense discussion between her and Herr Bamberger. Finally, they decided to perform as the concert centrepiece Handel's *Ode for St Cecilia's Day*, first performed in London on the 22nd of November 1739. Equally intensive had been the search for a tenor to sing alongside Arabella, a soprano. Herr Bamberger had selected several young tenors for Arabella to hear. They had eventually chosen Herr Stefan Fischer. In his late twenties, his height, experience and vocal depth had given him the edge over the other commendable candidates. For her part, though she had sung the *Ode* before in England, this time Arabella had decided to sing the libretto in German. The King might refrain from speaking his native tongue in favour of French but not everyone who might attend would understand the words in that language. The same applied to English.

News of the Camerata's second public appearance began to spread, so ensuring that the church would be full. On the evening of the performance the pews were packed tight, while latecomers stood at the side and the back. Behind the orchestra, which had been augmented by the church organist and a base drummer, were the Garrison Church choir. The church was illuminated by a multitude of candles, flickering in the draughts from the gusty cold wind outside. The Camerata entered to strong applause. Arabella followed, dressed in a yellow slim-fitting gown – without hoops, as was her now renowned style – with a white high bodice edged in lace, and sat to one side. The Countess von Schlegel was seated in the front row in a dazzling low-cut red gown. Nearby was Father Schmidt.

The concert began at five o'clock with Josef Haydn's *Fifth Harpsichord Concerto*, composed in 1763. Herr Kunzl, Arabella's former music teacher, had brought it to her attention in a letter several months before. Dorothea Winkler played the harpsichord. Handel's *Ode for St Cecilia's Day*, with words by the English poet John Dryden, then followed. The piece was well known to Arabella and her mother. Indeed, Monsieur Noverre, Arabella's former dancing master, had once suggested performing it as a masque at Meltwater.

After the first chorus, Arabella stood and moved to centre stage – tall, graceful and slim, despite the birth of her recent child, her hair loosely tied back. In the candlelight there was a lustrous mother-of-pearl gleam to her skin. She sang, in German, with effortless grace, each note cascading through the air, transfixing the audience.

What passion cannot music raise and quell!
When Jubal struck the chorded shell,
His list'ning brethren stood around,
And wond'ring, on their faces fell,
To worship that celestial sound.
Less than a god they thought there could not dwell
Within the hollow of that shell
That spoke so sweetly and so well.
What passion cannot Music raise and quell!

The audience were visibly astounded. The King, a musician of note, watching secretly from the organ loft, thought Arabella's lyrical interpretation exquisite – translating unlike any German singer he had heard the ordinary into the sublime. Her soft beauty, framed in the candlelight, the way she held the libretto, the way she lifted her voice so that it floated gently down the nave like softly falling snow, conveyed self-assurance tinged with a touching trace of physical vulnerability.

When Arabella had finished, Herr Fischer stepped forward and sang with great gusto.

The trumpet's loud clangour
Excites us to arms,
With shrill notes of anger
And mortal alarms.
The double, double, double beat
Of the thund'ring drum
Cries: "Hark! The foes come;
Charge, charge! 'Tis too late to retreat!"

At the end of the aria the clapping and stamping of feet was almost deafening, as many in the audience saw it as a rousing cry to

Prussia to take arms once more against its enemies.

To complete the work, Herr Fischer sang one further solo aria and Arabella three more, of which the second to last was even more beautifully rendered than her first, the words perfectly matching the gentle notes of the organ.

But oh, what art can teach,
What human voice can reach
The sacred organ's praise?
Notes inspiring holy love,
Notes that wing their heav'nly ways
To join the choirs above.

As she sang, there was a sharp gust of wind outside the church. The tall candles either side of Arabella almost blew out in the sudden draught. Drescher, sitting behind his master in the organ loft, took this as a sign of the impending denouement he had skilfully masterminded.

The prolonged applause at the end of the performance was principally directed to Arabella who, supported by Herr Bamberger, curtsied several times. The Countess von Schlegel and Father Schmidt added their own vigorous ovation.

Almost an hour later, as she prepared, despite the already advancing night, to leave for Herzberg, Waldemar Drescher handed her a sealed letter. Opening it she instantly recognised the hastily scrawled handwriting.

My dear Countess,

I heard you sing this evening.

The essence of you was visible to me in every note you sang. Your voice was what I imagine that of the angels to be. You moved me greatly.

How is the young one who bears my name?

Frederick
Potsdam, the 22nd of November

As they left her lodgings, the dark figure of Waldemar Drescher took her arm.

"At this late hour I will escort you to Herzberg. Nothing must happen to such a beautiful voice."

"You are most honourable, kind sir," replied Arabella.

On the way Drescher explained the arrangements for Arabella's departure to St Petersburg. The following morning he left Herzberg carrying a note from Arabella to the King.

To His Majesty,

Thank you for your most kind note of appreciation of my singing in Potsdam yesterday evening. I was greatly honoured to receive it.

And thank you for asking about the well-being of my son, Frederick Daniel. He is in good health. I hope there will be an opportunity for me to present him to you, his namesake, before too long. It would be a great honour to do so.

As you may know he and I are preparing to leave Schloss Herzberg shortly, to visit my husband in St Petersburg. I hope that all three of us will soon return to Prussia, where we will remain at His Majesty's service.

With my husband's and my warmest best wishes,
Arabella
Countess von Deppe
Schloss Herzberg, the 23rd of November, 1767

* * * * *

On Monday the 7th of December two small but well-built black coaches finally left Herzberg, as arranged by Waldemar Drescher. Arabella was accompanied in the first carriage by the Countess von Schlegel and Father Johann, both of whom – she had been told – had offered to escort her on the long journey ahead. In the carriage close behind was Frau Klein with Frederick Daniel and the wet nurse, Frau Weiser, together with Hanne, Arabella's personal maid, and a footman, Berthold.

The coaches – the first driven by a silent and morose coachman called Moser and the second by Herzberg's head coachman, Brenner – made early progress on the good Prussian roads. But as they journeyed further north-east towards the distant Russian border, the road surface deteriorated and daily progress became slower. Day after day as they travelled across grey featureless landscape Arabella often pondered, in between periods of polite conversation, questions she could not answer with any certainty. Why had she been obliged to leave Herzberg in bitter December weather, with a recently born child, to go to St Petersburg in the face of encroaching winter? Why had the King not permitted Carl Manfred to return to Herzberg to celebrate Christmas? Was there an ulterior motive of which she was unaware? Whatever the answers, at least she would soon be reunited at last with her husband.

* * * * *

The journey proved agonisingly long and arduous, broken by a stop for two days at Königsberg and another two at Riga. Once they were across the Russian border the weather worsened and rural poverty became even more striking. Eventually Moser, who said he had travelled the route before, announced that St Petersburg was only two or three days away. Later that day, in a heavy blizzard through which the two coaches struggled often at snail's pace, the coachmen agreed that it would be best to stop at the next inn, where there would be warm shelter, in order to let the storm pass and to refresh the exhausted horses. Only fresh horses would be able to tackle the deep snow the next day. That evening, in the warmth of the large low-timbered *dacha*, engulfed by thick driving snow, the travellers relaxed and enjoyed Russian hospitality in front of hot stoves, sipping tea from boiling samovars. Later they went to bed and slept soundly, wrapped in furs.

The following morning, before dawn, the lead coachman, Moser, rose early to check the horses. The snowstorm had thankfully passed. While it was probably better to shelter for another day he decided he could ill afford any further delay. For Russians an open sled was a more practicable means of transport in deep snow, but that would not be suitable at this stage of the journey. Besides, his passengers did not have sufficient warm clothing for exposed travel, and there was an infant, too. After instructing Brenner, Moser left the stable, saying he wanted to inspect the road from the village. With his lantern he walked along the edge of the nearby frozen lake in the direction of the route to St Petersburg. As he did so the first shaft of daylight of the winter solstice edged over the horizon. It was bitterly cold but the wind had dropped. Instead of continuing towards the road, Moser stepped onto the ice and began to head towards two islands of trees two or three hundred yards out from the edge of the lake, tracing the tracks of birds in the ripples of covering snow. He stooped several times to dip his gloved hand into the snow. The landscape was so silent, so beautiful and so appropriate. Occasionally he felt the ice crackle beneath his feet. After a short while, as the light grew stronger, he walked back the mile or so towards the inn.

An hour or so later, everyone was ready to leave. Moser suggested that, as after inspection it appeared they were closer to St Petersburg than he thought, there was time for the two countesses and the priest to take a walk to the lakeside to glimpse the rising sun and the fauna on such a peaceful morning. The Countess von Schlegel was unsure but Arabella and the priest, despite the ice-blue cold air, encouraged her to join them. Following Moser they walked along the edge of the lake and then onto the ice. The coachman urged Katherina von Schlegel and Father Johann to walk to the right, keeping to the footsteps he had made earlier, towards a small island of trees emerging from the ice. He told Arabella to walk to the left. That way they would each get a good view of some bison he had seen earlier amongst the trees. As the Countess von Schlegel and the priest passed the first island of trees, the coachman called out, beckoning them to walk towards him by the second island of trees.

"Just follow my footprints. The bison are here! Look, over here!"

As they approached where the coachman was pointing, two iron traps sprang shut: the first on the leg of the Countess and the second on the ankle of the priest. Both cried out in agony. The coachman looked towards them, both now on the ground, their cries of pain echoing across the lake. He smiled. Suddenly he heard the crunch of footsteps behind him. He spun round to see Arabella advancing towards him, in horror at what had happened.

"Countess, please stay where you are. Come no further!"

She stood still, her gloved hands clutched to her face, white with fear, thinking Moser was warning of cracking ice.

"Madame," he called out to her, pointing to the two figures on the ground and removing his beard to reveal himself as Waldemar Drescher. "Behold two enemies – to His Majesty and to you." From beneath his long thick coat he pulled a leather pouch. "In here are documents these two traitors were intending to reveal publicly in St Petersburg in order to denounce you at the Russian court as a foreign spy and an unfit person to enjoy the presence of His Majesty the King. They plotted in secret to destroy you. She" – he pointed to Katherina von Schlegel – "did it out of jealousy of you and your friendship with His Majesty. The other out of hatred and misplaced revenge, not Johann Schmidt but Jean, the son of Auguste Gaillard, a traitor like his father. I heard them behind the wall of a house in Potsdam laying their plans. This wretch," he said, pointing to the stricken priest, "proved to be no priest after all. He revealed to the Countess von Schlegel your confessions. With their accumulated false testimony, together they intended to drag you down, drive away your husband and poison the King's mind against you."

Arabella edged towards the two victims, flushed with anger at their betrayal. She spoke with rage.

"How could you? I gave you my friendship, Countess, an open heart. I was no threat to you. I respected you. My only sin was perhaps to be what you once were – a young woman in love, seeking happiness and fulfilment. The affairs of state are not for me. If these accusations are true, and I have no reason to doubt them, you betrayed my friendship with malice. As for you, Herr Schmidt – or perhaps I should say Monsieur Gaillard – I have nothing but contempt for you. It is a heinous sin to masquerade as a priest, to hear a private confession and to reveal its contents. You have earned my eternal hatred." Arabella moved closer but Drescher ran to restrain her. "I never wish to see either of you again."

"Madame," said Drescher, "you will not. Go back to the inn, gather your belongings together and be ready for immediate departure."

Arabella turned and walked quickly away, distraught, struggling to recover her composure and with the beseeching voices behind her gradually fading into the distance with each step she took. She did not know – and would never know – that Jean Gaillard was her step-brother, and that it was his father – her own natural father –

who had tried to kill her on the road to Magdeburg the previous year as she pursued Carl Manfred von Deppe, the man she loved. Yet another attempt to thwart her pursuit of happiness had occurred; yet again it had been foiled. On both occasions the King's spymaster had intervened.

Nearer to the inn, she recalled the words of her husband in the garden at Herzberg before their marriage: "We are all beset by profound difficulties and impossible situations not of our making. We see things in life that we could never have imagined . . . But however much we may be overwhelmed by what we have seen and by our guilt, we must try hard not to allow the past to stand in the way of our future happiness."

Arabella turned once more to look at the figures on the ice but they were suddenly enveloped in mist wafting towards the inn from the lake. Soon there was nothing to see; she could only hear the muffled sound of pistol shots. She crossed herself.

"Holy Mary, please protect me and my son."

As she breathed these words, they seemed to hang in crystal patterns in the freezing air.

Arabella stumbled through the snow towards the inn, half frozen by fear and the bitter cold. The mother of a young child whom she would fiercely protect, she was now more resolved than ever, whatever the danger, to live her life as she wished it to be and not as others wanted – a resolution she had written in her music book at Meltwater, a resolution she would now pursue with even greater determination. To do so would require tireless strength, constant vigilance for the malevolence of others, and the even rarer award of personal trust. But they would be tempered by an equally unbreakable commitment to the medium of music and through it the pursuit of true happiness, not just for her but for all within her compass. She recalled that Jean-Philippe Rameau had once said, "A good musician must abandon himself to all the characters he sets out to depict . . . but the music must speak to the soul."

* * * * *

As Arabella returned to the inn, the pools of blood from the injured traitors began to spread on the ice. The smell of it did not escape the sensitive nostrils of the ever-vigilant wolves. The

Countess and the priest begged to be released but Drescher was unmoved.

"You are two snakes full of venom, unworthy of mercy. But I will spare you from the wolves." He pulled his pistol from beneath his coat. "Let God have mercy on your wretched souls."

Drescher fired a shot into the ice, thinner by the trees where the victims lay. A crack appeared. He fired another. The crack began to widen. He fired yet again. The crack deepened, inching towards the water below, which slowly started to seep up and across the surface into the clothing of Katherina von Schlegel and Johann Schmidt. Drescher stamped his boot down hard. And again. More cracks appeared. The ice began to break beneath the weight of the bodies above. The two victims, now recognising they were beyond mercy, started to slide into the inky-black water below. Schmidt tried to snatch at a young sapling but it snapped in his grasp. The Countess von Schlegel, already overcome with cold, uttered no sound, simply closing her eyes as she sank into her watery sarcophagus.

Before leaving the lake, Drescher pulled a clutch of documents from the leather pouch, including the confession he had dictated to Philippe Robinet in Spandau citadel. He tore them into strips and lit a match from his tinderbox. The paper burned brightly for a moment or two and then he pushed the curled remnants into the water, which was already developing a new thin layer of ice.

* * * * *

As she mounted the carriage, holding her son closely to her, Arabella turned to Waldemar Drescher.

"Herr Drescher, yet again my life has been in your hands. Yet again you have saved me. I thank you from the depth of my heart." She kissed him on the cheek.

"Madame, I promised you I would hold your secret. I will continue to do so. Your life will always be safe in my hands. What has happened today has forged a further link in the unbreakable bond of trust between us. As long as I live, I will watch over you."

Arabella looked down into his face.

"Thank you, Herr Drescher," she replied, clasping his hand. "And the two who were with us?"

"Countess, they are gone into the kingdom of ice."

Arabella shuddered and looked away.

Resuming his seat on the coachman's box, Drescher cracked his whip over the horses. If they were quick enough they might even be in St Petersburg by mid-evening. He pondered the risk he had taken in breaching his vow of secrecy by disclosing information to Robinet about Arabella's previous life and then allowing Katherina von Schlegel to share its contents. The risk had led him to the very precipice of her trust in him. But he had decided it needed to be taken to protect the King and the woman inside the carriage. Yet who had been the more important in this instance – the King or her? He began to realise that, if he were not a lover of men and she were not married, he would be in love with her; and that he would fight any man for her hand. But she would never know that. In his tragic circumstances of unfulfilled love he could only be her warrior, her protector.

* * * * *

After an enforced overnight stop to replace a lame horse, the two carriages finally entered St Petersburg late on the afternoon of Tuesday, the 22nd of December, 1767, almost at the end of a momentous year. Arabella, still shaken by what had happened the previous day, looked in wonder from her carriage at the bustling city around her.

The coaches stopped at a house some distance from the Winter Palace. Drescher, travel-stained and clearly fatigued, explained to Arabella that after a further change of horses new but trusted coachmen, replacing him and Brenner, would take them to Count von Deppe's house in Dvortsovaya Naberezhnaya. A messenger was already on his way to the Admiralty Building, where an office had been put at the Count's disposal, to inform him that his wife and child would arrive shortly.

Having descended from her coach Arabella spoke to Waldemar Drescher as he helped to remove the weary horses from their traces.

"Herr Drescher, I did not sufficiently convey to you my deep gratitude for your protection yesterday. I was so shocked by what happened that I forgot to express my sentiments in the fullest way. Again, I thank you. And I do so from my heart."

"Thank you, Countess. To hear such warm words from your lips gives me great pleasure. I repeat that, as long as I live and am capable, I will defend you in whatever way I can."

As she turned to re-enter her carriage, taking the hand Drescher offered to help her mount the step, Arabella addressed him once more.

"Herr Drescher, did you know the real identity of the priest when you first sent him to me at Herzberg?"

"No, Countess, I did not. It only became apparent later, following a report I received that he was not who he claimed to be."

Arabella paused and then looked directly at him. She spoke with a candour she had never shown before – to him or anyone else.

"Herr Drescher, I will not be used by anyone for their purpose, even if it is the most noble purpose, without my knowledge. I will do as others wish but only as I wish it to be. That has been my abiding principle – always – and I do not intend to compromise it now. We trust each other well enough for me to speak with frankness. Share with me what you intend and I will give you my support, if what is required is for a noble and desirable cause. It cannot be any other way. I am sure we understand each other, Herr Drescher."

Arabella touched his arm in a gesture of friendship.

"Countess, I understand. On this matter we are agreed and it will always be so."

Arabella took her seat in the carriage. She turned and smiled at him.

Raising his hand in acknowledgement, he knew that he had just lied to her. In truth he had known about the young Gaillard, ready to masquerade as a priest in order to provide him (he had disguised his identity during their encounters) with information about the young Countess. Gaillard had been eager to spy on her because of his thirst for revenge for the death of his father, in which he had been led to believe the young English woman had played a part. Drescher had risked the Countess's life and her trust in him for the sake of unmasking and punishing two traitors. For days afterwards he could not remove from his mind her penetrating eyes as she asked him whether he had known of the priest's real identity at the time he had sent him to Herzberg. Drescher knew he was steeped in the craft of treachery but he vowed he would never lie to the Countess again. Her words and her gentle touch on his arm were perhaps her means of indicating to him that she knew he was lying but that she was willing to forgive him on account of the bond that existed between them. That bond was too precious to place in jeopardy again.

An hour or so later the two coaches entered the cobbled courtyard at Dvortsovaya Naberezhnaya. Stable-boys rushed to hold the horses and footmen opened the coach doors. As she stepped down into the bitterly cold St Petersburg night, the ground already covered in deep frost, Arabella recalled that a year before she had arrived by coach in a similar courtyard, in Paris, in the company of Carl Manfred von Deppe, a man with whom she knew she had fallen in love. Now, a year later, she was about to be reunited with him, her husband, after months of separation. The emotion from the strain of those months began to well inside her. She recalled what her mother had so often told her in the past: only reveal your feelings to those you love deeply, and do so in private, since from such control will come personal strength, which will win the admiration and support of those who observe from afar.

Taking Frederick Daniel from Frau Klein, Arabella entered the hall of the large spacious house. Coming towards her, arms outstretched, was Carl Manfred. Almost in tears, she placed the child in his arms.

Her voice breaking with emotion, she said, "You cannot imagine how much I have missed you, how much I have prayed for this moment of joy. My dearest Carl, here is our son, Count Frederick Daniel von Deppe, your heir to Herzberg."

Carl Manfred gazed down at the sleeping child.

"Darling Arabella, during the past months I too have prayed hard for this moment – you at last at my side, bringing with you our child. This moment means as much to me as it does to you."

Frau Klein stepped forward.

"Carl, this is Frau Klein, the excellent nanny I have chosen for Frederick, and Frau Weiser, his nurse. And of course you know Hanne from Herzberg."

"Frau Klein and Frau Weiser, it is a pleasure to meet two such important people in my son's young life. And Hanne, it is an equal pleasure to see you again."

"Count von Deppe, you and the Countess need time to be alone for a while," said Frau Klein.

Carl Manfred handed Frederick Daniel to her. Then turning to Arabella, he said, "Countess von Deppe, welcome to St Petersburg. Shall we go upstairs? I have arranged an early light supper before you rest after your long and tiring journey."

Arabella smiled.

"My dear Count, I should be delighted." Turning to Frau Klein and Frau Weiser, she said, "We will see you and Frederick Daniel in the morning. I thank you for your company and support during our long journey. Hanne, please lay out my sleeping attire and clothes for the morning. Then you too should rest."

Waiting at the top of the staircase was the Russian housekeeper, Alicia. She showed them into the library, where a table for two had been set near the fire. After an exchange of pleasantries, Arabella and Carl Manfred were finally alone. The next morning Alicia saw that the food had been barely touched.

CHAPTER 3

Intimate Conversations by Candlelight

Carl Manfred had left Herzberg in a royal coach on Saturday the 28th of February, 1767, with a heavy heart.

As the coach weaved its way north-east through deep snow, he had plenty of time to consider his predicament, as he had chosen to term it. He had received no adequate explanation for the King's decision to send him to St Petersburg. Moreover, his instructions – if you could call them that – were imprecise. He had been a professional soldier for most of his life. He was used to receiving unambiguous orders, defined tasks and planned outcomes. In contrast, diplomats dealt in words; they intrigued; they ducked and weaved; and often what they toiled for never happened or, at least, the consequences were unexpected. Such deceit and imprecision were not for him. But his aversion had made no difference. Whether he liked it or not he was bound for the Russian imperial capital.

The King had nearly lost everything in the previous seven years of war, but in the end his royal luck had prevailed – yet again. He had snatched victory from the jaws of defeat by the Russians and so gained the territorial prize he had long coveted. But still he wanted more. There was no sign he would ever give up. The King was as restless as ever. Whereas his dealings with the young Czar Peter III had flourished during the Czar's short years on the throne, those with the late Czar's wife, the formidable Catherine, had already become fraught since she proclaimed herself Empress of Russia; her husband, the Czar, had been found strangled shortly after. German by birth, the Empress had immersed herself in Russia following her arrival there eighteen years before. She had survived danger, isolation and intrigue. Now she sat on the imperial throne. It was reported she had spoken of the glory of Russia as her glory.

Since it was already plain to the King that persuading the tiresome Empress to act in concert with Prussia was proving difficult, Carl Manfred wondered how he, a mere soldier, could assist in the reversal of her policies – and, moreover, seek to do so without clear instructions. Despite Carl Manfred's personal remonstrations – including a request to speak to the King himself, which was refused – Drescher had insisted that the King would not entertain any delay in the Count's departure for Russia, even though his wife was expecting a child. He had been commanded to go, and out of obligation and deep respect for the King's judgement he should leave for St Petersburg as soon as possible. Now he was on his way. Mulling over what he would do after his arrival in the imperial capital, Carl Manfred had little choice but to draw on the limited information that had been given to him about the Russian court before his departure. Whether this information, from Drescher, portraying himself as the King's silent enforcer and chief spymaster, was as important as he conveyed was still open to question in Carl Manfred's opinion. But Arabella trusted him and he her. If she trusted Drescher, then Carl Manfred believed he had to do the same. But this reluctant trust did not remove his dislike for him.

The journey proved long, treacherous and tiresome. The weather worsened steadily the nearer the coach got to the Russian border. After two weeks of spending many hours each day on the road Carl Manfred finally arrived in St Petersburg, a city to which he had never previously been, on Sunday the 15th of March. Whereas spring might be showing signs of arrival at Herzberg, here it was bitterly cold and thick snow was falling. As soon as he was settled in the accommodation arranged for him, he wrote to his wife.

Dearest Arabella,

After an unpleasant and interminable journey I have at last arrived in St Petersburg. There is little to see as yet because the city is under a blanket of deep snow. It is bitterly cold and I must urgently find a warmer coat and a larger fire to sit beside. I miss you greatly. It is so cruel to be separated from you at this time. I think of you every moment.

Please take the greatest care in my absence. I insist that you let Maximilian carry the strain of the daily management of the estate. His bones may creak somewhat but he is diligent in his work. I know he respects you. On musical matters please contain your enthusiasm and let the energetic Herr Bamberger do as much of your musical preparation as possible. At all costs you must rest for what lies ahead.

I will endeavour to return to Herzberg and your side as quickly as I can from this city of ice and snow.

Your ever-loving husband,

CM

St Petersburg, Sunday the 16th of March, 1767

In the weeks following his arrival in St Petersburg Carl Manfred had further time to reflect on the country in which he now found himself. The incomplete map he possessed showed a vast land stretching ever eastwards and to the north. The woman who ruled this territory had to be admired, judging by the reports he had been able to piece together since coming to the imperial city. Sifting truth from mere gossip – always a difficult task – had been hard, but Carl Manfred, after many late evenings sitting by the fire in his study at Dvortsovaya Naberezhnaya, his new home, had managed to glean at least some of the facts that he as a military man had always been trained to acquire.

In 1741 the late Empress Elizabeth of Russia, daughter of Peter the Great, had seized the imperial throne in a coup d'état at the age of thirty-one. Ever fearful of being overthrown, Elizabeth had striven hard to retain her throne and to safeguard the future of the dynasty. One of her most important steps had been to make her nephew, Duke Karl Peter Ulrich, her heir. He was the son of Elizabeth's elder sister, Anna Petrovna, whom Peter the Great had married to Duke Karl Friedrich of Holstein-Gottorp, who was in turn a nephew of King Karl XII of Sweden. Elizabeth had brought her nephew to Russia at the age of fourteen to be prepared for his role as the future ruler of Russia. As he had to marry to have an heir, to everyone's surprise the Empress Elizabeth chose as his bride Sophie Frederica Augusta of Anhalt-Zerbst, a princess of a small German duchy. She and her mother, Princess Johanna Elisabeth, arrived in Russia in 1744. The young princess pleased the Empress Elizabeth and the Grand Duke Karl Peter. A year later, after converting to Orthodoxy and taking the patronymic Catherine Alexseyevna, she and the young Karl Peter were married. Catherine was only sixteen.

Though it was widely known the marriage was a disaster, Catherine had persevered with life in Russia. According to Drescher, she had learnt Russian well, read widely about Russia and philosophy, and had become adept at the art of survival in the treacherous waters of the imperial court. In September 1754 Catherine had given birth to a son, Paul. Speculation remained about the child's paternity as the Grand Duke Karl Peter had been rumoured to be unable to father children. One rumour had been that the father was Count Sergei Saltykov, who had received imperial blessing for the relationship and who had been despatched shortly after the birth on a long diplomatic mission. Once born the Grand Duchess Catherine's child was taken from her to be brought up by the Empress, while the Grand Duke pursued his own hobbies.

According to Carl Manfred's information, some of which had come from Drescher, with its authenticity subsequently confirmed by what he read and heard from other sources after his arrival, Catherine's life after the birth of her child had been precarious amidst the intrigues at court and in the face of her husband's disdain for her. But cunning, ambitious and astute, Catherine had survived, reading ever more political treatises and books on world history, philosophy and literature, and further improving her Russian. Though not allowed to write letters or to have any involvement in politics, she had been able to keep in discreet touch with matters concerning the delicate relationship between Russia and Prussia. Indeed, Catherine was almost compromised when her name had become linked with the withdrawal of the Russian army from Prussia, initiated by the Russian Chancellor Bestuzhev-

Ryumin just after the Russian victory at Gross-Jaegersdorf in 1757. Carl Manfred recalled the battle from his own military career serving King Frederick. Had the Russians not withdrawn, possibly on the grounds of supporting the Grand Duke, who greatly admired the King, it was likely that Prussia would have been obliged to capitulate to the Russian army.

As the health of the Empress Elizabeth deteriorated, Catherine began to prepare for the succession to the imperial throne. The Empress died in December 1761, after twenty years of sovereignty. The Grand Duke became Peter III and, fearing the country he now ruled, he turned at once to the leader he most admired – King Frederick of Prussia – with whom he entered into an alliance, so reversing the late Empress's treaties of cooperation with France and Austria, and nullifying the diplomatic and military gains of Russia during the earlier seven years of war that had ended in 1763. After becoming Czar he openly revered King Frederick. Indeed, he had reportedly adored publicly a portrait of the King; worn a ring with his image; replaced his Russian uniform with a Prussian one; and even donned the Prussian Order of the Black Eagle. The Russian army and court were not surprisingly outraged. Then in 1762 he publicly insulted his wife, his insult becoming the talk of the city. Deciding that the time had come to strike before her own possible removal, Catherine had declared herself ruler of Russia on the 28th of June, 1762. Her husband was subsequently arrested and a week later his death was reported to Catherine. She was crowned Empress in the Kremlin in Moscow in September that same year.

If all the stories and reports he had gathered were true, Catherine was an astute ruler and a worthy opponent of his King.

Some weeks after his arrival, Carl Manfred was present with many diplomats and other foreign guests at the Winter Palace, and still finding his feet. It was the first time he had been introduced to the Empress. In their brief exchange of pleasantries it was plain to him that she was intelligent, clever, well-educated and a most determined ruler. Her demeanour oozed ambition. She clearly had iron in her soul, just as he had long been aware of that same strength in King Frederick. Carl Manfred had already known, before this encounter, that in her dealings with the King she had become a formidable adversary in the promotion of Russia's interests. That evening at the Winter Palace also revealed that she was surrounded by people of great ability, not just Russian but from other parts of Europe too – many active in commerce, the arts and the building of palaces of state. Still without clear instructions, Carl Manfred found it hard to play – or indeed enjoy – his part in the swirling activity in and around the Empress's court. Frustrated at having to spend his time in St Petersburg where he felt uncomfortable and circumscribed, he often wished Arabella were with him if he could not be with her at Herzberg.

He met the Empress again several months afterwards in the garden of her summer palace at Tsarskoye Selo, which, under her predecessor, had become an impressive building but which Catherine was rumoured to consider an extravagance. Count Sokolov tapped him on the shoulder. He and Carl Manfred had spoken several times before and over dinner had discussed the art of warfare, a matter on which the Russian Count was well informed since amongst his many other accomplishments he was a high-ranking officer in the Preobrazhensky Guards, one of the imperial regiments that had supported Catherine when she proclaimed herself Empress in 1762.

"Count von Deppe, please come with me. The Empress would like to speak to you."

"What about?" asked Carl Manfred, somewhat taken aback that the ruler of Russia should wish to speak to him.

He followed Count Sokolov across the park.

"Your Majesty, I present Count von Deppe."

Carl Manfred bowed.

"Count von Deppe, how long have you been in St Petersburg?"

Carl Manfred looked into the Czarina's large expressive blue eyes with their long black eyelashes, took in her delicate nose and enticing lips, which it was said many men longed to kiss.

"Nearly half a year, Majesty," replied Carl Manfred, wondering what might lie behind her question.

"How long do you expect to be in Russia?" the Empress quickly replied.

"That is a question I cannot answer. I am here at the command of my King – and of course for as long as I am welcome in your imperial realm."

"How is His Majesty?"

"I do not have a current report but when I last saw him, before my departure from Prussia, he was in good health and continuing to work hard at good relations with you, Empress."

"And how is the Countess? I gather she is a highly talented musician and a well-read young woman. Born in England of a French mother, I believe?"

Carl Manfred was momentarily lost for words. How was it that the Russian Empress was so knowledgeable about his wife?

"Am I reliably informed or not, Count von Deppe?"

"You are well informed," replied Carl Manfred.

"Which is correct – her talents or her birth, or both?"

"Both," Carl Manfred hastily replied.

"I look forward to hearing before too long that she has joined you in St Petersburg, once she is able to travel following the birth of her child."

"I too hope so," responded Carl Manfred, still taken aback by what the Empress had just remarked.

With that the conversation came to an end. The Empress moved away.

"Count Sokolov, I am flattered Her Majesty should enquire after my wife. But with so many more important people at her side I am not sure it would matter a jot to her whether the Countess von Deppe were present in St Petersburg or not, though it of course matters greatly to me. Moreover, how is it that Her Majesty is so well informed about my wife's talents and present condition?"

"Dear Count von Deppe, I admire you greatly and hope that we can dine together again soon to discuss military tactics. Suffice it to say that some matters move in mysterious ways at this court. That is really all I can say. I think it is safe to venture the opinion that, before the year is out, the beautiful Countess will be amongst us. Now I must leave you. I believe the Empress requires my assistance. Please excuse me."

With that he was gone.

A month later Carl Manfred received a short message, signed with the letter D, to say that plans were afoot, at the request of a mutual friend, for the Countess von Deppe to travel to St Petersburg at the end of the year. The matter could not of course be formalised until after the birth of the Countess's child. Until then the intended journey should not be disclosed. That restriction extended to the Count's conversations in St Petersburg.

Carl Manfred recognised the handwriting. It was the King's, but the D beneath had been inserted by Waldemar Drescher. It was clear from the message that it was the King's intention for Arabella to join him in Russia rather than for him to return to Herzberg. He sensed a particular motive behind this proposed outcome, but what it might be was beyond him. What was certain was that he would be resident in St Petersburg longer than he had expected. He decided not to report the Empress's interest in Arabella but he continued to puzzle over who had provided the Empress with information about her. Might it have been Drescher – that man of secrets? Might it have been the King himself, in a direct communication with the Empress? If it was neither of them, then who else might it be? Was there a Russian spy at Frederick's court or a Prussian traitor in St Petersburg? If the latter, surely Drescher would have identified the traitor already? Then Carl Manfred recalled what Drescher had said to him in the garden of the Neues Palais about unmasking a spy and how Arabella might have to be involved. Anxiety quickened his heartbeat.

Whatever the answer might be, Carl Manfred would much look forward to Arabella's arrival – if she and her baby survived the impending birth. But he refused to contemplate alternative outcomes. Instead, the thought crossed his mind that if there were one person who might advance Prussia's interests at the imperial court better than him, it would be his wife. Her beauty, her musical skills and sharp mind might appeal to the Empress herself. Perhaps that thought had already crossed someone else's mind.

* * * * *

Carl Manfred was overcome with joy when – at last – his wife and child joined him in St Petersburg on the 22nd of December, 1767. He was shaken by the evident physical strain the long journey had imposed on Arabella, so soon after the birth of Frederick Daniel; then there had been the St Cecilia's Day concert in Potsdam, and her constant concern about the fate of Herzberg in their absence at St Petersburg. Shortly after her arrival Carl Manfred insisted that she rest in bed to regain her strength in order to celebrate the Feast of the Epiphany on the 6th of January. Arabella protested but eventually gave in to her husband's insistence.

While she rested Carl Manfred and Drescher met for supper one evening. Afterwards, over port, the Count posed the question uppermost in his mind following his wife's account of her journey.

"What happened to the Countess von Schlegel and the imposter priest after you unmasked their intentions?"

"They drowned," replied Drescher in a matter-of-fact voice.

"Despite their treachery did you not save them and send them back to Prussia?"

"No. I caught them with iron traps. Then they drowned."

"Good God, man, that is murder," Carl Manfred exclaimed.

"You, Count, may call it murder. I call it sentence of death for an act of betrayal."

"I suppose it was in the King's name?" countered Carl Manfred.

"What I do is always in the King's name and interest."

"And you did all this in my wife's presence?" said Carl Manfred.

"The Countess did not witness their final fate. She was never at risk. I saved her from that – because I have profound respect and admiration for her – and I saved you from public humiliation in this city."

"Drescher, if I understand you, you enticed the Countess von Schlegel and the priest to accompany my wife on this journey in order to kill them. You are utterly shameless. You live in a world of lies, half-truths and deception. You often describe the King's enemies as vipers. If they are vipers, you are the serpent. You say you conduct your business in the shadows in the King's name. I have never been convinced of that. I have never once heard him refer to you. I believe that most of the time you are settling old scores on a never ending list compiled by you for your own purposes. I cannot imagine that His Majesty knows half of what you do."

Drescher sat silent for a moment, gazing intently at Carl Manfred. Then he spoke in a quiet, deliberate voice.

"Count von Deppe, you are a soldier. Soldiers such as you are brave. But all of you perform in a different world to mine. You drill, you order formations, you execute battlefield plans, you fire, you charge, you kill, and with luck and good practice you survive to fight another battle. All such actions are to achieve a decisive victory, a routed enemy. That is what His Majesty likes, and soldiers such as you give him the results he seeks. But there is another world alongside that of military campaigns. It is a dark, bleak, friendless world full of duplicity. Everyone plays the game of deception. The French, the Austrians, the Swedes, the Poles, the other German states not under Prussia's authority and even those hypocrites the English are in the same game, seeking to undermine one another by finding out the secrets of others – most of the time by the foulest of means and indulging in betrayal and death. It is a game in which there are no rules, unlike your campaigns. Overnight, enemies become friends and friends become enemies. Alliances are built on shifting sands, here today and gone tomorrow. Like you I am loyal to His Majesty and, whether you approve or not, I will do whatever is necessary to protect him and to defend and advance the interests of his kingdom – regardless of the human cost."

"I find the means you advocate distasteful and reproachable," Carl Manfred replied.

"You may do so," said Drescher, "but they are essential. "That von Schlegel woman had been passing information about the King's intentions to someone in the Russian court for some time. Why else would she drag her aged husband around the Prussian court? She wanted to gather intelligence by eavesdropping on the King's conversations. I intercepted some of the messages she sent. Then her venom became more lethal. She became jealous of your wife, whom she thought would usurp her position at court. I saw her bitterness when she spied on you both as you went to the King's private apartment at the Palace of Charlottenburg a year ago. As for the priest, he wanted revenge for the death of his traitorous father, who had been in the pay of the French King. They had to die. So after hearing them plot to discredit your wife here in St Petersburg I lured them to their fate by asking them to accompany the Countess on a long and difficult journey. They fell into the trap and paid the price for doing so. It might have been helpful to have allowed the von Schlegel woman to reach this city, to see who her agent was. But I could not risk that. They wanted to humiliate the Countess – and you – by referring to her time in London, which you and I have promised will always remain a secret. You would not have wanted that for your wife and His Majesty would not have liked to be ridiculed in such a way. So you see, while a victory on the battlefield may be bloody but neat, it does not meet all the requirements of statecraft."

Carl Manfred made no comment.

"Now," said Drescher, "we have to plan how to achieve His Majesty's objective for your mission – which is to ensure the promotion of goodwill between Prussia and Russia in order to create a strong basis for achieving mutually acceptable territorial aims. I believe that the Countess von Deppe will be a most adroit person to do this once she is well. Her grace, sharpness of intellect and musical virtuosity are ideally suited for this task. I hope that before long she will have the opportunity to meet the Empress. I think they might enjoy one another's company. That, I believe, is the way to proceed. But we should share our intentions with your wife so that she is fully apprised of what has to be done."

Carl Manfred was about to question Drescher regarding what the Empress had said to him at Tsarskoye Selo when the door opened and Arabella entered.

"Herr Drescher, please forgive the interruption but I heard your voice. I wish to invite you to stay the night. The snow is falling even more heavily and I am told the wind is fearsome."

"Thank you, Countess, but I cannot stay," replied Drescher, "as there is urgent business to which I must attend."

"Herr Drescher, the hour is already late. That being so there is surely little to achieve before tomorrow morning. I am sure your urgent business can wait until then. As my much-valued guardian on our journey to this city you must stay. I insist. You agree Carl Manfred, don't you?"

"I do," replied Carl Manfred, hiding his reluctance to have the man he so disliked under his roof.

"Dearest Carl, would you be so kind as to ask Alicia to arrange a room immediately, one with a large warm fire, for Herr Drescher? As I feel cold I would like to warm myself by the fire here for a short while."

"Of course," said Carl Manfred.

After the door closed behind him, Arabella whispered to Drescher.

"I will be honest and admit I heard what you said to my husband about the Countess von Schlegel."

"Madame, you are picking up bad habits, listening at doors," he commented with a smile.

"Sir, while I confess I will never make a good spy, you should never underestimate the skills of a woman."

"Countess, I concluded long ago that you would be a formidable adversary. I thank the good Lord that you are on my side."

"Herr Drescher, that will remain the case as I believe there is a clear understanding between us on how we should approach matters of mutual concern in the weeks and months ahead."

"I agree. I remember your recent words to me on the subject," he replied.

"I am reassured to hear it," she said.

Carl Manfred returned to say that the room for Herr Drescher was ready. After a final exchange of pleasantries, the three retired. For Drescher's part, he was even more resolved to pursue his plan to uncover the traitor in the Russian court and to advance goodwill towards the Czarina in a way acceptable to King Frederick. The Countess would be his chosen instrument and ally, but he knew he could no longer take her for granted.

As they climbed the stairs, arm in arm, Carl Manfred observed that his wife had changed. Though still tired from her journey, she was more confident and strong-minded. Now a mother, aware of the King's great admiration for her musicianship and more striking than ever, she was no longer the hesitant and attentive young woman he had left in Herzberg. The woman beside him on the staircase had grown in self-assurance and maturity. The spell of physical attraction she had first cast over him in Paris was stronger than ever; his respect for her even greater. As for Arabella, she was relieved she had made clear, tactfully but firmly – not only to her husband, with whom she was deeply in love and whom she knew, out of concern for her, would listen at the door, but also to Herr Drescher – the precise terms on which she wished to approach her new role in St Petersburg and beyond. She recalled yet again the words she had once written in her music book at Meltwater and which she had echoed in her remark to Drescher on her arrival in St Petersburg: "I will do what people want but only as I want it to be." She would do all she could to ensure that happened.

Arabella took a last look at Frederick Daniel before going to bed. Gazing at her son in the flickering candlelight, she reflected on how much her life had changed since she had left Meltwater almost two years ago following the confrontation with her father about whom she should marry. She recalled not for the first time her arrival at Mrs Hallam's in London; her fear at being trapped in London's demi-monde; her escape from Mrs Rathbone's; her flight to Paris; singing to King Louis of France at Versailles; her long journey towards Potsdam in pursuit of the man she loved; her near despair in Magdeburg; her marriage; Herr Bamberger and the orchestra; the birth of her child. Now she was in St Petersburg. It had all happened with such breathless speed. Gently touching the sleeping child, Arabella realised that his birth, more than anything else, had changed everything. Her life would never be the same. But she felt stronger, more clear-sighted, more determined to pursue what she believed to be right.

As she closed the door she noticed a small white feather on the floor, probably from a pillow, she guessed, picking it up. It reminded her of the words of the Mother Superior with whom she had taken brief refuge on her journey to Potsdam the year before. She had told Arabella about something St Hildegard of Bingen had once written.

> *There was once a king sitting on his throne. Around him stood great and wonderfully beautiful columns ornamented with ivory, bearing the banners of the king with great honour. Then it pleased the king to raise a small feather from the ground, and he commanded it to fly. The feather flew, not because of anything in itself but because the air bore it along. Thus am I, a feather on the breath of God.*

Arabella had found a small white feather in the garden at Herzberg following her marriage to Carl Manfred and she had enclosed it in a letter to the Mother Superior as evidence that He had conveyed her safely to her destiny. Was this small feather at her son's door a further reminder of the life before her? She resolved that the next day she would go to the cathedral to pray for forgiveness and protection in the months and years ahead.

* * * * *

After his conversations with the Count and Countess and the rare night of warmth and comfort he had spent under their roof at Dvortsovaya Naberezhnaya, Waldemar Drescher disappeared back into the shadows to apply his spycraft. He was nowhere to be seen but Carl Manfred could scent his presence. While he still deeply disliked the man, he acknowledged that Drescher was right in one respect. You could see your enemy on the battlefield. In the corridors of the court – whether Prussian or Russian – you could not see your true opponent. Moreover, he had to confess it was reassuring to know he was close by. If Arabella were to be involved in a game of court intrigue and it were not handled well, Drescher would be the best means of escape. And there was still the surprising fact that no one had yet mentioned the disappearance of the Countess von Schlegel.

It was barely the beginning of January, 1768, when Carl Manfred received a letter from Count Sokolov inviting him and the Countess to join Countess Sokolova and himself at the Winter Palace on Wednesday the 6th of January for the imperial ceremony of the Blessing of the Waters on the Feast of the Epiphany, to mark Christ's baptism in the waters of the River Jordan. He would send a coach to Dvortsovaya Naberezhnaya to take them to the Winter Palace where he and Countess Sokolova would be waiting. There was little debate in the von Deppe household. The promptly written answer was yes.

The Winter Palace, a large and imposing building situated between the Palace Embankment and the Palace Square, had been the residence of the Russian monarchs since 1732. The dusk made the building more monumental than ever. Its massive front, lit by flares and flecked with snow, truly underlined the strength and power of imperial Russia.

Once inside the palace, Arabella shed the long black fur coat she had worn against the bitter cold. Beneath it was a purple almost off-the-shoulder gown, sprinkled with pearl dust and, as always, unhooped to reveal more of her slender figure. As she and Carl Manfred were ushered into a larger reception room, Count Sokolov stepped forward. He was tall, slim and good-looking, dressed in a rich military ceremonial uniform befitting a senior officer of the Preobrazhensky Guards, one of the first imperial regiments to show loyalty to the Empress Catherine. Beside him was a young, attractive woman with high cheekbones and drawn-back black hair, smaller in height than the uniformed Count and exquisitely dressed in a hooped white silk dress edged in gold.

"Count Sokolov," said Carl Manfred, "it is my pleasure to present my wife, Arabella, the Countess von Deppe."

Arabella curtsied.

"Countess, I have heard so much about you. Welcome to St Petersburg and to the palace," the Count replied in admirable French.

"It is a great honour and a privilege to be present this evening on such an important Feast Day," said Arabella, conscious that as she spoke the woman in white was looking at her intently but without expression.

"Count and Countess, I wish to present my wife, the Countess Kseniya Sokolova."

The two ladies curtsied to one another. Carl Manfred bowed.

"Come, let us go without delay to the foot of the Jordan staircase to await the arrival of the Empress, who has been to the Neva River for the Blessing of the Waters. We can talk later."

Count Sokolov offered his arm to Arabella and Carl Manfred his to the Countess Kseniya.

The imperial staircase was in the rococo style and of immense proportions. There was little time for small talk before a fanfare sounded and the Empress Catherine appeared at the top of the stairs accompanied by the Metropolitan and his priests, resplendent in their ceremonial vestments, and a large entourage. Watched by the assembled court, ambassadors and dignitaries below, the Metropolitan, assisted by his acolytes, again blessed his sovereign with the water of the Neva, consecrated at a ceremony on the bank of the river earlier in the day. The Empress then descended the grand staircase to be greeted by her honoured guests.

After the Blessing had ended Count Sokolov offered his arm once more to Arabella. They circulated through several rooms, followed closely by the Countess Kseniya and Carl Manfred. The Count introduced Arabella to many but paused only briefly with each. He led her with purpose towards a larger group at the far end of the throne room. As they drew nearer, he took a slip of paper from his pocket and discreetly passed it to an usher, who passed it on to another.

"Count Sokolov, you have been most attentive but perhaps the time has come for Count von Deppe and me to take our leave so you and the Countess Kseniya can enjoy the rest of this special evening with your friends and acquaintances."

"My dear Countess, it is rare that I have the chance to introduce such a beautiful and charming English countess to our friends."

"Count Sokolov, I am not an English countess. Whilst I was born in England I have become Prussian by marriage and therefore a Prussian countess."

"That may be strictly true but your veins pulse with English and French blood, which makes you in my opinion a rare acquisition to St Petersburg society."

"Sir, not only do you flatter but you are well informed as to my antecedents."

Before Arabella could continue an official whispered in Sokolov's ear.

A passage suddenly opened through the throng of guests. There before them was the Empress Catherine. Arabella curtsied deeply.

"Your Majesty," said Count Sokolov, "I wish to present the Count and Countess von Deppe from Prussia and my wife, the Countess Kseniya Sokolova. The Countess von Deppe has recently arrived in St Petersburg with her young son, born last year. She is a talented musician and singer. Count von Deppe was until some years ago on the military staff of His Majesty King Frederick."

There was a momentary pause before the Empress spoke.

"How is His Majesty?" she asked.

"I understand he is well," replied Carl Manfred.

"Still planning further territorial acquisitions?" the Empress enquired with a teasing glint in her eye.

"That is not for me to say, as I have not seen him for many months."

"I do not think the King has yet forgiven me for buying Gotzkowsky's pictures from under his nose."

"I am sure that is not the case," replied Carl Manfred, aware that the King was indeed still angry that the Empress had acquired a collection he had long coveted.

The Empress turned to Arabella.

"Countess, I have heard much of the musical skills to which Count Sokolov has referred. Where did you learn so well?"

"In England, I was well taught by my music teacher, Monsieur

Kunzl, and my mother, Lady Whitfield."

"We Germans get everywhere," said the Empress, chuckling. "What else do you do, besides being a young mother?"

"I formed an orchestra of young musicians last year. We have given two public performances. As my husband has been in St Petersburg for many months I have also been occupied with overseeing his estate. When I am not doing that, I like to read about art and philosophy, and I ride," replied Arabella.

"Side-saddle or astride?" interjected the Empress.

Blushing, Arabella replied the latter, whenever she had the chance to dress as a man to enable her to do so.

The Empress's eyes lit up at this remark.

"Do not be embarrassed, Countess. I ride astride as often as I can. It is far more enjoyable and a chance to wear a man's clothing. Perhaps we should ride together."

Some of those witnessing the conversation looked at one another, a few barely able to conceal a smile.

"I can see you are a busy young woman. And I compliment you on your gown – no hoops. Now there is an innovation. Count Sokolov, please arrange for the Countess von Deppe to come to the palace soon so she and I can have a longer and more private talk. I would like it to happen in days, not weeks. You understand?"

Sokolov quickly nodded.

With that the Empress turned away to talk to several other people awaiting presentation.

Slowly the Sokolovs and the von Deppes made their way back towards the main staircase, where Arabella and Carl Manfred prepared to take their leave.

"Countess," said Count Sokolov, "I will write to you shortly to fulfil the Empress's command. She meant what she said. And Count von Deppe, you and I should meet soon to have another discussion of military tactics. I will arrange that, too."

Arabella turned to the Countess Kseniya.

"Countess, it would give me great pleasure if you would join me for tea soon at our house in Dvortsovaya Naberezhnaya. We have hardly had time for private conversation."

"I would like that very much," Countess Kseniya replied.

"Then I will write tomorrow to suggest a date. Have you children?"

"I have a little girl, Natalya."

"I would be honoured if you brought her with you," replied Arabella.

"I will," said the Countess Kseniya.

In their coach from the Winter Palace, Arabella and Carl Manfred reflected discreetly on the evening just passed. In the privacy of their bedroom, Carl Manfred embraced and kissed his wife.

"My dearest Arabella, I marvel at your skills – a mother, a musician, the controller of our estate and already an accomplished diplomat. But above all you charm monarchs – first King Louis at Versailles, then His Majesty and now the Empress of Russia. Where this will lead I do not know. But I wish you to know that tonight you shone like the brightest star in the sky. I love you deeply."

He kissed her again.

"Carl, I am what you have made me. You are the love of my life."

"Then we should go to our bed without delay to prove I am worthy of the distinction," he replied.

"I would like that," she whispered.

*****

Three weeks later, on Tuesday the 26th of January, the Countess Sokolova and her young daughter, Natalya, came to tea at Dvortsovaya Naberezhnaya. They spent a pleasing hour together talking about matters women often speak of alone. While occasionally her eyes would come alive and she would smile with great warmth, the Countess Kseniya's demeanour was restrained and Arabella saw in her dark eyes a trace of sadness – perhaps for hope and joie de vivre diminished by disappointment, and perhaps for the betrayal of love. She held the young Natalya, barely two years old and as beautiful as her mother, tightly to her as though she were her only possession.

Before leaving, the Countess Kseniya handed Arabella a letter from her husband.

"Before you open it," said the Countess, "I have something to say. At the imperial court, like the River Neva, beneath the surface nothing is quite as it seems. The court is a place of intrigue, ambition and betrayal. Beware of those around the Empress. They will sell their soul for advancement and physical pleasure. Countess Arabella, I can see you are warm, open and honourable. Beware. Do not allow yourself to be tempted. The cost of doing so can be great, as I have witnessed. Please do not divulge that I have told you this."

"Countess Sokolova, I thank you sincerely for your warning. You have my word that what you have said will never pass my lips. I have already in my life encountered betrayal. Like you, I am vigilant for those who may attempt to use me for their own ends. My son, Frederick Daniel, is most precious to me, as Natalya is to you. I will not jeopardise my son's future happiness by foolish actions on my part. I hope that you will come again to Dvortsovaya Naberezhnaya."

"I would like that to happen," replied the Countess Kseniya.

After the Countess and her daughter had left, Arabella opened the letter.

Dear Countess von Deppe,

Her Majesty the Empress wishes to receive you in her private apartment at the palace this Saturday the 30th of January at five o'clock. She has commanded me to escort you. It will be my greatest pleasure to do so. I continue to have the warmest of memories of your presence at the ceremony of the Blessing of the Waters.

I am at your service.
Nikolay Sokolov
The Winter Palace, Monday the 25th of January, 1768

Arabella put the letter down. She had thought the Empress would forget what she had said to her on the evening of the Feast Day. She had not. She was obliged to attend. The prospect of going to the palace alone filled her with unease. Moreover, Sokolov had written directly to her rather than to Carl Manfred. Surely this was unusual. She showed the letter to Carl Manfred, who saw the apprehension in Arabella's face. They agreed that she was obliged to attend, but Carl Manfred advised it would be better for her to travel in her own coach. He would pass a message to Drescher asking him to take her.

With this advice Arabella replied.

Dear Count Sokolov,

I wish to thank you for your letter.

I am deeply honoured that Her Majesty the Empress would wish to see me on the 30th of January. As Count von Deppe and I will have other matters to attend to earlier that day it would be best if I were to arrive at the palace in my own coach to avoid any inconvenience to you.

Yours most sincerely,
Arabella
Countess von Deppe
Dvortsovaya Naberezhnaya, Tuesday the 26th of January, 1768

The next day there was a discreet handwritten note to Carl Manfred from Waldemar Drescher advising that he had arranged a suitable and secure coach to take the Countess to the Winter Palace.

* * * * *

More snow fell on Saturday the 30th of January. It was bitterly cold and few people were on the streets. A small black coach arrived at Dvortsovaya Naberezhnaya at four o'clock in the afternoon. A little later Arabella descended the staircase, accompanied by Carl Manfred. She wore a high-necked dark-blue velvet dress edged in gold; a complementary gold pendant was pinned above her left breast, a Christmas gift from Carl Manfred. Her hair was tied back at the nape of her neck by a matching velvet ribbon and covered by a loose shawl. Over her gown she wore a thick green full-length coat with a fur collar. Her face was drawn and she looked nervous as she kissed her husband. He clasped her hand.

"Everything will go well. I am sure of that. I will be waiting for your return, when we will have supper together."

He kissed her again. She placed her hands in her muff and boarded the coach. A voice whispered to her.

"Countess, I will be with you this evening – in the shadows – close by."

Arabella turned round. Above the muffled-up mouth and nose of the coachman were the eyes of Waldemar Drescher.

* * * * *

Count Sokolov greeted Arabella at the Winter Palace. He was resplendent in court dress, carefully tailored to portray his figure to best advantage.

"Dear Countess von Deppe, it is a great honour to greet you again and an even greater honour to accompany you to Her Majesty. She awaits you in her private apartments."

"Thank you, Count Sokolov. I am deeply flattered that the Empress should ask to see me. I am sure there has been a mistake, that she wished to see someone else more important than me."

"You are indeed mistaken, Countess. It is truly you she wishes to see."

They walked along many grand corridors before passing through a doorway that led to smaller corridors. At last they arrived at a closed door. Sokolov knocked. A footman opened the door. The room to which it gave access was large, with landscape paintings on the wall. A fire blazed in the great hearth. The footman took Arabella's coat, shawl and muff. Sokolov invited her to sit by the fire while he went to inform the Empress of her arrival. While she waited, Arabella heard distant men's guffaws and occasionally a woman's laugh. Almost a quarter of an hour had passed when the Count returned.

"The Empress is ready to receive you."

They passed through an ante-room into a large bedchamber. The room was warm. Thick elegant brocade curtains covered the windows. Candles burned. On the walls hung impressive portraits, evidently of past czars and generals. Facing the four-poster bed, which was draped in brocaded gold fabric, was an imposing, almost life-size painting, which Arabella instantly recognised as the Empress's forebear Peter the Great. Nearby was a smaller portrait, which Arabella identified as that of the Empress Elizabeth, Catherine's predecessor, who had greatly tormented Catherine following the latter's marriage to the Grand Duke Karl Peter, the late Czar Peter III. The Empress Catherine herself was sitting in a high-backed chair close to the bed, her feet on a dainty footstool and a small book open in her lap. Around her on silk-covered chairs sat several men, wine glasses in their hands, laughing and talking amongst themselves.

"Your Majesty, may I present the Countess von Deppe? You asked her to call on you this evening."

The Empress looked up.

"Indeed I did. Gentlemen, this is the Countess von Deppe – born in England of a French mother and English father. She has sung to His Majesty King Louis of France at Versailles and likewise to the Prussian King. She is married to Count von Deppe, whom some of you have met."

The men leapt to their feet and bowed. Arabella curtsied deeply.

"Gentlemen," said the Empress, "it is time for you to go. I wish to have time alone with the Countess to talk of matters that only concern women."

One of the men, Count Sakharin, asked if the Countess von Deppe might sing for them before they left.

"Countess, I apologise. Men can be such bores at time. You and I have much to talk about. Perhaps you would help me to remove them from the room by singing for us? There is a harpsichord near the window, which, sadly, few people play for me."

Arabella fumed inwardly. She had surely not come to perform. Yet there was little she could do but comply. Without her music book, though, what could she sing? She would have to rely on her beloved German-born composer.

She sat down to play. There was still some whispering amongst the men. Arabella looked at them with an icy stare. They fell silent. She began to sing, in Italian.

Where'er you walk, cool gales shall fan the glade;
Trees where you sit shall crowd into a shade;
Where'er you tread, the blushing flow'rs shall rise;
And all things flourish where'er you turn your eyes.

When she had finished a breathless silence fell over the room. Though she had sung for only a few minutes, her voice had been full of variety and invention – all the more remarkable as she had not expected to sing. The Empress spoke.

"Countess, thank you. Now, gentlemen, please go."

As each man left he bowed to Arabella, who stood by the harpsichord. Sokolov remained.

"Nikolay, even you must go. I will summon you when the Countess and I have finished."

He still hesitated.

"Go, Nikolay. Go or I will have the palace guard arrest you for insubordination. Go!"

He reluctantly left the room, entranced by the Countess.

"Watch that Sokolov," the Empress whispered as the door closed. "I can see he already has eyes for you. He has tried hard to get into my bed. But it is already taken. He will have to wait his turn for me, though in truth he may have to wait a long time. Beware of him in the meanwhile."

The Empress beckoned Arabella to come and sit facing her by the fire.

"Come and sit with me."

Arabella came towards the fire and curtsied.

"Please, enough of that."

Arabella sat opposite the Empress of All the Russias.

"You have a beautiful voice, Countess, and a light touch on the keyboard. I must confess I have been little interested in music. I should have done more with my music lessons before I came to Russia. And since my arrival there have been so many distractions. Now, tell me about your childhood. Where were you born?"

"I was born in eastern England, near the coast. The house faced north, so it was always cold in the winter as the winds blew directly from the north."

"That would be from Siberia," the Empress interjected, smiling. "Did you like your father?" she enquired.

Arabella hesitated.

"We are alone, Countess. You may speak freely. We can be intimate, woman to woman and mother to mother."

"No. I did not. He treated me as his chattel for disposal in marriage as he thought fit. I did not accept his insistence and ran away to London."

"I did not like my father either. But as his daughter I had no choice when the late Empress Elizabeth chose me as the bride of her nephew, my predecessor. I arrived here and though my mother stayed for a while I was miserable and lonely. I often wished in my early years that I could run away. But I could not. Did you like your mother?"

"Yes," Arabella replied. "I adored her and still do. I often think of her in England and wish she were with me. But that cannot be."

"Tell me about your husband, Count von Deppe."

"We met in London, by coincidence, in the difficult circumstances in which I found myself after running away from home. He was kind and gentle and helped me to escape from my predicament. With his assistance I fled to Paris, where I realised I had fallen in love with him. He is older than me and could not believe my affections for him. But I followed him to Prussia, where we declared our love for one another. We married in Berlin in March of 1766."

"What a love story!" the Czarina remarked. "Do you still love him?"

"Deeply," replied Arabella.

"Why?" asked the Empress.

"He treats me as an equal."

"A rare commodity indeed," said the Empress.

"I am perhaps still too inexperienced to judge, but I believe on the basis of my limited observation that you are right," said Arabella.

"Take my word for it. It is rare. I know from experience. Is he good in bed?"

Arabella blushed, hoping that her pink cheeks would not be seen in the candlelight.

"Yes, loving but respectful of my body," she replied.

"That is also rare. So often men behave like brutes in a woman's bed. They think admission means instant ownership and servitude." The Czarina momentarily looked wistfully into the flames. "And you have a child?"

"Yes, I have a son."

"His name?" the Empress quickly asked.

"Frederick Daniel," replied Arabella with some trepidation, knowing what response might follow.

"Why Frederick?" The Empress was again quick to question, this time with a twinkle in her eye.

"A family name, and my husband has been a loyal soldier in King Frederick's court."

"That wily old fox," replied the Empress. "My late husband, the Czar, adored him but it cost him his throne and his life. I respect His Majesty but he cannot have things all his own way. I won't let him. But that's between us, as indeed is all of this conversation."

Arabella nodded.

"Would you like some wine?" The Empress gestured towards the carafe and glasses on a small table beside her.

"No thank you," replied Arabella, wary of the effect it might have on her wits in a remarkably intimate conversation she had never imagined would take place.

A silence fell between them. The Czarina once again gazed into the fire, taking a sip of wine as she did so. She turned back to Arabella.

"You and I are alike. You are English by birth but now married to a Prussian with a young child. Your life is now committed to Germany, for better or for worse. Me, I am German by birth but now Russian for the rest of my life. Your marriage has so far been good. Mine was not. It made me profoundly unhappy and there were times when I wished I could run away. But I remained at court out of duty, as I am sure you will remain in Prussia in the face of whatever cruel winds may blow. My burden is to be Empress of Russia," Catherine continued. "I have a son, who will one day be my heir. Until that day I am surrounded daily by courtiers and suitors begging for my favours. But as a woman, in my private moments I sometime feel vulnerable."

"Is that truly the case?" interjected Arabella.

"Yes," the Empress replied.

"I have learnt from experience to award my trust with care," Arabella added, now becoming franker in her responses.

"My child," replied Catherine, "you are right to do so. Rarely can one trust any man. Everyone has their price. To survive, a woman – the weaker sex – has to be devious and manipulative. If you are not that now, mark my words, you will be soon – in order to survive, to get your way and to protect your son. Countess Arabella, I like you. We have much in common. Beneath that veneer of calm and sweet gentleness I can see a heart full of fire and passion, just like my heart. You must ensure that your husband inflames your passion. Do you read?"

"Yes," replied Arabella.

"Which books have you read?"

Arabella listed some of the books she had read in the library at Meltwater and some of the volumes she had added to her husband's library at Schloss Herzberg.

"Have you read Voltaire?" asked the Czarina.

"I have read *Plato's Dream*," answered Arabella.

"Read this," said the Empress, picking up from the table the first volume of Voltaire's *Dictionnaire philosophique*, published four years before. She thrust it into Arabella's hand. "What about art? Do you like art?"

"I do," said Arabella. "I am beginning to expand my husband's rather limited art collection."

"Splendid," replied the Empress. "I can hear voices outside. The men are back. We will meet again soon. I will send for you. I hope you will come. Please, our conversation is private. You promise me you will not divulge what has passed between us."

"I assure you our conversation will remain a secret."

"Good. Now you must go. I will ask Sokolov to escort you to your coach. Remember to watch out for his hands. He embarrasses his poor wife so often. And, Countess, I should like you and Count von Deppe to move to the palace while this bitter weather lasts. We can spend more time together without undue prior arrangement. We will find you comfortable rooms."

Arabella was momentarily lost for words.

"Of course, Your Majesty," she said, quickly regaining her composure. "It would be a great honour."

"And Countess, I admire your dress. You have no hoop. Your body is highlighted in a most attractive way. What do you call that style of dress?"

"I call it a chemise dress. My mother often pressed me to wear a hoop but I found it tiresome to do so, and that is still the case. So I choose to go without."

"And how many layers underneath, Countess? Come, tell me," the Empress asked with insistence.

Arabella was taken aback. What a question she had been asked!

"Countess, hurry please. Tell me."

Arabella knew she had no option. She had to reveal her dressing secret.

"First I put on my slip, followed by my stockings and garters.

Over my slip I wear a petticoat and over that my corset, laced at the back. My mother taught me to keep the bow ends of the lacing always shorter than the tail ends so that it can be quickly undone. Then I apply my corset cover, under which sometimes I might wear a small bustle pad. Finally, I put on another petticoat and over that my chemise, which is my dress."

"Thank you, Countess. Your undergarments will remain a closely guarded secret. But I might try your fashion one day."

There the audience with the Empress ended. Arabella declined Sokolov's arm on the way to her coach, purposefully placing her hands in her muff. After final farewell pleasantries at the door, she returned alone to Dvortsovaya Naberezhnaya. It was after ten o'clock. Carl Manfred was waiting for her. Although she felt a pang of disloyalty to her husband, she did not reveal over supper any of the remarkably intimate details of her conversation with the Empress. Drescher had reminded her, as she stepped down from the carriage, of the need for silence on whatever had transpired. Whether he knew what had been said, she did not know. There were rumours of spyholes throughout the Winter Palace. She and Carl Manfred retired late to bed, still recovering from the shock of their impending move to the palace. As for Drescher, he began to prepare for his new disguise as a personal footman to the Count and Countess at the Winter Palace – though only after he had sent a secret message to his master in Prussia.

* * * * *

Within the week the von Deppes and their entourage had moved to the Winter Palace.

February was bitterly cold, made all the icier by a fierce wind from the north. More snow fell. The apartment that had been made available had several large rooms, including comfortable accommodation for Frau Klein, Frau Weiser, Hanne, Berthold the footman and Josef, a *maître de service*, a sudden new addition from Dvortsovaya Naberezhnaya. But there were many draughts in the palace and it was sometimes hard to keep warm in the evening when outside the chill bit deep. There was little sign of spring at the beginning of March either as fresh snow fell.

Throughout these weeks the Empress Catherine frequently sent for Arabella. It was always in the evening and in the candlelit intimacy of the Empress's bedchamber. They spoke often about philosophy and art, but frequently too about Catherine's plans for the extension of the palace to provide space for her growing art collection and more private, informal rooms in which she could relax. Sometimes Arabella played the harpsichord for the Empress, often pieces by Bach, though she liked to hear Handel's *Sarabande* if her mood was careworn. Another favourite of Catherine's was the aria *Tristes apprêts, pâles flambeaux* from Act 1 of Rameau's *Castor and Pollux*, which she would ask Arabella to sing if she was waiting for her current lover, Grigory Orlov, or remembering her former lover, Stanisław August Poniatowski. Occasionally, the Empress would notice that Arabella was somewhat low in spirit.

"Countess, it is sometimes hard for us women. As I have remarked before, happiness and unhappiness are in the heart and spirit of each of us. If you feel unhappy, then you should place yourself above that and act so that your happiness does not become dependent on anything."

Arabella often remembered these words later in her life.

Men, also, were a frequent topic of conversation. Arabella was much the listener of the Empress's opinions, particularly on the brothers Orlov, who it was plain had a special place in her affections. On a few occasions Catherine's son, Paul, would join them, but not for long. Arabella sensed that, though the Empress was preoccupied all day every day with the affairs of state – about which she never asked and which the Empress never disclosed, except for inadvertently uttering odd snippets in moments of frustration – and at night was often visited by her lovers, she was at heart a lonely woman. Perhaps it was for that reason that Catherine, from a royal background and a different culture, enjoyed talking to Arabella in such an unguarded way. As the intimate evenings continued she became increasingly open in her opinions and so did Arabella.

On one such evening in early March the Empress asked Arabella how well she rode.

"I enjoy riding. It has always been my means of escape, to be alone," replied Arabella.

"And if I remember correctly, your preference is to ride astride, not side-saddle."

"Whenever possible," confirmed Arabella.

"In three days' time I am going to inspect Sokolov's regiment – the Preobrazhensky Guards. It is one of the rare occasions when I can wear a man's uniform and ride astride. I would like you to ride with me, in uniform, as my honorary equerry."

Arabella was speechless.

"But Majesty, that would surely be impossible and would lead to great and adverse comment. You surely do not want that?"

"On the contrary, Arabella," replied the Empress, using her name for the first time, "I would very much like it. I am surrounded by men. It would be so amusing to see my officers' faces when another woman joins their Empress on the parade ground. I am sure Sokolov would enter into the spirit."

Arabella again advised against it but the Czarina interrupted.

"Enough, Countess von Deppe, I have decided. You will join me at Tsarskoye Selo. Besides, I am reliably informed that you masqueraded as a French officer on the last part of your journey to Potsdam."

Arabella froze. How could the Empress know that?

Catherine summoned Sokolov.

"Sokolov, I have decided that the Countess von Deppe, who is an excellent horsewoman, will join me on the inspection parade of your regiment in three days' time. She will accompany me as one of my equerries. I trust you have no objection?"

Sokolov replied instantly.

"It is a capital idea."

"That is settled. Send a uniform to my chief seamstress so the Countess can be fitted in good time."

"Yes, Majesty," replied Sokolov, already relishing the idea of seeing more of the Countess's slender figure in a man's attire.

Later that day Arabella told Carl Manfred what the Empress had commanded. She repeated that she did not wish to do it, did not want to make herself a public laughing stock. He too was astonished by Catherine's command but concluded, on reflection, that there were possible, though risky, advantages to the forthcoming event.

"There are undercurrents in this palace of which we know little. You should do what the Empress has asked. You cannot refuse. Since she has already told Sokolov to prepare and he has agreed, apparently with alacrity, she would lose face if you refused. My dearest Arabella, you must do this. Moreover, the longer you are a confidante of the Empress the less likely it will be that she will create trouble for the King as she and he examine the possible acquisition of Polish lands."

"Carl, I will do it, but I am fearful no good will come of this."

"Arabella, we will take care of you. I promise."

Late in the evening Carl Manfred sought the advice of Drescher. The spymaster-cum-*maître de service* thought the risk of criticism was significant, but that if that were the price of the Empress's friendship, so it had to be. He would pass a message of reassurance to their master in Prussia.

"How did the Empress know that the Countess posed as a French officer when she passed through Magdeburg on her way to Potsdam?" asked Carl Manfred.

"I would think that the Countess von Schlegel passed that snippet of gossip, wherever it came from, to a person in this court who has the ear of the Empress. I hope before long – perhaps with the help of the Countess – to find out who the informer was."

"Drescher, I warn you again. Be careful. No harm must come to my wife."

"If you play the game with me she will be safe."

* * * * *

Two days later the Empress's chief seamstress arrived with the uniform for a final fitting. Skilfully altered it was a good fit but Arabella insisted that her breeches should be tighter, as should her boots. If she were to appear on a parade ground alongside the Empress, then her uniform should match that of any officer present, including no creases.

The next day, Wednesday the 9th of March, Carl Manfred left early for Tsarskoye Selo to watch the parade along with other high-ranking invited guests. Though the morning was still cold, the sky was blue and cloudless. The chief seamstress arrived shortly afterwards, to help Hanne dress Arabella. Hanne tightly bound her mistress's breasts, as once they had been bound during her escape from England. Her tight breeches – into which she was almost sewn – were of white chamois leather; her undershirt was white too, contrasting with her red waistcoat and the long blue gold-edged cutaway over-jacket with gold epaulettes signifying the rank of lieutenant. With her hair tied back in a tail, she put on a black fur hat bearing the regimental insignia. Lastly, she pulled on – with considerable assistance – her long black thigh boots, which glinted from the polish applied. Helped to her feet by Hanne and the seamstress Arabella looked in the mirror. She had to admit she was resplendent, her uniform and boots emphasising her slim, tall figure. If only her mother could see her, thought Arabella.

There was a knock at the door.

"Come in," said Arabella.

Count Sokolov entered, as proud as a peacock in his own dazzling uniform of a colonel of the regiment. He gazed in awe at Arabella.

"I have come to arm my fellow officer," he said.

He buckled a thin rapier around Arabella's slender waist. Then he draped over her shoulders a long black military-style fur coat which he fastened at the collar as he had done his own, saying as he did so that he would not want his young officer to become cold on parade.

"Now, Lieutenant von Deppe, let us attend the Empress."

They went first to the stable where Arabella mounted a tall white horse. After a brief rehearsal exercise in the yard, she and Sokolov joined other officers in the procession to the parade ground, led by the Empress, striking in her own imperial uniform. Arabella looked across to the far side and recognised Carl Manfred's coach; recognised too, close to him, the figure of Drescher in his *maître de service* uniform. Sokolov was near to her on her right, slightly to the rear of her horse, looking often at her long thin booted leg.

The parade lasted an hour. As the Empress approached the barracks for lunch, she pulled back until Arabella was level with her.

"Lieutenant von Deppe, you look quite handsome – one of the most handsome in the regiment, I would say. We will have much to talk about later."

In the mess hall Arabella moved towards a side table, increasingly conscious of the man's world in which she found herself. But Sokolov bounded across.

"Lieutenant, the Czarina requires her equerry to be close by. Follow me."

He placed Arabella next to him on the top table, in close proximity to the Empress.

They had barely sat down when the general commanding the regiment proposed a toast to the Empress. Carl Manfred had warned her that there would be several such toasts. She should sip, while giving the impression of drinking the vodka in one mouthful. It was hard to disguise her sips and on one occasion she accidentally swallowed the entire mouthful. But the vodka warmed her, even reaching her feet on the cold stone floor.

After food Arabella found largely inedible there were speeches in Russian. Sokolov translated for her. Then the Empress rose to her feet to praise the regiment for its valour and loyalty. While the Czarina spoke, Arabella felt Sokolov's hand brush against her thigh. She thought nothing of it as he had reached down for his napkin which had appeared to slip from his lap. A few minutes later it dropped again. Bending down to retrieve it, he inserted his hand inside the top of her boot.

"I hope, Lieutenant," he murmured in her ear, "we can spend time alone later. I have much to tell you about the regiment."

Feeling emboldened by the vodka she had drunk she turned to whisper back.

"Count Sokolov, before he left for St Petersburg my husband gave me a portrait of Athene. She was, as you will know well, a warrior, the protector of Athens. If I may be so bold as to speak as a warrior wearing this distinguished uniform, I guard jealously admission to my bed. My husband is most welcome but I have not given anyone else a key to my door and have no intention of doing so. I admire your military prowess, about which I have heard so much, and indeed there is much to admire about your other skills, but I would not want to trespass on Her Majesty's toes. I suggest you remove your hand and leave matters there."

The Count smiled broadly.

"I see I have encountered a formidable display of tactical skill. I admire that. I will indeed retreat, at least for the present, and view my most fetching adversary from the overlooking ridge." He withdrew his hand.

"So be it, Count Sokolov. I too will view my opponent from

afar. But I should add that however long you may camp on the ridge you will have no tactic to use to your advantage in the valley."

"Lieutenant von Deppe, you are indeed a formidable adversary. But we Russians are patient. Eventually we prevail."

"We will see, Count Sokolov. Let us drink to a stalemate."

"Indeed, let us do that."

They put their vodka glasses together.

At that point the officers rose to their feet to give the Empress three cheers.

Arabella rejoined the procession to ride back to the palace, proud of her reprimand to the Count.

At the palace, the Empress asked Arabella to join her in her bedchamber.

"Arabella, you look most captivating in your uniform."

"As do you, Empress."

"Come, let us admire ourselves."

Both women stood in front of the mirror, laughing, hugging and admiring their figures, while the painter, Fyodor Stepanovich Rokotov, sketched.

After a while Catherine dismissed the painter.

"Rokotov, you have enough of a drawing. Now go away and paint."

Once he had gone the two women were alone.

Much animated conversation later, the Empress was reminded through the locked door that her next visitor would soon arrive.

"Tell him to wait," the Empress bellowed. "Dear Countess Arabella, I know you wish to leave St Petersburg soon. Stay a while longer. I greatly enjoy our private talks together. Please, I request you."

"Empress, I will try to stay as long as I can but it is already spring in Prussia and my husband and I must return to our much-neglected estate. Please understand that I will be sorry to leave but our departure is inevitable."

"Thank you, Arabella. Now tonight, once out of these uniforms, we can surely have passion in our respective beds. Don't you think?"

Arabella smiled, made no comment, bowed, took her leave and withdrew from the Empress's private apartment.

Warmed by the vodka and comfortable in her uniform, Arabella returned to her own apartment. She was flattered and – dare she confess it – aroused by the thought that her body in its tight-fitting tailored clothes had captured the attention of a handsome senior Russian officer, though she had deeply disliked his physical touch of her knee. She had been even more flattered by Catherine's attentions to her. Arabella looked at herself in the mirror in her bedroom. For a moment she thought she saw the smiling face of Antoinette Badeau – her alter ego from her previous life – over her shoulder, whispering the taunting words, "Is that all you are going to do?"

"Far more than you might ever imagine, Antoinette," Arabella whispered with a sly smile. "Tonight I will spur my husband to make love to me with even more desire than before. If the Empress can enjoy unrestrained passion, so can Lieutenant von Deppe."

*****

Carl Manfred returned late to the palace after spending the evening with officers following the parade. Arabella was sitting by the fire in their bedroom, gazing into the flames, still wrapped in her long fur coat.

"My dearest Arabella, you were truly magnificent on parade. Who would have thought that beneath the uniform of Lieutenant von Deppe, equerry to the Empress, beat the heart of the woman I love."

He knelt down and kissed her.

"Sokolov tried today to lure me into his bed. The Empress warned me weeks ago he would. I told him I firmly held the key to my door. No one else other than you could enter."

"Arabella, surely you did not say that – in such blunt words? How could you! That is badly said."

"I did and I am proud that I spoke so."

Carl Manfred looked at her and smiled. How could he be angry?

"Arabella, you are a truly beautiful, remarkable woman. Not for the first time – nor, I am sure, for the last – I am struck by the prescience with which your mother chose your second name: Mariette – little rebel. You are more than a little rebel. You defy all human convention. You seek constantly to turn the world on its head. But I am slowly getting used to your utter unpredictability and shamelessness. I am aware too that almost every day of every week in this palace men are attracted to you like moths to candlelight. Some, like Sokolov, get burnt by you when they fly too close. I am truly blessed and honoured that such a captivating woman is my wife. I am the proudest man in this palace that so many men should covert you."

He bent to kiss her.

She looked up at him.

"Carl, please," she whispered, "use your key and unlock me. I beg you. Don't delay. I desire you so much. Do not hesitate – do it now." She stood up and seized the lapels of his jacket. "Please, I want you to do it now."

"Yes," he replied, stirred by how explicitly his wife had spoken.

She pulled the ribbon to release her hair and undid the buckle securing her long fur coat. It slipped from her shoulders revealing her half-unclothed body, dressed only in breeches and boots. Her eyes were piercing in a way he had never seen before.

"Carl, please, please I beg you. Make love to me – now. Please, I ask you, here by the fire."

He smiled but made no move as he watched her mounting impatience.

"Lieutenant von Deppe of the Preobrazhensky Guards commands you to follow an order," barked a smiling Arabella.

"Of course, Lieutenant," he replied.

She hastily spread the fur coat before the hearth and lay on it. He too felt the sudden impulse of lust as he looked down at Arabella's face and her breasts bathed in the shadow and light of the flickering fire. All those months he had been without her. And then there had been her slow recovery from the birth of Frederick Daniel and the journey, and, more recently, the long evenings she had spent with the Empress away from him. He lay beside her, gently fondling her.

"Carl, why do you torture me in this way?" she whispered. "Don't keep me waiting. I want you so much."

"Lieutenant von Deppe, you must be patient."

He slowly undid the fly of her breeches and eased them away. He ran the tips of his fingers, still cold, from her open lips down between her breasts to the now exposed soft place between her thighs and up again to her neck, just as he had done the night they made love in the royal bed in the Palace of Charlottenburg. Her body quivered with gathering expectation. She turned to him with half-closed eyes, her legs parted in anticipation. Suddenly, unable to wait any longer, Arabella pulled him onto her. As the fire crackled they joined together in divine pleasure.

"Antoinette, now be gone for ever. I have finally won," Arabella whispered later, staring into the flames, locked in her sleeping husband's arms.

In the distance a violin played the familiar chaconne by Nicola Matteis, the same refrain that was played that night at the Palace of Charlottenburg. Through a spyhole in the wall Count Sokolov watched the firelight scene. He vowed he would bed the English Countess before the month was out. If she would not come willingly, he would play his master card – blackmail – to force her to submit. And what an ace he held in his hand. She would know what had happened, on the road from the Russian border, to the Countess Katherina von Schlegel, another of his lovers, who had once said she would do anything to retain his favour, including the provision of secret information about the Prussian King and those around him. And she would know what had happened to Katherina von Schlegel's companion. She would confess in his bed how they had vanished. As he watched the bodies lying together asleep in the firelight and plotted what he would do to Arabella's unclothed body, he did not observe that all the while he was himself being watched by the violin player.

*****

Carl Manfred awoke early the next day. Arabella lay half uncovered and deeply asleep in the bed to which he had carried her in the small hours of the morning. Her fur coat, in which he had wrapped her, had slipped, exposing her breasts. She still wore her boots and breeches. Her rich dark flowing uncoiffed hair hid much of her face. He recalled for a moment how she had similarly lain, masked, in his bed in London – the day he had first seen her in the early-morning light. He pulled up the thick coverlet to warm her. She did not stir. As he left he kissed her cheek softly. She murmured but did not move. He gave orders to Hanne and Frau Klein that she should not be disturbed.

Within the hour, Carl Manfred received a note from Count Sokolov, while the Empress, excitedly wishing to reminisce about the events of the previous day and the night just passed with her lover, summoned her equerry from her bed. Unable to change in time, the Countess appeared in the royal apartment once again wearing her military jacket and clad in her rebuttoned breeches and boots – these particular items serving, if Arabella were privately to admit it, as a deeply sensual reminder of her provocative sexual behaviour the night before. Her actions had easily exceeded all that Antoinette Badeau, the imaginary woman behind whose identity she had hidden in London, had taught her; Arabella had nothing left to learn. The two women – the Empress and her coquettish equerry – spent several hours in private sharing indiscretions and secrets as women are inclined to do.

* * * * *

Dear Count von Deppe,

I would appreciate an opportunity to call on you at your convenience to discuss a most delicate matter requiring a mutually acceptable solution.

Perhaps you would be kind enough to inform me when might be a suitable time? We should meet alone.

With my felicitations,
Nikolay Sokolov
The Winter Palace, Thursday the 10th of March

Carl Manfred showed the letter to Drescher.

"You should know, Count von Deppe, that last night Sokolov spied on you in your bedroom."

"That is outrageous behaviour, unbecoming an officer and an official of Her Majesty's court," protested Carl Manfred.

"It is plain, my dear Count, that he wishes to bed your wife. He has been unable to keep his eyes from her since she arrived in St Petersburg. She has resisted his advances honourably. It is my opinion that this man, who is amongst the most lecherous at court, wishes to blackmail you."

"On what basis could he do so?" said Carl Manfred.

"It is my supposition that he was the recipient of information from the late Countess von Schlegel. If I am correct, and I believe I am for reasons I do not wish to disclose, he is likely to propose that you stand aside so he can take the Countess to his bed as his new mistress. But by doing so he would risk the anger of the Empress, who has chosen to keep him waiting a long time in the queue to her own bed. She would be incensed to think that he had withdrawn from the line to pursue a young woman whom she too happens to admire and who has become her close confidante. However, the stupid man would be prepared to risk the Empress's anger just to bed your wife to pursue his own ends."

"If you are correct – and I would imagine you are – what is to be done?"

"You should reply in the morning that you are ready to see him at Dvortsovaya Naberezhnaya on a forthcoming evening. That will give me time to lay a trap for him that he cannot possibly escape. You should say nothing to the Countess."

Carl Manfred agreed to what Drescher had proposed and accordingly wrote to Sokolov proposing that they should meet at Dvortsovaya Naberezhnaya at eight o'clock on Saturday evening the 12th of March, when Arabella would most likely again be with the Empress.

*****

Shortly after Arabella had arrived in the Empress's private apartment, Sokolov arrived promptly at Dvortsovaya Naberezhnaya dressed in his colonel's uniform. He sat down in the library opposite Carl Manfred. His manner was stiff and formal.

"Count von Deppe, I wish to broach a delicate matter. I received information some time ago that the Countess Katherina von Schlegel and a companion would travel with the Countess von Deppe to St Petersburg. On being given their description the frontier guards recall that both were in the coach occupied by your wife. Yet they were not in the Countess's coach when she arrived in this city. There has been no sign of either the Countess von Schlegel or her companion since. I can only assume that they are missing on account of something that happened to them after crossing the Russian border. Perhaps you or your wife could explain what that might have been?"

"My wife is not here to answer your question and even if she were I would not permit her to do so. The fact of the matter is that I do not know the current whereabouts of either the Countess von Schlegel or her companion, and nor does the Countess von Deppe."

"Count von Deppe, that is not what I asked. I would like to know precisely what happened to them after they crossed the border."

"I repeat, I do not know, and suggest that you conduct your enquiries elsewhere," Carl Manfred tartly.

"Count von Deppe, let me be even franker. I believe you do know what happened to the Countess von Schlegel and her companion. I believe they have been disposed of because they had certain information about your wife and indeed you that you were unwilling for them to divulge. Am I not right?"

"That is an outrageous and slanderous allegation and I am tempted to challenge you to withdraw it," replied Carl Manfred, struggling to contain his anger.

"A duel, Count, is not the outcome I am seeking in this case. I propose another solution. Perhaps it would be best if you were to withdraw from St Petersburg, leaving your wife here to provide continuing enjoyment to the Empress. And when she's not with the Empress, I could help her find other diversions that might amuse her. If this solution were to be agreed, nothing further would be heard about the fate of the Countess von Schlegel and her companion."

Carl Manfred could barely suppress his rage but he knew he had to restrain his inclination to strike Sokolov.

"Let me have time to consider your proposition. I suggest that you return in two hours' time to hear my answer," replied Carl Manfred – to the evident surprise of Sokolov.

"Thank you, Count von Deppe. I knew you would see reason as all good officers do."

Two hours later Sokolov returned to Dvortsovaya Naberezhnaya.

"I have found a way forward that I believe will resolve the situation. May I offer you a glass of vodka so that we can discuss the details in a convivial way?"

Carl Manfred pulled the bell rope to summon Berthold, the footman.

"Please bring two vodkas for Count Sokolov and me."

The two men exchanged pleasantries.

"I hope this will not take long, Count von Deppe. I have to return to the palace shortly."

"No, it will not take long, but we need to discuss the matter undisturbed."

Berthold returned.

"Count von Deppe, I can see you have taken to vodka well. These are generous shots, necessary on such a chilly night."

The two men raised their glasses and toasted the Empress.

"Sokolov, let me speak plainly," Carl Manfred began. "I cannot accept the proposal you made earlier this evening and I never would. What you said then was slanderous and untrue. My wife and I are blameless in the disappearance of the Countess von Schlegel and her companion. For a senior officer to blackmail another is worthy of court martial – at least in the Prussian army. So I am afraid the solution you have proposed is unacceptable and will always be so. The matter is closed."

"I am afraid you are mistaken, Count von Deppe. I will convey what you have said to the Empress without delay."

Sokolov rose to leave but fell back in his chair in sudden and evident physical discomfort.

"I feel unwell. I need some air," he said, trying to undo the top button of his tunic.

At this moment the Countess Sokolova entered the room. Tall and striking and dressed from head to toe in black fur, she looked down at her husband slumped in the chair, still struggling with his tunic and gasping for air.

"Nikolay Petrovich, I heard all that you said to Count von Deppe earlier this evening. You have betrayed me, your loyal wife, many times. Now you wish to dishonour my friend, the Countess Arabella, on account of your insatiable lasciviousness – she a friend and confidante of the Empress, no less. I poisoned your vodka, Nikolay Petrovich, and from the mixture you consumed you will shortly die. I promised to avenge your constant affairs but you would not listen. Now you will pay my price in a slow agonising death alone at our *dacha*. I hope that your soul, if you have one, rots in everlasting purgatory."

By now Sokolov was unable to speak.

Drescher and Berthold lifted him from his chair and carried him downstairs to a waiting coach.

"Thank you, Count von Deppe, for your assistance in this matter," said the Countess icily. "I have long wanted to see this day. My husband has paid the ultimate price for his betrayal. I will come by soon to say farewell to the Countess Arabella."

With that she left Dvortsovaya Naberezhnaya in the coach in which her husband had arrived, Count Sokolov himself leaving in the carriage behind, in the safe care of the man in the shadows, who had removed another enemy of the Prussian state. Carl Manfred returned to the Winter Palace.

Arabella returned late to the apartment after her private evening with the Empress.

"Has Count Sokolov been here?" she asked.

"No," replied Carl Manfred softly. "But he called on me at Dvortsovaya Naberezhnaya."

"What did he want?"

"What he wanted I could never give. He has gone and he will not cross your path again."

"What happened?"

"I assure you, nothing that need worry you at this late hour. I will tell you tomorrow. Come to bed."

* * * * *

The next morning, still unaware of what had happened the night before, Arabella spoke to Carl Manfred.

"There is something I wish to say."

"Yes, Arabella, what is it?"

"Carl, it is now spring in Herzberg. I wish us to leave Russia. I wish to go home. Whatever we were supposed to have done in this city, it is time to leave. You and I are more important than any affair of state – our love must not be consumed by the will or whim of a monarch. The King may be vexed by our departing when business is possibly still unfinished but so be it. I love you too much to put our happiness and the future of Frederick Daniel at risk. You, our son, Herzberg and even the Camerata mean far more to me than this city and, yes, the Empress. Our love for one another will come under even greater strain if we stay longer in this corrupt and corrupting city. So please, Carl, take me home without further delay."

He kissed her.

"I will," he replied, smiling. "We will leave at the end of the month, as soon as the necessary arrangements have been made."

"Thank you, Carl."

That night they made love even more passionately.

On Wednesday the 30th of March Carl Manfred and Arabella left St Petersburg for Schloss Herzberg.

The day before their departure Arabella called to say farewell to the Empress.

"Dear Countess Arabella, it saddens me greatly to see you leave. But I know you must go. I thank you for being such a true, discreet and faithful companion. You have taught me much. I wish you to have this gift."

She handed Arabella a copy of Voltaire's *Treatise on Tolerance*, published in 1763, in which the Empress had written:

To my friend and confidante Arabella Mariette
Арабелла Мариэтт
In warm remembrance of intimate conversations between an Empress and an English countess.
Never forget Russia. Never forget me.
Екатерина Алексеевна
Yekaterina Alexeevna

"And I wish to give you this."

The Empress uncovered a framed picture lying on the table beside her. It was an oil painting of the Empress and Arabella talking intimately to one another, hand in hand, in front of the mirror in Catherine's private apartment, as they had done on the 9th of March after the parade, each dressed in their Preobrazhensky Guards uniforms.

"Countess Arabella, I would like you to accept Rokotov's painting of us together on that recent special day. I will always regard you as an honourable officer in the regiment and a most cherished personal friend."

"Empress, your generosity has moved me greatly. I did so little," replied Arabella.

"I disagree. You have done much for me and for that reason I wish you to have this picture with you in Prussia. You had better not let King Frederick see it. It might make him jealous that he did not recruit you to the Prussian hussars first."

They both laughed.

Arabella gazed at the beautifully executed painting which suggested – nothing more – the possible existence of a close unspoken bond between the two embracing women, one perhaps comforting the other. The picture seemed to convey a narrative or meaning known only to the two uniformed subjects.

"Your Majesty, I am deeply touched by this picture. It will always be precious to me."

"As you have been precious to me," replied Catherine. "Play for me, Arabella, one last time."

"Of course," said Arabella.

She sat at the harpsichord. What could she choose at this poignant moment? It should be Bach and, as she had done sometimes at Meltwater when she was alone on a winter's morning, she played the composer's *Prelude No. 1*. The Empress looked at Arabella, playing the notes so softly. Arabella looked up. Their eyes fixed. They smiled at one another. Both had tears in their eyes.

As they completed their farewells Arabella curtsied and, rising to leave, whispered into the Empress's ear. A year later – from that whisper – Catherine the Great acquired the art collection of Count Heinrich von Bruhl of Saxony – a vast number of prints and drawings as well as over six hundred paintings from the Dutch, Flemish, French, Italian and German schools. Once again the Empress had outsmarted King Frederick in art acquisition. Not even Waldemar Drescher knew how the Empress had been so well informed of the impending disposal.

When Arabella opened the door to go, the Empress touched her sleeve.

"I was tired of him. There was no longer a place for him. Please tell your husband. He will know what I mean."

Catherine kissed Arabella's cheek and Arabella hers. After one final embrace, the door closed. Arabella fought hard to restrain her tears as she left the palace.

The last farewell at Dvortsovaya Naberezhnaya was from the Countess Kseniya Sokolova. She and Arabella hugged one another in the midst of another emotional parting.

"Come and visit us at Herzberg," said Arabella. "Promise me you will."

"I promise I will come one day."

CHAPTER 4

Death at Meltwater

It was Friday the 2nd of April, 1773.

Spring was slow to come to Herzberg after an unceasing bitter winter. Carl Manfred was once again closeted with the King at Potsdam. Despite increasingly cantankerous behaviour and a forbidding exterior, the monarch still retained the loyalty of a small – but diminishing – circle of close friends and confidants of whom Carl Manfred was one, though his patience with the King was often sorely tested. Yet while Frederick's moods frequently fluctuated and sometimes he kept Carl Manfred waiting for days at court without saying a word to him, the King always managed a winning smile and gentle words at the mention of his favourite English countess, Arabella von Deppe.

On this chilly though sunlit morning Arabella was in the library of a house now larger on account of a new wing that provided more room for her musicians and her slowly growing collection of paintings, the fruits of an appetite whetted by her first-hand knowledge of the Empress Catherine's extensive art-collecting habit in St Petersburg. In contrast to the Empress's ceaseless acquisitions regardless of cost, Arabella's choices – still limited by space and the Herzberg budget – were more measured and selective. Since their return from Russia, she had with her husband's approval bought several sixteenth- and seventeenth-century portraits and landscapes, which were widely admired – and often envied – by those who came to visit.

On the table in the library lay the latest musical score, which Herr Bamberger had delivered to Herzberg a day or so before with his recommendation that it might be added to the Camerata's expanding repertoire. Arabella played the first movement. Herr Bamberger was right in his judgement; it had a pleasant and refreshing melody. This was only to be expected of a keyboard concerto in F major from the Austrian composer, Haydn, courtesy of her old music teacher, Herr Kunzl. Haydn's fame as a composer was rapidly spreading. Arabella hoped that one day she might be able to meet him.

With a little time still to spare before lunch Arabella sat down in the library and leafed through some earlier scores that had lain untouched for many months. As she did so a loose sheet of paper fluttered to the floor. It was a letter written five years before by Herr Bamberger.

Dear Countess von Deppe,

On behalf of the Camerata I welcome you and Count von Deppe back to Schloss Herzberg from St Petersburg. We have missed you greatly. I wish to assure you that in your absence we have continued to practise, learning new musical selections we have been gathering for your consideration. Herr Kunzl has been most helpful in ensuring we do not slip in our commitment.

I look forward to calling on you at your earliest convenience. As news spread of your imminent return we received several requests to perform publicly. I would like to discuss these with you.

With warmest felicitations,
Albrecht Bamberger
Potsdam, Saturday the 16th of April, 1768

Rereading the letter Arabella recalled her and Carl Manfred's unalloyed pleasure five years earlier as their coach finally turned into the long drive at Herzberg. The journey from St Petersburg had been rigorous, and passing the lake where the Countess von Schlegel had drowned cast a dark shadow over their rising spirits as they headed for the Russian border. It struck Arabella more than once on the way home that every journey she had so far undertaken had been marked by bloodshed. Was it a bad spell cast upon her or just happenstance? That thought eventually passed from her mind as the Russian border receded behind them into the far distance. But five years later her warmer memories of St Petersburg and particularly of the Empress remained fresh in her mind. The small painting of her in Preobrazhensky Guards uniform standing beside the similarly uniformed Catherine remained a personal memento she very much cherished. And true to her promise to the Empress she had never disclosed to anyone the contents of their intimate candlelit conversations. They had been intensely private and would remain so.

Still casting her mind back to 1768 Arabella recalled the excitement of her first few weeks at Herzberg; the pleasure of seeing the young Count Frederick Daniel begin to become aware of his home; and informing Carl Manfred that she was bearing another child, conceived in Russia. Seven months later, on Thursday the 15th of December, she gave birth to a daughter, whom she and Carl Manfred named Elise Catherine Hildegard von Deppe, bearing like her mother the title of countess. As soon as she had recovered well enough from the birth, Arabella wrote two personal letters.

The first was to the Mother Superior of the convent near Maastricht where she had stayed for three days on her way from Paris to Potsdam, in the early weeks of 1766, in pursuit of Carl Manfred.

Dear Mother Superior,

You may not remember me but two years ago you and your sisters kindly and generously gave me refuge on my way east. You offered me comfort and before my departure recounted some words of the Abbess Hildegard, written so many centuries before. I still recall those words. In my letter of thanks, which I believe my mother delivered to you on her way back to England following my marriage to Count von Deppe, I pledged that if I ever had a daughter she would be called Hildegard.

I recently gave birth to a daughter, whom I wish to inform you now bears the names of Elise Catherine Hildegard. I believe she carries the name Hildegard with honour and humility. Our son, Frederick Daniel, is proud of his sister.

I often think of your open-heartedness at that time – to me, a stranger, uncertain of what the future held. Your prayers for me then have already given me so much strength and solace. I will continue to hold you and the sisters in the highest esteem and to keep you in my prayers to Our Lady. I hope that you will continue to think of me and pray to the Abbess Hildegard for my daughter, her namesake.
With my warmest wishes,
Arabella
Countess von Deppe
Schloss Herzberg, Monday the 2nd of January, 1769

The second letter was to the Czarina Catherine and was entrusted to Waldemar Drescher for safe delivery.

Most Personal
To Her Gracious Majesty the Empress,

This letter brings to you my warmest greetings and best wishes for the New Year 1769.

I continue to enjoy the most cherished memories of our many private conversations together, the contents of which will remain locked in my heart, inaccessible to others. I was deeply touched by your great kindness and patience towards me. There have been countless times – while reading the book by Voltaire you so generously gave me, or looking yet again at the painting of us together in our military uniforms – when I dearly wished to be back in St Petersburg to see your art collection, to witness all the new buildings constructed to your designs and to discuss more intimate matters as we did once before.

I hope that one day it might be possible for me to return to Russia and that I might bring with me not only my son, Frederick Daniel, but also our newly born daughter, Elise Catherine Hildegard, bearing the name Catherine in honour of yours.
From your friend and once-upon-a-time equerry, and with the greetings of my husband, Count von Deppe,
Arabella Mariette
Арабелла Мариэтт
Schloss Herzberg, Monday the 2nd of January, 1769

Arabella had considerable doubt that her letter to the Empress would reach its recipient, let alone that she would ever receive a reply. But Waldemar Drescher said he was sure it would since he was using his private means of communication. Within two months she received a reply.

To my personal friend Arabella Mariette
Арабелла Мариэтт
Thank you for your most kind letter. Its safe receipt brought me much joy, prompting with ease the memories of the private times we had together. I recall with special poignancy the music you often played to soothe me. No one can play Bach as you used to do. The pianists here play like donkeys.
I thank you for giving your daughter the name Catherine. I am deeply touched.
I urge you one day to come back to see me, to view my new gallery, now well under construction, and to make me laugh.
Your close friend and admirer,
Екатерина Алексеевна
Yekaterina Alexeevna
St Petersburg, Tuesday the 7th of February, 1769

Drescher assured Arabella and Carl Manfred that the existence of the exchange of letters would never reach King Frederick's ears. It never did. Arabella knew that Drescher was aware of the contents, but she trusted him.

A few weeks later a letter arrived from the convent at Maastricht.

Dear Countess von Deppe,
I wish to thank you for your gracious letter and for the joy it has brought to me and the sisters.
I assure you that you, Count von Deppe, your son and the newly born Elise Catherine Hildegard will remain much in our prayers to the Abbess of Bingen and Our Lady.
We hope that one day you will pass by us again.
In prayer,
The Mother Superior
Maastricht, Monday the 13th of February, 1769

The other notable event around that time was the first concert attended by Arabella, two months after the birth of Elise. It took place in the Golden Gallery at the Royal Palace of Charlottenburg. The Camerata played before a large audience. Even the King attended.

Arabella and Herr Bamberger chose the music with great care, the elderly Herr Kunzl adding his own opinions. The concert comprised:

Introduction in C Major by Pietro Antonio Locatelli
Concerto for Violin and Oboe in C Minor by Johann Sebastian Bach
Symphony No. 4 by William Boyce
Sarabande by George Frederick Handel
Harpsichord Concerto in D Major by Josef Haydn

There was strong applause as the concert ended, complete with calls for Arabella to sing. She took her place in front of the Camerata and sang with great tenderness and clarity *Where'er you walk* from Handel's *Semele*, the words of which she knew well, so hiding the lack of time she had had since her return to Prussia to practise and to learn new arias. The audience rose to their feet in delight. The King was visibly moved to hear her as he had been when she had sung on St Cecilia's Day in the Garrison Church at Potsdam.

Still the audience cheered Arabella and the Camerata, demanding yet more.

"To send us happily on our way the orchestra will perform the rondeau from Act Four, *Les Sauvages*, of Jean-Philippe Rameau's opera *Les Indes galantes*," Arabella announced. "Herr Bamberger, please play."

With those words the Camerata threw all musical restraint aside. Within a minute the audience picked up the rhythm and began to clap as the music bounced along like a ball. Then, to everyone's delight, Arabella sang the aria *Forêts paisibles*, accompanied by the young and handsome tenor Herr Stefan Fischer.

Oh, Arabella recalled, what a glorious occasion that had been! From that evening the fame and prestige of the Schloss Herzberg Camerata began to grow, with concerts in Berlin and beyond. Four years later the Camerata had become firmly established.

*****

Arabella began to play Bach's *Prelude*, while looking at the painting of her and the Empress hanging on the wall. She stopped mid-point. The memories remained warm and fresh but now, with spring imminent, it was time to put them aside and think of plans for the months ahead. She had written regularly to her mother, Lady Whitfield, during the past five years. The correspondence had often been amusing, with her mother frequently relating anecdotes about her friends, Meltwater and her husband's mistress, Lady Ward. Arabella hoped that, instead of further letters, her mother would this year return to Herzberg, where she had not been since March 1766. She decided that later in the day she would write to her mother again, pressing her to come without further delay.

She wrote to her mother care of the Comtesse de Caullery, who lived in Paris and was the sister of Lady Pamela Hartley, one of her mother's few London friends. It was Lady Hartley who had travelled with Lady Whitfield to Paris to search for Arabella at the beginning of 1766. As she believed Lady Pamela travelled frequently between London and Paris, where she stayed with the Comtesse de Caullery, Arabella thought that Lady Hartley would be best able to carry her letter to England and personally persuade Lady Whitfield to return to Herzberg to see her daughter and grandchildren.

Within two weeks Arabella received a letter from Lady Pamela who, as Arabella had surmised, was in Paris with her sister.

Dear Countess,

It is evident from your letter to me that you have not yet received the sad news of your mother's death.

I regret to tell you that Lady Whitfield fell ill during the past winter at Meltwater Hall. It was a long and bitter season, and your mother found it difficult to muster the strength to battle the chill that had afflicted her. As she grew weaker she asked me to go to Norfolk to be at her bedside. There was nothing her doctors could do. She died peacefully a month ago, on Sunday the 14th of March.

Before her death Lady Whitfield asked me to pass to you the enclosed letter and musical score. She expressed to me not only her profound love for you but also her highest admiration for your unswerving determination to achieve fulfilment in your life, for your continuing commitment to the Catholic faith and for your supreme love of music. She gave me, to hand to you personally, a portrait miniature of herself, which she kept with the portrait miniature of you that you gave her as a present on her departure from Prussia after your marriage and which she greatly treasured. She kept it close to her always, as a constant reminder of you. As they are most precious, I will hold them safely until you or a trusted messenger can collect it.

The Comtesse de Caullery and I will sincerely miss your mother, particularly her warmth of character, her adoration of music, which you have so richly inherited, and her strong ideals, firmly rooted in her quiet and unquenchable love of Our Lady. You have the Comtesse's and my deepest sympathy in your tragic loss.

I am spending more time with the Comtesse in Paris. She and I are ready to assist you in any way should you come to Paris soon in connection with your mother's affairs.

Lady Pamela Hartley

The 16th of April in Paris

Arabella put the letter down and wept.

A little later, when she had composed herself, she opened the second envelope. Within was the transcript of her first ever Bach musical exercise, which had held pride of place in the music book that she had returned to her mother as a personal memento at the time of her marriage to Carl Manfred. Affixed to it was a letter.

Arabella, ma fille très chère,

I fear I have not long to live but before I die I have entrusted Lady Hartley with this private communication and its musical enclosure, instructing her to ensure that it reaches your hands safely. She has also received two most personal items which I wish you to have.

I have played this simple Bach transcription often in my solitude at Meltwater, since it captures in fine relief my rich memories of our pleasurable times together at the keyboard before you left home in search of happiness, finding it at

Herzberg with your handsome and kind husband, Count von Deppe.

As I have so often written to you I have missed you greatly since we said goodbye after your marriage, now seven years ago. How the time has passed. But listening to others play music, and occasionally going to the theatre in Norwich – or even sometimes to London – to hear Monsieur Handel's arias, which you sang so well, have enabled me to reach out and almost touch you despite the great distance between us.

I have instructed that my remains should not stay in England but join those of my family in the crypt at Château de Rozac where the de Mirons have long lived. Perhaps one day you will come and lay a flower on my tomb.

I now say farewell and wish you continuing profound happiness at Herzberg. As the years pass, please do not forget me; do not forget Meltwater, despite its unhappy associations for you, because it will surely one day be yours by right, regardless of the possible machinations of others; and please do not forget to pray to the Mother of God that the Lord may have mercy on my soul.

Je termine ma lettre en t'assurant de mon affection la plus profonde.

Votre maman,

Thérèse

Meltwater, Friday the 12th of March, 1773

Arabella, overwhelmed by emotion, sat in silence in the library for over an hour, undisturbed in her grief. She had lost her closest friend, from whom she had learnt so much and from whom she had inherited so much: her stubbornness and determination, her love of music, and her respect for mankind and the equality of women. Her sorrow was profound. Her anger towards her father for his callous treatment of her mother during their marriage became even more unquenchable. Her mother's wish to be buried in France in the de Miron crypt represented a gesture of defiance and the utter rejection of the Whitfield family and all that it stood for.

The door opened. It was Elise Catherine. Frederick Daniel followed.

"Mama, why are you so sad?"

"Dearest Elise, I have lost someone very dear to me. That is making me sad."

"Mama, Frederick and I love you. We will help to make you happy again."

"Thank you, Elise," said Arabella as she stroked her daughter's long fair hair. "I know you will. Would you like to come to Paris with me?"

"Yes please, mama."

"Then we will go – very soon. I will speak this evening to your father."

Arabella held her daughter and son tightly. While she grieved for her mother, there were new young lives to nurture at Herzberg. Her future lay with them. Though she would have many warm and lasting memories of her mother the past was past. Helping her children to take their place in Prussia would require her continuing strength and dedication. Her grief should be put aside. She remembered what the Empress Catherine had said to her: "happiness and unhappiness are in the heart and spirit of each of us. If you feel unhappy, then you should place yourself above that and act so that your happiness does not become dependent on anything."

That evening Carl Manfred agreed without hesitation that Arabella and the children should go to Paris as soon as practicable to stay with his sister, Maria Louisa, in order to meet Lady Pamela Hartley and the Comtesse de Caullery. He would endeavour to accompany them, since he might well have business in Paris as Louis XV's reign neared its end. He and others were already pondering what the old king's grandson would bring fresh to France. If it were not possible to travel himself, he would ask Waldemar Drescher to ensure that they would be well protected.

* * * * *

On Wednesday the 28th of April, as they prepared, *toute la famille*, to leave Herzberg, Arabella received a formal letter from Mr Elisha De Hague, her father's long-standing attorney in Norwich. Arabella had met him only once, when she had accompanied her mother to sign some legal documents she had received concerning her family's estate in France. A portly, heavily wigged man smelling of snuff, he gave the appearance of great insouciance but behind the impassive face lurked an evidently sharp legal mind.

The letter read:

Dear Countess von Deppe,

You may recall that, before your unexpected departure from England in 1765, I was responsible for all legal matters concerning Meltwater Hall. Indeed, I once had the pleasure of meeting you in my chambers in Norwich when you accompanied your mother for the conduct of some notary business. I remain so responsible.

As you will already have been informed, Lady Whitfield died in March of this year following ill health of some months' duration. I convey to you my deepest condolences, particularly as it was evident to me that you were close to your mother, who in turn held you in deepest affection.

As she requested, arrangements have been made for her remains to be taken soon from England for interment in the family vault at Château de Rozac. In her will Lady Whitfield has bequeathed to you certain personal possessions, such as furniture, which your father, Sir Robert, has undertaken to ensure are delivered by suitable persons to your home, Schloss Herzberg. Lady Whitfield has also bequeathed to you an annual income of £3,000 from her personal estate at Rozac, which we will arrange to have paid to you annually by appropriate means.

With regard to the future of Meltwater Hall, Sir Robert has instructed me to inform you that, after a proper period of mourning for your mother, he intends to marry Lady Barbara Ward, and that she and her son, George Robert, will reside with him at Meltwater Hall. Sir Robert has also asked me to say that given the continued disappearance in France of his own son, George, possibly now dead, and your commitment to your own marriage, to your children and to your husband's estate in Prussia, he intends that upon his death Lady Ward and her son should assume responsibility for Meltwater Hall.

I am your obedient servant,
Elisha De Hague
Attorney at Law
5 Elm Hill, Norwich, Wednesday the 17th of March, 1773

Arabella's anger on reading this letter was immediate, palpable and intense. How dare her father compound his sins towards her and her late mother by instructing his solicitor to write such words! Her reply was swift and sharp and despatched the following day, ahead of her departure, with Carl Manfred and their children, for Paris.

Dear Mr De Hague,

I thank you for your letter of the 17th of March, offering your condolences on my mother's death and informing me of the contents of her will.

I am shortly to travel to Paris with Count von Deppe and my children in order to meet Lady Pamela Hartley, a close friend of my mother's. We are likely to remain there for some weeks and therefore all communications between us should until further notice be sent to 76 Rue St Louis. Before my departure from Herzberg, my husband's attorney will send to you instructions for the future payment of the annual income to me from Lady Whitfield's estate in France. Furthermore, I have received separate notification that two of my mother's most cherished personal possessions have already reached Paris and are in the safe keeping of Lady Hartley, awaiting my arrival, and that my mother's remains are on their journey to Château de Rozac.

Regarding the matter of the future of Meltwater Hall, I accept that as long as Sir Robert lives it is for him, as the inheritor and present owner of the estate, to decide who should reside there with him. But I cannot agree that upon his death the Hall should in effect become the property of Lady Barbara Ward by virtue of her and her illegitimate son's occupancy of the estate. While I do not know if there are any particular legal arrangements regarding the entailment of Meltwater Hall during previous generations of ownership, I doubt that any such arrangement would permit granting its legal title to an illegitimate line. As my brother, George, has not made any contact with his family since his disappearance late in 1765, I agree that it may be the case he is no longer alive. If there remains no contact whatsoever and if, on production of a certificate of death, he is pronounced legally dead, then upon my father's death I would surely become the inheritor of my family home and therefore the sole arbiter of its future, even though my

Catholic faith and my sex may be considered by some a legal impediment to the inheritance of land – a view that of course I would challenge as entirely and unjustifiably discriminatory.

I request you to inform Sir Robert without delay of my opinion on this matter, and to advise him that I will challenge as unlawful and therefore invalid whatever will he may draw up prior to his death for the disposal of Meltwater Hall and its estate to the exclusion of me or my family.

I ask you to place this letter in the relevant file. I have passed a witnessed copy to my husband's attorney so that it can be produced in a court of law should the need to do so ever arise.

Arabella
Countess von Deppe
Schloss Herzberg, Thursday the 29th of April, 1773

At the beginning of June, in Paris, Arabella received a further letter from Mr De Hague. It read:

Dear Countess von Deppe,

Thank you for your communication of the 29th of April, the contents of which I communicated without delay to Sir Robert Whitfield.

I have also received instructions from Count von Deppe's attorney in Potsdam regarding payment of the income from your late mother's estate in France. The first annual payment will be made within the next two months through the channels the attorney specified.

Sir Robert has instructed me to say that it is most unlikely you would be able to come to England to pursue any legal challenge to his will regarding the estate of Meltwater Hall on account of the allegations that remain outstanding concerning your alleged complicity in the unexplained death of an unknown man in Norwich in 1765 and a shooting incident near London shortly thereafter. It is Sir Robert's opinion that, to avoid further embarrassment to the family's reputation arising from the risk of renewed investigations into these incidents by the relevant authorities, it would be more appropriate for you to continue to pursue your life in Prussia.

I am your obedient servant,

Elisha De Hague
Attorney at Law
This day Wednesday the 26th of May, 1773, at 5 Elm Hill, Norwich

After seeking the immediate advice of Carl Manfred and the opinion of Lady Hartley, who was still in Paris and who was equally dismayed by the instructions Sir Robert's solicitor was obliged to convey, Arabella sent a terse reply.

Dear Mr De Hague,

I thank you for your communication of the 26th of May, 1773.

First, please advise Sir Robert Whitfield that I am blameless of the calumny that he has directed against my person in continued pursuit of his worthless defence of his inexcusable behaviour towards me over many years. His friends and acquaintances and others would be dismayed by the truth, which I stand ready to speak.

Second, please inform Sir Robert that it remains my position that, if there is any attempt upon his part to allow Meltwater Hall and its estate to become, through their physical occupancy, the property of Lady Barbara Ward and her descendants, I will seek immediately to contest in person such a position, taking my case to the highest court of the land if that proves necessary.

You should also be aware that I have asked Lady Pamela Hartley, a close friend of my late mother, to instruct lawyers in London to prepare for such an eventuality. Lady Hartley intends, on her return to London, to speak to this effect to her friend Sir Bernard Banks, who has chambers in Gray's Inn.

This letter and my earlier communication remain my firm and immoveable intention on this matter.

Please be aware that at the end of this month Count von Deppe and I will return to Schloss Herzberg, to which all future communications should be sent.

Arabella
Countess von Deppe
In Paris, this day Tuesday the 8th of June, 1773

Shortly before leaving Paris to return home Arabella received acknowledgement of her letter but no other contents. Legal lines had clearly been drawn.

*****

The vexing correspondence apart, Arabella and Carl Manfred much enjoyed being in Paris with his sister, Maria Louisa, and her husband, Etienne de Vervins, still aide de camp to General de la Rivière but now recently promoted to the rank of colonel, indicating that before long he would receive a prestigious command of his own. Their pretty daughter, Marie-Aurore, now aged nine, was precocious. With dark-green eyes, a turned-up nose and an abundance of curls, she spent considerable time with other children of aristocratic families in the royal residence at Versailles. But when at home in the Rue St Louis, in the grand building the de Vervins continued to share with General de la Rivière and his wife, Victoire, and daughter, Sophie, she sometimes played – patiently – with Frederick Daniel and Elise Catherine. Arabella and Carl Manfred observed that her manners sometimes revealed a trace of arrogance associated with behaviour at court. This was of some concern to Maria Louisa, but her husband dismissed her worries as just youthful boisterousness on their daughter's part.

In between Arabella's conversations with Lady Pamela Hartley and the Comtesse de Caullery and Carl Manfred's frequent meetings with the Prussian Ambassador and other acquaintances, there were soirées, often musical, at which Arabella was asked to play and to sing. Still deeply saddened by her mother's death, she frequently felt disinclined to perform, but as a guest of the de Vervins it would have been disobliging to refuse. Such evenings were also an opportunity to try new music she had found in Paris.

The musical highlight of the von Deppes' stay in Paris was attending a performance at the Palace of Versailles of Jean-Philippe Rameau's *Les surprises de l'Amour*, which he had composed between 1757 and 1758. Though his music had been overtaken by that of later composers, which she and the Camerata had chosen to explore and play, Rameau still retained a strong place in her heart.

Arriving by coach with the de Vervins, Carl Manfred and Arabella recalled their arrival at the palace seven years before to celebrate New Year, her presentation to King Louis and his invitation for her to sing. As she entered the Hall of Mirrors on her husband's arm, Arabella – who wore a yellow gown that, on the advice of Maria Louisa, was fuller than she was used to wearing – stared in renewed amazement at the long and seemingly endless gallery bathed in candlelight and glorifying France. Courtiers, diplomats and other dignitaries, accompanied by elegant women – all with elaborate coiffure designs, white complexions from the paste they applied and hooped dresses rippling in lace and pearls – mingled animatedly with one another.

While Etienne de Vervins, Carl Manfred and the Prussian Ambassador talked to soldiers and strategists, Maria Louisa introduced Arabella to her friends. Madame Victoire de la Rivière and her daughter, Sophie, joined them in gossip and laughter. Before long Sophie and Arabella were surrounded by several handsome young men. Maria Louisa whispered to her.

"If you and Carl Manfred had not fallen in love, I fear you would have been drawn into this milieu. All that these young men wish to do is to lure even younger women into their beds, to have their pleasure and then discard them. I often worry how Marie-Aurore will avoid such a fate. There will surely be less risk for Elise Catherine in Prussia."

"I do hope so," said Arabella. "Never forget, Maria Louisa," she added, "that you and Marie-Aurore will always be welcome at Herzberg. It is your home as much as ours."

"Thank you," replied Maria Louisa.

As they walked together to take their seats at the far end of the gallery, Arabella looked up at the painted barrel-vaulted ceiling where thirty allegorical compositions glorified France's military, diplomatic and domestic achievements. Maria Louisa recalled that three years before, the Hall had witnessed the masked ball for the wedding of the Dauphin and Marie-Antoinette of Austria. Mention of the name Antoinette momentarily reminded Arabella of Antoinette Badeau, but thoughts of her alter ego faded quickly in the sumptuous colour and drama of the evening. She admired the Rance marble pilasters decorated with gilded bronze capitals that divided the seventeen mirrored arches facing the windows; even more breathtaking were the three hundred and fifty-seven mirrors themselves – so much glass at so much expense. Arabella remembered the poverty she and Carl Manfred had seen on their journey through France – quite unlike what she had witnessed in Prussia and in sharp contrast to what she had witnessed in Norfolk. How long could this royal extravagance last?

At the end of the performance Arabella decided that she would seek copies of Rameau's composition so that the Camerata might perform it on her return home, now imminent. With His Majesty the King indisposed, the guests began to disperse.

* * * * *

For the last seven years, since her daughter's marriage to Count von Deppe and new life in Prussia, and her son's disappearance in Paris at the end of 1765, about which so little was known, Lady Whitfield had lived mostly alone in Meltwater Hall. She had become an acclaimed social figure and held many soirées at the house, though the annual balls she and her husband had given in the past were rarely replicated. And she had changed the décor of the Hall, reflecting much more the French style. Many of the more masculine possessions of her husband were relegated to unused rooms upstairs or to the attic. But the main rooms downstairs – the Long Gallery, the living room, the dining room, the Oak Room and the library – remained largely unchanged, as did the small chapel where Lady Whitfield, a Catholic, prayed every evening for her daughter's well-being and her son's safe return. Her daughter's bedroom remained as Arabella had left it when she ran away following the altercation with her father over his insistence that she should marry a husband of his choosing. On the dresser rested Arabella's cherished music book, which she had taken with her from Meltwater but which she had given to her mother as a keepsake after her marriage. Lady Whitfield would often go and sit in the bedroom, leaf through the book and think of her daughter, still hoping that one day she might return to Meltwater with Count von Deppe and their children.

Sir Robert Whitfield, whom his wife had never forgiven for driving their daughter away with his brutish behaviour, spent most of his time with his mistress, Lady Barbara Ward, at the family town house in Westminster, where she gave birth to a son, George Robert, in 1766. When Sir Robert visited Meltwater, approximately three times a year – to view the estate and to check that its income was keeping pace with the level of expenditure required to maintain two expensive residences and his estranged wife's own significant social expenditure – he was banished to a bedroom at the far end of the corridor on the first floor. This state of affairs only served to stoke Sir Robert's continuing resentment towards his daughter for what she had done to upset like a cart of apples his ambitions to become a Member of Parliament and thereafter secure a seat in government. The notoriety of Arabella's flight, the many months looking for her in London, the rumours that she had become a courtesan in Mayfair, her subsequent escape to France and now her marriage to a Prussian count had meant that his behaviour towards his wife and daughter had become a matter of some scandal in Norfolk and London. But Sir Robert had resigned himself to enjoying in London the company of Lady Ward, mingling with her wide circle of political and social friends, and of course earning yet more money from his increasingly prosperous Norfolk estate and other commercial investments. Though the dust from Arabella's actions had largely settled, he had resolved, unpleasant man that he was, never to forgive his daughter. He still hoped that his son, George, would one day reappear to resume his place, despite his weaknesses, as heir to Meltwater. But if he did not, he would do all in his power to ensure that the Hall and its surrounding estate would never be available to Arabella, whose name he could barely bring himself to utter. His mistress assisted by picking often at this raw self-inflicted wound.

The autumn of 1772 and the early months of the following year had been perniciously cold in Norfolk. For some time Lady Whitfield had not been her usual ebullient self, seeing fewer of her friends as a consequence. At the end of January Sir Robert received word that his wife had become noticeably poorly and that perhaps he should come to see her to ensure that her doctor was doing all he could to ensure her recovery. When he arrived in early February he was surprised to see signs of frailty. While Dr Spencer was confident that the spring would bring better health, Sir Robert was less sure. Before returning to London, he decided to go to see his attorney, Mr Elisha De Hague, in Norwich, doing so on Tuesday the 9th of February.

De Hague had served the family for a number of years, proving to be a sound lawyer whose judgement and advice he invariably accepted.

"Sir Robert, it is good to see you after so long. How are you?"

"I am well enough. As you may know I have been spending more time in London in recent years."

"How is Lady Ward?" responded De Hague, knowing in some detail the relationship between his visitor and Lady Barbara. There were no secrets of that nature in London. "I once had the pleasure of meeting her at a soirée during one of my visits to the capital to discuss a legal matter."

"She is well," replied Sir Robert. "But I have not come to discuss Lady Ward," he continued tartly. "I have come to discuss my wife."

"Sir Robert, as you will appreciate I cannot discuss Lady Whitfield's personal affairs. As her attorney, I can only discuss them with her."

"I know that," retorted Sir Robert. "My wife is most poorly and despite the optimistic opinion of her doctor I do not think she will survive the winter. I could of course be proved wrong and I have told Dr Spencer to do all that is necessary to assist her recovery. But I must face the fact that she may die. If that proves to be the case and if my son, George, remains unaccounted for, it prompts me to consider fresh arrangements for the eventual responsibility of Meltwater and the estate. That is where I need your action on my behalf."

"And what arrangements do you have in mind, Sir Robert?"

"That upon my death my future wife, Lady Ward, and her son – by me – George Robert, should become the stewards, if I may use that term, of Meltwater, followed in turn by their descendants."

Elisha De Hague was taken aback.

"Sir Robert, let me be plain. If your son does not reappear – and after seven years of no news perhaps the time has come to presume he is dead – your daughter would surely have a case to inherit Meltwater. It would be well-nigh impossible to persuade the Prerogative Court of Canterbury, which as you know sits in London on matters concerning disputes of wills, and ultimately the Chancery Court, to find in favour of your new wife."

"Mr De Hague, let me be equally plain. My daughter ran away from home against my wishes. I believe she may have lived a scandalous life in Mayfair, about which there are still allegations of possible criminal misconduct prior to her flight to France. She is now married to a Prussian count with a large estate and has two children. Her life is in Prussia and she is unlikely to wish to return to England with unresolved allegations still not withdrawn. Her bed is in Prussia. If my son does not reappear – though I still earnestly hope that one day he may return to England – my daughter will be unable to exercise any legal rights as I have already disinherited her, in time-honoured fashion, by bequeathing her a shilling in my will. So I ask you to write to her to explain the situation and to prepare a fresh will to reflect what I intend should happen."

"Sir Robert, I understand the resentment you may still harbour towards your daughter for the reasons you have given and I will write to her as you have asked. Moreover, I will draw up a fresh will for you to sign. However, it is my duty as your attorney to tell you that if you pursue your intention as you have outlined it to me, and if your daughter seeks to oppose upon your death the terms of your will, it is conceivable that your intended beneficiaries will lose. Of course if your son were to reappear then he would inherit the estate and its future would lie solely in his hands. But since there has been no word of him for the past seven years it would seem that outcome is becoming increasingly unlikely as each day passes."

"Mr De Hague, I thank you for your thoughts. My mind is made up. Please proceed as I have instructed you."

"So be it," replied the attorney. "But my record of our conversation will state that I have warned you of possible legal repercussions."

"So be it," growled Sir Robert in reply.

After Sir Robert had left his chambers, De Hague reflected that in his many years as an attorney he had never seen such bitterness in a family. In this case it seemed inextinguishable. Five weeks later Elisha De Hague received word from Sir Robert of his wife's death and the request that he should write as instructed to the Countess von Deppe. It pained him to do so and he surmised no good would come of the matter.

* * * * *

The funeral of Lady Whitfield took place at Meltwater's small and much-weathered parish church. Its round tower had been built in Saxon times but the nave expanded in size in the late fourteenth and early fifteenth centuries. Despite the church being ravaged during the Reformation, its rood screen remained largely intact and the trace of a mural remained. Set into the floor were the tombstones of earlier Whitfields and wool-merchant families who had once been ensconced in the area before them. Preceded by a private mass in the chapel in Meltwater Hall, said by Lady Whitfield's aged Catholic priest, Father James, the parish funeral service was conducted by the now gout-ridden Reverend John Blackett.

The church was full – with servants from the Hall, estate workers and tenants, as well as others from further afield – all wishing to pay their respects to a woman they had much admired for her generosity of spirit; her frequent attendance at the parish church, despite her Catholic faith; and the charity work she undertook, together with her daughter, Arabella, in the surrounding villages. Sir Robert sat alone in the front pew. His son had vanished seven years before and his estranged daughter was now in Prussia. However hard he had tried over the years to portray himself as a wronged father, the circumstances leading to the estrangement with his daughter and his wife were common knowledge. While in her last years Lady Whitfield had become one of the doyennes of the North Norfolk social milieu, tirelessly gregarious, there was much speculation that it was merely her way of coping with the sadness of Arabella's absence and her husband's cruelty towards her. It was also widely known that Sir Robert had a mistress in London by whom he had had a son. With mistresses amongst the wealthy two a penny, the pool of sympathy for him that day was shallow. To the many gathered in the church that day, the owner of Meltwater had shown no remorse for his actions.

The Reverend Blackett gave an eloquent oration, tactfully avoiding the disasters that had befallen the Whitfield family. The congregation nodded sagely in agreement with his sentiments. At the end Sir Robert stood at the church door receiving the awkwardly offered condolences as the congregation filed out. He knew their opinions of him but he cared little. The last seven years had brought him nothing but disappointment and setbacks – all of which he blamed on his daughter's unreasonable behaviour. It was now time to turn a new leaf with Lady Barbara Ward, whom he intended to marry within three months. Once married, he would introduce his new wife to Meltwater and make changes to his life and to the house. But nothing would erase his visceral hatred for his daughter.

*****

Some days after Arabella had written her last letter to Mr De Hague on the 8th of June, 1773, she received word that her mother's remains had arrived in France and would soon be interred in the family crypt at Château de Rozac. Leaving Carl Manfred and her children behind in Paris, Arabella arrived at the de Miron estate on Tuesday the 22nd of June. Monsieur Henri de Miron, her mother's older brother, greeted Arabella as she stepped from her coach. He was tall, distinguished and exquisitely dressed in a dark-blue frock coat and red breeches. His wig was white. Madame Véronique de Miron was a little younger, with a gentle face beneath her bonnet.

The château, not unduly far from the River Loire and situated in the lee of a small hill, was built of limestone. It was broad-fronted, with tall double windows on the ground and first floors. The high, steeply pitched roof was of slate, into which several substantial dormer windows had been set. At each end of the front façade was a circular, small-windowed tower, topped by a conical roof. The château was surrounded by a patio enclosed by a limestone wall, with a broad flight of steps leading down to a formal garden ornamented by a shallow pool and fountain. To one side of the château was the family *chapelle*, surrounded by trees, in which Lady Whitfield would be interred the next day. To Arabella it was a truly elegant house, radiating the same palpable generosity of spirit as characterised her mother. Its elegance was even greater within. All the downstairs rooms were high-ceilinged and many of the walls bore tapestries with scenes from mythology. An aura of understated wealth enveloped the château, its garden and the many hectares of the de Miron estate beyond.

After removing the dust of her journey, Arabella joined the de Mirons for tea. They were deeply impressed by her exquisite

French. For the next hour or so, they asked her many questions about her mother's life in England and about Sir Robert, and of course were eager to receive a description of Meltwater Hall. She answered their questions with great care as it was apparent that her mother had written selectively about her life in England, hardly revealing her husband's behaviour at all. Though Arabella wished to be open in her replies she decided that on such a sad occasion discretion was required. Soon other members of the family arrived and, after introductions, dinner was served, during which there were further questions to Arabella about her upbringing and her new life in Prussia, especially from Henri de Miron's son-in-law, August, and his charming wife, Roxanne. Arabella, in return, enquired about the estate and the state of the kingdom. The de Mirons were somewhat reticent in their replies, though it was evident that the rumours and reports of royal extravagance caused them some discomfort.

After dinner Henri de Miron invited Arabella to play for them, since Lady Whitfield had written with great pride of her daughter's musical accomplishments. She opened her music book – always with her – and chose to play an early suite by Rameau, which she had acquired in Paris.

Arabella spent that night in the bedroom her mother had used before she left for England. Madame de Miron said it had hardly changed since her departure. Arabella lay awake in the light of a candle set in a silver candlestick bearing her mother's initials, *T de M*. Next to it on the bedside table was an elegant silver goblet from which her mother had received her first Communion wine. Unable to sleep, Arabella cast her mind back to her own bedroom at Meltwater, recalling how her mother had often sat on the bed to read her stories, even when she was no longer a child. She recollected too how her mother had taught her to play the harpsichord; how they had gone shopping together for hats and dress fabric; and how she and her mother had clung to one another at Mrs Willoughby's lodgings in Norwich the day after her escape from Mrs Rathbone's establishment. Seven years later she was married with the title of countess, the mother of two children and living in Prussia where she had founded an orchestra. She had sung to the King of France, sung and talked often to King Frederick, and had been a confidante of the Empress of Russia – all in the space of just seven years. Her mother had often written of her pride at Arabella's achievements but urging her daughter never to relent in the pursuit of happiness, a mistake she had made at Meltwater with deep regret, and of course never to forget humility. While the final farewell to her mother at the interment would be difficult, Arabella would use it to renew her pledge to be strong and resolute, just as she had pledged on the shore of the ice-covered lake on her way to St Petersburg. Her mother would expect nothing less of her. As she finally drifted into sleep, Arabella decided that her next step in honouring her mother's memory would be to return to Prussia without further delay in order to devote her remaining life to her husband, to her children, and to Herzberg and its growing musical reputation. She would do so with all possible strength and willpower. Nothing would deflect her.

Early the next morning Arabella made her confession to the priest. Having received absolution, she joined the de Miron family gathered in the *chapelle* for a requiem Mass. After placing a white flower on the coffin and whispering the words "*Adieu, Maman*," she watched as her mother's remains were lowered into the crypt.

Later, in the warm sunlit morning, before she took leave of the de Mirons, Arabella walked in the garden with Madame Véronique at the latter's request.

"Comtesse," said Madame Véronique, "I am so pleased that you came to be with us on this sad day. I hope you will come back again before too long. I would so much like to talk to you more about Lady Whitfield."

"Madame de Miron, it would be an honour to return. I cannot say when it might be but I promise one day I will."

"You are so like your mother," said Madame Véronique. "She was sought by many men attracted by her joie de vivre and beauty. In the end it was your father who captured her heart and took her away to England. Her early letters were full of news and happiness. Your birth brought her particular joy, I remember. But I detected, as did Monsieur de Miron, that as the years passed the joy of life perhaps slipped from her grasp. I hope that you will have better fortune than she did."

"Madame de Miron, I promised this morning in my last *adieu* to her that I will strive in my remaining life to do all in my power to honour her memory."

Madame de Miron clasped Arabella's hands.

"Thank you, Comtesse. My husband and I are growing older by the year. We are blessed with a strong family who will do what they can to preserve this estate and its fortunes. But I fear – perhaps it is just a sign of old age – that difficult times may lie ahead in this kingdom. There are too many foolish individuals who do not care for the dignity of ordinary people. If matters are not put to rights soon, there may be a reckoning in which all of us pay a heavy price. Comtesse, I urge you to hold to your belief of equality – a belief that your mother once held – however hard you may find it to do so in the approaching storm."

"Thank you, Madame de Miron. I promise you I will not compromise. My mother gave me the second name of Mariette, one meaning of which is little rebel. As Count von Deppe said to me some years ago, I defy all convention. Nothing will change that, I assure you."

Madame de Miron kissed Arabella on both cheeks.

"*Au revoir, ma chère Comtesse*. I wish you *bon voyage*."

An hour later Arabella left Château de Rozac for Paris. Within two days the von Deppes were speeding back to Herzberg. Amongst their luggage were the silver candlestick and goblet given to Arabella from her mother's bedroom at Rozac. But in her hands was the portrait miniature of her mother, painted when she was young. Exquisite and of obvious quality, the portrait showed her head and delicate shoulders. Her mother's dark hair was pinned up, held in place by a ribbon in the ancient Greek style, but with curls down either side of her face, a fashion Arabella had not seen her adopt in later years. The face bore a beguiling smile that Arabella remembered from her childhood. On the reverse, inscribed in gold, were some words in French:

Dans ta face vivent sagesse, la beauté et l'esprit rare qui ni l'age ni froid doivent se désintégrer!
Du fond du coeur que vous avez rechauffé.

In thy face live wisdom, beauty and rare spirit, which neither age nor cold shall decay!
From the depth of the heart that you have warmed.

There was no indication of the painter's identity and certainly no clue as to the identity of the heart that had been warmed, the heart that had been inspired to commission such a well-executed miniature and embellish it with such tender words. Arabella could only conclude that it must have been her father, though the thought of him making such a gesture strained her credulity. Or perhaps it was a secret admirer. Though she would probably never know, it was a precious memento that she would keep safely. One day she would give it to Elise Catherine, together with the miniature of herself that Carl Manfred had already persuaded her to surrender to him to keep in his pocket.

CHAPTER 5

Endings and New Beginnings

In late January the snow lay deep at Schloss Herzberg.

Five years had elapsed since the von Deppes had returned from Paris in June 1773. Frederick Daniel would be eleven years old in September while his sister, Elise Catherine, would reach the age of ten some three months later. The children had flourished in their childhood under a young and inspiring French governess, Madame Plaquet. Beyond their studies they were nourished by the care, warmth and love of an attentive mother and the admiration of their frequently absent father. Beyond the well-furnished and pleasing house and the sound of children, the much-respected estate continued to be well managed; producing an appreciable income to support the family's accruing social and cultural responsibilities.

Music, not surprisingly, was ever present. Under the supervision of Herr Bamberger, it filled the house most days – including Frederick Daniel somewhat reluctantly playing the violin and Elise Catherine already dexterous on the harpsichord. Frequently the children attended performances of the Schloss Herzberger Camerata, now of considerable musical fame throughout the region thanks to Arabella von Deppe's patronage and frequent singing. There was also much dancing – and laughter – as the children were taught the steps of what Maria Louisa, a frequent visitor from Paris, reported were the latest dances at the French royal court.

Herzberg had further expanded to allow more space for boisterous children, for the growing picture collection, and for the creation of a concert room for orchestral practice and musical soirées at which the children were often allowed to be present. This room was known light-heartedly as the *Spiegelsaal*. A present from Arabella's indulgent husband, it was rectangular in shape with a painted ceiling depicting the Triumph of Flora and four ceiling coffers each containing one of the four seasons. Between the ceiling-to-floor windows were elegant gold-framed mirrors, a faint reminder for Arabella of the endless panes of glass in the Hall of Mirrors at the Palace of Versailles. The instruments in the *Spiegelsaal* were a spinet, a harp and an exquisitely painted harpsichord, to be joined soon by the newly fashionable pianoforte. It was in this room, and the library, that Arabella was most often to be found.

Despite the hostile wind and the daily dismal grey sky, the signs of growth on the trees near to the house suggested an early spring might not be too far away. Yet the promise of warmer times could not dispel an underlying air of gloom. To Carl Manfred the never-ending politics of European territorial musical chairs – and the tiresome diplomatic quarrelling that accompanied it – posed a threat to fragile peace. For him – an old soldier, as he called himself – the risk of possible misjudgement lurked beneath the surface of evident tranquillity, as he frequently remarked on his return from yet another visit to His Majesty the King. In conversations with Arabella in the privacy of their bedroom Carl Manfred spoke often of an unseen but inevitable drift towards war, with the King not seldom involved in machinations that he feared could easily go wrong through a false step. Frequent letters from Maria Louisa, now the Vicomtesse de Vervins after her husband's promotion at court, conveyed her own unease at events at Versailles following the accession of King Louis XVI in 1774. France had never liked the Austrians. Now the kingdom had an Austrian queen, Marie Antoinette, for whom there was little warmth. Furthermore, much to Maria Louisa's chagrin, her daughter, Marie-Aurore, now aged fourteen, had become ensnared in the web of the Queen's entourage. She would soon become a lady-in-waiting, which brought with it the prospect of marriage to a young courtier whose only concern would be bedding and then discarding her.

As each bitterly cold day was followed by another, delaying even further spring's once-promised early arrival, Carl Manfred's unease at the drift of events continued to increase. The King was full set on more territorial acquisitions. All that gave Carl Manfred pleasure in his deepening moods was the intimacy he and his wife never ceased to enjoy in their bed.

Carl Manfred's foreboding soon assumed a definite shape. Once more the King sent for him. He announced it was all to do with Bavaria. Arabella asked her husband why the future of that kingdom should matter. Did not the King have enough land to govern?

* * * * *

As a crisis began to develop, Carl Manfred explained to Arabella that when the young King Frederick ascended the throne in 1740, Prussia had consisted only of scattered territories in the west and in the east. By 1772, as a result of war, scheming and a large measure of luck, he had acquired more territory and at last had been able to fulfil his ambition and style himself King of Prussia rather than King in Prussia. But, said Carl Manfred, the old King's ambitions had not stopped there, nor had those of the Empress of Russia and the Empress of Austria. Just like these two far-aiming women, the King was not satisfied with merely retaining the sovereignty he had won. He wanted to extend it further still and had made clear – by his actions and his incessant plotting – that until his last breath on Earth he would never give up; he would always be vigilant for opportunities to seize the advantage for Prussia and to thwart the plans of others.

"Carl, why are you so concerned about the present situation? What is new?" Arabella asked.

"My dearest wife, here is where I have fears. A new opportunity for His Majesty has arisen from an unexpected quarter. A few weeks ago Maximilian Joseph, the last of the line of the house of Wittlesbach in Bavaria, died of smallpox, leaving no children. Charles Theodore, a scion of the senior line of the Wittlesbach family, holds the closest claim of kinship to Maximilian but he too has no legitimate children to succeed him. This leaves his cousin, Charles August, with a legitimate legal claim to the Bavarian throne as Charles Theodore's heir presumptive. But across the border in Austria the Holy Roman Emperor Joseph and his mother and co-ruler the Empress Maria Theresa, a formidable and scheming woman, also have eyes on Bavaria. Indeed the Emperor Joseph went so far as to marry Maximilian Joseph's sister, Maria Josepha, in order to extend an eventual claim. He has even, according to Drescher's information, agreed with Charles Theodore a plan to partition Bavaria, so refusing to acknowledge any claim of the heir presumptive, Charles August. As you might imagine, Arabella, the empty Bavarian throne has suddenly aroused the attention of all the King's territorial opponents, so inevitably increasing his own determination to ensure he is a player in the game he thinks is about to ensue. In my opinion, all this spells trouble, which is even more likely because, according to Drescher, the French want to poke their noses into the problem as well."

"Why should the French worry about Bavaria?" Arabella asked.

"Arabella, it is to do with yet another woman!" Carl Manfred exclaimed.

"Now now, Carl Manfred," admonished Arabella.

"My dear Arabella, there are three women who, whether they realise it or not, are slowly dragging us to the battlefield. First, there is the Empress Maria Theresa who, as I have already explained, wants Bavaria. King Frederick fears that if she were to control that land it would limit Prussian influence in wider German affairs. Only a few days ago the King insisted in a testy conversation at the palace that Prussia's territorial gains had been hard won and, banging the table, said he was damned if he was going to sit by and let the Austrians steal such a rich slice of cake off his plate. He had made Prussia a European power and he would do everything he could to ensure his conquests were not reversed. To make matters worse, his insistence is shared by Frederick August of Saxony, who considers that any division of Bavaria would be against his territorial interests. Then there is a female dimension in France. The French Foreign Minister, Charles Gravier, has said that a war over the disputed succession to the Bavarian throne would upset his country's preoccupation with helping the rebels in America to defeat the British in the struggle for independence. But, according yet again to your Herr Drescher, the real reason for French interference is that an unsuitable solution to Bavaria would disrupt the delicate diplomatic relationship between France and Austria which, once upon a time hostile, has become sensitive ever since the marriage of the Austrian Marie Antoinette to the French Dauphin, now Louis XVI. The third woman in the troika is your dear friend in St Petersburg, Yekaterina Alexeevna, as you like to call her. She fears that a war in the centre of Europe would mean a change in the existing balance of power – a fact she could not accept. So, Arabella, three powerful women and an ageing king are gradually edging us towards an abyss in a dispute over whose bottom should sit on the Bavarian throne. Of course Drescher relishes all the manoeuvring and the interception of diplomatic messages. But if war breaks out it will not be him in the line of fire but ordinary decent soldiers – all because of the vanity and greed of monarchs."

"Carl, I have never heard you speak with such vehemence before. Please do not worry. I am sure there will be a peaceful solution."

"Arabella, I hope so but I have my doubts. Here's the rub. You should realise that if there is war, the King will seek my assistance. I have already suggested to him that perhaps it is time for me to retire gracefully. But he won't hear of it."

They talked no more of war but anxiety began to fill Arabella.

* * * * *

Carl Manfred's fears soon came to pass.

Within the first few weeks of 1778 news arrived in Berlin that Charles Theodore had claimed the Bavarian throne and, moreover, that Austrian troops had crossed the Bavarian border – but going further into Bavaria than had been specified in his earlier agreement with the Emperor Joseph. Charles Theodore realised that he had been tricked.

On receipt of this disturbing news King Frederick began to mobilise an army near the Prussian border with Bohemia. During the next four months intensive negotiations took place between Vienna, Berlin, Dresden and Munich, and by early spring large Austrian and Prussian armies faced each other, so increasing the risk of war. It soon became clear that there would be no diplomatic solution and before the end of April King Frederick completed his preparations for invasion. He gathered supplies, set out his field tactics, brought up his artillery and drilled his soldiers, deploying in total some 80,000 men on the border between Prussia and Bohemia. His younger brother, Prince Henry, formed a second army of over 75,000 men to the north and west. By the end of that month King Frederick and the Emperor Joseph were in the field. In July the King entered Bohemia. The following months saw frequent skirmishes and many military gains and setbacks. Eventually, after depleting the surrounding countryside of all provisions, the main opposing armies withdrew without a clear victory on either side. The absence of a decisive outcome – military or diplomatic – meant there would be further inconclusive confrontations pending further diplomatic negotiations. For the troops left holding the line in the field the conditions were miserable and led to growing starvation and resulting disease in the absence of adequate supplies to feed the soldiers.

It was towards the start of these developments, at the beginning of February, that, as Carl Manfred had warned Arabella, the King summoned him to his side as one of his most trusted and experienced senior officers and, since his secret mission to London in 1766, one of the most loyal members of the monarch's still-diminishing inner circle. With profound sorrow Carl Manfred informed Arabella of his necessary departure from Herzberg.

"Dearest Arabella, as I predicted the King has written to me, insisting that I join him in Berlin as soon as possible and, if certain diplomatic negotiations fail, be at his side in the field as he raises an army to counter the threat from Austria. I cannot refuse his order. But I wish you to know that it causes me great anguish to leave you – the more so because I may be away not just for some days or even some weeks but for much longer. While I am absent I will write to you often. You, Frederick and Elise and this house will be in my thoughts and prayers every day."

He took her hands and kissed them.

"Dearest Carl, when I saw the King's messenger arrive with a letter for you and saw your name in the King's handwriting I knew your departure from Herzberg was inevitable. Though I would embark on any stratagem to keep you with me I know I cannot stop you from going. The King's command overrides whatever wish or desire I may have. What a monarch requires a monarch receives. In your absence, which I hope will not be as prolonged as you fear, I will ensure that the children remember you every day and that this estate flourishes in the way you desire. As for me, what can I say? It almost breaks my heart to see you go. I assure you that you will leave with my love, my respect and a deep longing for your early and safe return."

They spent the evening sitting together in front of the fire in the library, planning the year ahead at Herzberg and what they would do together on his return. At midnight they went to their bed to share a tender and deeply intimate farewell.

The following morning, Wednesday the 11th of February, 1778, Carl Manfred left Herzberg for Berlin. His wife and children stood on the steps of the house to wave him good bye.

* * * * *

On his arrival in Berlin Carl Manfred had much to do, assisting the King and his brother, Henry, in the creation and deployment of two armies. Everyone hoped that the diplomatic negotiations taking place would find a solution, but as the weeks passed the prospect of such an outcome receded by the day. By early April Carl Manfred was in place on Prussia's border with Bohemia, heavily engaged in the establishment of an army of some 80,000 men, ensuring they were well drilled, well instructed, well-armed and well provisioned. Whilst he greatly missed his family and Herzberg, he relished being in the thick of planning for a war, though he, like others, hoped that it would be avoided. He much enjoyed reading Arabella's amusing letters, reporting on the affairs of the estate, the progress of the children in their studies and her continuing concerts in the *Spiegelsaal*, in Potsdam and, for the first time, at the Hofoper in Berlin, the city's main concert hall.

Before his departure for Bohemia, Carl Manfred and Waldemar Drescher had supped together in the back room of a Berlin tavern.

"I will confess I have never liked you, Drescher. I do not know who you really are. I do not like what you do. I have said before that I have never been sure on whose orders you act – the King's or your own. Your hands are steeped in blood. By your own admission you live in the shadows. You are a bringer of death."

"Count von Deppe, death comes to us all," Drescher

interrupted. “But it is true that in my hands it may come earlier than expected to those who deserve it. I am not judge and jury. I am merely the prosecutor and the executioner, submitting irrefutable evidence then carrying out the sentence fitting the judge’s guilty verdict. That’s the way it is. I do the unpleasant examination – the persuasion, the torture, the hanging by the wrists though perhaps not the burning with irons as in the days of old – and the eventual disposal of the body so everyone else’s hands are clean.”

“What you have just said, Drescher, makes you even more reviling. But whatever may be your motives you have been loyal and protective, especially towards the Countess, and I am thankful for that, just as I would be thankful if an unpleasant ally enabled me to achieve victory on the battlefield. I would have preferred it if our paths had diverged after London. But that was not to be. While I can barely tolerate you, the Countess admires you, though why escapes me.”

“Come to the point, Count von Deppe. Why did you ask to see me?” Drescher asked impatiently.

“I do not know where this confounded business in Bavaria will lead. I hope common sense will prevail. Who on earth would wish to see blood spilt for the sake of such a petty quarrel? But the King has spoken and people like me have to dance to his tune.”

“To some, Count von Deppe, that would be dangerous talk,” Drescher interrupted again. “It could imply a lack of loyalty.”

“I am as loyal as the next man,” Carl Manfred replied sharply. “But I thought my days as a soldier were over long ago. Now, as a consequence of that wretched business in England, I find myself ever more at the King’s side than at my wife’s. I married late. I want to be with the Countess, rather than drilling soldiers in Bohemia. There are plenty of younger men better able to take my place.”

“The King says he needs you,” replied Drescher. “Besides, many of these younger men lack your military experience and you know the King’s mind. You should be flattered, von Deppe. With you as part of the King’s command there is perhaps a better chance of a faster resolution.”

“It is you who flatter me, Drescher. I’m too old for this work.”

“Count von Deppe, the young don’t have your wisdom. They

rely too much on books. I think it was Cardinal Richelieu who once said, "Nothing is as dangerous for the state as those who would govern kingdoms with maxims found in books." The King heeded that advice long ago. He wishes to succeed with people who have practical experience, like you, at his side. Anyway, you are not too old if you enjoy a young wife in your bed."

Roused in anger Carl Manfred grabbed Drescher by the lapels of his jacket.

"Drescher, you are foul-mouthed. Next time I will hit you hard."

Drescher smiled.

There was a pause in the conversation. Both men drank some wine. Drescher gestured as though to encourage Carl Manfred to speak.

"Count von Deppe, tell me the real reason why you invited me here."

"Very well, I'll come to the point, Drescher. If anything happens to me on this campaign I want you – despite your many other preoccupations, about which I do not wish to know – to protect the Countess, to see that she comes to no harm. She trusts you and I think you trust her, far more than you do me. As you have often said, this world is full of vipers, and a widowed woman with young children, wealth and Herzberg as her inheritance will be vulnerable. It is for her to live her life as she wishes, but I want her to have the freedom and protection to do so. I want someone to watch over her without her knowledge, but at the same time to be someone to whom she can turn for advice and protection. I have decided that you are best able to ensure this happens. That is my instruction. Do you understand? That is what I want you to do."

"Count von Deppe, you have said you do not like me. To be honest, the more this conversation continues the more I have come to dislike you. I have always found soldiers hard to bear. They see everything in black and white. The world is not like that. It never has been black and white and it never will be. The truth is we are governed by what happens in the cesspit. And someone has to be there, despite the stench. That's my job. I receive no recognition for what I do, but what I do achieves solutions in the significant interests of the Prussian kingdom. Yet all that is beside the point. You will return to Herzberg once this quarrel is resolved.

But if you do not, then, much as I dislike you, I give you my solemn promise, if that is what you wish, that I will protect and defend the Countess von Deppe to my last breath and that I will offer her my counsel. Whether the Countess would ever seek it is of course another matter."

"It is my wish," replied Carl Manfred.

"So be it," replied Drescher.

"There is one last matter," Carl Manfred added.

"And what is that?" Drescher asked wearily.

"When Sir Robert Whitfield dies, the Countess intends to seek to inherit the family estate. Her father intends that she should not. Instead, he has stipulated that it should pass to his second wife and the illegitimate son she had by him. Drescher, if this matter is not resolved in a satisfactory way, it is possible that the Countess may seek to fight for her inheritance in the English court. If she were to go to London to do so, there is a risk that those who would oppose her might seek her arrest, on the grounds of her alleged involvement in what we did thirteen years ago on His Majesty's behalf, in order to close the matter in their favour. Even if there were no legal opposition, there is still the risk that her emotions on this matter might cause her to decide to spend the rest of her life in England with my children. Drescher, let me be plain: in the event of my death I wish her to remain in Prussia, to bring up my children in Prussia, to make her chamber orchestra famous in Prussia, and to ensure that Herzberg remains in safe hands. She must not be allowed to return to England under any circumstances. Her father's lands are of no importance. Mine are."

"What do you want me to do about it?" said Drescher, looking intently into Carl Manfred's eyes.

"I want you to find out what happened to the Countess's brother after we finished with him in Paris. I am not sure whether he left our presence dead or whether you and your accomplices put him in some oubliette to be forgotten, which, knowing a little of your methods and duplicity, might well have been the case. If Whitfield is still alive, I want you to secure his release and send him back to England to reclaim the family estate, so removing any reason on the Countess's part to choose between Prussia and England. She remains aware that her brother tried to abduct her in Paris in order to deliver her into her father's and, ultimately,

Bolton's hands. But that is all. Under no circumstances must the Countess ever know what happened in that cellar in Paris and afterwards. She has never asked and I have never said. Many times I have felt great guilt at hiding such a terrible secret from her – the murder of her brother at worst or, hardly less appalling, if he survived the cellar, the possibility of his lifelong incarceration. If she ever found out what was done, her trust in you and me would be irreparably shattered. With that knowledge she would not, in the event of my death, turn to you for advice and protection, and without you she would become vulnerable to those who might want to bring her down because of envy. Disclosure of our secret would surely increase the chances of her renouncing Herzberg and Prussia. That would be an unbearable outcome. Above all else you would no longer be able to honour your promise – just made to me – that in the event of my death you will protect her to your last breath. So, Drescher, do whatever is necessary to stop the Countess from returning to England. Use any subterfuge, use your cunning, use any means at your disposal. Do you understand me?"

Drescher did not speak. He sat impassively looking directly at Carl Manfred with his dark hooded eyes, inwardly surprised – indeed deeply so – that the Count should reveal a darker side, uttering the chilling words "*use any means at your disposal*" in respect of the woman he claimed he loved so much.

"There is much darkness in my world," Drescher replied slowly. "In that darkness there are many voices – echoing voices of the long-since dead, still repenting their treachery, and those of the living dead. It remains to be seen which part of the underworld Whitfield inhabits. Of one thing you can be truly sure, Count von Deppe. In the event of your death on the King's business – and your survival lies largely in the quality of your military preparations – I repeat: I will serve your wife as her protector and counsellor, and I will do so with personal honour – but only as long she desires it. I will see to it that nothing befalls her and that at the end of her life, which I hope will be long, her children and her grandchildren and Prussia itself, not England, will look upon her with pride."

"Drescher," replied Carl Manfred, "you would make a good diplomat if you were not so steeped in blood. Diplomats rarely speak with clarity. The implication of their words has to be dissected to get closer to the meaning of their deviousness. But in this case I will leave this room knowing, I believe correctly, that you have understood what has to be done and that you will do it."

"Go to war, Count von Deppe, and leave the rest to me. I can say no more."

Drescher proffered his hand. Carl Manfred hesitated but returned the gesture. With that both men finished their wine and went outside into the cold wind.

* * * * *

The excitement of the early months in the field began to pall as the crisis over the succession to the Bavarian throne dragged on week after week, month after month. In early July General Johann Jakob von Wunsch led the first military foray but had to withdraw as the tactic proved unsuccessful. Shortly afterwards King Frederick personally led his 80,000 troops into Bohemia. Carl Manfred was close to him. Thereafter the fighting ebbed and flowed inconclusively. The two Prussian armies remained in the field until September, eating as much of the food available in the surrounding countryside as possible, while secret negotiations resumed between Russia, Austria and Prussia. In October, as winter approached, the main Prussian and Austrian armies withdrew, leaving small forces on each side to watch the other. The King instructed Carl Manfred to remain on the battlefield as his principal eyes and ears. Throughout the miserable cold winter there were periodic clashes and some notable Austrian raids on Prussian positions. Eventually, as the spring of 1779 took root, peace was agreed at Teschen.

With a treaty imminent, finally the remaining Prussian forces returned home. The overall campaign, in which no major battles were fought, had not gone well. Many officers had died and several thousand soldiers were killed, wounded and captured. Starvation and disease had also inflicted death, not just on the soldiers of both sides but on the civilian population.

Over a year after his departure Carl Manfred returned to Herzberg at the end of April 1779. Arabella was deeply distressed by his appearance. He had aged; he was thin; he was weary. She immediately summoned a physician, who in turn asked others to join him for their opinions.

"Countess von Deppe, the Count is very sick," the physician

said. "He has been worn out by the exertions of a long and harsh military campaign and, more recently, by rampant disease due to poor food. He now requires rest and much gentle nursing, which I know you will provide. But I must warn you that unless he can soon repair his strength he may not survive the damage that the conditions in which he has been living for so many months have inflicted on him. He has gone for too long without proper nourishment, preferring to make do with the same meagre rations that the soldiers under his command endured. His recovery is in peril and the long and painful journey home has not helped. We will come daily to assess his progress and to assist where we can."

"Thank you. We will do all that it is necessary."

That night and for hours every day Arabella sat by Carl Manfred's bedside, feeding him and urging his spirits back to life. In the first two weeks of May he became strong enough to sit on the patio in the sunlight, wrapped in blankets. His condition seemed to improve further. His smile returned, he began to ask questions about the estate and enjoyed having his children sit with him. But his wretched cough never left him. Towards the end of May his condition suddenly worsened and, despite the best efforts of the physicians to reverse his decline, he became delirious. Arabella sat with him throughout, holding his hand, praying for him constantly. But his weary body no longer had the strength to fight the final stages of the illness he had contracted in Bohemia. Finally, shortly after losing consciousness, Carl Manfred von Deppe died in the early hours of Sunday the 30th of May, 1779, leaving behind a heartbroken Arabella.

* * * * *

Late in the afternoon, after Carl Manfred's body had been removed to be made ready for burial on the estate, Waldemar Drescher arrived at Herzberg. Arabella was in the library, reading to her children, together with their governess, Madame Plaquet.

"Children, please go with Madame Plaquet for a walk in the garden. I will join you soon and then we will have supper together. We have much to do in the days ahead and we must all be strong."

Frederick Daniel and Elise Catherine followed their governess reluctantly.

"Countess, please accept my deepest condolences on the death of Count von Deppe. I am at your service at this most tragic time."

"Herr Drescher, I thank you for coming. The last weeks have been sorely testing. I thought my prayers for my husband's recovery had been answered but it was not to be. He is gone. I am left only with memories and those pieces of music he particularly liked to hear. I am lost, Herr Drescher, completely lost."

"Madame, you are not lost. The Count is no longer with you but you are mother to his children, you are the chatelaine of Herzberg and the creator of an accomplished orchestra. You are much respected, admired and loved by many. I would fight hard to be the first to praise your accomplishments – as indeed would His Majesty, who will be deeply distressed to hear of your husband's cruel death. But from your sadness you will surely emerge with added strength – drawn not just from memories of the Count but from your continued determination to add to his legacy. It will not be easy in this dark and difficult world but you will prevail."

"Herr Drescher, thank you for your kind words. My heart is truly broken and the time ahead will be testing, but I will remember what you have said."

"Countess, I wish you to know that a year ago, on the eve of his departure for Bohemia, Count von Deppe asked me to do whatever was necessary to protect you if he were not to survive the battles he foresaw ahead. I promised solemnly to him that I would. I repeat that promise to you today. You may not always see me but I assure you I will always be close to you, ready to guard you from any danger you may face or any malevolence directed against you, and to advise you – but only if you so wish it."

"Herr Drescher, my mind is in such turmoil. I find it hard to decide where to turn, what to do. The responsibilities I face appear overwhelming. But you are the one landmark left. My late husband may not always have agreed with you but, as I have said before in all honesty, you and I are already bound together by a bond of mutual respect and trust. So, Herr Drescher, I welcome the comfort of knowing that you will be a source of advice and protection, beginning now at this dark place in my life. Please, Herr Drescher, stay at Herzberg tonight. It will be a great solace to know you are here."

"Countess von Deppe, I will do as you ask."

Later that night, by the light of a single candle, before going to sleep in her empty bed, Arabella wrote some words in French, the language of her mother.

Il est mort!

J'ai été vraiment amoureuse de cet homme qui me rendu profondement heureuse. Je l'ai aimé de tout mon coeur, parce que c'était le meilleur des hommes. Cet homme m'a compris; il était charmant et si gentil.

Ce que je souhaite le plus c'est de conserver dans mon coeur son chaleureux souvenir. Il restera avec moi, tous les jours de ma vie.

He is dead.

I was truly in love with this man who made me profoundly happy. I loved him with all my heart for he was the best of men. He understood me; he was kind and gentle.

What I now wish above all is to keep in my heart his warmest memory. He will be with me for the rest of my life.

She placed what she had written in her music book, alongside a letter that had arrived during the evening from the King in which he mourned her loss and the loss to him of a trusted friend.

Waldemar Drescher lay awake, listening to the distant sobbing of the woman he had promised to protect.

* * * * *

Within the month Maria Louisa de Vervins arrived at Herzberg from Paris to comfort her sister-in-law. She brought with her a letter from Lady Pamela Hartley.

Dear Countess von Deppe,

I have asked the Vicomtesse de Vervins to convey to you directly my and the Comtesse de Caullery's deepest sympathy on the death of Count von Deppe. This is a cruel tragedy, robbing you and us of a man of great honour and distinction. We will pray that you have unending courage and fortitude to face the future without him at your side.

I hope that before too long you and your children will come to Paris so that we can help to comfort you in your distress.
Lady Pamela Hartley
Paris, Tuesday the 15th of June, 1779

Slowly, as each day passed, Arabella adjusted to her new life alone. While Herzberg was full of those who came to support her in her grief, which she did her best to mask, and Herr Bamberger encouraged her to resume her interest in the affairs of the Camerata, she found the nights alone the hardest to bear. Not even Frederick Daniel or Catherine Elise could assuage her loss. Decisions had to be taken about the affairs of the estate but Arabella found it difficult to make them. Daily life had become so empty that not even the words of the Empress Yekaterina Alexeevna, which she had often recalled, could raise her spirits.

*****

Before the end of June, Waldemar Drescher summoned a young man to see him in Potsdam. Anton Kiefer was tall, good-looking, somewhat feline in his features and finely dressed. The two men were well-acquainted, judging by the relaxed manner in which they spoke to one another.

"I want you to go to Paris without delay. Leave tomorrow. Take the fastest horses. When you arrive, you should go to this address in the Rue de la Cité and ask for Monsieur Bertrand. He is one of us. When you meet him – he is identifiable by a scar on his right cheek – hand to him this sealed letter in which a name is written. Ask him to enquire of the head jailer at the Bastille whether a prisoner of that name is still being held in solitary confinement on the instruction of a *lettre de cachet* signed by the late King Louis. Stay close by until you receive an answer. If the answer is no, return here quickly. If the answer is that the prisoner still lives, send me a message and I will come to Paris with all speed. Do you understand my instructions?"

"Yes," replied Kiefer.

Drescher spoke again.

"If the prisoner is alive, do not attempt to see him and make clear to Bertrand that he too should have no contact. This matter is most secret. Under no circumstances must you disclose the purpose of your journey."

"Yes, I understand," replied Kiefer.

He got up and moved towards Drescher as though to embrace him.

"Not now! You must go," Drescher barked.

*****

Within the week Kiefer had arrived in Paris. As instructed he went direct to number 5 Rue de la Cité.

A poorly dressed scullery maid answered the door.

"I have come to deliver an important message to Monsieur Bertrand."

"He is sleeping," replied the sullen-looking woman.

"Please wake him. My business is urgent."

"I will try," said the maid. "He went to bed drunk last night. Who shall I say wishes to see him?"

"Tell him a friend from the east."

Some minutes later a dishevelled middle-aged man stumbled down the narrow staircase, smelling of alcohol.

"Who are you? What do you want?"

"I come from the east, Monsieur Bertrand. I hope that is who you are."

"Yes, it is."

"I have something for you – from a long-standing friend of yours, I believe. Is there somewhere we can speak in private?"

"Come in here," growled Bertrand.

They sat down at a table littered with bottles from the night before. Bertrand poured himself a drink. His visitor declined.

"Our mutual friend in the east has asked me to give you this."

Kiefer handed Bertrand the letter. He broke the seal and read it, suddenly straightening himself and pushing his wine glass to one side. Kiefer thought he detected a momentary look of fear cross the man's face.

"This matter is urgent and of the greatest secrecy. Your instructions are merely to confirm to me whether the man whose name you have before you is alive or dead. You must tell me as quickly as possible."

"I will go immediately to the jailer at the Bastille," said Bertrand, slightly sweating.

"I will wait here until your return," said Kiefer, placing his pistol on the table.

"Of course," said Bertrand. "Marie, bring my visitor some bread, cheese and fresh wine. He has come a long way."

Bertrand, an exquisite forger by profession, went by sedan to the Bastille as quickly as he could. As he was carried, he recalled the man with no name who some years ago had come to Paris in search of those with dirty secrets who might be blackmailed to become agents for a foreign power. Bertrand had a secret which, if exposed, might lead to his incarceration for life or even his execution. He had agreed to the bargain, receiving money in return for the provision of assistance and privileged information. The money he had received was good; it settled his debts. But in accepting money he believed he had dealt with the devil himself. Some years later he had been approached by the nameless stranger to do another favour. Subsequently, a man called Dressler asked him to dispose of a body delivered to him on the banks of the River Seine. Again he was paid. It had been a murky business in the dead of night. He had done what he was instructed to do, very nearly getting caught as he did so. He had heard nothing further and assumed he had seen the last of the nameless man. His new visitor was evidence that he had not gone away. He was now asking for yet more.

On arrival at the Bastille, Bertrand asked to see the chief jailer. After some hesitation, he was taken down a wide, dingy and foul-smelling corridor and shown into a large room. There were many bunches of keys hanging on the wall, with books of different sizes on shelves between them. He also observed some items of ironware hanging from the wall at the far end of the room. They appeared to be instruments of torture. The jailer gestured to his unexpected visitor to sit down at the table.

"Do you have a prisoner of this name on your book?" asked Bertrand nervously.

"Why do you want to know?" said the jailer.

"A friend has asked me. I owe him a favour. I just want to know if the man on this piece of paper is still here."

"What's it worth?" said the jailer.

Bertrand pulled a leather pouch from his coat pocket and tipped two gold coins into the jailer's hand.

"Is that all?"

"Yes," replied Bertrand, still apprehensive.

The jailer got up and after running his finger along the shelf pulled down a large leather-bound book – a ledger, it seemed. He thumbed through the pages.

"Yes, we do. He is here indefinitely under a *lettre de cachet* – yet another person no doubt disowned by his family and conveniently forgotten about."

"Thank you," said Bertrand, anxious to escape into the street.

"Does anyone want the prisoner? No one has been to see him in the fourteen years he has been here."

"No one wants him – at least for now."

Bertrand hurried back to the Rue de la Cité.

"The man whose name is in the letter you gave me is alive in solitary confinement in the Bastille under a *lettre de cachet.* No one has been to see him in fourteen years, according to the chief jailer."

"That is of no interest to me," said Kiefer. "Monsieur Bertrand, I will pass on your answer. Shortly, we will return so you can provide further help."

"Who is 'we'?" asked Bertrand.

"I will return with the man who has no name."

Bertrand turned white.

"Have no fear, Monsieur Bertrand. Just do as we say and you will come to no harm."

* * * * *

On the 13th of July Arabella received a letter from Mr Elisha De Hague, the Whitfield family lawyer in Norwich.

> *Dear Countess von Deppe,*
>
> *I was deeply saddened to hear recently of the unexpected death of Count von Deppe. I extend to you my deepest sympathy on your tragic loss.*
>
> *I regret that I have to add to your distress at this time. I wish you to know that your father, Sir Robert Whitfield, is now in poor health and not expected to live many more months.*

He is at present in London, in the care of Lady Barbara Whitfield, but they are expected to return soon to Meltwater Hall, where Sir Robert wishes to spend his last days.

As foreshadowed in my letters to you in 1773, it remains Sir Robert's intention that, upon his death, Meltwater Hall should become the home of Lady Whitfield and of their son, George Robert, and that thereafter the property be used by any descendants of his arising from any marriage into which he may enter. It is still your father's firm opinion that, as your life is now in Prussia and is likely to remain so, for the sake of your children, despite the death of Count von Deppe, the steps he has proposed are the most suitable in the circumstances.

He has instructed me to inform his barrister, Sir Quentin Fobb, accordingly. You may wish to bear this in mind in any response you may have to this letter and in any instructions to your barrister, Sir Bernard Banks. Sir Robert hopes that you will acquiesce in this matter.

Elisha De Hague
Attorney at Law
5 Elm Hill, Norwich, Monday the 21st of June, 1779

The receipt of the attorney's letter released Arabella's long-suppressed emotion. It blew away in a single gust of wind the dark mist of despair in which she had been wrapped since her husband's death. Her anger was palpable. She would not allow her father to strip her of her perceived right of inheritance in favour of his second wife and bastard son. Though now alone, she would fight her father's will in the English court to secure possession of Meltwater, to which her late mother had devoted so much of her life. However hard the legal battle might be and whatever the risks, she would fight her corner tooth and nail. As Maria Louisa was about to return to Paris, Arabella decided that she would go with her in order to seek the support of Lady Hartley, whom she hoped was still there with her sister, the Comtesse de Caullery. Immediately, Arabella asked Madame Plaquet to prepare the children for their journey. Later in the day Arabella wrote to Waldemar Drescher to inform him of her intention. Thereafter, she replied to the attorney's letter.

Dear Mr De Hague,

I acknowledge receipt of your letter of the 21st of June.

My response to this matter remains unchanged. I will contest strongly any such step to execute Sir Robert's will as he has proposed.

I will leave Herzberg shortly for Paris, to consult with Lady Hartley. It is likely that, after further consideration, I will travel to London to call on Sir Bernard Banks to lay the matter before him and to seek his representation in court.

Please write to me at the Rue St Louis in Paris, the address you have used before for this purpose should you have further news to report to me.

Arabella
Countess von Deppe
Schloss Herzberg, Tuesday the 13th of July, 1779

Two days later Drescher called on Arabella at Herzberg. He asked why she was going to Paris in such haste.

"I wish to consult with Lady Hartley and to send from there a further reply to this outrageous letter," she said, thrusting it into his hand, "where it can be delivered to London more quickly. Indeed, I may go to London in person to see Sir Bernard Banks and, if necessary, to plead my cause in court. I will not bend in this matter. Meltwater is mine. I will not let my scoundrel of a father bequeath my home to a pompous woman, previously his sordid mistress, and her illegitimate son. I will not have it."

"What of Herzberg?" asked Drescher.

"I will defend this estate with honour and determination as I promised Count von Deppe I would in the event of his death. Herzberg is my home, Prussia is my homeland by marriage and my children are Prussian. But Meltwater is mine too once my father is dead and I will do all that is necessary to ensure that my home in England is in my name, that it becomes my possession, and that it is mine to share with my legitimate children, not awarded to a bastard boy."

Drescher had never seen Arabella so angry. Colour, passion and spirit had returned to her face. The sadness and grey pallor of the past weeks had suddenly evaporated in an explosion of rage.

"Countess, I believe you are right in what you have decided.

You should indeed go to Paris. I will make arrangements to ensure that you, your children and the Vicomtesse have a fast but safe journey. I should inform you that I am likely to have business in France myself. Perhaps our paths may cross."

"Herr Drescher, I hope they will," replied Arabella.

Drescher left Herzberg quickly to prepare for his own departure to Paris. He sat back in his coach, pondering what he was about to do. He had destroyed many plots against the state, killed many victims in his deadly web of intrigue. He lived in the twilight, unseen and largely unappreciated by those he served. Now, at the request of her dead husband, he was engaged in a scheme to stop the Countess von Deppe from going to England. Drescher realised that the possible consequences of her doing so, particularly if her efforts to secure her family home led her to appear in an English court, could be unpredictable and potentially dangerous. There was a risk that her vengeful dying father could indeed cause her arrest for accessory to murder, as the late Count von Deppe had feared. If that were to happen the connection between what he and the Count had done in England and his King could conceivably become public knowledge. If she were put on trial and found guilty she might be hanged. To fulfil his promise to the late Count – and keeping promises had never been his forte – he had been obliged to arrange the release of George Whitfield (for such was the name in the sealed letter he gave to Kiefer), who in his opinion deserved to languish forgotten where he had put him all those years ago. His plan further required him to engineer an encounter between sister and brother in order to ensure that the latter, upon his release, would not seek retribution against her for his long incarceration in the Bastille but would return instead to England to seek the inheritance of Meltwater Hall. And he needed to persuade the Countess to commit her remaining life to Herzberg and Prussia.

Why should he risk such a precarious undertaking? Why should he bother with a promise he had once given to the Count, who was no longer alive – a promise, moreover, about which no one else knew? Why should he care about a woman? But he had to confess that, though he was a lover of men, in other circumstances he would be deeply in love with the Countess. If he could not have her because of his sexual inclination he still wanted her near to him in Prussia where she could be his to protect, where he could gaze upon her – indeed, where she could be his to cherish as an object of beauty, a unique jewel. Through the many years he had come to know her well, he had become increasingly jealous of the Count's possession of such a beautiful woman. If he could not have the man he had loved all his life, why should another man be more fortunate, claiming the widowed Countess in a second marriage? He wanted her to be his, no one else's. Could he be so selfish? Could he use the tricks of his trade to have his way in this matter?

For now there was much to do. But as he made his plans he realised that if he did not unpick carefully what had been done in the Paris cellar fourteen years ago, the personal consequences of any slip on his part would be unimaginable – he would lose what he wanted to possess and he would destroy the Countess's cherished memory of her husband.

* * * * *

Arabella, her children, Madame Plaquet and Maria Louisa arrived in Paris on Tuesday the 20th of July. The Vicomte de Vervins now lived almost permanently at the Palace of Versailles in attendance on the King. Though he missed the comfort of the Rue St Louis he felt obliged to suffer the incommodiousness of an attic room at the palace in order to be close to the King and to play his part in judging the loyalty of the nobility, all of whom were similarly encamped in the cramped corridors of royal power. Maria Louisa still insisted that her daughter, Marie-Aurore, carry on her education with her governess, Madame de Bouchon, but it was becoming increasingly hard to achieve as the Queen's court continued to divert the young woman's attention. The Vicomte tried to solve the conundrum by prevailing upon his wife to join him at the palace, so the family could spend more time together. But Maria Louisa was adamant that she would remain in Paris, away from the intrigue and the insanitary conditions of Versailles.

Waiting for Arabella was a letter from Mr De Hague informing her that her father had died in the first week of July. As instructed by his late client in his last will, he would proceed to brief Sir Quentin Fobb in anticipation of her avowed intention to contest the matter in court.

Later in the week, on Thursday the 22nd of July, Lady Pamela

Hartley and her sister, the Comtesse de Caullery, came to tea at the Rue St Louis. The topic of conversation was the future of Meltwater and what Arabella should do, now that her father was dead. After long discussion and despite gentle attempts at dissuasion, Arabella said that her mind was made up. She would travel to London, accompanied by Lady Hartley, to instruct Sir Bernard Banks. She understood the risks of doing so, arising from the circumstances of her departure from England fourteen years before, but insisted no woman should be crushed by the bullying of a man – even from his grave. In an age of reason it was surely time to assert the equality of a woman's rights. She was ready to fight such a cause in memory of her mother. Lady Hartley and her sister were deeply impressed by Arabella's strong purpose of mind. They saw in her fiery and unrelenting response her mother's temperament. Whatever caution they advocated made no difference. Nor did Maria Louisa's gently expressed concern about the welfare and future of Herzberg cause any hesitation in Arabella's judgement. She was determined to go to England and to take her children with her.

It was accordingly agreed that Arabella, accompanied by her children, Madame Plaquet and Lady Hartley would leave for Calais on Monday, the 26th of July.

On Friday afternoon, the 23rd, Arabella received a message from Waldemar Drescher to say that he had arrived in Paris. He hoped that they could meet as he had some important information. She replied that he should meet her in Calais on the 28th, before she boarded a boat for Dover. Her mind was made up. She intended to leave for England. He confirmed that he would do so at the Lion d'Or, near the harbour front. It was now time for Drescher to act – and to do so swiftly.

* * * * *

Later that evening Drescher and Kiefer went to the Rue de la Cité where a nervous Monsieur Bertrand was waiting.

"Bertrand, I have two tasks I wish you to undertake with all speed," said Drescher. "I want you to accompany us to the Bastille, to persuade the chief jailer to deliver the prisoner Whitfield into my hands. But before we go, to help achieve that outcome, you must forge a *lettre de cachet* in the King's name, granting the immediate release of the prisoner for an unspecified onward journey. You forged the original *lettre de cachet*, so you must do this one."

"But," said Bertrand, "I gave up such forgery some years ago. My hand is no longer as good as it was."

"Stop snivelling, man. Do it. I will dictate. You will write. Get on with it." Drescher took from his satchel a sheet of paper bearing the French royal coat of arms and handed it to Bertrand. "Don't make a mistake!"

Within the hour a sweating Bertrand had produced the required *lettre de cachet*, granting a Monsieur Duplantier possession of the prisoner Whitfield. Drescher pulled a stick of red wax from the same bag and the seal of the King of France. The document, bearing the date the 22nd of July, 1779, was duly stamped and tied with blue ribbon.

"Now, Bertrand, I need a cellar where I can interrogate Whitfield. It must have a secluded access. Do you know of one?"

"Yes," stammered Bertrand, his face covered in oily sweat. "There is one at the end of the street by the riverbank. I rent it."

"Good. Let me see it."

An hour or so later, after inspecting the cellar and taking some refreshment, Drescher and Bertrand left for the Bastille in a black unmarked coach. It was four o'clock in the morning when they woke the chief jailer, demanding urgent action.

"What the hell do you want at this hour in the morning? I was asleep."

"You're not now. We have come to collect a prisoner."

The jailer continued to remonstrate.

"Damn you, man, open the letter," said Drescher.

The jailer undid the ribbon and read the document. It was not often he saw a paper bearing the King's signature. He straightened himself.

"And who exactly are you, Monsieur Duplantier?"

"Never mind who I am. I have the King's authority to remove the prisoner and I will have him, if you please."

The jailer reached up for some keys on the wall.

"Standards are slipping. I remember the day when such documents were delivered by men in uniform. Now under this king things are going to the dogs. It is all because he married that

Austrian woman. The Hapsburgs used to be our enemy, now we are in bed with them – or at least the king is."

"Shut up. Get on with it," interrupted Drescher.

The jailer took his three visitors down long, dark, dimly lit corridors descending into ever greater darkness. The stench was almost overpowering. Finally they came to the last cell. The jailer turned the key and opened the door. He kicked a figure huddled on the bench.

"Get up. You have visitors."

George Whitfield stirred and slowly emerged from a foul-smelling blanket. Drescher looked at him. The eyes were glazed, his face unshaven; unkempt clothes hung from his thin frame.

"These men have received the King's authority to take you away. Come, get up. You have to go now."

A look of fear crossed Whitfield's face.

"Where are you taking me?" he asked plaintively.

"Somewhere else," replied Bertrand.

"What is going to happen to me?"

"You will see soon enough," answered Kiefer.

"Handcuff him, jailer," said Drescher.

Minutes later, Whitfield was thrown into the coach blindfolded. Within the hour he was in the cellar in the Rue de la Cité, once again shut away in the darkness.

The next day, on instructions, Bertrand went to the house above the cellar to boil some water which he poured into a large tub. He laid out a set of clothes and prepared a razor and a bowl of lather. He then went down to the cellar and, assisted by Kiefer, dragged Whitfield upstairs.

"Get undressed and wash yourself. You stink!"

Still with the handcuffs on, Whitfield climbed into the tub and lay back in the warm water. He could not remember his last bath. Bertrand thrust Whitfield's head under. He thought he was going to be drowned but his head was yanked back up. A sullen-looking elderly woman who had entered the room washed Whitfield's back and his hair. Her hands were rough and calloused. Bertrand then shaved him and cut his hair, after which he removed the cuffs so Whitfield could dry himself and put on the fresh clothes and some shoes. Then he was recuffed and pulled across to a table on which there was some bread, cheese and a mug of wine. He sat down and ate greedily. Afterwards he was taken back to the cellar and fixed to a chain pegged to the wall.

The whole day passed without a visitor to the cellar. Then at a late hour the door opened and Drescher and Kiefer entered. Whitfield looked frightened. They unchained him and sat him down at a table. They sat opposite him.

"George Whitfield, fourteen years ago I and another man sat opposite you. Hours before, you had attempted to abduct your sister and return her to England for possible imprisonment – perhaps even worse – on the instructions of your father, the late Sir Robert Whitfield, and a man called Bolton, who was an agent of the King of France and subsequently murdered. You and Bolton conspired in this matter. France has long been – and still is – an enemy of your country of birth. Yet you persisted in treachery and conspiracy to murder for the prospect of money. And in case you have forgotten we played pharo, a card game still illegal in France and which often carries the sentence of death. Last but not least, many years ago you murdered a certain Herr von Deppe on the streets of Paris over an alleged unpaid debt. I should have finished you off long since, but decided – in an error of judgement – to place you in the custody of the Bastille, in the expectation that your incarceration would last for the rest of your life. Now I find myself in the position of having you in my hands once more. Just beyond this cellar wall is the river. I could drown you. Or I could put you in a box and post you back to England to stand trial for treason. Or I could place you in an oubliette, of which there are many in this city, and brick you up so that you die of hunger and thirst. Or you could do as I tell you. Which would you prefer?"

Drescher leaned forwards and stared into Whitfield's eyes.

Whitfield rocked to and fro in his chair, his emaciated face racked with fear, his eyes moist with tears.

"I want to live. I want to atone for what I did. I will do anything you ask. I don't want to die."

Drescher said nothing. He continued to stare into Whitfield's eyes, pulling out a knife as he did so. He placed it on the table.

"Please, please," begged Whitfield, "I don't want to die. Please don't kill me. I have suffered enough."

"Before I decide on your fate you must write your confession," said Drescher, without showing any emotion towards the shrivelled figure in front of him.

"Yes, yes I will."

Drescher pulled some sheets of paper from his bag and took a pen and ink from a cupboard. He put them in front of Whitfield.

"Now confess. The degree of mercy you will receive will depend on the quality and honesty of your confession."

Uncuffed, Whitfield proceeded to write. So great was his fear that his hand shook as he wrote. Drescher watched him carefully and asked him at one point to rewrite the second page as it was almost illegible.

"Write clearly, man. This may be read by an English court with you in the dock."

"I th-th-thought y-you –" stammered Whitfield.

"Stop talking. Write."

Whitfield's ordeal lasted for over two hours until Drescher was satisfied he had exactly what he wanted. He then asked Whitfield to sign the confession, after which he sealed it with the stamp of a Monsieur Fournier, notary public appointed by the King of France – whose seal was also affixed, for good measure.

With that Whitfield was once again cuffed and chained to the wall.

"We will return before long to tell you your fate."

On the morning of Monday the 26th of July Drescher, Kiefer and Bertrand returned to the cellar.

"Tonight, Whitfield, you will leave Paris for Calais and Dover. On arrival in England you will be free to do as you wish, including pursuing your claim to Meltwater. The solemn promise you will now make is that you will never speak of your business in France fourteen years ago – and in England before that – and that you will never seek contact with your sister. You will repeat this promise to her in Calais before you board your ship. Your promise and your act of contrition will be witnessed, and your sealed confession, here in my hand, will be lodged with an attorney in London. We will watch you wherever you go. You are a marked man, just like the cards you used to mark. If you break your promise, the attorney will be informed. He will follow his instructions and break the seal on your confession. He will see to it that you are arrested, charged with treason and murder, and tried before the Lord Chief Justice. There will be no escape from the noose."

His hand trembling on the Bible Bertrand placed in front of him, George Whitfield made his solemn promise. Drescher again leaned forward and peered into Whitfield's terrified eyes; Bertrand knew how that look bored into one's very soul. Drescher took his knife and pressed the point into the side of Whitfield's neck. A tiny trickle of blood began to run down to the collar of his jacket.

"If you break your promise, Whitfield, you will surely die. So help you God."

With that chilling reminder to ponder, Whitfield was locked away once more.

That night George Whitfield, still handcuffed but better dressed, left Paris by coach escorted by Kiefer. Ahead of them, in another coach, sat Drescher, also destined for Calais. He had safely delivered Whitfield from the Bastille and believed he had done enough to convince him to remain silent. Now he faced the final step – to convince the Countess von Deppe to turn back to Prussia.

* * * * *

Arabella, her children, Madame Plaquet and Lady Hartley arrived in Calais late on the afternoon of Tuesday the 27th of July. They took rooms at the Lion d'Or and after a short walk along the harbour wall – to show Frederick Daniel and Elise Catherine the sea, which they had never seen before – retired for the night.

As she was about to blow out the candle Arabella saw that a note had been pushed under the door. It was from Drescher, asking her to see him alone the next morning, at seven o'clock, in a room at the end of the corridor on the floor above. It was essential that she should come. Arabella blew out the candle. She knew it would be one last effort by Drescher to dissuade her from leaving France. He would not succeed. Her mind was made up. She would go to England regardless of the consequences. Besides, she had no wish to linger in Calais. This was the place where, over fourteen years ago, she had arrived on a ship bound and gagged in a box to escape England and her father and brother.

* * * * *

The next morning Arabella dressed quickly. She asked Madame Plaquet to see that the children ate a good breakfast as they had a long journey ahead of them. She climbed the narrow stairs to the floor above and walked to the door at the end of the corridor. She knocked.

"Enter," answered Drescher's voice.

"Herr Drescher, you will not change my mind. I am going to England today. The sea is calm and Lady Hartley has arranged a suitable boat. We leave on the tide at mid-morning. I have to go."

"Countess, please sit down. I have some important information you should know."

"Herr Drescher, there is no point. Nothing will dissuade me. I intend to go."

"Countess, please sit down," he repeated, with a firmness she had not heard from him before. "Please, Countess. I insist."

She sat down.

"Your brother is alive. He is here, in a room you have just passed."

Arabella looked in disbelief at Drescher.

"Please don't be so cruel. He is dead!"

"Madame, he is alive. I know this because five days ago I removed him from the Bastille prison on production of a *lettre de cachet.* The letter countermanded the earlier *lettre de cachet* that had consigned him to prison fourteen years ago not only for his attempt to abduct and return you to England for possible imprisonment but also for playing the illegal card game pharo and for the murder of your late husband's brother. I and others have examined him and have decided that he should now return to England to do as he wishes."

Arabella sat motionless, still shocked.

"How is it that he has been locked away for so long without news of him or explanation?"

"Countess, the Prussian prison system has serious faults but the penal code in France is far more undesirable. A *lettre de cachet* enables anyone – an individual, a family, His Majesty the King of France – to remove and hide any person they do not wish to have in their way. After his attempted abduction of you in the Bois de Boulogne, I decided that your brother would best be removed to a place where he and his co-conspirators – such as Bolton and

Gaillard – could not reach you. I am responsible for what happened to your brother, not, to pre-empt the possibility of it crossing your mind, your husband."

Arabella attempted to speak but Drescher interrupted her.

"My dear Countess, I have taken steps to ensure that your brother never reveals what happened fourteen years ago. He knows that if he does so his sealed confession will be opened by an attorney in London and he will be arrested and charged with the murder of your late husband's brother, your attempted abduction, and with aiding and abetting a foreign power. Countess, the past is the past. Let it go. We all have to look to the future. Do not go to England. No good will come of it. Return to Prussia, which eagerly awaits your return."

Arabella became distressed.

"Please help me, Herr Drescher. I do not know what I should do." Her eyes were full of tears. "I do not know what to do."

"Madame, do not return to England," insisted Drescher.

She buried her face in her hands.

"Your brother wishes to see you."

"I have no wish to see him."

"I believe you should. You may not forgive him but surely you should hear his declaration of repentance. You will regret it later if you do not. Surely the Holy Mother of God would expect that of you?"

"What do you know of religion, Herr Drescher?"

"More than you think, Countess." Drescher paused. "I will bring him to you," he said, touching her arm as he left the room.

George Whitfield entered. Arabella was standing. Her brother was thin, pale and had significantly aged.

"Sister, I beg your forgiveness. All those years ago I was full of pride, arrogance and disdain for others. I thought I was better than most people. I took our family's wealth for granted. I drank too much and I enjoyed the pleasure of women. I committed many sins. I killed your late husband's brother and I attempted to abduct you in order to hand you over to our father, who was determined to see an end to you for what he believed were the wrongs you had done to him. For the last fourteen years I have thought constantly of what I did and prayed for an opportunity to make amends. Now I have that opportunity. Please forgive me. I beg you. Forgive me."

Arabella looked at her brother, now on his knees in front of her. Her face was white, drawn and mask-like. Her eyebrows were arched, hinting at a proud, even cruel, presence. There was no display of emotion.

Then she spoke.

"It is not for me to forgive you. You should seek the intercession of Jesus Christ – if you still believe in the Christian faith in which you were brought up. But I accept your apology for what it is. Before you leave for England, I ask three things of you. First, you must never seek to make contact with me again. Though I strive hard to be free of prejudice, I could not bear to be reminded of what you did. Second, I wish you to go to Meltwater without delay and remove that woman by the name of Lady Barbara, who was once our father's mistress, and her bastard son from the estate. Meltwater belongs to us true Whitfields and to no one else. Third, I urge you to seek an honourable marriage and to have children of your own, so returning happiness and true inheritance to Meltwater. If you do, perhaps one day our families can be reunited. But that, I fear, cannot happen in my lifetime because the pain you and our father inflicted on me is too raw to heal. Now please go."

George Whitfield rose to his feet and sought to kiss his sister's gloved hand. She allowed him to do so.

Two hours later Arabella stood with her children on the dockside, watching as her brother, Kiefer and Lady Hartley boarded the packet for England. The morning was warm, the sea as smooth as a mirror. In the distance she could see the cliffs above Dover. As the boat cast off, she saw her brother on the deck. He waved to her. She half raised her hand in response.

"Mother," said Frederick Daniel, "can we go home now?"

"Yes," Arabella replied. "Let us go home to Herzberg."

As she turned to walk away Arabella gave a gentle wave – not to the disappearing boat but to the distant cliffs across the English Channel. She knew that she would now never return to Meltwater or England in her lifetime. She had made a decision; the door had firmly shut behind her and was now locked. She had heard the sound of the turning key. But it was she who had turned it.

Waldemar Drescher came towards her, doffing his tricorne. He attempted to speak but Arabella put her finger to his lips.

"Herr Drescher, please take us home to Herzberg. There are now many things that have to be done."

"With pleasure, Countess," he replied.

*****

On Wednesday the 29th of September, 1779, the Schloss Herzberger Camerata played at St Hedwig's Cathedral in Berlin.

This was the orchestra's first public performance since Carl Manfred's death and was widely attended by the city's Catholic community, now swelled by immigrants to Prussia. Under the circular dome and surrounded by a multitude of candles the orchestra played Johann Sebastian Bach's *Brandenburg Concerto No. 1*, followed by the *Oboe Concerto in D Minor* composed by Tommaso Albinoni, a piece that Herr Bamberger had recently added to the Camerata's repertoire. To end, the orchestra, joined by the cathedral choir, performed Bach's *Cantata No. 140*, *Wachet auf, ruft uns die Stimme.*

Arabella sat alone with Frederick Daniel and Elise Catherine, largely unrecognised in the congregation as she had wished. Listening to the Bach cantata she once again retraced her life. Her childhood at Meltwater with her mother and warm memories of Carl Manfred filled her thoughts. For a moment she believed she could sense his presence close to her, so much so that she turned to look. But he was not there. She was alone – a widow, the mother of two children and the inheritor of an estate in a country that would never be her true home. Her brother had come back from the dead in circumstances she did not yet fully understand. She still missed her mother. The remainder of her life would be in Prussia, far away from England. It was now her task to ensure that her children grew up prepared to seek their own happiness and accomplishments. She believed she would never overcome the loss of her husband but, despite his absence from her life, she would fulfil her earlier pledge to leave a legacy worthy of his name. To do so, she would have to be brave, bold, poised and passionate in her beliefs. In the words of the cantata, "Sleepers wake, the voice is calling".

While Arabella was congratulating the Camerata, she received a note in handwriting she recognised, asking her to go to the palace at her convenience. Within the hour she was in the King's presence.

"Where are your children?" he asked. "They were with you in the cathedral."

"In the ante-room, Sire," she replied.

"I would like to meet them," he said, beckoning to a footman to bring them to him.

"Your Majesty, I wish to introduce my son, Frederick Daniel, who is twelve years old, and my daughter, Elise Catherine, aged ten."

Frederick Daniel gave a deep bow and Elise a well-practised curtsy.

"Countess, you have charming children. You should be proud of them, as would be your late husband if he were here."

"Thank you," replied Arabella.

"Countess von Deppe, I admire your courage. I admire all that you have accomplished since I first met you. It may be hard for you now – to be alone in a foreign country, so far from the land of your birth – but I wish you to know that I hold you in the highest esteem. You will always be welcome at my side. And I will honour and help guide your children."

"Your Majesty, I am deeply touched. Prussia is now my home and whatever happens in the years ahead all that I do will be for the well-being of your kingdom."

She curtsied. The King took her hand.

"Countess, I have a request of you. I wish you to sing for me at the Hofoper."

"Sire, I have not sung in public since before Count von Deppe's death. And I am older. My voice is no longer as strong as it used to be."

"Countess, you underestimate your ability. I beg you, please sing for me. The *Staatskapelle* will accompany you."

"If it is your wish, I will do so."

"Now, it is late. You and your children should go home and rest. I hope you are staying in Berlin tonight."

"Yes, Sire, we are."

With that they said goodnight.

* * * * *

A month later, on Friday the 29th of October, 1779, Arabella arrived at the Hofoper, the court opera house, on the Unter den

Linden in Berlin, to sing accompanied by the Staatskapelle Berlin, the court orchestra whose roots went back to the sixteenth century. Her children were present, accompanied by Madame Plaquet and Herr Bamberger. The opera house filled quickly, encouraged by the rumour that the King would attend.

Though she had rehearsed with the orchestra Arabella was apprehensive. Not only would she be singing in public for the first time since Carl Manfred's death; she knew that members of the court and distinguished Prussians would be looking closely at her demeanour. Fulfilling her pledge to be bold, Arabella decided no longer to wear the sombre clothes she had been favouring in mourning for her husband. That night in the Hofoper she chose to wear, as she was sure he would have wished, a cream off-the-shoulder chemise dress edged with white fur, offset by a low-slung white shawl. Her shoulders and dark hair, now revealing streaks of grey and pinned up, were sprinkled with pearl dust.

Arabella sang three arias from Handel. The first was from the opera *Rinaldo*:

Lascia ch'io pianga mia cruda sorte,
E che sospiri la libertà!

Il duolo infranga queste ritorte
De' miei martiri sol per pietà.

Let me lament my cruel destiny and yearn for liberty!
May grief in its mercy shatter the bonds of my torment.

The second aria was from the opera *Xerxes*:

Ombra mai fou
di vegetabile
cara ed amabile,
soave più.

Never was the shade
of a plant
dearer and more lovely,
or more sweet.

Her last aria was from *Giulio Cesare*:

Da tempest il legno infranto,
Se poi salvo giunge in porto,
Non sa più che desiar.
Così il cor tra pene e pianto,
Or che trova il suo conforto,
Torna l'anima a bear.

When a ship, battered by storms,
Reaches safe harbour,
It desires naught else.
Thus when a heart, riven by grief and sorrow,
Finds consolation at last,
It bids the soul revel in its joy.

Wreathed in candlelight, Arabella sang each aria with purity and assurance, seemingly unaware of the audience beyond, who were mesmerised by the quality of the notes she produced and by her almost translucent beauty. The timbre of her voice was deeper and mellower than before. They applauded each aria with great warmth and admiration. At the end the King and the entire audience stood to praise her performance, joined by the *Staatskapelle* who wished to demonstrate their respect for her personal triumph.

Calls rang out for Arabella to sing again. They were so persistent that she sang once more, an aria she had never performed in public before but which Herr Bamberger had encouraged her to practise in case it was necessary to add it unexpectedly to her repertoire for the occasion. It was the aria *Vedrò con mio diletto* from the opera *Giustino* by the Italian composer Antonio Vivaldi, some of whose music Herr Bamberger had discovered on a visit to Austria. He accompanied her on the harpsichord.

The next morning as Arabella prepared to return to Herzberg she received a simple handwritten and undated note from the King. It simply said:

Thank you.
Frederick

PART TWO: MENUETTO (ALLEGRETTO) EVENING 1786–1793

CHAPTER 6

The Old Order Ends

Following her performance at the Berlin Hofoper in October 1779 Arabella became increasingly preoccupied with three consuming tasks: ensuring the proper care and well-being of the Herzberg estate by endeavouring to fulfil the plan she and her late husband had made for its secure future before his ill-fated departure for Bohemia; continuing her patronage of the Schloss Herzberger Camerata, which continued to grow in fame as its repertoire expanded, including performances of works by new and talented composers across Europe; and being an enlightened mother to her children, Frederick Daniel and Elise Catherine.

Her dedication to the stewardship of the estate and her extensive agricultural knowledge, much admired by the King, were widely noted and were reflected both in Herzberg's financial success and the way others used it as a model. Even greater was her commitment to the Camerata, which had increased in size and musical variation. It was evident to all that Arabella's love of music knew few bounds. Her enthusiasm, constantly urged on by Herr Bamberger, matched the intensity of any movement *allegro molto*. At the same time, as a wealthy, much-respected and highly eligible widow, her hand in marriage was frequently sought. Some admirers even wanted to paint her. While Arabella was flattered by such proposals, not least on account of her unspoken desire for renewed physical intimacy, and while she sometimes coquettishly flirted with men for her amusement, none of her suitors seemed able to break the emotional grip that her late husband's memory continued to exert over her. She appeared – in the eyes of many who enjoyed her company and her patronage of music and the arts – charming and approachable but ultimately beyond reach, as though on a pedestal, though that was never her intention.

Remembering her own childhood and closeness to her mother, Arabella devoted much care and attention to the upbringing of her children, sharing with them her love of music, art and poetry. Madame Plaquet had proved an excellent governess, to whose teaching Frederick Daniel and Elise Catherine had responded well. They spoke excellent French, English and German; had learnt diligently their geography; were sound in arithmetic; and had become avid readers of books on art and philosophy. Arabella had ensured that music featured strongly in their lives – encouraging them to sing and to play a variety of musical instruments to the point where they were sometimes able to play with the Camerata. There were also the obligatory dancing lessons – often a source of great merriment. Not least, both son and daughter were encouraged to take an interest in the affairs of the estate. For this purpose, and to stifle any inclination on the part of her children towards pride, Arabella often invited the children of those who worked on the estate to come to the house to play with them, thus exposing them all to her deeply held principle of equality.

At the beginning of 1786 Frederick Daniel, who would be nineteen in nine months' time, was already tall. Slim and with light-brown hair, dark-brown eyes and strong, handsomely drawn features, he was carved much in his father's image, a daily reminder to Arabella of the man she had so deeply loved. Frederick Daniel was attentive, energetic and open-minded. He would shortly go to university to study law, not in Berlin as his father had once done but in Strasbourg which, though a French city, still remained a beacon of German language and culture. What career he would follow afterwards neither mother nor son had yet decided. It would greatly pain Arabella to see him leave Herzberg.

Elise Catherine was equally tall with an exquisite figure and pleasing bust. With thick, light-ash-coloured – indeed, almost blonde – unpowdered hair, which she wore more often pinned up than long like her mother's, high cheekbones and a pink-and-white complexion with no hint of rouge, she was already a striking young woman. From hours spent with her dancing master, reflecting her notable interest in ballet, her posture was delightfully feminine, particularly the way she delicately used her hands. Her singing was of high quality and her fingers feather-light on the keyboard. Like Frederick Daniel, Elise Catherine had developed an independence of mind and, contrary to her demure appearance, was often outspoken in her thoughts, already on occasions surprising her mother. Arabella knew that soon Madame Plaquet's task would be completed, thus bringing to the fore the question of whom her daughter might marry and, indeed, the similar question of whom Frederick Daniel would wed, though being a man there was less haste. These were matters Arabella would need to resolve before long – but with care and sensitivity.

* * * * *

Though Arabella had been received by the King several times following her Hofoper performance, more recently she had seen and heard little of him as he neared the end of his life. He had become ever more solitary. His already much-diminished circle of friends had become even smaller in the face of yet more frequent arbitrary behaviour and intolerance. According to Waldemar Drescher, who often called at Herzberg, the King dismissed with a wave of the hand the frustration of those around him attempting to conduct state business, preferring to enjoy the company of his pet greyhounds – his marquises de Pompadour, as he called them, in a jibe aimed at the mistress of the French King. Drescher believed that King Frederick's death was not far away.

It was not long after Drescher's most recent visit that the monarch died in an armchair in the study of his beloved Palace of Sanssouci on Thursday the 17th of August 1786. He was succeeded as king by his nephew, Frederick William II.

Two days later Drescher arrived at Herzberg, his spirits low like a slack tide.

"Countess, my master is dead. My life's work is done."

"Why should that be?" asked Arabella. "Surely the new King will wish to benefit from your vigilance? The person seated on the throne may have changed but not the enemies of Prussia."

"Countess, nephew and uncle were as different as chalk and cheese. One was ascetic, the other has always enjoyed the pleasures of life, as you will have heard people say, married twice and with a mistress by whom he has had five of his twelve children. The new King's interests will be different. There is no longer a role for me in protecting the House of Hohenzollern."

"If that is your judgement, what do you intend to do?" asked Arabella.

Drescher paused before he answered.

"I intend to leave Prussia for a while, as I once did a long time ago."

"Herr Drescher, I wish you well but please know that I for one will regret your departure. I would also like you to know that if you return to Prussia, or your intentions change, you will always be welcome at Herzberg."

"Countess, why should you wish to extend such an invitation? My hands are dipped in the blood of others and I am nearing the end of my life. You have children still to care for. You have your music and fond memories of Count von Deppe. And you are chatelaine of this estate. I have nothing to show for my life, other than to recall the lives I have ended in the interests of the state. I loved only one, but someone always beyond my reach. It is time for me to wander and to reflect on a life past."

"Herr Drescher, it is for you to decide the course of your remaining life. It is not for me to implore you to stay. But I will repeat that I would be honoured if, at the end of your travels, wherever they may take you, you were to consider Herzberg as a place of peace and ease where in private – alone or with another of your choice – you can continue your reflections upon life, as I often do in the quieter moments of the day."

"Countess, I am deeply touched by your words."

The conversation paused. The only sound was that of the ticking clock.

"Herr Drescher, as I too grow older – an inescapable truth as my children visibly leave their childhood behind – I reflect on time. The clock you and I now hear records the hours, the days and the weeks passing by in an unstoppable carousel. The passing of each hour, marked by the chimes of the bell, is the audible sound of the universal tyranny of time, reminding us that our lives are fleeting and transient. Every human life rises and dies and this pattern will continue until the end of time."

She waited but still Drescher made no response.

"I do not know how much of my life is left and you do not know what remains of yours. Uncertainty hangs over us like the sword of Damocles. But though we are governed by the sound of the clock and the inexorable never-stopping passage of time, each of us possesses free will. It is ours to use as we wish, for better or for worse. I am determined, through the exercise of my free will, to make the best use of my remaining life, despite my fears and prejudices. Herr Drescher, I urge you to do the same. While I have no wish to enquire into the dark secrets of your past, I do wish you to know I consider you a good and trusted companion to me – *ein treuer Begleiter*, I think you might say in German. We may travel different roads but I hope that from time to time those roads will cross here at Herzberg. I will say no more on the subject."

"Thank you, Countess. I will reflect on what you have said. I would only say now – and I wish to speak most honourably – that you still have much road to travel, much life ahead of you, much to offer others. Unlike me, cut from a different physical fabric, you still have time to find fresh love and companionship. I encourage you not to deny yourself such an opportunity."

"Herr Drescher, I will speak frankly as I know that you will never breach my confidence. I do indeed seek the love and companionship of a man. But I am afraid to love again because I fear I may soon forget in new-found pleasure the memory of a man I cherished. But that is not the sum of it. I fear too that if I were to love again I might have to endure afresh the pain and sorrow of a love once more cruelly removed. I intend to make the most of my life but, in this personal matter, I feel trapped as in a spell, trapped between the past and the future."

"Countess, I had a lifelong love for which I sacrificed every moment of every day. Now that love is gone. I am left like a shrivelled autumn leaf blown in the wind. But you, Madame, still have beauty, a passion for life and music, the love of your children and the admiration of so many. And you have the gift of time. The hands of the clock have much further to travel before your final hour is struck. I have little time. You once travelled alone in great danger in search of what you dearly wanted. You had the courage of your convictions and persisted. Unleash that courage again now, Madame. Break the spell that you say binds you and seek afresh what you want."

With that he rose, took his leave and departed from Herzberg.

* * * * *

"Herr Bamberger, I think the Camerata should mark the accession of King Frederick William with a concert at Herzberg. By all reports he greatly admires music, is a talented cellist and his court orchestra has a good reputation throughout Europe."

"Countess, I agree. What a splendid idea. Is it your intention to invite His Majesty as guest of honour?"

"Yes, it is, Herr Bamberger. I will write to His Majesty and also to the King's master of music, Monsieur Jean-Pierre Duport, to tell him that I have done so. Whether the King attends or not, it is important that we present a programme worthy of the occasion – and do remember that Monsieur Duport is a much-acclaimed cellist, as we saw when I sang at the Hofoper in 1779."

* * * * *

The Camerata performed in the *Spiegelsaal* at Schloss Herzberg on Tuesday the 3rd of October, 1786. As twenty years before at the *fête champêtre* – some three months after Arabella and Carl Manfred had married – the great, the good, the wealthy and the curious attended from neighbouring estates and further afield, including the new British Ambassador, Viscount Dalrymple. They came to pay their respects to the new King and Queen Frederika Louisa; to mingle; and to witness what display of warmth the new King would show to the widowed English countess, who had enjoyed the friendship and esteem of the late King Frederick.

"Your Majesty, Schloss Herzberg is deeply honoured by your and Her Majesty's attendance," said Arabella with a low curtsey. "It is our wish today to recognise your great patronage of the arts and your notable love of music, which has so inspired the wide and much-acknowledged success of your own orchestra. As a humble gesture, my Camerata welcomes this unique opportunity to greet you and Her Majesty in music. My guests, the orchestra and I warmly welcome you both."

"Countess von Deppe, the late King spoke to me of his great respect for you and your late husband. He referred warmly to the dexterity of your fingers on the keyboard and to your beguiling voice, which I hope the Queen and I might enjoy today. I have also received many reports of the satisfaction the Herzberger Camerata gives to those who hear it perform."

"Your Majesty, I thank you for your kind words. The Camerata bears no comparison in experience or quality to your own orchestra, which has played across Europe. We are no rival. We play only for pleasure, and we hope to give you and Her Majesty much enjoyment this evening."

"Countess, our orchestras should perhaps be rivals – but friendly ones, as would be right."

"Sire, I say again we are no rival, since we have not been tested beyond the borders of Prussia. We seek simply to be purveyors of enjoyment within your kingdom to those who wish to hear us play. I believe it was Plato who said, 'Rhythm and harmony find their way into the inward places of the soul.' That is what we seek to do – to convey rhythm and harmony to those in whose presence we have the honour to play."

"Countess, you have spoken of a noble aim. Let us put it to the test."

In close consultation with Arabella, Herr Bamberger had chosen a musical selection to portray the Camerata's talents. The programme began with Johann Sebastian Bach's *Brandenburg Concerto No. 5*, with its extended cadenza in the opening movement – almost making it the first harpsichord concerto in the history of music – enabling Arabella to display her virtuoso keyboard skills. Her assured performance was followed by George Frederick Handel's *Oboe Concerto* and after that Carl Philip Emanuel Bach's *Concerto for Cello*, featuring the excellent musicianship of Wilhelm Scholz, the Camerata's cellist since its foundation. Aware of the King's knowledge of Mozart, whom Arabella had seen perform as a boy in London in 1765, the Camerata played the composer's *Quintet for Piano and Winds*, composed in 1784 and performed two days later at the Imperial Court in Vienna. After an interval the Camerata performed Antonio Vivaldi's *The Four Seasons*, an almost complete copy of which Herr Bamberger had found on his recent travels in France. It was an evening of musical variety – a mixture of the old, the new and the forgotten.

"Countess, I congratulate you with great sincerity on the Camerata's performance, including most notably your own. Please accept our warmest and heartfelt compliments. My orchestra does indeed have an accomplished rival. Perhaps one day you will play for us? Meanwhile, Madame, we cannot depart without hearing your voice. Please sing for us – a Handel aria, perhaps?"

"Sire, my voice is not as strong as it used to be."

"Come, Countess, do not disappoint us. Please, I ask you. If not Mr Handel then perhaps Monsieur Rameau. The late King told me he was deeply touched by an aria you once sang for him from Mr Rameau's opera *Castor and Pollux*. Perhaps you could sing it for us?"

Arabella was reluctant to perform because of the sadness it would evoke for her, but with strong encouragement from Herr Bamberger she sang the aria *Tristes apprêts*. As she did so, it brought back memories of when she had sung it twenty years before in the royal chapel at the Palace of Charlottenburg in Berlin – the night that she and Carl Manfred had spent together in Queen Elisabeth's royal bedroom. Though her voice was now deeper and mellower, Arabella's vocal range and interpretation of the words of sorrow remained as striking, penetrating and affecting as they had been all those years ago. The King and Queen and all those present were visibly moved. The audience rose to their feet, calling for her to sing again.

Arabella, deeply touched that they should do so, chose to sing *Laudate Dominum*, which Mozart had composed in 1780 as part of his *Vesperae solonnes de confessore*. She had heard it performed at St Hedwig's Cathedral in Berlin and thereafter had often sung it privately at Herzberg. For her the andante represented a sublime manifestation of her Catholic faith.

"Your Majesty, I have already detained you and the Queen for too long but with your permission I wish as an epilogue to invite my son, Frederick Daniel, soon to leave Herzberg to study at the university in Strasbourg, and my daughter, Elise Catherine, to play with the Camerata the *Canon and Gigue* by the German composer Johann Pachelbel. While it is music from a previous century, my son and daughter represent, like you, a new generation. It is they,

Your Majesty, who will help you and others to take Prussia in new directions. I commend them."

As she sat watching, with pride, Frederick on the violin and Elise on the harpsichord – both no longer children – playing with the skill and confidence she and Albrecht Bamberger had taught them, Arabella suddenly recognised that the future of Herzberg was visibly passing from her hands into theirs, just as it had passed from Carl Manfred's into hers. His death, which she still mourned, and the unexpected departure of her *Begleiter*, Waldemar Drescher, had left her alone. Yes, she continued to have admirers and suitors, but none could replace what she had lost. She was becoming aware that one by one the landmarks of her life had disappeared or were receding from sight. Only her children were left.

Her remaining task was not to become reclusive but, in the years left to her, to begin to step with confidence and strength into the background so Frederick and Elise could take her place and make whatever they wished of their lives and of Herzberg, which they would in due course inherit. While she would continue her stewardship of the estate and of the Camerata, and, accordingly, determined to remain a staunch defender of both, it would be in their name not hers. She decided at that moment, as a first gesture, that she would no longer sing in public. It was time for Elise, with her own sweet voice, to take over. For Arabella, it had therefore been appropriate that her last public vocal rendering had been the *Laudate Dominum*. Though her religious discipline had been inconsistent, her commitment to her Catholic faith had nonetheless remained steadfast despite many setbacks and distractions. The words she had sung were a small gesture of gratitude for the gift from her mother of a strong conscience, which she had possessed since childhood.

She was stirred from her thoughts by the warm applause for the young performers.

"Countess, we thank you again with even greater warmth," said the King. "You sang with great expression, beauty and reflective sadness. If I see Herr Mozart I will tell him that you would be an excellent singer for one of his operas. And had he been here, Monsieur Rameau would have been full of praise for your rendition of his aria, as I am. Your son and daughter would be worthy members of my orchestra. Thank you for such an impressive evening of music. Schloss Herzberg is a true oasis of musical brilliance, do you not agree, Monsieur Duport?"

"I do agree, Sire."

The King and Queen departed. Herzberg, the Camerata and the Countess von Deppe had transcended the new royal order in Berlin.

* * * * *

Shortly after the concert and Frederick Daniel's departure for Strasbourg Arabella received a letter from a Mr Charles Gray.

> *Dear Countess von Deppe,*
>
> *I have arrived in Berlin on private business.*
>
> *The British Ambassador, His Excellency Viscount Dalrymple, with whom I recently dined, has told me of the splendid musical evening you hosted at the start of this month in honour of His Majesty the King.*
>
> *Please forgive my unprecedented boldness but before my departure from Prussia for St Petersburg it would greatly please me if you would grant the honour of allowing me to call upon you at Schloss Herzberg in order to make your acquaintance. Your musical reputation in Prussia is such that it would be a privilege to discuss matters of mutual interest.*
>
> *Yours most sincerely,*
> *Charles Gray*
> *This day Wednesday the 11th of October, 1786, at Berlin*

Waldemar Drescher had advised her long ago to be vigilant for the unexpected. She had never heard of Mr Gray but he claimed he had dined with Viscount Dalrymple, with whom she was well acquainted, and it would be pleasant to hear reports of England. Besides, he was travelling to St Petersburg and she would be interested to know for what purpose. If he were returning to Berlin afterwards he might bring news of the Empress and perhaps even of the Countess Sokolova. So Arabella agreed that he should call on her on the morning of Tuesday the 17th of October.

* * * * *

Charles Gray, a man in his late thirties, was markedly good-looking, elegantly – indeed expensively – dressed, and distinctly well-mannered, as his gestures and conversation immediately indicated. His hair was deep brown and tied back in a tail, just as Arabella often used to wear hers, though in recent years she had taken to wearing it pinned up, while still resisting, like her daughter, the application of any adornment. She had vowed she would never wear a widow's bonnet. It was so on this occasion.

Mr Gray and Arabella drank coffee in the library before she took him to the *Spiegelsaal*, at his request, to see the room in which so many concerts had taken place, including the most recent. He asked her knowledgeable questions about the Camerata, its steadily expanding repertoire and the contribution Herr Bamberger had made. She showed him the gallery to which, over the years, she and her late husband had added some fine and distinctive pictures.

"Countess, I have been travelling in Europe for some months – first to Italy, of course, and then further, to Vienna and Prague, and, more recently, Berlin. Shortly, after a hurried visit to St Petersburg, I begin my journey back to England. I have seen many fine buildings and made the acquaintance of many fine people on my journey around Europe. But it has been truly an honour to meet you and to see this impressive house with its gallery and concert room. Viscount Dalrymple is right. You are a most gracious lady who – with the late Count – has done a great deal to advance the cause of music in Prussia, bringing to the task a unique English approach. You may not be aware, Countess, but you have done much to strengthen understanding between the two kingdoms."

"Mr Gray, I thank you for your kind words. You seem, if I may so, to be remarkably well informed about Herzberg and while I am flattered you should come this far on your way from visiting the great capitals of Europe, I sense there may be another motive for your presence here today. Perhaps you would be kind enough to share that motive with me. Let us return to the library for you to do so."

As they walked from the gallery, Elise Catherine came to see her mother to seek some musical advice.

"Mr Gray, I wish to introduce my daughter, the Countess Elise, an accomplished musician and singer in her own right. She is shortly to sing at the Hofoper in Berlin."

"I am honoured to meet you, Countess von Deppe." He bowed and she curtsied.

"Mr Gray, provided your forthcoming disclosure is not distressing, would you care to join a mother and her daughter for lunch, so you are well fortified for your onward journey?"

"I would be greatly honoured to share the company of two such beautiful ladies," he replied with a smile and another bow.

Arabella smiled wryly while Elise's natural pink-and-white complexion revealed the slight trace of a blush.

"Good, that is settled. Elise, please would you tell Weisser that there will be three for lunch, which should be light, I suggest."

"Yes, Mama," replied Elise.

"Now, Mr Gray, tell me, why have you really come today?"

They had returned to the library. The autumn sun was now hidden behind dark clouds beginning to advance from the west.

"Countess, I wish to assure you that I am truly interested in music and while I was in Vienna I had the honour to meet Herr Haydn. He told me he had already heard of Herzberg and its musical tradition through his brief acquaintance with Herr Bamberger. I therefore decided that as I was coming to Berlin and it would be only a short distance, I should divert to Herzberg. Viscount Dalrymple encouraged me to do so. I am pleased I have."

"Mr Gray, I think your musical interest, though clearly genuine, is by the bye. Please, I ask you to come to the point. I always prefer clarity to the opaque."

"Countess, my business affairs in London take me widely across Europe. I share the view of others that the present condition of the continent of Europe is not good. The Austrian empire is showing distinct signs not only of wear and tear but of unpredictability in its actions. The situation in France, as you might perhaps be aware if you have been in recent touch with your sister-in-law in Paris, the Vicomtesse de Vervins, is beginning to reveal growing discontent amongst a heavily taxed people. The King and his Austrian Queen are less popular than they once were. The Empress of Russia, whom you have had the privilege of meeting – and what a splendid picture of you and her I see on the wall – still exercises significant influence in the affairs of Europe and her territorial ambitions continue to flourish. I believe it was the late King Frederick who said of the Empress, 'She wept and she wept but she took and she took.'"

Arabella smiled.

"In England," Charles Gray continued, "the loss of the American colonies has left an indelible mark and there is unpleasant confrontation between Whig and Tory not just in Parliament but on the streets. Last but not least, there is a new King on the Prussian throne, different in approach and style to his late uncle. So there exists a strong recipe for possible instability. In London we prefer to see stability on the European mainland – or should I say, the existence of a balance of power where no one has a particular advantage over another. Such balance is hard to achieve but a worthy aim nonetheless."

"Please forgive me, Mr Gray, but why are you telling me this? I am a citizen of Prussia, a country where I have lived since my marriage to my late husband in 1766. Uppermost in my mind are the well-being of Herzberg, the welfare of my children, the interests of the kingdom and, of course, the propagation of the appreciation of music. The wider affairs of Europe are surely the concern of men such as you, particularly since there is no taste, either in England or in Prussia, for the views of women. Whatever opinions we may have are often regarded as out of place or frivolous."

"That is not an attitude to which I subscribe," retorted Gray. "It is not just your beauty and musical reputation that led me to ask to call on you, but your intellect also."

Arabella smiled again.

"Come, come, Mr Gray. Flattery will not get far with me. Please come to the point."

"Let me be frank, Countess."

"I invite you to be frank," Arabella quipped.

Gray smiled.

"It is my opinion – and that of others with whom I associate – that the situation in Europe is slowly, imperceptibly, deteriorating in an undesirable way. The clouds of possible upheaval are gathering in the distance. Such upheaval may lead easily to war and continental dislocation, and war never ends quietly. As I have already stated, England has always believed in the principle of balance in the affairs of Europe. The rise of one power over another and the instability that might provoke are dangerous and never in England's interest – indeed, not in anyone's interest. I include Prussia. Imbalance sparks conflict, intentional or unintentional. In such a situation no one really wins. Even if one country seems to do so, those who have been defeated plot fresh conflict to recover what they have lost. In the circumstances of instability and, heaven forbid, conflict, alliances are crucial – to avoid war or, in the event of hostilities, to deter aggression. In the time left at our disposal, my friends and I believe it is highly desirable to use all means to recreate previous worthwhile alliances and, where necessary, create new ones. You, Countess, have a much-respected reputation at the Prussian court. We hope you may be well disposed to use it to good effect now that a new monarch sits on the throne. An alliance between Prussia and England remains necessary."

"Mr Gray, on whose authority do you speak in these matters?"

"Countess, I would prefer not to say, but they are influential and well-intentioned."

"I respect your reticence but I imagine you are referring to the government of my country of birth."

For a moment Gray did not respond. But he thought better of it.

"Yes, Madame, I am."

"If you are asking me to become an advocate at the Prussian court of your people in London then I must refuse. If I were ever to be at the new King's court I could not speak in favour of England. That would be discourteous and deemed by those regularly in attendance as unacceptable. To act as an advocate of England must surely be the task of Viscount Dalrymple and others. Even if I were to agree to utter any word in the direction you have described, my position in Prussia – let alone at court - would be compromised. If you are asking me to spy for England by eavesdropping on conversations at court and reporting what I have heard, as I was asked to do once before, that is even more impossible. I could not even contemplate such an undertaking. Born in England of a French mother and a citizen of Prussia by marriage I have steered with great care through shallow and treacherous waters hiding dark rocks beneath. I have survived so far. I wish to add that twice in the past I have seen duplicity and betrayal at work – the perpetrators and the victims. Intervention is best left to others."

"I understand," Gray interjected swiftly.

"As a widow alone in Prussia I too am aware that old certainties are no longer reliable. The old order, if I may use that phrase, is indeed fast disappearing. It is evident even at Herzberg. If continental upheaval comes, I will do all that I can to ensure the safekeeping of this estate and the well-being of my children, as well as to rally to the cause of my present homeland, doing whatever is asked of me. However, I assure you that, while those will be my primary preoccupations in such circumstances, I would never act in a detrimental way against the country of my birth, so long as the aims of England are not inimical to those for which I have always stood – most notably the principle of equality for all. In that regard England has a good reputation, for which I am ready to speak up as a patriot, though I am reluctant to use such an emotive word. You may consider what I have said to be selfish, Mr Gray, but that is the judgement I have to make and I have had much time in recent years to consider it. Let me say in conclusion that you may rest assured you and the others with whom you say you associate are always most welcome at Herzberg to share my table and to discuss the affairs of the world in which I, a woman, do take an interest but to listen rather than to advocate. I thank you for listening with great patience and politeness to what I have said."

"Thank you, Countess. You have spoken with admirable clarity. I will convey to those concerned that your kind hospitality awaits them. If you ever need to seek our view on any matter the Ambassador will know best how to provide it."

"I thank you, Mr Gray, for your kind offer. Who knows what advice an ageing widow may require in the future?"

"Come, come, Countess, your beauty and wisdom will be ageless."

"I can see, Mr Gray, that you are a masterful exponent of flattery. Now let us join my daughter for lunch and talk more about our shared interest in music."

"Countess, before we do so I would like to add that, if war were to come to Europe, it may embrace all corners of this continent, spreading across frontiers without discrimination for its victims. Frequently, a new order is born out of chaos and much destruction. If the worst were to happen, I hope you would ensure that you and your family survived in safety in order to contribute to such a new order."

"If you mean, Mr Gray, would I wish to die defending my late husband's estate, the answer is no. But I would do all that I could to preserve what is here up to the time such a decision were necessary."

"Countess, there is one other matter. I have been asked to deliver to you this personal letter. I do not know the contents, nor do I know the writer. All I can say is that the letter has nothing to do with what we have discussed."

Gray placed the letter on the table.

"How intriguing, Mr Gray. I have something to read after lunch while my daughter shows you our garden."

*****

After lunch, while Elise Catherine – as her mother had proposed – walked with Mr Gray in the garden, Arabella opened the letter he had given to her.

> *Dear Sister,*
>
> *When we said goodbye in Calais, I agreed to your condition of no further contact between us. I have honoured that condition. However, as several years have since passed, I wish to break it – not to instigate correspondence between us, which I believe you would still consider undesirable, but to advise you of events at Meltwater, which I would like to think still has a place in your heart. Was it not Mary Tudor who said she would die with Calais engraved on her heart?*
>
> *Six years ago I arrived in London penniless and in some ill health as a consequence of my incarceration in prison for fourteen years. On my way to meet our late father's attorney, Mr Elisha De Hague, in Norwich, I remained full of rage at what had happened to me. There were moments when thoughts of revenge filled my head. But after many weeks I came to see that the indignity I had suffered bore no comparison to the injustice that our father, Sir Robert, had done to you, with me as an accomplice, unaware of what he was doing because of my*

own selfish preoccupations. I came to realise that he had driven you from home on account of his own ends and of his failure to tolerate your strongly held principle that women should not be treated as chattels, a principle to which he was blind, as was I. Though you married a man who gave you the love and respect you had been seeking, but who sadly died, and though you have children and comfortable circumstances in Prussia, the fact remains you live in exile as a consequence of the actions of others. I apologised to you in Calais. I do so again by means of this letter. However many times I may do so, the events all those years ago will continue to weigh on my conscience.

You may wish to be informed that upon my return to Meltwater I asked Lady Barbara Whitfield and her son to leave the estate and to return to London. I believe they were relieved to do so, as the conduct of the estate was proving beyond their interest or capability. With the assistance of Mr De Hague, who disclosed that the estate was entailed, it was agreed amicably by me, after some discussion, that Lady Barbara should be allowed to reside at Sir Robert's town house in Westminster, while I became the legally acknowledged owner of the Meltwater estate, which now benefits from a new and highly experienced land agent, Mr Blackwell. The estate flourishes in his safe hands.

Two years later I married Mrs Sophie Charmley. She was previously Miss Skipworth, one of the young ladies with whom you may recall I danced at the Meltwater ball, the last soirée of that sort to be held at the Hall. She married Mr Stephen Charmley soon after that event, but her husband died in a riding accident some years later, leaving her alone with a daughter, Alice.

Lady Sophie and I remain happily married. We have a son, whom we have called Robert Stephen, known to all by his second name. He is a bonny child, and he and Alice do well together. In my will, lodged with Mr De Hague, I have stipulated that upon my death Meltwater should remain in entail to my son, but that if anything were to happen to him before my demise and there were no further male heir from me and Lady Sophie, the estate should pass to you as far as legally possible upon my death. If such a circumstance were ever to arise

I earnestly hope you would look kindly on Lady Sophie and my step-daughter, Alice.

I have been assured that you will indeed in due course receive this letter. I do not hold out hope of a reply in view of the understandably bitter feelings you displayed in Calais. But I hope that, even if you do not respond, what I have written will bring you some comfort. I might add that my written confession still resides in the lawyer's chambers in London and it will do so until my death. I have instructed that upon my death the document should be burnt unopened and with it my disgrace, which remains a personal shame not shared with others.

Your brother,

George

Meltwater, Friday the 26th of May, 1786

Arabella put the letter down. Its receipt had been entirely unexpected. She walked to the window. Elise was returning to the house with Mr Gray. They were laughing together. Beyond the garden the clouds were darkening still. There would be rain soon.

She remembered what Mr Gray had said before lunch about the possible prospect of renewed conflict in Europe and recalled a recent letter from Maria Louisa in Paris, expressing further worry about increasingly troublesome undercurrents at the Palace of Versailles and signs of widening discontent beyond the palace gates. Arabella suddenly felt more alone. She still missed her mother greatly; an unnecessary war had taken her husband's life; her father had died unmourned; King Frederick had been a friend but was now gone; and Waldemar Drescher had disappeared upon the King's death, his whereabouts unknown. Frederick Daniel was studying law in Strasbourg and had already spoken of joining the Prussian army as his father had once done. Only Elise was left, and soon she would wish to marry and so leave Herzberg. Was it right in such circumstances to continue to harbour a grudge against her brother after all these years? While she still could not bring herself to utter words of forgiveness, it was surely time to hold out her hand to acknowledge with some suitable gesture what her brother had written.

After asking Mr Gray to delay his departure a short while, Arabella wrote to her brother. As she began she heard Elise in the

Spiegelsaal playing Bach's *Prelude and Fugue No. 1 in C major* to their guest. The sound reminded her of the many times she had played it to soothe the Empress Catherine in the Winter Palace. It now caused her to write in a soft vein to her brother.

Dear Brother,

I thank you for your letter, which I received today by the hand of Mr Charles Gray.

I convey to you and Lady Sophie my happiness at your marriage, of which I had no prior notion, and my equal measure of happiness on the birth of your son and the acquisition of a step-daughter. I wish you, Lady Sophie and your children much good fortune in the years ahead.

I am relieved that Meltwater is restored to its rightful ownership. That is as it should be and it is all that I ever wanted.

We are both older and wiser, as the saying goes. Moreover, as we advance in years we benefit from our children, brought up with kindness and understanding as we wish it to be, not as others might insist on account of pride and destructive ambitions. I do not know what the uncertain future holds for me in the remainder of my life in Prussia. But whatever may befall me I now have the comfort of knowing that Meltwater, of which I indeed have some happy recollections from my childhood, will survive in good hands. I will never see my childhood home again, or even England, but I hope that one day in the future our descendants will meet and by so doing lay a strong foundation for true and lasting friendship between our two families and our two countries, so assuaging the bitterness and rancour of the past, which for me is now a closed book.

In reconciliation,
Your sister,
Arabella
Schloss Herzberg, Tuesday the 17th of October, 1786

An hour later, Mr Gray left Herzberg for St Petersburg, promising to deliver her letter to its recipient before the end of the year.

That evening, over supper, mother and daughter made plans for a soirée at Herzberg, to take place shortly before their departure for Strasbourg, to see Frederick Daniel; the family would then travel together to Paris, to spend Christmas with the de Vervins.

"Elise, I have decided that the soirée should be in your honour, so please tell me soon which young men you would wish me to invite."

"I will, Mama, with pleasure. Thank you."

After supper Elise played Bach's *Partita No. 4* to her mother, as Arabella had once done to her mother. The wheel had turned full circle.

That night, alone in her bed, Arabella could not remove from her mind Charles Gray's fears at the prospect of upheaval and possible conflict in Europe. His words had been chilling and unsettling. He was clearly well informed, just like Waldemar Drescher had been. She had told Gray that in the face of any threat she would choose to stay at Herzberg to protect the estate in her husband's memory, until she were forced to decide between life and death. But how far could she go in such a test of resolve, a woman on her own? There was no answer. She could only wait to see whether his prophecy came true. Only then would she be able to decide. But at least she had made peace with her brother.

CHAPTER 7

A Musical Encounter

After the distinct bustle of a morning, and with the prospect of evening enjoyment in the ambiance of candlelight still some hours away, there is a time in the day, in the still of mid-afternoon, when sometimes the hands on the clock seem to slumber. For a casual observer, that was the impression of the two and a half years since Arabella had written to her brother. There was little news of note during this time. The handsome Mr Gray made occasional visits to Herzberg, to which Arabella always looked forward on account of his humour and well-informed conversation. As for the estate, it continued unhampered its seasonal rituals, watched over by its attentive chatelaine. Music, however, remained the activity from which Arabella derived most pleasure, seeking the offerings of new composers but still enjoying those of the past, a taste the Camerata was pleased to indulge. The lightness yet inherent mellowness of Johann Joachim Quantz's *Concerto for Flute, Strings and Basso Continuo in G Major* and Tomaso Albinoni's *Sonata in C Major for Two Violins, Two Violas and Basso Continuo*, two compositions she frequently asked to be played at this time, accurately conveyed her still confident but equally reflective mood during these years. But now it was 1789 and the movement of the hands on the clock became more perceptible.

Though preoccupied with her daughter's future, Arabella was

intrigued by a report in early April from Herr Bamberger that the Austrian composer Wolfgang Amadeus Mozart was likely to come to Potsdam to pursue King Frederick William's patronage in order to boost his musical reputation and to earn more money.

Arabella had seen the young Mozart – when he was only nine – perform twice while she had been residing at Mrs Hallam's house in Mayfair as a young masked courtesan, in hiding from her father. The boy's musical genius had been immediately apparent. She had even asked him, on the second occasion, to play from the *Gradus Ad Parnassum*, a treatise on counterpoint which the Austrian composer Johann Joseph Fux had written in 1725 and which her music teacher, Herr Kunzl, had often made her play in her own piano lessons. Mozart had responded eagerly to her request, playing without slip or hesitation – and adding some ornamental flourishes of his own – part of the *Gradus* for the elegant lady in the mask. He had entranced her. Now, according to Herr Bamberger, Mozart would soon be in Potsdam, accompanied by his aristocratic friend, Prince Karl Lichnowsky, and Josepha Duschek, a Bohemian soprano for whom Mozart had composed music especially for her to sing.

Arabella promptly decided that she would write to the composer to invite him, together with his two companions, to Herzberg.

Dear Herr Mozart,

Please forgive my impertinence but I have heard of your imminent arrival in Potsdam to wait on His Majesty's pleasure.

I write to invite you and your travelling companions, Prince Karl Lichnowsky and Madame Duschek, to visit Schloss Herzberg while you are in Potsdam. Herzberg is not far by fast coach, which I should be honoured to provide, from where I believe you may be lodging. The Herzberg Camerata, reports of which you may have received on your travels, was formed at the Schloss over twenty years ago. I have asked Herr Bamberger, its esteemed leader, to ensure that this letter reaches you safely.

I wish to add that I have heard some of your compositions and have great admiration for their skill and originality. Indeed, I sang the Laudate Dominum *from your* Solemn

> Vespers *to His Majesty three years ago at Herzberg. Because of my great respect for your music, and as I had the privilege of hearing you play on two occasions in London in 1765, it would be a great honour and pleasure to make your acquaintance to discuss matters of mutual musical interest. Of course I would understand if you were unable to accept my invitation because of your prior preoccupation to seek audience with His Majesty. However, I will hope that you may have some available time while you are in Potsdam for us to meet.*
> *With cordial greetings,*
> *Arabella*
> *Countess von Deppe*
> *Schloss Herzberg, Thursday the 9th of April, 1789*

"Herr Bamberger, please do all you can to see that this letter reaches the hand of Herr Mozart. I so want him to come. Please do not depend on Monsieur Duport for that purpose. He is haughty and unreliable and, if I may say so, envious of the Camerata's reputation and therefore unlikely to help speed my invitation to its rightful recipient."

"Countess, I will make every effort to deliver your invitation personally to Herr Mozart."

* * * * *

Herr Bamberger's persistence bore fruit, his success aided by King Frederick William's failure, so far, to receive Herr Mozart. Accordingly, Wolfgang Mozart arrived at Herzberg on Wednesday the 29th of April, accompanied by Prince Lichnowsky and Madame Josepha Duschek. To Arabella, the composer bore little resemblance to the boy she had seen perform so long ago. He was short in stature, his skin was pockmarked and he had protruding eyes. But he was bursting with expression and curiosity.

"Herr Mozart, welcome to Herzberg. It is a great honour to receive you. I believe you have already met Herr Bamberger, the leader of our Camerata. May I introduce my daughter, the Countess Elise von Deppe?"

"Thank you, Countess von Deppe, it is a great pleasure to meet you, to see Herr Bamberger again and to make the acquaintance of this charming and most elegant young Elise," the composer replied, his eyes twinkling. "I wish to introduce my great friend and patron, Prince Lichnowsky, and Madame Duschek, for whom I compose arias."

"You are all most welcome. Let us have lunch."

There was much laughter and merriment over lunch, of a volume not heard at Herzberg for many years. Everyone was in high spirits, pleased to escape the so far fruitless waiting on Monsieur Duport for word of an audience with the King.

"Elise, perhaps you and Herr Bamberger might wish to take Prince Lichnowsky and Madame Duschek for a walk in the garden while Herr Mozart and I exchange memories of London in the *Spiegelsaal*."

"Yes, of course we will," said Elise, looking at Herr Bamberger to help her fulfil her mother's plan that she and the composer should have time alone.

"Indeed we will," Herr Bamberger hastily added.

"Cannot I stay with you?" said Madame Duschek with an imploring look at Mozart.

"No, Josepha, you may not. Only this morning you had one of your tantrums and said I was insufferable and wished me to go away. So I am turning the tables on you. You can walk with the amusing and talented Herr Bamberger so I can enjoy the company of the beautiful Countess Arabella in the *Spiegelsaal*. And Lichnowsky will have the pleasure of walking with the equally beautiful Countess Elise. Josepha, please don't put on one of your sour faces. Be a good girl and go into the garden. Lichnowsky, please make her do what I ask," said Mozart, laughing and putting his hands together in feigned supplication.

"Yes, we will go," said Lichnowsky. "I would like very much to accompany the Countess Elise. Herr Bamberger, you may escort Madame Duschek. Perhaps you have a composition ready for her to try amongst the trees?" he suggested, laughing.

Once the walking party of four had disappeared, Mozart admired the *Spiegelsaal* and then sat down at the pianoforte.

"Do you play this instrument, Countess, or do you sing? Or perhaps you do both."

"Yes, I used to sing and play, but not any longer," replied Arabella.

"Why should that be?"

"Because I have become too old to do so," answered Arabella.

"Absolute rubbish," Mozart riposted. "You should see some of the ugly old ducks that come to ask if I would let them sing in my operas. Countess, you are truly beautiful and with an equally beautiful voice I am sure, which I will soon put to the test!" He gave a loud laugh. "But first things first," he added. "Who taught you music?"

"First it was my mother, who was French, and a great lover of music and a fine exponent of its art. She was followed by my German music teacher, Herr Kunzl."

"Ah! Yet another German! Was he any good?" enquired the composer.

"I thought he was. And he had met some of the Bachs."

"But was he plonky on the keyboard?"

"No, he certainly was not. He played with great skill and had an impressive voice – at least, I thought he did."

"Show me," said Mozart, examining the pianoforte closely. "Not a bad instrument," he muttered. "I have a similar one in Vienna."

"I did not expect to be auditioned," replied Arabella.

"Why not?" said Mozart. "I want to hear how good you are. That's the price of asking me to lunch! Now, Countess, please sing. And by the way, come and sit beside me at the keyboard."

Arabella sat beside Mozart – a little nervous. What could she choose? Why not play the Bach *Prelude*, softly and quietly as she had done to the Empress Catherine. Though a simple composition, it was expressive. She played, her fingers hardly touching the keyboard. Closing her eyes she recalled those intimate candlelit evenings with the Empress Catherine in the Winter Palace. When she had finished they sat side by side without a word.

"You are an accomplished player," said Mozart, breaking the silence. "Now listen to this!"

He played the allegro of a piano sonata based on the musical scale.

"Repeat that from memory!" he said with a guffaw.

Arabella repeated the allegro with the composer conducting beside her. He made her go faster and faster. Then he played the andante movement while Arabella watched intently.

"Now, Countess, I will play the rondo and you will repeat it."

Under Mozart's guidance she reprised the bars as best she could.

"Bravo! You pass that test. Now sing for me," he said.

"But Herr Mozart, I have not sung –"

He interrupted her.

"Please, Countess, sing for me. Just me, for no one else."

What could she sing after three years of vocal silence? She chose *Where'er you walk* from Handel's *Semele*, again her fingers like feathers on the keyboard. Her voice flowed gently, the notes sung with ease.

"What a choice, Countess! Mr Handel understood effect better than any of us. When he wants to, he strikes like a thunderbolt. Now, as you are an accomplished singer, sing me something else. Tell me what it is and let's see if I can play the tune."

"I have sung several times *Vedrò con mio diletto* from Mr Vivaldi's opera *Giustino*. Do you know it?"

"Does it go like this?" He began to play.

"Yes, Herr Mozart! That is it exactly."

"Then sing, Countess!"

She stood beside him. The words and notes flowed effortlessly.

Unknown to her and Mozart, Elise and Prince Lichnowsky were listening at the slightly open window leading to the garden. Both were spellbound. Singer and pianist were oblivious to the world around them. As Arabella finished, the two bystanders tiptoed away in silence to tell Herr Bamberger and Madame Duschek what they had heard.

"Countess, again please. You are perfect but I need to be entranced again. Please sing it again. Take me to heaven!"

"If you insist, Herr Mozart."

"I do, I do, Countess. And please be a little more expressive with your hands."

Arabella repeated the aria.

"Thank you, Countess, you are a worthy musician and singer. You are a miracle from heaven."

"Herr Mozart, you are mocking me."

"Countess, why should I mock a vision of beauty and the voice of a heavenly angel?"

"Now it is your turn to perform, Herr Mozart. It is my wish

that you do so, to sing for your supper as they say."

"Countess, I am not a performing monkey," he retorted, laughing.

"And I am not either, Herr Mozart, but you tricked me into playing and indeed into singing – singing twice, for that matter. I am letting you off lightly by only asking you to play. Come, it is your turn. I have spoken," said Arabella smiling, beginning to get the measure of her guest and enjoying the game – a flirtatious one at that – they were playing.

"I see I am cornered by a beautiful and determined Countess. I surrender," he said, holding his hands up. "Have you heard this silly tune?"

He began to play.

"Yes," said Arabella. "Is it not composed by Monsieur Duport, the King's musical major domo?"

"Yes, Countess, you're right – by the old fart himself! It is so boring, don't you agree?"

Arabella just smiled.

"Let's see whether we can spice it up," said Mozart.

He played, laughing as he did so. Then he played the melody again but with another variation.

"That's two variations!" he counted.

"Surely a clever composer like you can devise more?" said Arabella, once again sitting beside him.

"Countess, I accept the challenge – but with your help."

Arabella watched in delight and growing amazement as Mozart played three more variations, then yet another.

"I've lost count. How many is that?" he asked Arabella.

"Six," she replied. "Maybe there's another," she added.

"Show me," said Mozart. "Countess, I dare you."

Arabella played.

"Hmmm, that's not bad. Perhaps we'll add a tweak here and one there . . ." he said, as he recapitulated from memory what Arabella had just played.

"And here's another," she said, laughing, much enjoying the spirit of the game. She played a further variation.

"That's very good, very good indeed. You're getting good at this. Now it's my turn," he said, producing yet another variation.

"Herr Mozart, that's nine variations altogether. Well done."

"If only old Duport could hear us. He really is a boring po-faced old fart, keeping me hanging around in Potsdam. He and that old sack Salieri would make a good pair of smelly old shoes."

Arabella burst out laughing.

"Oh, Countess, what fun we've had! What an enjoyable day this has proved to be."

"But Herr Mozart, how will you remember what we have just composed?"

"Easy-peasy, Countess. That's not a problem. I need some paper, ink and a pen."

Arabella fetched them and sitting at a nearby table Mozart scribbled furiously. A few minutes later he stood up in triumph.

"Here we are – nine variations on a tune by Monsieur Duport. Let's play them! Come, sit beside me again. Let's go! I'll play mine and you play yours."

And so they played – the English countess and the Austrian composer.

"*Voilà*! All played, all correct," he exclaimed. "Don't you agree?"

"Yes, I very much agree," said Arabella, surprised and delighted.

The exuberant Mozart hugged Arabella.

"Oops. I hope you didn't mind that?"

"I did not, Herr Mozart, not at all." It was the first time she had been hugged by a man in a spontaneous gesture of affection. "But, Herr Mozart, how will I remember what you and I have composed?"

"Countess, more paper please!"

Mozart proceeded to write out the variations again – not copying what he had already transcribed, but from memory. Again they sat side by side as they played.

"Correct?" he asked Arabella.

"Yes, perfectly correct."

"Allow me," he said.

Picking up the pen, he took the first copy, which Arabella was holding in her hand, and wrote:

> *I dedicate to the beautiful and elegant Countess von Deppe these amusing variations, which she composed with me. By so doing she helped to raise my low spirits with fun and her delightful*

company at Schloss Herzberg. Let us hope these musical trimmings will presage a momentous year for both of us.
WAM
Wednesday the 29th of April, 1789
Schloss Herzberg
PS I would love you – the heavenly voice of the Annunciation – to sing for me in my next opera. I won't let you say no.

"Herr Mozart, I am deeply touched. But I could not sing for you in public. What about Madame Duschek?" she protested.

Mozart simply put his finger to his lips.

"Hush, Countess. We will see. I am good at getting what I want."

He smiled and kissed her hand.

Just then they heard voices. Elise, Herr Bamberger, Prince Lichnowsky and Josepha Duschek entered the *Spiegelsaal.*

"The Countess and I have greatly enjoyed putting some life into a silly and dull melody by Duport. Bravo for the Countess."

Arabella appeared to blush a little. Lichnowsky and Elise smiled knowingly to one another.

"Countess, you, your charming daughter – who smiles like the sun – and Herr Bamberger must come to the performance of my opera *Die Entführung aus dem Serail* in Berlin on the 19th of May. I insist. Promise me you will come – all of you. Please promise me."

"Of course, we will come. I promise," said Arabella.

"Yes, of course we will come," echoed Elise.

"Now, will you stay to eat?" asked Arabella.

"I would very much like to, as would Karl and Josepha. Then we must return to Potsdam just in case old man Duport summons us to meet His Majesty."

Later that evening, after Mozart and his companions had departed, Arabella played the nine variations to her daughter, smiling in amusement as she did so. Once upon a time she had heard a nine-year-old boy play in London. He had rekindled her love of music in those dark, despairing days, inspiring her to escape to a new life that had eventually led her to Carl Manfred and her children. That afternoon the talented Herr Mozart had sat beside her and together they had composed a delightful sequence. He had even hugged her. If only her husband could have seen her.

"Mama, you look so happy," said Elise.

"I am, Elise. I am happy. Herr Mozart has truly lifted my spirits. Should we speak of Herr von Schellenhorst tomorrow?"

"Thank you, Mama. I would like that, as I believe he wishes to call upon you at your convenience."

"Does he? Do you wish me to receive him?"

"Yes, Mama, I would like that very much."

"So be it."

* * * * *

Herr Joseph Lange von Schellenhorst came to Herzberg the following week.

He had first met Elise Catherine almost two years before, at a ball at the royal palace in Berlin. He was immediately taken by the poised, elegant, simply dressed and highly attractive young woman who bore little comparison to the other young women at the soirée with their fussy dresses and powdered hair. They had danced twice together but then she had disappeared from his view for the rest of the evening.

Aged twenty-eight, von Schellenhorst was tall, well-dressed, quietly mannered and softly spoken. A lieutenant in the army, he had become acquainted with the young Prince Frederick William, heir to the Prussian throne, through Count Hans von Blumenthal, owner of the Paretz estate, not far from Berlin, which the young Prince regarded as his home. While on the Grand Tour, which so many of the younger generation undertook, von Schellenhorst had met a suave but remarkably well-informed Englishman, Charles Gray. They had enjoyed each other's company and after parting in Rome had subsequently corresponded about matters of mutual interest. When von Schellenhorst mentioned in a letter that he had met a dazzling young woman, the Countess Elise Catherine von Deppe, in Berlin, he received an early response in which Gray reported his visit to Herzberg, where he had enjoyed lunch with the young Countess Elise and her mother, the English-born Countess Arabella. He urged the young man to pursue the daughter, if he were so inclined, as she came from a remarkably talented family. Gray added that he wished to ensure their future was secure as stability in Europe continued to weaken.

Joseph Lange von Schellenhorst took no immediate steps to do so because of other preoccupations, but some months later he met Elise at another soirée and thereafter at a musical evening at the Hofoper, in the company of her mother, to whom he was introduced. Many attending the event said that mother and daughter had shone like stars in the night sky. The young Joseph was captivated. Over subsequent weeks and months the young officer and the Countess's daughter shared many occasions together. One of the most impressive was a performance of a selection of Bach's *Concertos for Harpsichord and Strings* at Herzberg, with Elise as the harpsichordist. As he watched her, attired in a simple white-and-gold dress with her long hair, usually pinned up, loosely tied behind with a gold ribbon and with her delicate fingers flying across the keyboard, Joseph Lange von Schellenhorst suddenly realised he had fallen deeply in love with this remarkable, strong-willed young woman. More weeks passed as he began delicately to reveal his feelings towards her. Elise at first seemed to pay little attention but almost imperceptibly she let her mask begin to slip. At yet another musical soirée at Herzberg their fingers touched as they sat side by side. A frisson of sexual chemistry flowed through the veins of each. Von Schellenhorst looked at Elise in some apprehension. She said nothing; only smiled. No word was uttered but the meaning of her smile required no explanation.

* * * * *

On Friday morning, the 8th of May, dressed in his uniform, Lieutenant Joseph Lange von Schellenhorst called on the Countess von Deppe. She received him in the library, her favourite room.

"Countess, it is most gracious of you to receive me. I know you are very busy but I much appreciate this opportunity to discuss with you a matter of great personal importance to me."

"Please, Lieutenant, be seated. Would you care for some coffee?"

Von Schellenhorst, obviously nervous about what he was preparing to ask, declined.

"How may I help you, Lieutenant?"

"Countess, I have come to ask you whether I may have your

permission to request your daughter's hand in marriage. I have known her for nearly two years. In recent months my feelings towards her have become unmistakable. I will come to the point. I am deeply in love with her and I have reason to hope that my feelings may be reciprocated. I wish to ask her to become my wife. I hope you will allow me to do so."

"Tell me, Lieutenant, have you any indication of her feelings towards you? Has she given you any sign?"

"Countess, though I am young and inexperienced in the affairs of the heart, when we are together I sense a strengthening bond of mutual appreciation and harmony between us, such a closeness as I have observed between your daughter and the keyboard."

"Lieutenant, what are your prospects?"

"Countess, I believe they are promising. My father owns an estate from which he gives me an annual income. I am not sure how long I will remain in the army. And I am acquainted with the Crown Prince and, as we are becoming good friends, he has asked me to assist him in certain matters at Paretz. While I would be unable, at present, to provide your daughter with the same measure of comfort she enjoys at Herzberg, I am confident that with my modest means I would still be able to make her happy. I would wish, of course, to encourage her to pursue her musical interests, whether at Herzberg with the Camerata or elsewhere. I would not wish to stand in the way of her ambitions in that regard. I hope that what I have said will give you adequate assurance."

"Lieutenant von Schellenhorst, thank you for your response. I welcome your honesty. Let us ask Elise for her opinion."

Arabella rang the bell for the butler and asked Weisser to invite Elise to the library.

"Elise, Lieutenant von Schellenhorst has called on me this morning to ask if I would agree to him putting to you a most personal question. We have discussed the matter and in your presence I wish to tell him that I have no objection. I suggest that you and he walk in the garden and, if there is any outcome I should be aware of, perhaps you would be kind enough to let me know. I will be in the *Spiegelsaal*."

Elise and Joseph Lange von Schellenhorst walked in the garden. They sat on a seat under a large tree where, unknown to them, twenty-three years ago Carl Manfred von Deppe had proposed marriage to Arabella Whitfield. Elise accepted with profound pleasure the Lieutenant's proposal. They walked back towards the house arm in arm.

"Elise – if I may use your name now we are engaged – I am overjoyed that you have agreed to be my wife. Yet I am concerned our new life together will mean you see less of your beloved mother, and she less of her cherished only daughter. With her son also away from home, she will be increasingly alone. It is small compensation but I have described the Countess and her extraordinary qualities to the Crown Prince. He is a painfully shy man but he has said he would like one day to meet her and to hear more of her musical achievements. He has remarked that her bravery following your father's death has been exemplary. The Prince does not enjoy simple social conversation, because of his shyness, but I am sure you and the Countess would put him at ease."

"Lieutenant von Schellenhorst, you may indeed call me Elise if you allow me to call you Joseph. We should not be stuffy or conform to old out-dated social conventions. It is time for new attitudes, as my mother often says. It is important to be openly affectionate and loving to one another."

"My dear Elise, I promise to be so with all my heart and please, from henceforth I am Joseph." He took her hand in his and kissed her.

"Dear Joseph, before we speak to my mother, let me say this. Throughout her life in Prussia, she has selflessly pursued three resolutions. The first was to be a faithful and loving wife to my father. It is clear to all that she was, and he loved her deeply for it. The second was to cherish and nurture her children. She has done that too, for which my brother, Frederick Daniel, whom you will meet soon, and I deeply thank her. We are who we are because of her. All that we have learnt and now practise is a consequcnce of her example and commitment to us. Her third resolution, which she still pursues with all her strength and determination, is to uphold the well-being of Herzberg and its reputation as a source of impressive music for all to appreciate. Underlying all three resolutions is her wish to do well for her adopted home of Prussia. My mother is unshakeably loyal, wary about whom to trust but, once sure, trusting completely, and, while some may envy her achievements and friendships, few despise her and few hate her. She has the kindest and warmest heart. I intend to do all in my power to follow her example, and to continue to support her as much as I can, and I trust, Joseph, that you will honour my wish to do so."

"Dear Elise, you have my promise. Now let us tell the Countess our good news."

As they entered the *Spiegelsaal*, the Countess was playing the first spirited movement of a Bach harpsichord concerto. The news she received made her playing even more spirited. Arabella had achieved what her father had never permitted. She had allowed her daughter to make her own free and informed choice of husband. The next day plans began for the marriage of Elise and Joseph at the Garrison Church in Potsdam.

On Tuesday the 19th of May Arabella, her daughter and Herr Bamberger attended as they had promised a performance of Herr Mozart's opera *Die Entführung aus dem Serail* at the Hofoper in Berlin. The composer conducted and Madame Duschek sang the lead role of Konstanza, whom the hero, Belmonte, attempts to rescue from the seraglio of the Pasha Selim. Arabella and Elise were captivated. Afterwards they bade farewell to the composer, who repeated his determination to return to Berlin within months to persuade Arabella to sing for him in public despite her reluctance to do so.

"We shall see, Herr Mozart, we shall see!"

"Countess, if I cannot secure the King's patronage, I will secure your presence on the stage. So there!"

But Mozart's intentions and the impending marriage of Elise to Lieutenant von Schellenhorst were soon to be overshadowed by disturbing news from Paris.

CHAPTER 8

Revolution in Paris

The Countess Elise Catherine Hildegard von Deppe married Lieutenant Joseph Lange von Schellenhorst at the Garrison Church in Potsdam on Friday the 12th of June, 1789. The next day, at Herzberg, there was a musical soirée to celebrate. A seemingly endless line of carriages arrived, bringing the rich and the famous, the great and the good to an occasion perceived by all as one of notable prestige. There was constant dancing to lively music played by the now much-expanded Herzberger Camerata, still led tirelessly by Herr Bamberger.

Amongst the guests that evening in the *Spiegelsaal* was the shy Crown Prince Frederick William, who had come at the request of his friend Lieutenant von Schellenhorst and with the strong encouragement of Mr Gray, who had also arrived with the Crown Prince. During the musical interval and noticing that the Crown Prince appeared to be finding conversation difficult Arabella invited him to join her in the library, together with Mr Gray, so they could sit for a few minutes in some peace.

"Your Royal Highness, I am greatly honoured that you have come all the way to Herzberg from Paretz to be with us on this special evening. All of us here are deeply touched by your gesture, no more so than my daughter and Lieutenant Joseph Lange von Schellenhorst, her husband."

There was a pause before his reply.

"I am pleased to be here, though these are not occasions I particularly enjoy. Von Schellenhorst is a good companion. I hope he will remain so. I wanted to meet you, Countess. I have had several reports of your musical interests and the hard work you do at Herzberg to ensure it is well maintained. It is indeed a most impressive house. This room is most comfortable, not as large and intimidating as the others. I would like one day to have a room such as this, where I can sit and consider matters in peace. Tell me about the picture on the wall of the two women in uniform."

Arabella smiled.

"His Majesty the late King Frederick sent my late husband, Count von Deppe, to St Petersburg on diplomatic business – in 1767, if I recall the year correctly. I joined him there after a while and became acquainted with the Empress. We would often talk together alone in the evenings, about personal matters, never those of a political nature, I assure you. Sometimes, I would play some Bach to her – at her request. One day she asked me to be her honorary equerry at a parade of the Preobrazhensky Guards, with both of us to be dressed in regimental uniform. I resisted her invitation but she insisted. Following the inspection she asked her court artist to paint this picture of us, discussing the day's events in the intimacy of her private room before we changed back into women's clothes after our male masquerade. She gave me the painting as a parting gift."

"You both look very handsome in uniform, but what an extraordinary thing for the Empress to ask you to do," he replied.

"Thank you, Sir, I am flattered you should think the picture pleasing. Yes, it was an extraordinary thing for her to ask of me. But she was insistent and I decided I had to oblige her. After all, she was Empress of All the Russias and I was her personal guest in the Winter Palace."

"I accept your explanation," the Crown Prince replied in his well-known curt manner of speaking. "I am pleased von Schellenhorst has married your daughter. She is very attractive and most accomplished."

"Just as you are, Countess," interjected Gray.

"Indeed," the Crown Prince added. "The Countess Elise and von Schellenhorst will be most welcome at Paretz. And I hope that one day soon you will come, Countess, and tell me more about Russia and France, which I think you also know well as your mother was French."

"Thank you, Sir. I can see that Mr Gray has informed you well. But then he is well informed about most things. At least that is my impression."

"And mine too," added the Crown Prince.

After an exchange of further pleasantries, the Crown Prince returned to the *Spiegelsaal*. As the Countess followed the young Frederick William, Mr Gray whispered to her.

"I wonder whether I might return to Herzberg tomorrow as I would like us to have a further tête à tête about matters of mutual interest."

Arabella smiled.

"Mr Gray, I see you are persistent. As I said when you last came to Herzberg, I can be neither spy nor informant. So there can be no further discussion of that matter. However, with Elise now married and, with her husband, shortly to leave their temporary lodgings on the estate, I will be alone and ready to be amused by other topics. So I would much enjoy your company tomorrow. We might go for a walk or even ride, if you feel so inclined."

"Countess, we will do whatever takes your fancy. I greatly look forward to your choice."

"Mr Gray, when you return, please, I ask you, do not paint too dark a picture of the affairs of Europe."

"Countess, we will discuss Europe *un petit* because the clouds, which we cannot see tonight, are ever darker in France. I fear that, if a storm breaks, we may all be engulfed. But after that *petit*, Countess, I wish to talk only about you – the beautiful, charming and elegant English countess."

Arabella smiled.

"Mr Gray, flattery of that proportion will not get you far."

"We will see, Countess. We will see."

The evening's entertainment culminated first in Muffat's *Florilegium Secundum* which, although over a hundred years old, allowed elegant dancing similar to the style Arabella and her mother had inspired at Meltwater; and then finally in a rendition of *Forêts paisibles* from Act Four, *Les Sauvages*, of Rameau's *Les Indes galantes*, with everyone in circles of ten moving first clockwise and then anti-clockwise in rhythm with the throbbing beat of the music. Even the shy Crown Prince joined a circle. As the tempo increased, Arabella, joined by Herr Bamberger, with his surprisingly strong baritone voice, sang the lyrics. As the pace became faster and faster, the circles almost seemed to spin in a blur, with the dancers repeating the chorus of each verse. The *Spiegelsaal* had never seen such a scene of joy.

*****

Mr Gray returned late the next morning. He and Arabella rode together; they talked together; and she played Bach to him. He stayed another day and the day after that, with the newly married couple often joining them. A day later, Elise and her husband left for Berlin. For Arabella it was a deeply emotional parting which she found hard to bear. With her son still in Strasbourg, she would now be alone at Herzberg. That evening Charles Gray told her that the next morning he too would have to leave.

"Must you, Mr Gray?" she said.

"Countess, I have been here almost a week enjoying your company. It has been most pleasurable. But I fear I must go. I have to attend to certain matters and you will wish, I am sure, to see me leave. Guests should never outstay their welcome."

"Of course, I understand, but I will miss our lively conversations," said Arabella with a hint of coquettishness in her eyes.

"So will I," he replied.

After supper they went to the *Spiegelsaal* where Arabella played a Bach partita and a Haydn keyboard composition. Neither spoke. Gray sat near, watching her long delicate fingers lightly touching the keys.

"Mr Gray, do you play?" she asked.

"Not well, Countess," he replied.

"Show me," she said with a smile.

He sat beside her on the stool, their two bodies almost touching.

He played skilfully.

"Mr Gray, you should be less shy about your skill on the keyboard. Perhaps you should be just a little lighter on these notes."

As she showed him he suddenly placed his hand gently on hers. She stopped and looked at him as he withdrew it.

"Countess, please forgive me for my impertinence. I apologise for any offence I may have caused you. Please let me explain. The fact of the matter is that I have become deeply attracted to you. It has been the case since I first met you, even more so in recent days. If the truth be known, wherever I am I find it difficult to put you from my mind. You are the most beautiful, most sensuous woman I have ever met. There is no other way to explain it."

He reached for her hand and kissed it softly.

Arabella removed her hand from his and resumed playing, trying hard to conceal her surprise at the boldness of his actions and, even more, the frankness of his words. She sought to collect her thoughts. It was a fact that she enjoyed flirting with men in order to see for her amusement how they would respond. But never before had a man reacted in such a way. She continued to play, though aware he was looking intently at her for any sign of a response to what he had done and equally aware that he knew she was biding her time before replying. Since she had not so far remonstrated with him for his behaviour, he was likely to be thinking that he had not gone too far. For Arabella, the truth was she had indeed been attracted by him. She had found his handsome countenance pleasing from their first encounter, as other women no doubt did judging by the way they had responded to the attention he had given them at the celebration of her daughter's wedding. She had to admit that she enjoyed his company, being close to him. How should she respond to what he had said and done? Should she show she had been affronted? But as she had not responded in such a way the moment he had put his hand on hers, that course of action was no longer plausible. Should she encourage him in his action? If so, what should she say?

As she played, considering what to do, Gray too was reflecting on his actions. Had he gone too far? Should he have apologised and left? But perhaps his judgement had been right. He had struck when she was vulnerable. An older woman she might be but she was still a great beauty with a sensuality and physical magnetism he could not resist.

Arabella ceased playing. She turned to Gray.

"Are you always so bold with women, Mr Gray?"

Her eyes were dark but rich in expression. Encouraged by her response, he again placed his hand on hers.

"With you I am," he replied with a smile.

"That is plain to see," Arabella rejoined.

There was silence as they looked at each other. Then Gray leaned towards her, his eyes fixed on hers. He kissed her cheek. She gave no response. Again he looked at her intently and taking both her hands in his he kissed them. She did not withdraw her hands from his.

"Perhaps, Mr Gray, we should say goodnight."

"Of course," he replied.

They went upstairs, side by side; his hand brushed against hers. They spoke not a word.

*****

Some minutes later, after gently tapping on the door and receiving no response, Charles Gray entered Arabella's bedroom, as magnificent in its splendour as it had been on her first night at Herzberg as Countess Arabella von Deppe. Having closed the door behind him he paused for a moment. A fire burned in the hearth. She stood in front of it gazing into the flames, wearing only a silk slip. As he slowly approached her, she could not believe what she had done. To have disrobed, all but her shift, to await the arrival of a man she wished to make love to her – all on account of him placing his hand on hers. He was handsome, amusing and flirtatious. She had responded coquettishly to his flirtations and for some time had wondered what it would be like to be held by him, to be kissed and caressed by him. But the touch of his soft skin on hers had suddenly aroused her. She desired him. In truth, she wanted him to see her body. She sought to create excitement.

Now he had come. Would what she had done diminish his opinion of her? How would he respond – with callousness, taking her for his own selfish enjoyment, or caringly, bringing her pleasure because he wanted her, while still respecting her, as much as she wanted him? Or might he reject what he saw? After all, she had more than once remarked to herself in the mirror that she was like a glass of water that had been left standing for a long while.

She turned but said nothing as he began to undo the ribbons on her shoulders and let her shift ripple to her feet. He kissed her softly before carrying her to the bed just as her husband had once done. Arabella uttered no word, nor did he.

Lying beside her, Gray fondled her breasts, kissing her as he did so. Bathed in the soft light of the bedside candle, she responded with increasing purpose. He caressed her breasts with his lips before gently running his manicured fingertip down her body, in ever decreasing circles, to her secret part, where he lingered. He kissed her now hardened nipples. She took his finger.

"I need more than this. Make love to me," Arabella said softly.

Gray responded wordlessly. Now locked in his arms beneath his warm slim body, a sudden vicious lust unleashed itself within her, surging forward like a rush of overflowing water. She tried to suppress the mounting tide of irresistible desire but, despite her years of rigid self-imposed chastity, her grip of self-restraint buckled. Her body began to tremble as Gray continued to tease and cajole. She slid slowly towards the edge of the abyss, their bodies locked.

"I don't know what to do. I am in such turmoil," she murmured as she pulled Gray ever more deeply into her. "I don't know what to do."

Gray whispered, "Yes you do. Let go. Don't hold back. Let go. It is what your body wants so much."

As Gray uttered those words, her final defence crumbled. Her body shook as she fell into the dazzling void, succumbing to the triumph of her earthly desire. She spiralled downwards like a leaf in a gust of wind into a vortex of pleasure. She cried out in an ecstasy of pain. Her heartache, the sadness long present in the deepest recesses of her being, was suddenly extinguished.

"Hold me, please don't let me go," she whispered to him.

"I won't – ever," he whispered back.

Gray looked at the woman facing him, clutching his hand while he caressed her skin. He had bedded many women but the Countess was different. She was clever, deeply sensuous and expressive, and had revealed confident sexual enticement and accomplishment in their intimacy. Her body was slim and her breasts still sculptured and firm. And then there was her radiant natural beauty. Though an older woman – and he had made love to no few – she was not faded.

As she gazed at the younger man who had just made love to her, Arabella acquiesced to the likelihood that she was no doubt just one of his innumerable conquests. But perhaps she had shown him she was unlike other women whose beds he had shared. He might not know that she had learnt the art of provocative lovemaking in London's demi-monde. Or maybe he did know but, as the most discreet of men engaged in spycraft, he chose to remain silent in order to enjoy the fruit he had just picked. She kissed him and ran her fingers across his cheek. They lay together without speaking. It was Arabella who broke the silence.

"Mr Gray, again," she said.

"Perhaps you would like this," he enquired.

With her willing compliance he blindfolded her. Lying beside her, he took her index finger and, after dipping its tip in the glass of water beside the bed, he guided it to her mouth and within. Then it softly traced the shape of her neck and, as commanded by his hand, followed the contour of each breast, the tip of each nipple. Her finger, now joined with his, slowly explored every ridge and dip of her body as it rose and fell with each agitated breath she took. She remembered, beneath her silk blindfold, reminiscent of the mask she had once worn to conceal her identity, what she – as Antoinette Badeau – had done long ago at Chesterfield Street. As their entwined fingers explored ever deeper, the fear and loathing of the demi-monde had gone, replaced by erotic, indeed profane pleasure at what Gray was doing. Again and again their locked fingers teased the ever-mounting physical expectations of her body – so near and then withdrawal.

"Let me come. Please let me come," she pleaded.

He pulled her to him, this time placing her astride him, her breasts cupped and fondled in his hands. He slipped into her and again she was overwhelmed by her lust. She slowly sank into his arms, his hands lost in her rich dark hair.

"Let me remove your blindfold."

"Not yet, Mr Gray, not yet," she whispered. "Though I want so much to see your face I want for a minute or so longer to enjoy being a blind captive of your wickedness."

They kissed.

"Mr Gray, you wicked Mr Gray, what have you done to me?" she murmured as she lay on him, locked in his arms.

"Countess, I have seduced you," he replied.

"Mr Gray, you have indeed. What would people say if they only knew?"

"They will not know from me. As for you, Countess, our secret is yours to keep or reveal."

"It will remain my secret, along with the many other unspoken secrets that I have never revealed," Arabella replied.

"And so it will be with me, except in one regard," he answered.

"And what is that, Mr Gray?"

"Your beauty, your appeal to men is plain for all to see. That is no secret. But what I have seen and done beneath your slip is beyond any man's expectation. What you have revealed there will be my secret."

"I am flattered, Mr Gray. But I have a question."

"And what is that, Countess?"

"Would you seek me as your mistress, if that office is not already occupied by another, or merely *une liaison temporaire*?"

"Countess, neither is a term I would use in the situation in which we find ourselves. But I would be flattered if you were to regard me as your lover – that is, of course, if you wished me to fill that particular office for you."

"Mr Gray, we will see what may happen. You may now give me back my sight."

They kissed again.

Arabella woke the next morning, alone in her bed, soon remembering the night before. Her body felt cleansed, renewed by the physical intimacy she had shared. For the first time in many years she had allowed her body to be entered – and by a man younger than her. She had fallen from her pedestal of rectitude and sexual repression. Should she be ashamed of what she had done, breaking her vow of chastity to the memory of Carl Manfred? But that thought did not linger long. She could not be chaste for the rest of her life. She did not feel tarnished; she felt no regret; she would not care what people might say if they knew what she had done. She wanted physical love in her remaining years from someone who would cherish and respect her.

Charles Gray did not leave that morning as he had planned. In the immediate days that followed, Arabella spent each night in the arms of her lover, each night more erotic and uninhibited than the one before. But suddenly one morning he was gone. On her dressing table she found a note, tied in blue ribbon, in which was written:

Shall I compare thee to a summer's day?
Thou art more lovely and more temperate:
Rough winds do shake the darling buds of May,
And summer's lease hath all too short a date:
Sometime too hot the eye of heaven shines,
And often is his gold complexion dimmed;
And every fair from fair sometime declines,
By chance, or nature's changing course, untrimmed;
But thy eternal summer shall not fade,
Nor lose possession of that fair thou ow'st,
Nor shall Death brag thou wander'st in his shade,
When in eternal lines to time thou grow'st;
So long as men can breathe or eyes can see,
So long lives this, and this gives life to thee.

Only Mr Shakespeare can express my love for you, oh beautiful Countess.
I will return once I have attended to pressing business.
CG

The suddenness of his departure seemed to be like that of Theseus leaving his beloved Ariadne to wake up alone and abandoned.

During the following days, and nights, she greatly missed Gray, his embrace, the way he provoked her lust. Just what had he done to her? In bed with her lover she had indulged in shameless eroticism that had once been second nature to her, as a high-class courtesan in Chesterfield Street – a sexual abandon she thought she had ceased long ago. By day she masqueraded behind her elegant aristocratic exterior – untouchable, much respected, standing on her pedestal of modesty admired by all. But as she lay in bed, unable to sleep, longing for Gray to return, she asked herself again and again who the real Arabella was. Was it the dark, wilful sexual predator within her that had been suppressed for so long but was now released, only to become trapped in a vortex of sexual desire fanned by the provocative Charles Gray? Or had she in truth become a victim, like the beautiful Andromeda, stripped and chained naked to a rock to sate the monster that was Gray? What was she to do? Should she surrender her principles, acquiesce to the monster's demands and so become his possession? Or should she resist the monster and remain a prisoner like Andromeda, unable to escape her chains until freed by Perseus? If it were to be the latter, what chance was there that Charles Gray would transmogrify into a different shape to become the hero? Whatever the answer, their affair – with all of its sexual profanity, if that were not too strong a term to describe the circumstances – had opened a Pandora's box of unquenchable atavism.

Then in early August came disturbing and distracting news from Paris, brought by an unexpected messenger.

* * * * *

In the earlier months of 1789 Arabella had received few letters from Maria Louisa in France.

At the beginning of the year she had written about the freezing weather in Paris, the rise in bread prices and increasing allegations of a conspiracy by the nobles to withhold flour from the hungry. In the spring, another letter reported that, while the weather in Paris had improved, the mood amongst the poor continued to worsen – becoming more hostile as each week passed, inflamed by the growing torrent of untruths from the *libellistes* using their pamphlets and posters to pour yet more poison into the swollen lake of royalist denunciation.

A further disturbing letter, written in obvious haste in early May, spoke of a riot late the previous month, sparked by the decision of a wallpaper maker to cut wages at a time of further exorbitant increases in the price of food. According to her sister-in-law's account, some three hundred people had been killed. The steadily deteriorating situation had led to the first meeting of the Estates-General in 175 years. The letter ended with Maria Louisa's decision to leave Paris to join her husband, Etienne, at Versailles, together with her daughter, Marie-Aurore, her son-in-law, Comte Armand de Puyraveau, and their young son, Antoine. Arabella knew that Maria Louisa had long resisted living at Versailles, a vast sprawling palace open to the public with little privacy for the court and most unsanitary living conditions. That she had decided to move there from her comfortable Paris residence was worrying. Since then there had been no further letters, but Arabella received some unsubstantiated reports from visitors to Herzberg of yet more unrest in Paris and even deeper hostility towards King Louis and Queen Marie-Antoinette. These added credence to Gray's earlier opinion of a worsening situation in France, with possible consequences beyond its borders. However, in one or two eventual brief communications from Versailles, Maria Louisa still seemed optimistic that the storm would soon blow itself out, once common sense prevailed and the King had taken decisive practical action to show that he really cared for the people of his kingdom.

"Madame, there is a visitor to see you," said Weisser.

"Did he give a name?" she asked.

"No, Madame, but you will recognise him."

"Please show him in at once."

Arabella stood by the fireplace in the library in anticipation. Her lover had returned.

The visitor entered. It was not Charles Gray but Waldemar Drescher.

Drescher had much aged since Arabella last saw him in 1786. But, though he was stooped, gaunt and his long hair was cut short, she still recognised the strong fierce-looking man with piercing eyes she had first met in 1765 on her flight from England. He took her hand and bowed to kiss it.

"Herr Drescher, what an unexpected pleasure to see you," she said. "I thought you had disappeared from my life never to be seen again. Where have you been for the past three years?"

"Dear Countess, I have wandered Europe like a gypsy – listening, observing, noting and enjoying the company of a few as fancy took me. But old age caught up with me and I decided that as I approached the final years of my life it would be both apt and right to return to France to witness the twilight of a regime, and to consider its possible repercussions for our country, which I still continue to hold dear despite the neglect from which it suffers at present. I wished to see – as a bystander – whether my fears had been borne out. So for the past months I have been in Paris, watching the gradual collapse of the French state. Countess, I wish to inform you that France is unravelling and if it continues to do so it will have, in my humble opinion, catastrophic consequences for us all. I decided that if our indolent King would not listen you would. While there is little that you or I can do in the face of present events, the preservation of Herzberg and, more importantly, your own well-being are uppermost in my mind. It is for that reason that I have returned to bring you this news and to urge you to be vigilant and to take certain steps."

"What has caused you to reach your conclusion that France is doomed?" asked Arabella. "Earlier this year," she added, "I received letters from the Vicomtesse de Vervins. She said conditions were hard, causing her concern, but I have received no recent reports that would suggest I should have deeper disquiet. Herr Drescher, tell me, what are the events to which you allude?"

"Countess, there were serious riots in Paris on the 12th and 13th of this month. The following day the Bastille fortress was stormed by crowds of protestors looking for weapons and gunpowder. Nearly one hundred people were killed and many injured. Paris is now lawless. The country is starving. The King and Queen are isolated in their palace at Versailles, their enemies multiplying by the day. Some nobles have fled France, while others have stayed with the King. The Vicomte and Vicomtesse de Vervins, and their daughter, the Comtesse de Puyraveau, her husband and their son, are amongst those remaining at the side of the King and Queen. It is hard to see where this mutinous situation will lead."

Already surprised by his sudden reappearance, Arabella was shaken by Drescher's account. Preoccupied with her daughter's future and the affairs of the Camerata, and then diverted by Charles Gray, she had allowed herself to forget the world beyond the boundaries of Herzberg. Her distress was evident to him.

"Madame, please do not chastise yourself for not being aware of what I have told you. Recent events have fallen upon us all with extraordinary speed. I urge you not to regret but to authorise me to take urgent action."

"What action is that, Herr Drescher?"

"Countess, the contagion in Paris is spreading beyond the city. The first step must be to ensure the safety of your son, Count von Deppe. As the disaffection and lawlessness sweep quickly through

France like a heath on fire it is important that he brings his stay in Strasbourg to an abrupt end. I believe he has been there for three years or perhaps longer. It is an agreeable city and, though under French ownership, our young have always found it a most desirable place in which to live, to study and to have fun as Herr Goethe once recommended. But hatred of the Austrian-born Queen Marie Antoinette may soon cause no distinction to be made between German and Austrian neighbours. It is my strong advice to you that he must return quickly to Prussia, where he will be safe. May I have your leave to travel will all speed, taking a message from you requiring him to return to Herzberg without delay?"

For a moment Arabella said nothing. Then she answered.

"Herr Drescher, you have always spoken the truth to me, even though I have never penetrated the inner recesses of your mind. You have always advised and protected me well. My son and daughter are deeply precious to me. I would like both of them near to me at this time. You have my authority to go to Strasbourg to urge him to return. Perhaps I should come with you?"

"Countess, I ask you please to stay at Herzberg. Nothing will be gained if you come. If the situation in France deteriorates further, we may have to take other steps. Please remain here and prepare Herzberg for further blows."

"But Herr Drescher, Frederick Daniel is my son –"

Drescher interrupted Arabella before she could complete her sentence.

"Madame, your son is almost twenty-two years old, surrounded by friends of his own age. He would not want a tearful mother on his doorstep. Please, I beg you, leave this matter to me if you confirm that you wish me to act as I have recommended."

Arabella visibly smarted at his response but knew Drescher was right.

"Herr Drescher, please go to Strasbourg with all haste and bring my son home. You go with my trust."

"Thank you, Countess. I will not fail you."

He waited while Arabella wrote a letter to Frederick Daniel. After she had sealed it, Drescher took his leave of her. Hauling his aching bones into the saddle he left Herzberg and was soon on his way to the French border.

Arabella sat alone afterwards in the library. As dusk fell she stood by the window looking out across the garden towards the tree where she and Carl Manfred had once sat twenty-three years ago, pledging their love for one another. He was gone; Elise Catherine had married and left Herzberg with her new husband; and gone too was Charles Gray, who had given her such warm physical intimacy only weeks before. The remaining sunlight disappeared into the grey sky and then nightfall. A profound unease filled Arabella.

* * * * *

It took Drescher longer than he had planned to reach the French border – he lacked the agility and strength of past years – and then he had to overcome difficulties in crossing the River Rhine. He finally entered Strasbourg, dominated by its famous cathedral, on Monday the 24th of August. For long in the past a German city, Strasbourg had been in French hands since 1678. Despite over a hundred years of French occupation, however, its language and roots remained strongly Germanic, particularly in its Lutheran university. Drescher recalled as he walked the streets that it had been here that the young German Johann Wolfgang von Goethe and his philosopher friend, Johann Gottfried Herder, had advocated the unique passion and expression of the German language, claiming that French education had deformed and misguided German minds, an opinion with which Drescher strongly agreed.

The city was swirling with activity, gossip and open criticism of the monarchy, fed by the arrival of frequent reports of mounting disaffection in Paris and in the provinces. Vigilante groups of *patriotes*, wearing the tricolour cockade, had begun to appear, formed to seek out nobles trying to escape from France, allegedly in their efforts to spirit away money. The rallying cry was that the King and Queen and those around them had stolen from the French people.

After recovering from the journey, Drescher soon established the whereabouts of the young Count Frederick Daniel von Deppe. He first spotted him on Tuesday the 1st of September in a tavern, mingling with students and young revolutionary activists debating the latest events in France. Tall, with light-brown hair and good-looking like his late father, he was the centre of attention as he argued the case for reform of out-of-date institutions and the lessons such reform might offer not only for France but more widely in Europe, including Prussia. Von Deppe spoke with fluency and passion. The debate lasted several hours. Drescher watched from the shadows. Late at night the debaters said farewell to one another and gradually drifted away into the night, in twos or threes or alone, as Frederick Daniel did. Drescher followed him.

Becoming aware of the closing footsteps at his back, Frederick turned to confront the figure nearly upon him.

"What do you want? If it's money, I have none."

"It's not your money I want but your attention," replied Drescher curtly. "I have in my pocket a letter from the Countess von Deppe, your mother. She asked me to deliver it personally to you."

"Who are you? What is your name? If it is a game you wish to play, I will not comply," responded Frederick Daniel.

"Count von Deppe, this is no game. I know exactly you are."

"I don't recall ever seeing you before," stammered the young man.

"There is no reason why you should. But I have watched you grow up. Now I bring a letter from your mother, with whom I have been acquainted for many years and before that with your late father. I have not ridden all the way from Herzberg to amuse you or to steal whatever meagre possessions you might have. I want to give you the Countess's letter and to answer any questions you might have. I suggest that we go into the tavern across the road so I can give it to you without further delay. Time is against us. So let's get on with it."

Frederick Daniel was taken aback by the sharp response of the unknown man. Though he was much older and possibly no physical match, there was something menacing about him. He decided to obey.

* * * * *

They sat down facing one other across the tavern table, each with a jar of wine. Drescher pulled the letter from his coat pocket and pushed it across the table. Frederick immediately recognised the distinctive Herzberg seal and the way his name had been written. It was his mother's handwriting. He broke the seal and read the letter.

Dear Frederick,

The bearer of my letter is Herr Waldemar Drescher. A most close confidant to the late King Frederick and a respected acquaintance of your father, he has twice saved me from the profound malevolence of others. For that reason, he has earned my trust and accordingly I asked him to deliver this message to you by hand.

It is now some three years since you left Herzberg for Strasbourg. I have greatly enjoyed reading your letters about what you have studied, the friendships you have made, including with Herr Goethe, and your refreshing views on the rule of law, freedom of speech, history and philosophy. Those of my sex greatly envy the independence of thought that a university education bestows upon young men. I continue to pray that one day women will be similarly able to study in institutions of learning.

As Herr Drescher will elaborate, the news from Paris is deeply disturbing. The Vicomte and Vicomtesse de Vervins, their daughter, Marie-Aurore, her child and her husband, the Comte de Puyraveau, are restrained at the Palace of Versailles by the daily crowds of protestors besieging the throne. While the King and Queen may in some measure have contributed by their past actions to the ruin of royal authority, some of the vile insults against their name may not have been justly earned. The fate of France now hangs by a more slender thread. If the monarchy were to collapse and a new tyranny of rule by the mob were to emerge in its ruins, I fear the consequences may quickly spread far beyond the borders of France. Prussia would not be immune if there were such an outcome.

I ask you to return to Prussia without delay, to help me prepare for the defence of the principles of freedom and tolerance that the late King applied during his reign and to which I continue to adhere. But even more may be necessary to defend Herzberg and Prussia. If you were able to fulfil my wish, my heart would be deeply gladdened that I would also see you again after such a long absence.

Your loving mother,
Arabella
Schloss Herzberg, Thursday the 6th of August, 1789

Frederick Daniel put down the letter. He was about to speak when Drescher forestalled him.

"The Countess is remarkable and brave. She has given Herzberg an enviable reputation because of her widely respected stewardship of the estate since your father's death and the unquestionable success of the Camerata she founded with the encouragement of the late King. Though of English birth she has for over twenty years dedicated herself unselfishly to Prussia. The late Count loved her deeply and admired her commitment to her new country. His early death was a devastating blow to her but she has persevered. Now testing times lie ahead for all of us. Unless we are well prepared, Prussia will suffer in due course. I too urge you to return. You are done with Strasbourg."

Frederick looked once again at the letter and then at Drescher before replying, carefully picking his words.

"Herr Drescher, I too deeply respect my mother and what she has achieved for my sister and me, for Herzberg and for Prussia. But I am not sure I share her opinions about the adverse meaning of present events. The turmoil in Paris and the intention of the Assembly to place limits on King Louis's conduct are surely to be welcomed after years of tyranny. For too long the French people have been sorely taxed and misused. That has to end and a new constitution prepared with new freedoms put into place. If the English can do it, surely the people of France can do so as well. We should not allow these noble aims to be thwarted. You may think that a simplistic view but it is one I hold nonetheless. I believe in the better side of human nature and the dignity of man. I do not believe I am threatened in this city. I see no reason to leave yet."

Drescher replied with characteristic bluntness.

"Count von Deppe, it is indeed desirable to pursue noble aims. But too often such aims, however noble, do not combine well with the dark side of human nature and the selfishness of mankind. Was it not the English philosopher Thomas Hobbes who wrote that without strong government the life of man would be 'nasty, brutish and short', and that to avoid the inevitable consequences of such a condition man should surrender his right of self-determination to a superior authority? It is always difficult to make comparisons but our late King Frederick tried hard to strike a balance. While not perfect, he achieved a strong and improving State, which met with the general satisfaction of those living within its borders. They enjoyed freedoms based on tolerance of one another.

"By contrast, the kingdom of France has been governed by a blinkered autocracy with an ever-widening separation between the governed and those who govern. King Louis and his father before him failed to see the deadly disaffection, born out of extreme poverty, spreading beneath the veneer of apparent resignation to what life had to offer. That veneer has now been stripped away by recent events, revealing the rot beneath. The more the rot is exposed the more the demands of those wanting a more satisfactory structure will be drowned out by the greater clamour of those bent on revenge and insurrection. Their numbers multiply by the day. Tomorrow may be quiet in this city but I have no doubt that within its secret places plotting has already begun. The throne of France will fall before long, to be replaced by the rule of the mob and an ensuing bloodbath, not just in Paris but throughout the country. Who will talk of noble aims then? Who will speak of tolerance then? And it will not stop there – for history tells us that from chaos there always emerges a new tyrant with ambitions for repression and territorial acquisition. So it will be with France. Some monster will fight his way to the pinnacle of the pyramid and once in place will cast an eye beyond the borders of France. Prussia will once again be confronted by the strutting French *coq* that just over a hundred years ago stole this city from us. Once upon a time I observed the result of national weakness from the shadows, from where I schemed for many years to bring down the King's enemies. I assure you that in this imperfect world there are few friends but a multitude of foes.

"So, Count von Deppe, we stand on the edge of the abyss. A peaceful and gradual revolution, for which I have heard you argue, will never happen. Instead we must suffer and then overcome the consequences of this present upheaval. It is therefore important that you return to Prussia in good haste to help protect what we have from this contagious French infection. And remember, much of the disaffection in Paris is driven by hatred of the Queen. It is inevitable that in any bloodshed no distinction will be drawn between us and those damn Austrians. I regret to be so blunt – bloodcurdling, you might say – but the time has come to be so. Repay the kindness of your mother by putting her mind at rest. Don't be selfish. Put her first."

Frederick Daniel bridled at this last remark but held his tongue. The old man's piercing eyes revealed a cunning and coldness that made him shiver. If this man had saved his mother twice, then perhaps his judgement should be respected, even though he did not accept the premise of Drescher's rebuttal of his opinions.

"Herr Drescher, I will not quarrel with your opinion at this late hour, nor question the high esteem in which my mother holds you. Whatever may be the outcome of the present disaffection, I am a true Prussian and as proud of my country as you. So I agree – albeit reluctantly – that to satisfy my mother's wishes we should leave France as soon as I have put my affairs in order."

"And when will that be?" asked Drescher.

"The day after tomorrow," replied Frederick Daniel. "I have lodgings at Stissen, not far from the city. I need to pack and say farewell to friends."

"So be it," said Drescher. "But be discreet in what you say to your friends. Do not tell them you are returning to Prussia. And take not a day longer or else the noose may tighten. I will meet you at the tavern Au Petit Bois Vert on the Quai de la Bruche at five o'clock in the afternoon the day after tomorrow. We will try to cross the River Ill and the Rhine later that evening."

"I will be there," Frederick Daniel replied.

He did not know that the cunning Drescher would follow and from the shadows closely observe him to make sure he kept to his promise.

The following evening, the 2nd of September, Frederick Daniel met his friend Robert Trudaine.

"Robert, tomorrow I must leave Strasbourg. I hope to return soon, once the present situation has calmed. You must take care while I am gone. How can I keep in contact with you?"

"I cannot believe you are leaving France, that you're going back to Prussia, that you are leaving us for good. I can see it in your face. I thought you intended to stay to see the outcome of the revolution for better or worse. Tell me the truth, please, friend to friend. Why are you suddenly leaving France?"

"My mother has written, asking me to return home," said Frederick Daniel. "She is worried about the precarious state of this country and the possible consequences for Prussia if there is a general war. I cannot leave her alone."

"Your opinion has suddenly altered. What information have you received to cause your change of mind? What information does your mother have?" Trudaine demanded. "If you are going, something must have happened to cause you to leave so abruptly. Until yesterday you were convinced moderation would prevail in Paris. My parents in Reims are concerned about the rule of the mob – they are landowners – and the shortage of food. Even in Strasbourg stocks are running low. Frederick, I repeat, why is it you are going when yesterday you were confident of a good and rational outcome?"

"I am not fleeing, Robert. I have received a letter from my mother by the hand of a messenger. It is clear that I must return to Prussia without delay."

"I wish to cross the border with you. If you go, I will go."

"No, you should stay in Strasbourg. Nothing will happen to you."

"Frederick, please take me with you. I beg you."

Frederick Daniel paused. Trudaine was one of his closest friends. He could not leave him.

"I will see what I can do," he replied.

"I will take that as yes."

The young Count von Deppe returned to his lodgings to pack a few belongings into a leather satchel. An hour or so later there was a single knock on his room door.

"Who is that?"

"It is I, your escort." Drescher entered. "I think you have something to tell me."

"Yes, I do. But how did you know?"

"It is my business to seek out all information that concerns me," replied Drescher.

"My friend, Monsieur Trudaine, knows I am leaving Strasbourg tomorrow. He wishes to accompany us. I ask you to agree," urged Frederick.

"You told him, didn't you? I told you not to do so. Who else might he tell?" said Drescher, fixing Frederick with his cold piercing eyes.

"I trust my friend. He will not tell others."

"You did not do well," replied Drescher.

Frederick Daniel looked uncomfortable.

"I told you explicitly to keep our departure secret. Strasbourg is full of informers and valuable information is worth money. Tell me about Trudaine."

Frederick Daniel explained that he was the son of a wealthy landed family near Reims. They had become close friends at the university in Strasbourg. Trudaine was worried by the reports from his family of the deteriorating situation – the diminishing supply of food and increasing civil disobedience.

"I want to meet him. Please bring him here – now – so I can judge for myself whether we should take him."

Within the hour Trudaine appeared. He was a handsome young man with fine-cut features, elegantly dressed and with delicate mannerisms. The three talked for a while. Then Drescher delivered his verdict.

"Monsieur Trudaine, you may come with us. Bring no baggage, only a few light personal items in your pockets. The *patriotes*' vigilance on the border is increasing by the day as their search for escaping courtiers intensifies. No one is safe. So we will need to move with stealth, not weighed down by luggage."

"*Merci*, Monsieur . . . I am afraid I do not know your name."

"You do not need to know my name. The less you know the better. I have decided that our meeting place tomorrow night should change. We will now meet in the cathedral at six o'clock, mingling with those attending Mass. Both of you should sit in the tenth pew on the left-hand side of the nave. Dress simply to avoid drawing attention to yourselves. You will receive a signal from me when to move. Now, Monsieur Trudaine, be gone."

Robert Trudaine left hurriedly.

"Count von Deppe, please, no more additions."

"You have my word, Herr Drescher. Why did you decide to let him come with us?"

"I can smell traitors. But he had a good smell."

The following evening, Thursday the 3rd of September, there was a large, noisy and seditious crowd outside the cathedral, with the tricolour cockade widely worn; the chants reflected the latest news from Paris of further riots and demonstrations. The mood in Strasbourg had suddenly become more menacing and less good-natured than in previous days. Many of the demonstrators were drunk, calling for the arrest of the King and Queen, for them to be put on trial for their crimes. Frederick Daniel began to realise that Drescher was right: it was time to leave.

He took his place in the tenth pew on the left-hand side of the nave, as instructed. Drescher, unshaven, looking dishevelled in old clothes and wearing a cockade in a battered hat, sat two pews further back, watching for the arrival of Trudaine. The young man, who reminded him of the young Crown Prince Frederick, arrived, dressed in a shabby coat with a leather satchel slung over his shoulder. Both von Deppe and Trudaine knelt to pray. Within minutes a second young man and a young woman entered the same pew and sat next to Trudaine, who turned to them in recognition. They too knelt, but it was evident that the four were conversing with one another rather than praying. Drescher realised that instead of two people in his care there could now be four. He left his place in the eighth pew and sat beside von Deppe, who did not recognise him.

"Who is sitting beside Trudaine?" Drescher whispered.

Frederick Daniel was startled but after a moment identified Drescher by his eyes.

"Mademoiselle Jacqueline d'Anville, a friend of Trudaine's. She is the daughter of the Comte and Comtesse d'Anville. The other is Monsieur Jean-Marie de Vancy, son of the Comte and Comtesse de Vancy and also a friend of Trudaine's. Both families have been arrested. In the mêlée at the place where they were being held Mademoiselle d'Anville and Monsieur de Vancy managed to escape. They made their way to Villedom, where Trudaine has lodgings, and sought refuge with him. They believe they are being pursued."

"Von Deppe, I came to take you back to Prussia alone. I agreed to one extra. Now our party has grown to four. As the number increases, so does the risk to our safety."

"Herr Drescher, I agree with your opinion. We should leave. But we cannot leave Trudaine's companions to the mercy of the *patriotes*."

"So speaks the man who a few days ago was arguing in favour of revolution. Now you see first hand the consequences of fear and misplaced ambitions. Tell Trudaine that after the Mass is ended his two friends should follow him, not too closely, to number 31 rue des Charpentiers. He, Trudaine, should walk in your footsteps at a suitable distance and you in mine, to avoid any suspicion. I will observe if any of you are followed. On arrival at the rue des Charpentiers knock three times in quick succession. The door will open. We will leave immediately from the rear of the house in the direction of the *les ponts couverts*. If I smell any whiff of treachery from the girl and her companion, I will kill them. Do you understand?"

"Yes," whispered Frederick Daniel.

"Good, now pray hard that we will cross the Rhine tonight in safety."

*****

The four made their way to number 31 rue des Charpentiers. An elderly woman, tightly wrapped in a badly stained shawl to which was pinned a tattered tricolour cockade, answered the door as each of them knocked. Without saying a word she led them to a small back room lit by a single candle. Drescher was already sitting at a table. His gaunt face, coated in stubble, highlighted his strong pale-blue eyes which seemed to dance with exhilaration in the light of the lantern on the table. Once all had assembled in the room, he issued instructions.

"Listen carefully, as there is no time to repeat what I am going to say."

He looked at the four – von Deppe's strong, handsome, chiselled features, revealing no sign of fear but an intentness his mother had often displayed; Trudaine's fine almost feminine face, betraying perhaps a hint of apprehension; de Vancy, in his early twenties, maybe, with puffy features already suggesting early signs of corpulence from dissolute living and with it a touch of arrogance often found in the *noblesse de robe* at Versailles; and the girl, Jacqueline d'Anville, possibly aged seventeen or eighteen, a beauty with wild hair, translucent skin and large eyes full of terror at what lay ahead. He saw von Deppe cast surreptitious glances at her.

"In a few moments we will leave through the door behind me out into the night and a narrow alley. It will lead into another alley and yet another and another. Each alley will lead us towards the covered bridges. The alleys will be slippery from human waste. Don't look to avoid excrement. Just walk. There must be no talking, no whispering. My lantern will be covered to minimise the risk of anyone seeing us. I will go first, followed by you" – pointing to von Deppe – "then the mademoiselle, followed by you" – this time pointing at de Vancy – "with the monsieur" – looking at Trudaine – "at the rear. Once outside the door, we will pause for a moment so you can adjust to the dark. At the side of the bridge we are making for is an even narrower passageway. That will lead to a door and a further passageway down to the level of the river. There we will board a small boat and drift down the Ill until we reach the Rhine. Then we will attempt to cross it. It is a large and swift-running river so you must sit still. Any movement and the boat will capsize and we will all drown. You and you" – pointing at von Deppe and Trudaine – "will help with the rowing. Throughout you must keep silent. If I discover any of you seeking to alert the *patriotes* I will kill you."

"What about the old woman next door?" asked Frederick Daniel. "Won't she give us away?"

"She is one of us," Drescher replied. "Now we must go."

After covering his lantern with a scrap of greasy sailcloth, he opened the door and stepped out into the alley. The four fugitives followed. Drescher began to walk quickly, with the lantern in his left hand and his right hand already poised to reach inside his long shabby coat for his narrow-bladed knife. The others dutifully followed in the prescribed order. After walking for several minutes down numerous dark alleys, each seemingly darker than the one before, and splashing through puddles of waste, they reached the narrow passage close to the *les ponts couverts*. They could hear voices nearby and raucous singing. Almost at the end of the passageway, with the riverbank just around the corner, Drescher took a key from his coat pocket and opened a wooden door. Once all were inside he relocked the door and uncovered his lantern. At their feet was a narrow stairway covered in slime. Below in the darkness they could hear the sound of water.

"At the bottom of these steps is a further short flight leading to our boat. Hold tightly to the chain on the wall as you descend. Tread slowly and no talking. And keep to the same order as before."

Just then some voices passed the other side of the locked door.

"Did you hear, fellow *patriote*? They have just strung up another of those fat pigs from Versailles. He was caught with his wife, some comtesse or another, trying to make their way to Switzerland. In their baggage they had several bags of money and jewellery. The Committee are going to share it out tomorrow. As for the Comtesse, they have put her to work in the wash house. That will help equality."

The other voices cheered and laughed. The four behind the door shuddered, the girl's face frozen in fear.

"Monsieur," whispered Trudaine, "thank you for your act of mercy." He tried to embrace Drescher but the latter pushed him back.

"Concentrate on what you are doing, man! We are far from safety yet, so don't tempt fate."

One by one the fugitives followed Drescher down the steps that brought them to a stone platform set within an arch of brick. He re-covered his lantern. The smell of fresh air and the sight of stars in the sky above the high stone river embankment opposite brought a moment of relief. Drescher pointed to the even narrower flight of steps below. Holding on to the slimy chain he descended slowly and then, with one foot on the edge of the gunwale and the other on a narrow ledge, he stabilised the boat as one after another the four boarded and sat down two abreast. No one spoke a word. Once all were seated, Drescher loosened the painter and the small boat began to drift noiselessly downstream. At the stern he used an oar to guide the boat and to make sure it did not strike the balustrade of *les ponts couverts*. No one spoke; each fugitive sat motionless, hardly daring to breathe. The only sounds were the occasional swish of the oar and voices from the riverbank above, interspersed with more distant cries for revenge against the criminals of Versailles and occasional gunshots. Jacqueline d'Anville, her hands clasped tightly, was trembling. Frederick Daniel placed his hand on hers and gave her a comforting smile. De Vancy saw what he had done and attempted to speak but von Deppe put his finger to his lips and then slid it across his throat.

Gradually the sounds of the city faded and the river widened. Soon they would be at the mouth of the Ill and out into the Rhine.

A few minutes later, as the small boat cleared a bend in the riverbank, a lantern appeared and a voice called out.

"Who goes there?"

Drescher whispered to his passengers.

"Leave this to me."

"I said who goes there?"

Drescher shouted his reply in coarse French.

"While you celebrate I'm trying to catch some fish to feed my children. I will be back at dawn and give you some."

Another voice called out.

"Come here. I want to see your permit. No one is allowed to fish at night. Come here at once!"

"I can't hear you," Drescher shouted back. "I'll return at dawn. See you then!"

Two or three lanterns moved to and fro along the riverbank but there were no more shouts. Drescher uncovered his lantern.

"In a few minutes we will move out into the Rhine. You three men should pick up the oars at your feet and get ready to row on my command."

Just then Drescher became aware of a sailing boat behind them and moving closer. He covered his lantern again and ordered the men to row hard. But before long the sailing boat caught up and prepared to move alongside. Drescher counted two lanterns and three shadows. He whispered to his "crew" to cease rowing and to crouch low in the hull.

As the sailing boat came closer, a dark figure holding a lantern called out.

"When I say come, you come! I want to see your papers."

A grappling hook at the end of a rope landed in the boat, hitting de Vancy. As it was pulled it dragged its sharp points across his back, causing him to cry out in pain.

Only a few feet separated the two boats. Then the voice called out again.

"Hey, Bertin, this is no fishing boat. It's a bunch of aristocrat pigs trying to escape."

Bertin, a larger figure, came up to the side.

"Some catch for the hangman and a woman amongst them. She

will be a fine addition to the brothel."

The two boats were now side by side.

De Vancy was still in pain from the grappling hook. Drescher pretended to be similarly injured.

"Auguste, step into the boat and secure the line. Then throw the two injured overboard."

The man called Auguste stepped into the small boat and as he did so it dipped, causing him to lose his balance and drop his lantern in the water. In a second Drescher rose and plunged his knife into the man's back. The other man, Bertin, pulled a pistol and fired into the rowing boat, aiming at Drescher. But the boat was still rocking and he missed. Drescher drew his pistol from his coat and in a second fired it. Bertin fell to the deck. His body rolled until it was resting lifelessly across the narrow gap between the two boats.

"Von Deppe, hold the line and keep everyone low."

Drescher jumped into the sailing boat to find the third figure he had seen. He could smell his quarry and found him crouched in the wheelhouse.

"Get up!" shouted Drescher.

As the man did so, he fired a pistol. Drescher ducked but the shot hit his left shoulder.

"You bastard!" cried Drescher.

As the man tried to reload his pistol Drescher plunged his knife into his chest. Then he ran back towards the smaller boat.

"Drescher, you've been hurt," said Frederick Daniel.

"It's only a shoulder wound. With your help, we will move the three bodies into the small boat and we will sail this one. It should make our passage across the Rhine easier and faster."

Frederick Daniel helped to roll Bertin's body into the rowing boat. De Vancy screamed.

"Get him away from me!"

"He's dead, de Vancy, you fool," replied Drescher.

"I did not escape to be a party to murder. I want to go back. I can't take any more of this," said de Vancy, whimpering in a state of deepening panic.

"Shut up and sit down," yelled Drescher.

The two remaining bodies were dragged and rolled to join Bertin's. Then Trudaine helped Jacqueline d'Anville into the sailing boat. Only de Vancy was left to board.

"Are you coming, de Vancy? There is no time to lose," said Trudaine.

De Vancy did not speak but as he stood up the left hand of one of the men in the bottom of the hull grabbed his ankle. De Vancy screamed and in his panic lost his balance, falling into the widening water between the two boats. Frederick Daniel dived into the river, ignoring Drescher's shouts not to do so. He caught hold of de Vancy's body in the inky blackness of the water but it did not respond. De Vancy was dead. Frederick William resurfaced. For a moment he could see nothing but then he heard Drescher's voice.

"Over here! Over here!" the voice repeated.

He struggled to the sailing boat where outstretched arms hauled him aboard.

Drescher crouched beside the young Count, wrapped in a rough blanket stinking of fish.

"I pledged to your mother the Countess that I would return you safely to Herzberg. Never, so long as you are with me, do such a foolhardy thing as you have just done. In war, never let your judgement be clouded by the most basic fact of existence. On the battlefield and in life it is your survival that matters, not theirs. Your father accepted that, as did King Frederick. Follow their example. Now I suggest that you comfort the girl. I need Trudaine's help in the wheelhouse."

* * * * *

The next day, Friday the 4th of September, after sailing north for several hours, keeping close to the east bank of the Rhine – the larger craft indeed making the Rhine crossing far less treacherous and difficult than it would have been in the rowing boat, as Drescher had predicted – they finally tied up at a hamlet close to Rastadt on the road to Stuttgart. With the help of some local fishermen they made their way to the village where Drescher had an old friend whom, as a precaution, before entering Strasbourg, he had alerted that he might need help on his return. In a small but comfortable dwelling Drescher had his wound dressed, and Frederick Daniel and Trudaine received a change of clothes. Jacqueline d'Anville, still recovering from the previous night's ordeal, was given the clothes of a peasant woman. They ate a simple but welcome supper and after a night's rest left by carriage for Stuttgart, the home of the Counts of Württemberg, known to Drescher. Within hours of their arrival they were guests in the old castle where they were able to rest and change into more suitable clothes.

While Drescher and Robert Trudaine became better acquainted, quickly becoming good companions, Frederick Daniel spent time with Jacqueline d'Anville. Soon after their arrival they were alone in the library.

"You were most brave in our escape, Mademoiselle. You displayed great courage. Please tell me a little about what happened to your family."

"I am happy to oblige, Monsieur, after all you have done for me, though the events that have brought me here are still almost too painful to bear and cause me much anguish to relate. You will see it is not I who have shown courage and bravery, but those I have left behind. My family have lived in Lorraine for many generations. We own land, which my father has tended well. We have done our best to be good landlords. Yet earlier this year we became aware of local rumours that we and other landowners were agents of a grasping King and Queen, that we had hidden amounts of money due to our tenants but which were destined to go instead to the Palace of Versailles for the Queen to spend on more dresses. In our case it was utterly untrue, as we tried to explain to our tenants. We think they believed us. Then agents arrived from Paris and began to agitate. One night as we were preparing to go to bed a large crowd arrived at the gates of the château demanding their money. My father and mother said they did recognise a few local tenants amongst the crowd but that those who spoke did not have a Lorraine accent. We pleaded with them to wait until the morning so we could assemble what little money we had to meet their demands. But they would not listen. They seized my mother and father and me but killed my brother when he resisted. As we left the château, handcuffed in a cart, I looked back to see our home in flames. My mother wept. Later we were locked in a house with other landowners to await public examination. With us in the small room in which we had been confined were two elderly couples and the Comte and Comtesse de Vancy and their son, Jean-Marie. My father and mother knew them but I did not care for them. They spoke of revenge for what had happened to them. In the morning we were let out into the courtyard. There was much confusion at that time – peasants were coming into the courtyard to watch the examinations and possible executions, while others were leaving to confront more landowners. No one seemed to know what was happening. It was then that Jean-Marie's father and, following his example, mine urged us to escape and make our way to the south. Jean-Marie and I were doubtful but we were pressed to go. And so during one particular commotion we escaped, making our way on side roads and pathways towards Strasbourg where Jean-Marie said he knew a friend, Monsieur Trudaine. The rest of the story you know. Monsieur, I have no home and I do not know what has happened to my mother and father and my brother is dead. I do not know what I will do next."

Frederick Daniel looked at Jacqueline. Though overcome with grief and much fatigued, she was a beautiful young woman, tall and slim with long reddish hair and almond-coloured eyes. In some ways she reminded him of his mother as she appeared in the painting completed at the time of her marriage to his late father.

"Mademoiselle, thank you for telling me what you and your family have suffered. Your story is most sad. I hope that soon news may come of the release of your mother and father. But I could not bear to think of you alone in this city. I wish you to accompany me to my home at Herzberg, near Potsdam. My mother will care for you until your future is clear."

"Monsieur, I am afraid I do not know your real name. I thank you most kindly for your generous offer but I could not do that. I will find a family here in Stuttgart who may need a French governess. And then perhaps when the present madness in France is over I will be able to return and search for my mother and father."

"Mademoiselle, I am Count Frederick Daniel von Deppe, at your service. I insist that once Herr Drescher is returned to good health he, you and I – and possibly Monsieur Trudaine – will set out for Prussia. You will come as my guest. I insist. My mother, the Countess von Deppe, is English by birth and a long time ago she arrived in Paris homeless on account of a dispute within her family. My aunt, now the Vicomtesse de Vervins, and her husband, the

Vicomte, offered her hospitality. Later she went to Prussia and married my father. The Countess will sympathise with your plight. Once the present trouble is over, you can return to France to pursue your life. Now we will hear no more of it. You will travel with us."

"Monsieur le Comte, your suggestion is most kind and generous. Let me consider what you have said. I believe it is important to remain close to the French border and as close as possible to my parents, wherever they may be. But I will consider what you have proposed, I promise you."

A week later, on Friday the 11th of September, Waldemar Drescher insisted he was well enough to travel. It was time for them to head north, towards Berlin. Robert Trudaine had already announced that he would accompany them in order to assist Drescher in any way necessary. It was now time for Jacqueline d'Anville to decide.

"Mademoiselle," said Frederick Daniel, "I know Strasbourg well. I studied there for over three years and made many friends. But they, the city and all of France are being overtaken by madness, inspired and driven by fear, hunger and outright lies peddled by the *libellistes* in Paris. Since we have been in Stuttgart Herr Drescher and I have sought out the latest reports from across the Rhine. The news worsens by the day. The *noblesse* continues to be a target of revenge. Examinations of the sort your family and the de Vancys faced are now commonplace and often lead to summary executions. There are few survivors from this madness. France is becoming increasingly stained by the spilt blood of the innocent. While your mother and father may still be alive, they would wish you to put as much distance between you and the *patriotes* as you can. I urge you, Mademoiselle, to come with us. If you do not, you will be alone in Stuttgart. That should not happen to such a beautiful young woman."

Jacqueline d'Anville looked out of the window at the city below.

"Mademoiselle, I beg you. Come with us. There is no time to lose."

She turned to give her reply, her eyes moist with tears.

"Though it pains my heart to put more distance between my parents, if they are still alive, and me, I will come with you, Monsieur le Comte."

Frederick Daniel offered her his arm and they left the room.

By midday they had said farewell to the Count of Württemberg and were on their way by the first of many coaches towards Prussia. Frederick Daniel felt guilt that he had applied pressure to Jacqueline d'Anville to accompany them. While he was truly concerned about her safety alone in Stuttgart he was also attracted to the striking young woman beside him.

*****

On the last part of the long and at times tedious journey from Stuttgart to Herzberg Waldemar Drescher had ridden ahead, with Robert Trudaine, to announce to the Countess that he had fulfilled her wish and returned her son to Prussia. Arabella thanked him and insisted that he and his companion should stay on the estate for as long as they wished, to recover from the vicissitudes of the past weeks. Drescher told Arabella of the young woman accompanying her son. When she showed irritation at Frederick Daniel's actions, he reminded her of the warm welcome she had once received from Maria Louisa de Vervins in Paris all those years ago as the young Arabella Whitfield. Arabella at once scolded herself for being so ungenerous and thoughtless. She would welcome the young woman with warmth and kindness.

The next afternoon, on Tuesday the 29th of September, a mud-stained black coach arrived at Herzberg. Frederick Daniel leapt down to greet his mother, who was standing at the bottom of the steps leading to the main entrance of the house. They embraced after three years' absence from one another's company.

"I believe you have a travelling companion. Don't leave her sitting there. Bring her to me. I wish to meet her," said Arabella with a smile.

"Yes, Mother, it is my pleasure to do so."

Frederick Daniel returned to the coach. As he opened the door Arabella remembered that moment twenty-four years earlier when Carl Manfred had opened the door of her coach and introduced her to his sister. Maria Louisa's warm welcome had begun Arabella's new life. Here she was, many years later, seeing history repeat itself – her son introducing a young woman for whom, according to Drescher, he possibly had an affinity just as she,

Arabella, had had a close affinity to the man in Paris who was to become her beloved husband.

"Maman, I wish to introduce Mademoiselle Jacqueline d'Anville, daughter of the Comte and Comtesse d'Anville. Her parents –"

"Frederick Daniel, I know. Herr Drescher explained the circumstances to me yesterday."

Jacqueline, with her hair tied back in a tail and wearing beneath a jacket and long open coat a simple chiffon-style dress – now increasingly the fashion in Europe, which Arabella had foreshadowed many years before in her own manner of dress – curtsied.

"I am deeply honoured to make your acquaintance, Madame la Comtesse. Monsieur le Comte insisted that I should come. It is most kind and generous of you to receive me. I promise I will not remain with you long."

"Mademoiselle Jacqueline, you are most welcome. I would have been cross if my son had not insisted you come as our guest. Hanne will take you to your room and help you change for supper."

As Jacqueline d'Anville went upstairs, Arabella turned to her son.

"What an attractive young woman you have brought with you. She obviously holds some appeal for you." Arabella smiled.

"I am sure the Vicomtesse de Vervins said the same to my father about you," he quipped.

They both laughed.

Just over two weeks later Arabella, Frederick Daniel and Jacqueline, who to the young Count's obvious pleasure was wearing a low-cut décolleté dress to reveal a fine bust, were joined for dinner by Elise Catherine and her husband, Joseph. Towards the end of their meal Arabella received a note to say that Waldemar Drescher had an important message to give her when she was ready.

"Weisser, please ask him to join us now."

"Yes, Countess," replied Weisser.

Drescher entered. He was clean-shaven and dressed in an elegant frock coat. He bore little physical resemblance to the man who had been their guide and saviour in France.

"Herr Drescher, you have important news. Please share it with us all."

"Countess, I have received a reliable report that the market women of Paris marched on the Palace of Versailles on Monday the 5th of October to protest their poverty and hunger. A large crowd besieged the palace and in the early hours of the next day they broke in and ransacked the Queen's bedroom. She was not there as she was with the King but in the attack two bodyguards were killed and it is reported that her bed was pierced with pikes in case she was hiding beneath. The crowd forced the King and Queen to go with them to Paris, where they are now in the Tuileries, effectively under house arrest since the royal bodyguards have been replaced by the National Guard under the command of General Lafayette. The National Assembly is now in charge of the government of France. Some are calling for the King to be put on trial. The vilification of the Queen is ever greater. The prospects for the return of sanity in France look more remote than ever."

"Thank you, Herr Drescher, for this deeply disturbing news. Perhaps you will join us after breakfast tomorrow morning to discuss the situation further? I would welcome that as your information is trustworthy and up to date."

"Countess, I will return in the morning as you wish, but before I leave I have one other report."

"Yes, Herr Drescher. Please tell us."

"The Vicomte and Vicomtesse de Vervins and the Comte and Comtesse de Puyraveau and their child are with Their Majesties in the Tuileries. The crowds besieging the palace insisted that they should accompany them. So they too are now prisoners in the Tuileries."

"Thank you, Herr Drescher. That is profoundly distressing news. There is all the more reason to meet tomorrow morning as I have asked, to discuss what might be done. I hope, Joseph, you will join us before your departure to join the Crown Prince. Mademoiselle d'Anville, you were right to come with my son to the safety of Herzberg. I urge you to remain with us."

"Thank you, Countess, for your generosity," Jacqueline d'Anville replied. "I will gladly do so. If Their Majesties have been arrested the prospects for my mother and father look bleak."

"They are indeed," said Drescher as he left the room.

Later that evening, to ease the sombre mood that had now enveloped Herzberg, Arabella played the harpsichord. She performed the nine variations she and Herr Mozart had composed earlier in the year and then sang *Vedrò con mio diletto* from Antonio Vivaldi's opera *Giustino* – an aria that had become a favourite of hers. Afterwards Jacqueline d'Anville played a courante and sarabande from a suite for harpsichord by Rameau, then accompanied Arabella as she sang another of her favourites, *Tristes apprêts*, from Rameau's *Castor and Pollux*. Elise and her husband held hands in a display of their deep love for one another, while Frederick Daniel looked at Jacqueline d'Anville. To end the music for the evening Arabella and Jacqueline played together on the keyboard the chaconne by Nicola Matteis that the Camerata had first played long ago at the Palace of Charlottenburg, the night she and Carl Manfred had made love in the royal bed. As she played Arabella secretly longed for Charles Gray to return, while Frederick Daniel longed to kiss Jacqueline with whom he was falling in love.

As she lay in bed thinking of Charles Gray and longing to have the comfort of his body next to hers, Arabella resolved that if Maria Louisa and her daughter were to be in mortal danger as a result of their continued close proximity to the King and Queen, then she would do everything within her power to secure their freedom, whatever the risk may be.

CHAPTER 9

Entr'acte

More than a year passed with little encouraging news from Paris.

Though the French King and Queen enjoyed a measure of freedom at the Tuileries they remained under the thumb of the Constituent Assembly – itself subject to demands resulting from periodic violent upheavals on the streets of the capital. There were graphic reports of the celebration of the first anniversary of the fall of the Bastille prison. At the same time the Committee of the Constitution continued to debate the future role of the monarchy, resulting in July 1790 in the King's acceptance of a constitutional monarchy. The Assembly's supervision of the institution, in accordance with the revolutionary principles of liberty, equality and fraternity, extended to those who remained with the King, either out of loyalty, such as the Vicomte de Vervins – with the reluctant compliance of his wife, Maria Louisa – or because they had no choice but to do so – a restraint that applied to the de Vervins' daughter, Marie-Aurore, the Comtesse de Puyraveau, who, with her young son, had already been stopped once, trying, with her husband's and Maria Louisa's encouragement, to leave without written permission for Switzerland.

Most distressing for Jacqueline d'Anville was the unconfirmed report that her parents had been executed for attempting to escape. Though there was much confusion in France, feeding rumour and counter-rumour, the account of what had happened to them – and to others among the aristocracy – had the undeniable ring of authenticity. As no contrary report of her parents' safety reached her, Jacqueline reluctantly accepted the probability that they had indeed perished. Frederick Daniel and Arabella did their best to console her, offering assurance that she would have a home at Herzberg for as long as she wished.

Against the darkening backdrop of France in turmoil the seasonal life of the Herzberg estate remained largely untroubled. Arabella continued to ride regularly around its boundaries and villages, sometimes accompanied by Frederick Daniel, to demonstrate her commitment to those who worked on the land and to ensure that the farming practices she had pursued for many years remained in place. She was proud of what she had achieved and enjoyed the respect for her efforts shown to her by other landowners. Behind her mask of confidence Arabella knew that the threat of war would have heavy consequences for the estate, particularly if Prussia were required to mobilise a large army to confront its enemies. Military recruitment would deal a devastating blow to the labour the estate required to ensure Herzberg continued to flourish.

The Camerata remained another of Arabella's preoccupations. The orchestra played regularly in Potsdam, in Berlin and further afield in Magdeburg and Halle. Herr Bamberger remained its leader, a responsibility he had held for over twenty-four years. Now almost fifty years old he was looking for a suitable successor, perhaps his son, to guide the much-enlarged orchestra forward. As the news from France grew more disturbing Arabella and Herr Bamberger recognised that the time would come when the Camerata, with other orchestras, might be required to help lift the national spirit. Whereas the music of Rameau and Lully had once been popular in Prussia, the taste for French compositions obviously began to wane. The Countess and Herr Bamberger began to consider other composers, past and present, from Germany and the Empire, for inclusion in the Camerata's repertoire. The need to do so was highlighted by the treaty signed by the Emperor Leopold II and King Frederick William of Prussia in Reichenbach on the 27th of July 1790 in order to settle old differences and to lay the basis for a new alliance in the light of the perceived threat from France.

Much earlier in the year Arabella had travelled to Vienna where she attended the first performance of Mozart's new opera, *Così fan tutte*, in the Burgtheater on Tuesday the 26th of January – accompanied by her son, Frederick Daniel; her daughter, Elise Catherine, and son-in-law, Joseph; Herr Bamberger; and Jacqueline d'Anville. The opera greatly impressed Arabella. The aria *Soave sia il vento*, sung by Dorabella and Fiordiligi as their fiancés leave for military service, touched her deeply as it brought back poignantly Carl Manfred's departure for war and his subsequent death; she still missed him acutely. Though staying in the imperial capital for only a short while, Arabella received a visit from the composer at her lodging the following day, and much enjoyed his company. They laughed together, particularly as she remonstrated with him about the premise of the opera's title, with its implicit meaning "Thus are all women *fickle in their love*". They played the harpsichord side by side as they had done at Herzberg the previous year. Mozart lamented that had he known his English countess would be present he would have asked her to sing the role of Fiordiligi instead of the arrogant prima donna Adriana Ferrarese de Bene, whom he claimed dropped her chin on low notes and threw back her head on high ones.

Shortly before Arabella's planned departure from Vienna for Prague on Monday the 1st of February she received at her lodging a private letter, the handwriting of which she instantly recognised.

My dear Countess,

Our paths will finally cross in Prague in the next week. Once I have received confirmation that you have arrived safely at the Clam-Gallas Palace, I will send word in order that we might meet at your convenience.

I have greatly missed you. I envied Mr Mozart's pleasure of your company.

Charles G

Vienna, Friday the 29th of January, 1790

Arabella slowly put the letter down.

This was the news for which she had longed. But how could she see Charles Gray in Prague, accompanied by her family, Herr Bamberger and Jacqueline d'Anville? Of course she could receive him over tea and pretend that it was simply renewal of a past acquaintance. Or she could avoid Prague but stay longer in Vienna or indeed return to Herzberg another way. But since he knew she was in Vienna he would follow her wherever she went. Why avoid him? She wanted his intimacy. So without more ado Arabella decided to continue with her plan to pass through Prague as she intended and to meet Gray there in whatever circumstances were possible. She reread the letter, her fingers tracing his handwriting as though to touch him. Physical feelings for him had already stirred within her. She looked at herself in the mirror. Was a woman of her age still able to have a lover? If so, and their previous intimacy resumed, how could she conceal it? The smiling face of Antoinette Badeau briefly appeared in the mirror above her right shoulder.

"Be bold, Arabella, as I once was. Take your lover! If you do not, you will regret it."

"Go away, Antoinette. I will decide, not you."

"Arabella, don't be such a hypocrite. Be honest, you have already decided to reply positively to his note as you wish once again to be with him!"

"Hush, Antoinette, be gone!"

The face faded. She had indeed already decided to renew her acquaintance with Charles Gray and to let him share her bed if he wished to do so.

Later that day, before supper, Arabella received further unexpected news, this time from her son.

"Mama," said Frederick Daniel, "I wish to inform you of two matters."

"And what are they?" replied Arabella, still preoccupied with thoughts of Charles Gray.

"First, I request your permission to ask Mademoiselle d'Anville to be my wife. I have considered the matter for many months, since her arrival at Herzberg. I have fallen in love with her and did so almost when I first met her."

"Do you know what her feelings are towards you?" enquired Arabella.

"Mama, you with a woman's intuition may be better informed than me in that regard. But I believe we have an affinity, a friendship, that would, if declared, bring us together in much happiness."

"Frederick, are you proposing this match out of pity for her because of the death of her father and mother?"

"I feel truly sorry for the news she has received but my feelings towards her became apparent long before that blow," he replied.

"If you are sure that this is what you wish, I have no objection. She is a beautiful and graceful young woman who I am sure will make you content. But you will be under a supreme obligation to make her happy and to treat her with the deep respect and love she will deserve."

"Thank you, Mama. I promise you I will fulfil my obligation in that important regard."

"Before you ask for Mademoiselle d'Anville's hand, Frederick, what is the other matter you wish to share?"

"Mama, I have decided after much consideration that I should join the army to help prepare for the defence of Prussia. I have discussed it with Joseph and I believe it is the right step for me to take. Moreover, I would be following in my late father's honourable footsteps. That is my decision and nothing will persuade me otherwise."

Arabella had dreaded hearing such words from her son but she knew she could not oppose his decision. He had clearly made up his mind. Besides, if there were a call to arms the King and those who advised him would expect him to serve his country.

"When did you make this decision?" she asked.

"As I left Strasbourg," Frederick Daniel replied. "I had high and idealistic hopes that the revolution in France would prove a noble venture. But from what I saw before leaving that country, and from the reports I have received since my return to Herzberg, the fulfilment of the noble aims I once hoped for appears to have turned to dust. Now we must consider protecting and upholding what we have achieved in our homeland."

"Frederick, is your decision to join the army yours alone, or have you been influenced by others such as Herr Drescher?"

"Mama, I have made up my own mind uninfluenced by any others except you. You have often spoken of your commitment to the country that has adopted you with such open arms, and how you wish to continue serving Prussia until the end of your life. Your music and the Camerata are dedicated to Prussia and you treasure Herzberg for what it represents. I wish to follow in your footsteps as well as my father's by making this decision and therefore I beg you not to oppose me."

"Of course I will not oppose your decision, even though as a mother I will worry that in the event of war your life will be in danger. You are my only son and the inheritor of Herzberg. But I understand your reasons and therefore will not stand in the way, not that I could do so anyway."

"Thank you, Mama. I will discuss what has to be done with Joseph on our return to Potsdam. He will advise me how to proceed."

"And Mademoiselle d'Anville? When will you tell her of your decision?"

"I will tell her when I ask for her hand in marriage."

"Frederick, I thank you for sharing your plans with me. I am deeply honoured that you should do so. Please go to Mademoiselle d'Anville and without delay declare your love for her, so that later in life, if she says yes which I am certain she will, you will be able to look back on this special day in Vienna with pride and happiness."

Within the hour Frederick Daniel returned with Jacqueline d'Anville.

"Mama, it is my pleasure to tell you that Mademoiselle d'Anville has accepted my proposal of marriage and agreed with my decision to serve in the army in the defence of liberty for Prussia."

Arabella took Jacqueline d'Anville's hands in hers.

"Are you truly content and ready to accept my son's proposal of marriage? Marriage is unique and based on respect for one another. Are you sure he will bring you the happiness you have every right to expect?"

"Madame la Comtesse, I am truly convinced he will. My love for your son, Count von Deppe, is deep, genuine and heartfelt. I wish to become his wife and for him to become my husband."

"Then so be it, with my blessing," replied Arabella. "Welcome to our family. Henceforth, I will call you Jacqueline. None of us, Jacqueline, knows what the future may hold in these increasingly dangerous times. I will long feel sorrow for your mother and father but I wish you to know that whatever may happen in France, a country for which I have long had affection as my mother was French, Herzberg will always be your home, your refuge and, I hope, your inspiration for a long, fulfilling and fruitful life."

"Madame la Comtesse, I thank you for your kind words."

"Frederick Daniel, it is already late. Let us have some supper and share your good news with Elise and Joseph. We will celebrate on our return to Herzberg."

That night Arabella went to bed in some sadness, but with her feelings partly assuaged by a measure of happiness. She was sad that her only son would soon share his life with his new wife and join the army where he would face danger as his father had done long ago. And she was sad that she had passed another milestone in her life: her two children had grown up to pursue their lives, ambitions and happiness with others away from Herzberg and her side. Following Carl Manfred's death they had – when they were young – been her preoccupation, a source of comfort and therefore her protection from loneliness. Now she would be truly alone. But in the midst of her sadness she also felt a degree of happiness – not just at the prospect of her son marrying a young beautiful French woman but also at the thought that soon she would see Charles Gray.

*****

Four days later on the afternoon of Thursday the 4th of February, 1790, Arabella, still accompanied by her son and his fiancée, her daughter and her husband, and Herr Bamberger, arrived in Prague, a city that still showed some of the consequences of the extensive Prussian bombardment in 1757, to stay at the Palace of Clam-Gallas, originally built for the Viceroy of Naples almost seventy-five years before. Later that evening, after supper, Arabella received a further handwritten note.

My dear Countess,

Welcome to Prague.

I hope that I may have the pleasure of calling upon you in the morning and that perhaps later in the day you might do me the honour of walking with me for a short distance.

I await with great anticipation an early reply and to that end have instructed the messenger to wait for such a communication.

With my warmest felicitations,
Charles Gray
Prague, Thursday the 4th of February, 1790

Despite the late hour and since it would be disobliging to send the messenger away empty-handed Arabella replied.

Dear Mr Gray,
I thank you for your letter received this evening. How observant you are about my comings and goings.
I will await with pleasure your call on me tomorrow morning at eleven o'clock.
Please accept my felicitations,
Arabella
Countess von Deppe
Prague, Thursday evening, the 4th of February, 1790

She reread the letter, wondering whether she might have replied in warmer terms. But she decided to leave her words unchanged and handed the letter to the messenger.

As her son and his fiancée and her daughter and son-in-law had decided to go sightseeing in the old town, and Herr Bamberger, dedicated as always, was engaged in a quest to secure copies of the latest compositions for the Camerata, Arabella was alone when Charles Gray arrived at eleven o'clock the next day. He was handsomely dressed, his hair revealing a touch of silver that she had not noticed before. He smiled warmly as he kissed her hand in greeting.

"I deeply regret that I have not been in touch for such a long time. My business has caused me to travel widely in Europe and in some cases it has been difficult to write securely. I ask your forgiveness."

"You are forgiven, Mr Gray. I hold you no grudge for the absence of any communication following the most personal one you left on my dressing table at Herzberg. May I ask where you have travelled since we last met?"

"I have been to St Petersburg, where I had the honour of meeting Her Imperial Majesty, who still has fond memories of your many conversations with her, and to Sweden, and, after a short interval in London following the death of my father, Sir John Gray, to France, where the situation becomes more unsettled as each day passes. But throughout this time you have been often in my thoughts. That is why I was so pleased that our paths should cross in Vienna and now more directly in Prague. As I believe you may be staying in the city for several days I hope that it might be possible for us to spend some time together."

"Mr Gray – or Sir Charles, I should say, as I believe you are your late father's eldest son and as such inherit his title – I extend my sympathy on his death. I never had the pleasure of meeting him but according to my acquaintances he was a distinguished and most kind man."

"Countess, you are well informed. And I thank you for your sympathy."

"Sir Charles, I thought of you many times following your departure from Herzberg but as I had not received word from you I assumed after a while that I had become a relic of your past," Arabella said teasingly.

Gray's face reddened momentarily.

"Countess, you – such a beautiful and most charming woman – are no relic of my past. Far from it, you have become a pivot of my life."

"If that is the case, Sir Charles, I might have expected more following the note you left on my dressing table."

Again, Gray's face reddened at the further chastisement he had received. The Countess was offering him little quarter.

"Countess, as I believe we are alone, please let me be open with you in the expectation that you will hold what I am about to tell you in confidence."

"Sir Charles, I have told you before that I am the keeper of many secrets. Whatever you may reveal now I will add to my store of the undisclosed."

"Thank you, Countess. As you may have suspected before now I am engaged in diplomacy on behalf of the British government. But my activities are conducted out of sight, with as few people as possible knowing what I do. I listen, I watch and I gather intelligence, which I convey to London as often as circumstances allow. I do what your friend Herr Drescher has done for many years. But my methods are somewhat different from his. The peripatetic nature of what I do means that regular communication is not always feasible. But I accept that in this instance I have served you badly by not keeping in regular touch. I stand reprimanded. It should not have happened. I wish earnestly for your forgiveness and hope that we might now spend some time together before your return to Herzberg so that we can resume what abruptly ended."

"Sir Charles, I thank you for your honesty and for your trust in my discretion. You have my word that I will not disclose to anyone the nature of what you do."

"Countess, my affection for you has not diminished during my long absence. What I said to you at Herzberg remains as valid now as it did then. Indeed, my affection is even stronger than it was then."

"What do you propose to do, Sir Charles, to demonstrate this affection? Am I after all *une liaison temporaire* to be used at your convenience? If that is your intention, I am not sure what my response would be."

"Countess, you toy with me. I do not consider you some *liaison temporaire*, as you phrase it, but a strikingly attractive woman whom I greatly admire, profoundly respect and with whom I wish to enjoy the fruits of friendship, if you were to permit that. Where my affection might lead is in your hands, Countess, not mine. For the present I can see you are playing with me, as it is a woman's prerogative to do. I treat you as an equal because you are my equal in every respect. Please, Countess, I beg you to be open with me as I have been with you."

Arabella did not respond but stood as though to bring their conversation to an end. Gray rose to his feet too. They looked at one another, each holding the other's gaze. He moved towards her, his hand held out ready to say farewell, his entreaties having appeared to fall on stony ground. She took his hand and then drew him towards her.

"Kiss me, Sir Charles," she whispered.

He kissed her, placing his hands around her slender waist, pulling her against him.

"What shall we do, Sir Charles?" she said as they kissed again.

"Before you reach Dresden on your return to Berlin you may wish to accompany me to Karlsbad on the 9th of February. We might linger there for a day or so at our pleasure. Few people will be there to take the waters. We would be almost alone. I am ready to ride ahead and make the necessary preparations while you decide how best to arrange your entourage."

Arabella paused, her body close to his. Was such a plan really what she wanted? What would she tell her travelling companions? But the thought of being with Gray sent a frisson of physical excitement through her. She looked up and kissed him.

"Sir Charles, I accept your invitation."

"Countess, I am deeply honoured and touched by your decision."

They kissed again.

"I have one request, Countess. When we meet, please be free to love. Do not allow your love of a memory to be an obstacle to your happiness."

"Sir Charles, my love for a memory will not cease but I will do all in my power to ensure it does not interfere with the intimacy of what we may intend. But you should know that my wish to love and be loved is distracted by another concern. It is the plight of my sister-in-law, Maria Louisa de Vervins, and her daughter, the Comtesse de Puyraveau, and her young son, in Paris. Their current predicament is heavy on my mind. You should know also that I have resolved, should their position worsen, to do whatever I can to secure their freedom. I dread the receipt of any news from Paris, fearing that whatever I might decide to do will be too late. I will look forward to our visit to Karlsbad but this matter weighs greatly on my mind."

"Countess, I am aware of their plight. I pledge to you that if their position worsens I will do all that I can to assist you in their escape, which hopefully would include the Vicomte de Vervins and the Comte de Puyraveau also. I should warn you that their situation will most likely worsen. Before long we will make a plan, I assure you of that. However, it will require much consideration and detail. Too many schemes of that nature have come to grief, leading to further tragedy. But I am sure that whatever plan we conceive can succeed, despite the great danger involved. But for now let us look to the coming days. You will receive word from me en route regarding the arrangements I have made for your stay."

They kissed once more and then parted.

*****

The next day Arabella announced to Frederick Daniel, Elise

Catherine, Joseph and Jacqueline that on their return journey she intended to travel to Karlsbad in order to spend time alone to consider the future. It was many years since she had been to the spa town and though it was the depth of winter she wished to see it again since she was not sure when such an opportunity might arise again. There was unanimous agreement that they should accompany her. But Arabella insisted that was not necessary. She would ask a guide to escort her to Karlsbad and subsequently to ensure that she would be protected on the resumption of her journey to Dresden, where she would be reunited with her family. She repeated her wish to be alone.

And so on Saturday the 6th of February the entourage left Prague. Before the final departure Elise Catherine spoke to her mother.

"Mama, I wish you, as do we all, a safe journey to Karlsbad. We will miss you on our journey to Dresden."

"Dearest Elise, thank you. I wish you a safe journey too. We will not be parted for long but this is an obligation to myself I must discharge."

"Mama, I understand why you wish to travel alone to Karlsbad. I hope that you find great peace, serenity and happiness while you are there. You have my blessing. I hope your heart is healed as a consequence."

She kissed and embraced her mother.

"Thank you, Elise. I hope I will."

Arabella knew that her daughter was aware she would not be alone.

* * * * *

The weather in Karlsbad was bitterly cold but the sky was blue, the sun bright and the air crisp. Arabella and Gray walked arm in arm, talking in hushed tones as lovers do, seemingly oblivious of others around them. As there was none to take the waters, there was a minimum of risk they would be recognised. They strolled along pathways, along the riverbank, through trees, through the snow, sometimes on the ice of the frozen river. Arms linked they appeared carefree. Arabella looked striking in her ankle-length black fur coat and matching hat, her hands in her fur muff and her long black boots occasionally revealed in the swagger of her coat. They ate alone in their near-deserted lodgings, which Gray had taken under assumed names. In the evening she played the piano to him; sometimes he played to her; or they sat together, still arm in arm, as a lone pianist played. Sometimes they played cards or just talked. And when they talked it was about the past, the present and the darkening future.

At night they slept together in a large ornate four-poster bed hidden behind thick brocade curtains. Charles Gray continued to show he was an accomplished lover of women, well used to exploring avenues of intimacy to bring pleasure by touch and by word. He remained fascinated by the woman whose body he caressed and entered. She was beautiful, elegant, exquisite and full of sublime musical notes when she sang. She had delicate feminine mannerisms and her deportment made her even more striking. Beneath her façade, however, was an unbridled sensuality. She was unrestrained, whether beneath or above him, encouraging him to explore and inspire her body. For her part, Arabella was even more entranced by Gray, his gentleness, his graceful body, his silkiness, his almost hypnotic manipulation of her senses – physical and emotional. He led her to extremes of physical intimacy not even she had experienced at Chesterfield Street. Their closeness revealed to her that, beneath that veneer of sophistication for which she had become renowned at Herzberg, the grain of her body – even her inner being – had been irreparably stained by the demi-monde. She might hide its traces but she could not remove the stain itself. But it did not matter. In the arms of Gray, why should she not go with the grain? She had chosen since the start of their affair to relinquish all resistance. She and Gray became in those days in Karlsbad the exponents of the erotic.

On their last night together – overshadowed by their impending farewell – their closeness became yet more intense. They played together Ludwig Abeille's *Piano Concerto for Four Hands*. Their proximity side by side at the keyboard and the close harmony of their fingers visually emphasised the sexual current between them. At the end of the slow movement he stopped and placed his hand on hers.

"Come to bed, Arabella," he asked her."I want you."

She smiled at him.

"Yes, I will come," she replied.

As he undressed, she played the slow movement of a Bach piano concerto.

"Arabella, come please," he said.

"Why should I come?" she asked him in the coquettish way he had come to know so well.

"Because I want to make love to you – now," he said with a slight trace of irritation.

"Charles, *dans un petit instant*," she replied in French.

* * * * *

He lay on the bed, stripped, looking towards her and thinking. Tomorrow they would leave. Their privacy would be over. What next? What was to become of them? Arabella sat in front of the large fire, unclothed except for her fur coat draped over her slender shoulders. The flickering flames cast dancing shadows on the light and dark contours of her breasts. Her hair was loose about her face. She too was thinking of their departure. Tomorrow she would resume her journey back to Herzberg. He would go – disappear for weeks or perhaps months without a word – while she would be left alone with just memories.

"What is the nature of love?" she suddenly asked him.

Gray did not reply.

She asked again.

"Is it the beauty of a sonata? Is it the romantic love of a chivalrous knight for a damsel in distress? Or for us is love that which is manifested by the physical touch of your skin against mine?"

"Arabella, why do you ask such questions? I am not a philosopher," Gray replied. "I can only speak about what I see and feel. The bond between us, Arabella, is physical – mutual irresistible attraction. If I remember my school Greek the word *eros* surely best describes our intense physical desire for one another, though I recall also that Plato held *eros* to be a desire that seeks transcendental beauty. If he was right then your beauty, Arabella, is not just what I see with my eyes and enjoy in our bed. It is also a reflection – like the flames' shadows on the wall of this room – of a higher beauty. In that definition, Arabella, you are beauty on earth and a representation of what surely is heavenly beauty. That is the best answer I can give to your question."

Neither spoke.

He hoped he had answered her question; that she would not persist. As for Arabella, should she, she thought, pursue his answer? She could not resist pushing him further.

"Charles, does real love exist between us? Or is our intimacy merely an unquenchable satisfaction of earthly desire? There are those who hold that real love has an intrinsically higher value than physical desire. What verse are we contributing to the poem of life? Or is what we are doing selfish foolishness?"

"Are you speaking of romantic love? Is that what you seek but think you do not have?" Gray replied irritably. "If so, in the Middle Ages such love was not to be consummated, out of deep respect for the lady, whose beauty was instead admired from afar. Whereas our love is consummated in fulfilment of the desire we find in each other."

"Charles," Arabella countered, "I am speaking of romantic love, but a romantic love that two people find in each other's virtues – one soul and two bodies, as Aristotle once defined it. In Monteverdi's *Vespers of the Blessed Virgin*, one voice sings *Gloria Patri* echoed by a distant singer – two separate voices but both praising the Almighty. That is my conception of romantic love – two in one, of earth and heaven. What is your opinion?"

"Arabella, if you speak of the soul, then you speak of heavenly matters of which I have frankly no knowledge, as I imagine would be the case with you. Such things are surely beyond our understanding – beyond time and the distance of the stars above us. Only Lazarus could answer that question and he is not here to do so."

"Charles, you mock me."

"I do not mock you. It is just that I am fixed on us in this room at this very moment."

"I am searching for an answer, Charles. You do not help me."

"Arabella, you can be infuriating at times – no more so than now when our precious time together is slipping away."

She showed irritation at his reply.

"I have not heard Monteverdi's *Vespers* performed," continued Gray wearily. "As you have done so, and using them as a yardstick, how would you describe us against that lofty definition?"

"I do not know," said Arabella. "I have become obsessed by you. Every time we are together, skin to skin, you demolish my defences, compromise all my principles of personal conduct. You have made me shameless, a prisoner of intense physical desire. Every time you make love to me you bring me into a paradise in which I am caressed by an indefinable sweet tenderness. It is an ineffable experience I cannot explain. It is as though I am on an island where there is no wind, no shadow, only warmth and a tinted sky. Then I return to my confusion. My predicament – whenever I am with you – has stood all my notions of love, all notions of my being on their head. My whole world has been turned upside down."

"If you are confused, Arabella, so am I. I seek to go about my work but I confess I cannot concentrate on it as I should. If I have obsessed you, you have obsessed me."

"So what are we to do?" she asked, turning to look at him for an answer.

Her shadowed profile beguiled him. What was he to say, to do?

Again he beckoned her to the bed. She leaned over him. As she did so, the fur slipped from her shoulders; her hair fell about his face; and her breasts brushed his chest. She slowly lowered her body onto his, her legs either side of his thighs. She stretched out his arms, placing the palms of her hands in his and locking his fingers with hers. There she lay, he quiet beneath her. Then suddenly – almost in a flush of anger – he roughly put her beneath him. She did not resist. He kissed her slowly and deliberately – first her lips, then lingered on her nipples, then down across her stomach to her sweet spot and beyond to her feet. Then stretching out her arms and locking her hands into his as she had done to him, they made love – intense love, so intense she cried out in her moment of illuminating affirmation.

She lay beside him.

"Charles what are we do? What does our friendship, our companionship, really mean? Where is it leading us? Where will it end?" she asked as she caressed his body.

"Arabella, please, no more questions. But let me say this. If the truth be known, you are not my companion. You have so bewitched me that sometimes it seems I must succumb and become your slave or I must exert myself and become your master."

Arabella raised herself and looked into Gray's eyes, deep anger on her face.

"Charles, if I were your slave – whom I could never be, even if I survived without your physical love – I would despise you. If I were your master – and I would equally despise you for allowing me to be so – I would seek to punish you for your cruelty, leaving me alone for months without a word. The concepts of master and slave are not part of my world. They never have been and never will be. The fact is, Charles, you and I are equals in all that we do in life and as equals we must conduct ourselves accordingly. Yet that is not easy as our desire for one another is so intense that we are feeding on each other. Our desires for one another have become frenzied. I fear that if we do not find a higher love, which releases us from sole dependence on physical desire and which embraces higher perceptions of beauty and fellowship, then the deep regard in which we hold one another, perhaps even our love for one another, might one day be extinguished. I hope that will never happen."

"And so do I," said Gray, rising from the bed. "Come, Arabella, enough of debate. Let us not quarrel. Tomorrow we must leave. We will see what it brings."

They sat by the fire, she wrapped in her coat and cradled in his arms, her face against his chest. Neither spoke. Her questions remained unanswered as she fell asleep to the sound of the crackling fire and the moan of the wind outside.

*****

On Saturday the 13th of February, 1790, Sir Charles Gray and the Countess Arabella von Deppe left Karlsbad in a closed carriage in the direction of Dresden. On Monday the 15th of February they embraced and kissed one another on the outskirts of the city. After a final goodbye he left the coach to go in another direction. Arabella asked the coachman to pause while she dried her tears and prepared to rejoin her family for a concert that night. As the coach moved slowly into Dresden with its distinctive architectural silhouette she knew that she was more in love with Gray than ever.

If there had been any doubts in her mind beforehand there was none now. He had promised they would soon be reunited but his absence in the meantime would be hard to bear.

That evening the reunited party attended a performance of Mozart's *Great Mass in C Minor* in the Frauenkirche. Composed in Vienna during the years 1782 and 1783 but still incomplete, the *missa solemnis* was scored for two soprano soloists, a tenor and a bass as well as a double chorus and large orchestra; it was the first time that Arabella had heard the grand work performed. She was deeply moved by the sublime aria *Et incarnatus est*, part of the unfinished *Credo*. Born a Catholic, Arabella had clung to her faith. She still possessed her missal, one of the few personal belongings she had packed, along with her music book, when she ran away from Meltwater in 1765. Although practising her faith in Protestant Prussia had not been easy, and she had been to confession infrequently, she was comforted by the music she heard that evening as she recalled her life, her love of music, her late husband, her children, now grown-up, Charles Gray and Herzberg. Her birthplace had become a distant memory. She had made many decisions, fought hard for what she believed was right and suffered tragedy amidst happiness. Gray and, before him, Drescher had reminded her of the approaching clouds of possible war. She feared even greater tests ahead and doubted sometimes she had the will or courage to prevail. But prevail she must. The *C Minor Mass* reminded her that her faith would be a solace as she summoned the strength that would be needed.

Elise Catherine was seated beside her mother. At the end of the Mass she took Arabella's hand.

"Mama, I hope you found in Karlsbad the peace and happiness you sought. You looked sad but so serene when you rejoined us earlier today."

"Thank you, Elise, I did. But I am pleased to be with you again and on our way back to Herzberg."

"Mama, I am sure he will return," said Elise with a gentle smile, still clasping her mother's hand.

Arabella looked at her daughter and smiled in return.

"I hope so, Elise. I hope so."

She squeezed her daughter's hand and turned away, almost succumbing to her emotions.

* * * * *

Two major events marked the arrival of early summer at Herzberg.

The first was Frederick Daniel's admission as an officer into the Prussian army. Watched by his mother, his fiancée, his sister and her husband, and the Crown Prince, he received his lieutenant's commission from His Majesty King William Frederick. It was a proud day for Frederick Daniel von Deppe and indeed for his family, but Arabella's own pride masked her anxieties at what might happen to him. Her anxieties were a precursor of the growing concern and outrage the monarchies of Europe were openly displaying towards the revolution in France. They were deeply troubled by its upheavals and by the increasing risk of the spread of revolutionary infection throughout Europe.

Shortly afterwards, on Friday the 18th of June, 1790, the newly appointed Lieutenant Frederick Daniel von Deppe married Jacqueline d'Anville in the Catholic Cathedral of St Hedwig, built with the permission of King Frederick for the numerous Catholic immigrants that had arrived in Berlin and completed in 1773. The circular cathedral was full that day, such was the prestige of the von Deppe family and the respect in which they were held. Though a day of great joy for Jacqueline d'Anville, it was for her also tinged with sadness by the tragic absence of her family. After celebrations in Berlin, including a musical performance by the Camerata at the Hofoper, Arabella, now the Dowager Countess von Deppe, returned to Herzberg accompanied only by Herr Bamberger. That night she sat alone in the library, lost in thought.

* * * * *

Since Drescher's return to Prussia from helping her son escape from Strasbourg, Arabella had seen little of him and his companion Robert Trudaine. She had offered them lodging on the estate, which they had used in the early months after his return to recover from his exertions, but more recently their visits had been rare.

It was at the end of June that Drescher returned to Herzberg with a short letter from Maria Louisa, which his old contact in Paris, Bertrand, had delivered into his hands.

Dear Countess von Deppe,

I wish you to know that the Vicomte and I are well. We are lodged in the Tuileries with simple rooms not far from those occupied by Their Majesties and the Dauphin and Dauphine. The Comte and Comtesse de Puyraveau and their son are nearby. I miss the comforts of our house in the Rue St Louis but it has now been requisitioned by the authorities, which is as it should be.

His Majesty is patient with the demands made upon him and is supported by the Queen. What the future holds is unclear but we are all hopeful that once there is agreement on a new constitution it will be possible for us to have more freedom to travel.

With my warm felicitations,
Maria Louisa de Vervins
Paris, Thursday the 13th day of May, 1790

The letter was simple, without detail and restrained in affection.

"Herr Drescher, it is a sad letter."

"Indeed it is, Countess. The Vicomtesse was aware that it could be intercepted and possibly perceived as information being passed to an enemy of France. But though my informants are ageing, like me, they remain reliable."

"How far did you travel into France, Herr Drescher?"

"To a point east of Paris," he replied. "I had wished to enter Paris itself, but I decided that in such a volatile situation as now prevails on the streets of the capital it was wise at that moment to go no further."

"Were you alone?" Arabella enquired.

"I was accompanied by Monsieur Trudaine," Drescher replied in a matter-of-fact tone.

"You used the words 'at that moment'. Does that mean you intend to return to France at some stage?"

"Countess, France is sliding inexorably towards disaster. It could happen soon or it could be some years away. But disaster there will be and in those circumstances many innocent people will suffer, including amongst the *noblesse*. The time is approaching when Prussia will be called to arms to defend its borders and to seek with others to eradicate the scourge now beginning to afflict Europe. I hope that before too long His Majesty, our King, will realise that at present we are woefully unprepared for what may happen. In the meantime, we must acquire the best information we can so that we have good knowledge of what may confront us and when. I am ready to share my information but few pay attention. Only you, Countess, listen and understand."

"Herr Drescher, your words are chilling but you have not answered my question. Are you intending to return to France and, if so, why? Why would you wish to expose yourself to unnecessary danger and Monsieur Trudaine too?"

"Madame, together with the letter I received information, which I believe to be reliable, that the Comte de Puyraveau is plotting to escape from the Tuileries with his wife and child. The King still has freedom to leave his present lodgings and the Comte often accompanies him. The plan is full of risk, not least because the Comte is not amongst the most well-liked of the King's circle and, if his intention is discovered, or he and his family are intercepted in their flight across France, they could pay a heavy penalty."

"What is to be done?" asked Arabella.

"Nothing for the present," he replied. "But if I receive word of the date of the intended escape and their route, Monsieur Trudaine and I will cross the border to meet them and bring them safely across the Rhine as we did the Count. In order to be ready, he and I will travel immediately to the border to await information."

"Herr Drescher, your valour and courage are limitless. I am deeply honoured that you should wish to undertake this mission. But I urge you to take the utmost care and to turn back if the circumstances become too dangerous. You have been a most loyal friend and a great guardian of all that for which Herzberg stands. I would not wish to lose you now. Do you require money?"

Drescher shook his head.

"Countess, I am deeply touched by your words. I have not been a warrior like your late husband but a man who deals with the world of darkness, treachery and betrayal – the traits of human nature at its worst. That is the cloth I cut for myself when I was young. Although I have found contentment, the cloth I cut then is the cloth I continue to wear. I cannot change the habits and attitudes of a lifetime. I will do my best to secure the freedom of this family if that is possible and to bring them to Herzberg. If I fail I wish you to think well of me."

"I will, Herr Drescher, I will. God speed on your journey."

"Thank you," he replied. "I have one last word, Countess. You have shown yourself to be a keeper of secrets and able to survive surrounded by vipers. You have learnt well from the hand of cards life has dealt you. You have learnt too that in the midst of comfort and privilege you must exercise constant vigilance. I admire you for your steady hand, your warm heart and your strength – the strength of a man. If I do not return you would be right to place your trust in Sir Charles Gray. He may come from different stock, his methods may be different, but they are nonetheless well chosen and when necessary they are deadly. I believe he thinks highly of you, just as I do. I must now be gone. We do not know when the escape may happen but we must be ready, even if we have to wait many weeks."

With a deep bow Waldemar Drescher left Herzberg and, with his young companion, departed for France. Arabella mulled over his words. How much did he know about her and Gray's recent companionship? Indeed, always well informed, did he know about their stay in Karlsbad? Had he been there? What contact had there been between Gray and Drescher? These were questions she could not answer. But even if Drescher were aware, she knew that her secret would go no further.

* * * * *

The escape of the Comte and Comtesse de Puyraveau and their son took place on Saturday the 30th of October, 1790, as the King and Queen and their entourage left St Cloud, where they had stayed during the summer months in relative peace and freedom, for the enclosed world of the Tuileries.

The Comte, a somewhat arrogant man, had decided, unlike the Vicomte, to put his personal ambitions and needs above his loyalty to the King. He could not bear the thought of spending the winter months in an enclosed palace, cheek by jowl with dozens of other courtiers. His wife, Marie-Aurore, was less sanguine about the chance of success and her mother, Maria Louisa de Vervins, shared the same doubts. But the Comte prevailed and shortly after the royal entourage left St Cloud for Paris the coachman of the small unadorned carriage in which the Puyraveaus were riding claimed a problem with the harness of one of the two horses. By the time it was allegedly fixed it was almost nightfall. Resuming their journey they managed after a short distance to give their few guards the slip and, resorting to side roads, turned eastwards, changing into simple clothes as they did so. After spending the night hours in a forest they moved closer towards Chalons-sur-Marne, changing horses before reaching town. It was at this point that a passer-by told the coachman there were delays ahead as the *patriotes* were conducting yet another search for absconding *noblesse.* If his business was urgent he should prepare for a long wait. The Comte decided that, though it would be more arduous, it was necessary to avoid the town and resort once again to side roads in order to move south of Chalons-sur-Marne and then, after some distance, to once again turn east, in the direction of Nancy, provided it was possible to find a suitable place to cross the River Marne.

Drescher and Trudaine, who had been in eastern France since July, had been separately observing several routes that they thought the Puyraveau family might take. The road to Chalons-sur-Marne had become much used by those escaping and was therefore under close *patriotes* scrutiny. Drescher's network of spies and informants had greatly diminished since the death of King Frederick, and with little money left it was proving increasingly difficult to bribe those who still remained in touch. As a consequence his sources were becoming unreliable or had taken their information elsewhere. As the small black coach failed to appear in Chalons-sur-Marne, Drescher – now joined once again by Trudaine – decided that it would be best if they rode south-east looking for the Puyraveau family. Wearing shabby clothes and cockades in greasy hats they announced to those who bothered to listen that they would follow the west bank of the Marne to see what "vermin" they could find.

By now the disappearance of the Comte and Comtesse had become public knowledge and it was not long before word was passed down the line for their apprehension and return to Paris for examination along with the Vicomte and Vicomtesse de Vervins. For nearly two days the small black coach edged nearer the River Marne while Drescher and Trudaine followed the riverbank. It was on Tuesday the 2nd of November that as the coach attempted to cross the river by ferry a *patriote* became suspicious and ordered the ferryman to halt. Within a few minutes the coach was surrounded and the Comte and his wife and son were arrested and taken to a nearby village in a cart. Drescher and Trudaine, who had finally caught up, witnessed the arrest from the top of a nearby hill. They followed the cart. In the village square the Comte and Comtesse were manhandled from the cart into a tavern, their hands still bound. The child was crying as he was dragged behind his mother. The summary proceedings were chaotic, the first witness being the Puyraveaus' coachman who had, it appeared, betrayed his master. Then certain contents of the coach were displayed – some correspondence, several small bags of money and items of jewellery. A self-appointed magistrate listened to the evidence presented to him and without providing any opportunity for the Comte to speak sentenced the family to death for treason.

Drescher got to his feet and drew himself up to full height, flicking his long greasy grey hair aside from his face. Though aged, he was still a formidable presence.

"Citizens, I hear your verdict but justice is not solely in your hands. These people may be a cog in the royal wheel but the whole machine must be judged in Paris. That's where the wheel of justice is turning and for it to grind the corrupt into the ground these malefactors must be returned to Paris to receive their final judgement there. I have in my pocket the instruction of the Assembly in Paris authorising me and my companion to take back to the capital anyone who would escape. With your support I wish to take these prisoners now and commence our return to Paris. Citizens, it is your duty to assist the revolution in this way. When the time comes for the prisoners to meet their end I will make sure that some of you will be present as representatives of your village. You will be able to throw your hats in the air and say we delivered them to their just deserts."

The court fell silent as it examined the crumpled document Drescher had waved before the magistrate. It was an impressive forgery, which convinced those able to read it and those who heard its contents that citizen Morin and citizen Roussel had been appointed rat-catchers. After some debate it was agreed that Morin and Roussel would receive custody of the prisoners and, assisted by three local *patriotes*, would return to Chalons-sur-Marne where the prisoners would be placed with others to await return to Paris. Though it was now late afternoon it was decided, on the instruction of Morin and Roussel, to begin the journey without delay. So as dusk fell and the weather turned icy the prisoners, once again bound and back in the cart, and their guards began the journey north – the *patriotes* on horseback and the prisoners huddled together for warmth, with three additional horses tied behind the cart in case those pulling it became lame. Later that evening the grim procession reached a village where the horses were changed, the prisoners given some bread and water, and the *patriotes* offered wine to cheer their spirits. As midnight approached Morin and Roussel summoned everyone to prepare to move on as there was no time to waste. Shortly after midnight the prisoners were once again bundled into the cart and the journey resumed, accompanied by raucous singing from three *patriotes* much the worse for wear.

As the weather deteriorated Morin ordered that they take refuge in an abandoned cottage close to some woods. He and Roussel insisted that the three *patriotes* rest so they would be ready for the long haul to Chalons-sur-Marne in the morning. They soon fell asleep. Morin turned to the prisoners.

"Monsieur le Comte, you must follow my instructions explicitly. In a few minutes, we are leaving here – neither for Chalons-sur-Marne nor Paris but for the Rhine, which it is my intention we should cross. Until I deem it safe you will remain bound, to give the impression to any who may be curious that you are prisoners of the revolution. Madame la Comtesse, I know it is difficult for you but you must do all you can to keep your boy quiet so that he does not make undue noise and draw attention to what we are about to do."

The Comte and Comtesse nodded.

With that Drescher and Trudaine changed the horses on the cart and, with the de Puyraveau family once again on board, they moved off in a new direction, through woods, and led by an old man on a horse whom Drescher had drawn from his pool of old informants. Later the next day Trudaine managed to find some food and the old man found saddles, which were placed in the cart. Drescher pinned cockades to the de Puyraveaus. By Sunday the 7th of November the procession, which had kept rigidly to forest tracks and pathways, had reached the banks of the River Meuse south of Nancy. In the remaining woodland before the river the cart was abandoned and the five fugitives – for that is what they now were as the alarm had been raised – mounted the horses and proceeded along the riverbank where they took their place in a long queue to cross. It took more than two hours to reach the head of the queue but by late afternoon they had crossed the Meuse. Strasbourg, the south-east and the Rhine were now within striking distance.

Drescher was weary. Their progress had been slower than he had wished. Three days later, on Wednesday the 10th of November, the tired, bedraggled riders reached a village several miles south of Strasbourg, close to the Rhine. He had warned the Comte and Comtesse many times that loose talk could cost them their freedom. It was that evening that the boy remarked in his innocence that when they had travelled with the King their journeys across France were more comfortable. The comment was overheard by the tavern-keeper and two drinkers. Drescher, also hearing the boy's remark, made immediate preparations for what he knew would happen. The tavern-keeper's information was worth money. He stole outside and prepared the horses for their escape. Returning to the tavern he summoned the others, but the tavern-keeper and the two other occupants of the inn tried to stop them leaving. Drescher and Trudaine subdued them and bound them with some rope. The fugitives then slipped quietly into the night.

By the early hours they were on the bank of the Rhine. Drescher searched for an empty fishing boat but there was none. Fearing pursuers may not be far behind he decided to capture an occupied boat. They walked further along the bank until they reached a larger craft being prepared for departure. The two *patriotes* on board were hauling up the sail. Drescher and Trudaine boarded.

"Hey you, get off the boat. We're getting ready to sail and don't need any more crew. We need space for our fish."

"We want to cross the river," said Drescher. "Will you take us?"

The man who was obviously the captain replied that he would not. Then looking over Drescher's shoulder he noticed that the Comte, close behind, had reversed his cockade to reveal its white material. This was the sign the Bourbons used to signify their contempt for the revolution.

"You're bloody monarchists trying to escape," the captain said, struggling to pull a pistol from his belt.

Drescher flicked back his long shabby coat and in a flash fired at the captain. He fell backwards, collapsing in a supine heap. The second *patriote* ran forward. Trudaine fired his pistol. The man slumped to the deck. By this time the firing had attracted attention along the riverbank and before long figures started to run towards them.

"Quick, de Puyraveau, slip the moorings," Drescher ordered. "If they board we are done for. Come, Comtesse, you and the child must step aboard instantly."

The Comte de Puyraveau undid the first rope and then the second as pistol shots began to whistle above their heads. He pushed the boat away from the jetty with his bare hands. The boat began to edge out into the open river, the wind catching its sail.

"Trudaine, take the tiller and steer towards the other side. Everyone keep down."

More shots were fired from the bank and further back up the river Drescher could see another boat setting sail.

Gradually, the current seized the craft and it began to move faster towards midstream. Another shot rang out as Drescher and the Comte de Puyraveau pulled hard on the lines to stretch the sail to full capacity to catch the light wind. Drescher fell back. Glancing off the narrow deck, his body slid into the water.

"Puyraveau, take the tiller and my pistol and use it if that boat gets any nearer!" said Trudaine as he plunged into the water. With considerable effort he caught hold of Drescher and, despite the man's heavy coat, dragged him to the side of the boat. In spite of his wound Drescher managed to pull himself out of the water with the help of the Comte, who had given his place at thc tiller to his wife. By this time a stronger breeze had caught the sail and with rowing from Trudaine and de Puyraveau the boat gradually got closer to the eastern bank of the Rhine and safety. The smaller boat had pulled back from pursuit. An hour or so later they had taken refuge in a small village, free of France.

The following morning they began their journey towards Stuttgart, as Drescher and Trudaine had done the year before. By now Drescher's health had worsened. The pistol shot had passed through his body causing significant bleeding which, valiant though the efforts of the villagers were, had not stopped. His condition obliged them to halt their progress in the next village they came to. Two days later, despite further attention and care, Waldemar Drescher died of his wound in the arms of the young man he had come to admire and love in the short time they had been together. He was buried by the family he had rescued. Before he died he gave to Trudaine a sealed letter, which he instructed him to hand personally to the Countess von Deppe. This was the last act of love he wished Trudaine to show him.

* * * * *

On Wednesday the 1st of December, 1790, Robert Trudaine arrived at Herzberg to inform Arabella, to her joy, that her niece, the Comtesse de Puyraveau, the Comte de Puyraveau and their young son would arrive at Herzberg the next day. But her joy was overwhelmed by sadness when Trudaine, close to tears, told her that Waldemar Drescher had died from a wound he had received during the escape across the Rhine. The man in the shadows, her protector, had gone. She comforted the heartbroken Trudaine and urged him to stay at Herzberg at least until the winter was passed. As she held his hand Arabella thought of her own mortality.

Later that evening, after supper, Trudaine handed her the letter from Drescher.

"Countess, he asked me to give you this and to urge you to read it in private."

Arabella withdrew to the library. The handwriting was uneven and in places hard to read, revealing the difficulty and pain of writing. There were two or three brown marks on the paper, which Arabella realised were drops of blood.

> *Dear Countess von Deppe,*
>
> *Throughout my life I have been used to reading in secret the letters of His Late Majesty's enemies. I wrote few letters of my own because I believed that the fewer words I committed to paper the less incriminating would be the contents of my correspondence if intercepted by an adversary. But now the time*

has come for me to write a final letter and, though I am unskilled in the art, it is appropriate that it should be to you.

When you receive it by the hand of my companion, Monsieur Trudaine, I will no longer be of this world, relieved at last of the personal physical burden I have carried throughout my life. I will at last be able to sleep undisturbed and untroubled. I have long been a man oppressed by sin. Where my soul might go will be a matter for the Almighty to decide in his infinite wisdom, weighing as he will the many sins I have committed – and the blood I have shed – in the earthly interests of Prussia and its King. I will accept whatever punishment he considers I deserve.

Before I begin my journey to final judgement and likely damnation I wish you to know that from the moment you saved my life on the road to Magdeburg I realised that you were different from so many others who had crossed my path. Since that time I have witnessed in you bravery, steadfastness and strength of character to match that of any famous warrior. You listen, you observe, you consider and you decide according to the noblest principles of this world. But most of all you are loyal and a beacon of unblemished trust, a true keeper of secrets.

I wish to confess that I fell in love with you long ago. It was not for me the physical love of a man for a woman, though I often wished it could have been. I came to love you because of who you were, because of your fierce pursuit of what was right and honourable, and because you were never the carrier of malice. I deeply envied your late husband, Count von Deppe, and soon became jealous whenever I saw him and you together, enjoying the fruits of a friendship and a love I could never have and which once I believe he may have betrayed by a certain use of words in a moment of weakness. My jealousy of what he had, of what he possessed, and, moreover, my anger towards him for what he had said became so overwhelming that I chose not to do all that I could to protect him, though he did not seek it, from the danger to which the late King had exposed him in Bohemia. I had promised him before his departure that I would protect you, but I did not protect him when I could have easily saved him from the attrition of war. I left him exposed just as King David placed Uriah in the front line of his army because of his love for Bathsheba.

My sin did not stop there. After the death of Count von Deppe, I considered you – without you ever knowing – my personal possession, like a collector of a precious painting that no one else should have. In the poem Orlando Furioso *an old hermit fell in love with the beautiful Angelica and tried to abduct her. When she resisted his advances, he gave her a magic potion to drink so she would fall asleep and he could admire her beauty. I had become similarly obsessed. Ultimately the hermit had to admit defeat. In my case, that was the moment when Monsieur Trudaine arrived in my life. Through his wise words I realised I was guilty of the cardinal sin of envy, which Dante once defined as "Love of one's own good perverted to a desire to deprive other men of theirs".*

I am now an old man, dying and riddled with the aches and pains of life, and plagued with regrets for not doing many things in my life that I should have done. My greatest regret of all was my lack of courage to confess my sin to you earlier and to seek your forgiveness. What a coward I proved to be, hiding behind the deception that in wartime the truth is so precious that she should at all times be attended by a bodyguard of lies. Instead I should have honoured the promise I made to you in St Petersburg that I would always be honest with you. I was not.

My hour is nearly come but I ask you, if you can bring yourself to do so, to forgive me and perhaps pray for my soul as I descend towards purgatory to receive due punishment for an unworthy life.

I have one final wish, which it may be easier for you to grant. Do not leave Prussia as its hour of need approaches. One day my country – your country – will again be great. When it is, your grace and devotion to our country will have contributed to such an outcome.

Waldemar Drescher
The 14th of November, 1790

Arabella put the letter down. She was swept by swirling anger, derision, prejudice, pity, sorrow – and a deep sense of betrayal. How could her most trusted friend – the man who had saved her life more than once, the man who had brought her son safely back from France and who had now delivered the Puyraveau family to safety – write such a letter, asking her forgiveness? How could he have left her husband unprotected? How had her husband betrayed her in a moment of weakness? Why had Drescher not revealed the secret further? She turned towards the fire, scrunching the letter in her fist, tempted to consign it to the flames. But she stayed her hand.

She had knelt more than once in the confessional to confess the sin of pride. Who was she to judge others? Smoothing out the letter she reread it, and began to understand the torment and rejection Drescher had endured throughout his life – the absence of the love he had needed for fulfilment and happiness. He had asked for her prayers in his last letter, written shortly before his painful death. Who was she to deny him that? She folded the bloodstained letter and locked it away in her secretaire. Before leaving the room, she gazed into the fire.

"Herr Drescher, I will miss you. God have mercy on your soul."

* * * * *

In the early afternoon of the next day the de Puyraveau family arrived at Herzberg. Tired from the long journey, they took some days to recover from the circumstances of their escape and Drescher's death.

The Comtesse Marie-Aurore de Puyraveau, now aged twenty-seven, took longer to raise her spirits in freedom, not least on account of her worry about the continued detention of her mother and father. The possibility that they might be punished for the escape weighed heavily on her mind. But in her lighter moments she was an attractive, softly spoken and much-refined young woman, well rehearsed in court etiquette from her position as a young lady-in-waiting to King Louis's daughter, Marie Thérèse, the Dauphine. Her features and slim build more resembled her mother's than her father's. Her son, Antoine, looked more like his father.

The Comte, some years older than his wife and rumoured to have had several mistresses, was tall, broadly built, good-looking but, having lived at the Palace of Versailles since his birth, he was well attuned to the intrigue, banter and good living that thrived in the shadow of the throne. From the moment of his arrival he displayed the supreme self-confidence and lack of sensitivity often to be found amongst those who served the Bourbon King. Within days he had noisily pledged to return to France to help the beleaguered King stay on his throne, slay the King's enemies, and secure the release of the Vicomte and Vicomtesse de Vervins and the restitution of their property. His swagger, his attitude and his boastful pronouncements irritated Arabella. Several times she had cause to hush him in the presence of her servants. As she discreetly pointed out, while the Prussian King may be deeply sympathetic to the French King's cause, that did not mean all Prussians were immune to bribery for the provision of information that could be useful to the enemy. He took her reprimand in good spirits but her advice was soon cast aside by his pride.

* * * * *

A week later the occupants of Herzberg gathered to honour in prayer the man whose name had been inscribed on a simple stone at their feet.

An
Waldemar Drescher
Ein treuer Begleiter
Gott sei mit ihm

To
Waldemar Drescher
A true companion
God be with him

Afterwards, while the others walked back to the house, Arabella paused to say an additional prayer for the man she had never really understood but who, second only to her late husband, had been a valiant friend and defender. Then in the gathering gloom she walked a short distance to her husband's grave.

"Dearest Carl Manfred, I still miss you – even if you betrayed me in some way as Herr Drescher claimed you did. The past is the past and I will never forget that it was you who saved me from despair and degradation. I forgive you for whatever you might have done. I ask you now to be with me in spirit as I continue to protect Herzberg in your name. You made me what I am and, despite my frailties and distractions, I will continue to strive to serve Prussia with honour to the end of my life, in gratitude to all those who have supported me since I first came to this land and we pledged our love for one another under these trees. God be with you and with me in whatever further tests I may face."

* * * * *

In early December Arabella received word from Sir Charles Gray. He was on his way back from diplomatic business in St Petersburg and, as his journey had taken longer than expected and travel through France remained unpredictable, he had decided to stay in Berlin until early the next year. He hoped that it would be possible for him to pay his respects to the Countess before the end of the month. She sent immediate word to his intended lodgings in Berlin, inviting him to join her for her planned pre-Christmas musical soirée and to stay as her guest for a few days. Over a week later he replied that he would be delighted to do so but that his stay would be short.

On Saturday afternoon the 16th of December, 1790, a long line of carriages arrived at Herzberg to hear a performance in the *Spiegelsaal* of Handel's sacred oratorio *Messiah*, played by the Herzberg Camerata, with Elise Catherine as the soprano soloist and her mother, Arabella, as the mezzo. Herr Bamberger's son, Philip, destined to follow in his father's footsteps as the orchestra's *Leiter*, took the tenor part; the redoubtable Herr Heinrich Bergman was the baritone. The singers were supported by members of the choir of St Hedwig's Cathedral in Berlin. Amongst the audience were the Crown Prince Frederick William; the fourteen-year-old Luise of Mecklenburg-Strelitz, accompanied by her grandmother; the new British Ambassador, Sir Morton Eden; and Sir Charles Gray. Sung in candlelight in the gloom of the late afternoon, it was a fitting oratorio with which to draw 1790 to an end. Many were conscious that day that France was slipping further into uncertainty and ever-deepening recrimination against the monarchy. The implications were chilling.

Christmas Eve was celebrated quietly at Herzberg. Arabella was joined by her son and daughter-in-law, the Count and Countess von Deppe; her daughter, Elise Catherine, with her husband, Lieutenant Joseph Lange von Schellenhorst; the Comtesse and Comtesse de Puyraveau and their son, Antoine; Monsieur Trudaine; and Sir Charles Gray. Over the next two days they walked, talked, played cards, and sang and played music. In the depth of the night Arabella shared her bed with her lover.

CHAPTER 10

The Shedding of Blood

Throughout 1791 news from Paris provided little hope to the von Deppe family that the revolution had run its course. To the contrary, it appeared to gather strength with each passing month as different protagonists, egged on by the scurrilous *libellistes* and the activities of street mobs, fished in a deepening pond of hostility towards King Louis and his wife, Marie Antoinette.

In March came news of the abolition of the royal guilds and monopolies. Three months later came reports that the King and Queen had escaped from Paris only to be intercepted at Varennes and forced to turn back to the capital. At the beginning of July the Austrian Emperor, Marie Antoinette's brother, declared a set of principles in accordance with which a coalition of French émigré nobles and European powers – Austria, Prussia, Britain, Spain and Russia – would invade France and end the revolution. Later that month the National Assembly declared the King inviolable and restored his prerogatives. Shortly afterwards it was reported that the National Guard had fired on crowds protesting against the King's restoration; there had been many casualties. Late in August, at Pillnitz, the Emperor Leopold II declared the support of the Holy Roman Empire and Prussia for the beleaguered French King. The following month, news came that King Louis had accepted a new constitution. By November the French National Assembly ordered that all émigrés return to France under threat of death, only for King Louis to veto it two days later. As report after report reached the von Deppe family the prospects for peace seemed to get bleaker by the day.

The Vicomte de Vervins and his wife, Maria Louisa, remained at the Tuileries – along with many dozens of other courtiers – out of loyalty to the royal family, having survived their examination following the escape from France of their daughter and son-in-law with their child late in the previous year. The plan of the elder de Vervins to escape in the hubbub following the King's own attempted flight never materialised.

* * * * *

Meanwhile, at Herzberg, the spring of 1791 brought fresh colour and vitality to the estate. Arabella von Deppe intensified her supervision as war clouds gathered in the west. Her other task, with Herr Bamberger, was to plan their new "season" for the Camerata, with yet further changes to the repertoire as French composers became increasingly unpopular.

The Comte de Puyraveau, whose company Arabella did not always enjoy – though concealing it for the sake of his wife, Marie-Aurore – spent considerable time travelling in order to meet other French émigrés to discuss the restoration of the rights of the Bourbon monarchy. Though Marie-Aurore had recovered from her escape from France, her spirits remained low because of anxiety about the possible fate of her mother and father. Shedding some of her French court etiquette and becoming more relaxed, in keeping with the simple style at Herzberg, she proved accomplished on the harpsichord, though not as dexterous as Elise Catherine; Arabella's daughter liked to play whenever she came to stay from her home near the Potsdam military garrison during the absence of her husband, now a major, on army manoeuvres. Another frequent visitor to the estate in her husband's military absence was Frederick Daniel's wife, Jacqueline. The women became known, when together at Herzberg, as the Three Graces. Their laughter, beauty and limpid femininity made them the envy of the many other women who came regularly to the house. Male visitors, for their part, found it hard to divert their gaze from the slender figures before them, often emphasised by their slim-cut chiffon dresses and low décolleté. One visitor remarked that when Arabella was present it was akin to visiting Venus's palace. Another commented that to see the Countess and the Herzberg girls together was like watching a performance of Gluck's *Dance of the Blessed Spirits*. Robert Trudaine's own spirits lifted. Though he continued to occupy a small house on the estate, he mysteriously came and went – sometimes for periods of many weeks – but when present he added to the laughter and informed debate, whether the subject were light-hearted or more serious.

In their garrison at Potsdam, Frederick Daniel – now with the rank of *Rittmeister* in the cavalry – and his brother-in-law, Joseph, had become increasingly aware of the growing shortcomings of the Prussian army, no longer the efficient machine it had been under the late King Frederick and his father before him. The failure of the present King to begin reforms had added to the army's declining prestige. The two young men, together with others in a small coterie around the shy Crown Prince Frederick William, began to consider ways in which the army might be improved, though they knew that the steps they envisaged would be hard to implement.

Military reform aside, when the two came to Herzberg, now not far by fast carriage on the good road from Potsdam, they were occasionally accompanied by the Crown Prince. The three would sit for hours in the library discussing the latest reports from France. Sometimes the news and examples of the latest *libelliste* outpourings were brought to Herzberg by the always well-informed Sir Charles Gray, in whose company the Countess Arabella seemed greatly at ease. This ease went largely unnoticed, except by Elise Catherine, who had sensed ever since their visit to Prague – and her mother's diversion alone to Karlsbad – that their companionship was closer than many might think. Aware of the need for discretion, Arabella and Charles Gray were at pains to eschew any action or mannerism that might possibly disclose or even hint at intimacy between them. But they were not always successful. On one occasion Elise Catherine glimpsed her mother's hand appearing deliberately to touch Gray's as he held her chair at the dining table, and noticed the resulting pleasurable physical frisson the touch seemed to cause her. She was tempted to tease her mother about her possible feelings towards Sir Charles but decided that it would not be appropriate to do so – at least not for now.

Charles Gray was not a frequent visitor to Herzberg, as his undisclosed diplomatic activities kept him regularly occupied, but it was obvious to all how much he enjoyed his visits to the estate. He could relax, listen to excellent music, discuss matters in private without fear of disclosure, as well as browse the ever-expanding Herzberg library and, not least, observe the slow evolution of the Herzberg generations. He particularly enjoyed sharing the company and intelligent banter of such attractive women around the dining table, but most of all he relished his physical intimacy with the Countess Arabella, whose sophistication and sexual needs remained unalloyed pleasure to him and, of course, to her.

*****

The year wore on, spring into summer and hot and pleasant summer into autumn. As 1791 moved to a close, music was played, the army drilled, and the Herzberg estate looked with relief on its successful harvest. No devastating news arrived from Paris. The monarchs of the other European states continued to huff and puff. But as everybody went about their daily business they continued to fear a disaster. The first revolutionary shoe had dropped in July 1789 but when would the second fall? To everyone's relief it had not done so by the end of 1791.

*****

The previous year's perceived intermission in the downward spiral of events in France soon came to an end at the beginning of 1792. In January came reports of persistent food riots in Paris. The growing agitation on the streets of the capital against the occupants of the Tuileries was further fuelled by the defensive treaty between Austria – in the person of Marie Antoinette, perceived in France as its arch enemy – and Prussia. By March the guillotine had been adopted as the official means of execution and put to use soon after. The bad blood between France and Austria became worse when on the 20th of April King Louis was obliged by popular sentiment to declare war on the homeland of his wife. Three days later France invaded the Austrian Netherlands. The revolution was now spreading beyond the borders of France as Charles Gray had predicted.

Within France the situation deteriorated further. Yet more disturbing reports reached Arabella. On the 20th of June the *sans-culottes* had invaded the Tuileries and humiliated the King, obliging him to wear the *bonnet rouge*, which had become the popular street insignia of the revolution. On the 5th of July the Legislative Assembly had declared the fatherland in danger. Later that month the Brunswick Manifesto, issued by Charles William Ferdinand, Duke of Brunswick and commander of the allied army, added more fuel to the fire by warning the people of Paris that an "exemplary and ever-memorable vengeance" would follow if the royal family were harmed. This had the counter-effect of spurring the radicals in Paris, the so-called Girondins, to further humiliate King Louis and to seek a war against the enemies of France. At the same time petitions began to circulate calling for the abolition of the monarchy. On the 30th of July Austria and Prussia invaded France and by the end of July it became compulsory for all men to wear the tricolour cockade. In August the strains of the *Marseillaise* were heard for the first time in Paris with the arrival of the revolutionary volunteers from Marseilles. The news from France seemed to be worsening by the day.

* * * * *

On Wednesday the 25th of July a sombre and fatigued Charles Gray arrived at Herzberg from Berlin, following an audience with the King. He was accompanied from Potsdam by Frederick Daniel and his wife, Jacqueline, and by Elise Catherine and her husband, Joseph. Gray told Arabella and the Comte and Comtesse de Puyraveau, also present, that so bitter and intense had become the already inflamed hostility in France towards the monarchy that he believed the institution would not survive the remaining months of the year. There was little doubt in his mind that the combination of public malevolence and revolutionary fervour was about to push the country over the edge of the abyss. If that happened, war in Europe would be inevitable. Frederick Daniel and his brother-in-law, Joseph, agreed with Gray's opinion. While they had yet to be summoned to the war front, they knew that it would not be long before they would be required to go. This filled Arabella with dread. She had lost her husband as a result of war. Frederick was her only son and it would be catastrophic if he were to die. Though filled with inner turmoil, she dared not reveal her fears and risk condemnation for her perceived selfishness at a time of national sacrifice. At Herzberg almost daily Armand de Puyraveau spoke of the need for the restoration of Bourbon pride. That night, Arabella lay in Charles Gray's arms. His intimacy was more of comfort than of physical enjoyment.

The next morning Sir Charles and the family gathered for breakfast. There was further discussion of the prospect of war. The Comte de Puyraveau spoke with his usual verbal bluster.

"War is unpleasant and people get killed but it is essential that firm action is taken against the monsters in Paris – such as Mirabeau and Danton – and so this revolutionary nonsense brought to an end and the Bourbon King restored to his rightful throne. France has always been a monarchy and that historical fact cannot be reversed by individuals pursuing personal ambitions. They and the Duc d'Orléans – that traitor to the royal cause – should be sent to the guillotine. Prussia has a crucial role to play in the defence of the monarchy in France. I for one will set an example and support the Bourbon King and indeed take my place in the front line. *Aux armes*! I say."

For a moment no one spoke, though everyone's discomfort at Comte de Puyraveau's gauche and insensitive remarks was palpable. Arabella intervened, unable to suppress her anger.

"For the past year I have listened patiently to the news that Sir Charles and others have kindly brought to me and for which I am truly grateful. Like everyone else my hopes for peace and common sense have risen and fallen over the many turbulent months. But it has been evident to me – a mere woman – that this revolutionary die was cast long ago. Though I fear the prospect of war and its possible consequences, I will, like everyone in Prussia, do everything I can to support His Majesty's decisions, whether it is providing more from the estate or the greater availability of music to raise the spirits of our people.

"But there are two particular matters on which I wish to be frank. My mother was French. I adore France as she did – its traditions, its literature, its music and its beauty. The language of France is second nature to me, as indeed it is to all of us around this table. I have been to my mother's family estate at Rozac. It has epitomised France for generations. But France has been sorely tested by the present King and indeed by his father. They failed to make reforms and improve the well-being of the nation. I regret, Monsieur le Comte, if I offend your support for the Bourbon dynasty but no one – even the French King – can push back the tide of history.

"There is another and more personal matter. The Vicomte and Vicomtesse de Vervins remain under guard in Paris. It is not for me to judge the reasons for those circumstances but I owe it to my late husband to bring liberty to his sister and her husband. They took me into their home long ago with great kindness and generosity. It was in the same spirit and with pleasure, Monsieur le Comte, that I welcomed you and Madame la Comtesse into Herzberg two years ago. You may stay here as long as you wish. But I cannot sit here in any peace of mind without the release of Etienne and Maria Louisa from their captivity and bringing them here. That is more important than the fate of the French King.

"Please all of you continue to discuss and plan but for me the release of these two dear people from the Tuileries is uppermost in my mind. And I intend to give it urgent thought since if you are correct, Sir Charles, there is little time left in which to take action. If you are shocked, Monsieur le Comte, by what I have said, I ask your dispensation. But as I once said to my father when he provoked me to anger, '*Je suis comme je suis.*' I am as I am."

Everyone around the breakfast table sat in stunned silence. No one had ever heard Arabella speak in such a forthright manner before.

Frederick Daniel broke the silence.

"Mama, we understand your feelings, but seeking to free the Vicomte and Vicomtesse would not be easy. The Prussian army is already in France and it is possible that together with the Austrians we may be able to lance the boil."

"I respect what you say, Frederick Daniel, but please do not humour me because I am a woman. I repeat, something must be done soon about Etienne and Maria Louisa. I could not bear to think that their lives might end in bloodshed because I did nothing."

"Madame la Comtesse," said de Puyraveau, "I apologise for any ill-judged remark I may have made. Your hospitality towards us has been generous. But it remains my view that King Louis must be restored to his throne as a step towards the restoration of sanity in France and for the greater protection of Europe."

"Armand," said Elise Catherine, "there is no need to apologise. We are all under great strain. But my mother is right. We must consider soon what is to be done about Marie-Aurore's mother and father. Sir Charles, we know you have many preoccupations but we should all be grateful if you would assist us with further advice as soon as you are able."

"I will indeed," replied Gray, "and as quickly as I can."

Shortly before his departure later that day for a destination he could not disclose he spoke alone to Arabella.

"Dearest Arabella, like you I find de Puyraveau a buffoon. King Louis will not survive and I doubt neither will his wife. I will see what I can do about the de Vervins. It will not be easy. The Vicomte nailed his colours to the royal mast long ago out of loyalty and affection and at the time those were noble virtues. But the *sans-culottes* do not make sophisticated judgements. De Vervins is now in dire danger. As for the Vicomtesse, because of her German accent she is perceived by the *sans-culottes* – wrongly, of course – to be Austrian and, thus tarred, the efforts of the Prussian Ambassador to secure her release have fallen on deaf ears. Those driving the revolution for their own ends see the de Vervins and others like them as mere disposable pawns on the chessboard of revenge. Please, Arabella, I know the strength of your views but in my absence do nothing rash and stay guarded in your opinions. Even close friends can be unreliable. Remember the late Herr Drescher's advice: be vigilant and trust no one – advice you have always followed and advice I too would commend. Drescher was a good man and I got to know him well in his last years. He earned my respect and I trusted him. I urge you to continue to do so. Do not drop your guard now. Remember, terror makes people not only frightened but ingenious, not least selling information about others to protect themselves, if not to gain from the misfortune of others."

"I will, Charles, I will. I find your departures so painful. Once you are gone, I feel so alone, no one to turn to for advice."

"Dearest Arabella, I will be back with all speed. In the meantime, Monsieur Trudaine is likely to return soon from his own travels. He may have more news to share and so help us to decide how best to act."

During the remainder of that week and the one following, people came and went. While Arabella did her best to ensure, as calmly as she could, that daily life at Herzberg carried on uninterrupted, and continued to prepare for the impact of army recruitment on the estate, she began to assemble a plan in her mind to secure Etienne and Maria Louisa's liberty. She chose to keep it secret, mindful of the renewed advice from Charles Gray to be vigilant and to trust no one, not even Marie-Aurore de Puyraveau, lest she reveal the plan to her bellicose husband.

On the 20th of August Arabella received news she had been dreading. Robert Trudaine arrived on horseback – breathless, travel-stained and worn out – to tell her that the Vicomte Etienne de Vervins had been massacred earlier in the month, along with the King's Swiss Guard and loyal soldiers, while defending the Tuileries Palace from an attack by the National Guard of the Paris Commune. The King and Queen had sought refuge with the Legislative Assembly. The Vicomtesse had been separated from the royal family and taken to La Force prison. He added that there were now rumours that coalition troops, led by the Duke of Brunswick, had already invaded France. Arabella sat in shock in the library, her face drained white. Then her anger exploded.

"Monsieur Trudaine, I have sat in this room for over two years listening to news brought from France and to dire warnings of bloodshed. For two years I and others have sat on our hands doing nothing to rescue the Vicomtesse de Vervins, a lady immeasurably dear to my heart, and her husband. I cannot speak for those others but I am ashamed of myself for being so idle and selfish. Herzberg has earned great respect over the past years but while we have served and saved others we have not saved our own blood. What has become of us? Just what has become of us? If only Herr Drescher were here."

Tears filled her eyes.

"Please, Countess, do not distress yourself. You are beyond reproach. You inspired Herr Drescher to save your son and then the two of us to rescue the Comte and Comtesse de Puyraveau.

There is nothing more you can do. But if you think there is, I am at your service."

"Monsieur Trudaine, I despise this accursed revolution. There is talk of the rights of man – a noble aim – but these rights have become selective. Where are the rights of the innocent before the law? People require inspired and honourable leadership, not the leadership of the vengeful and the ambitious, ready to pursue personal aims and to sacrifice those who have caused no offence. Mark my words. I swear revenge on the revolution for the victim, Etienne de Vervins, it has claimed, just as Electra swore revenge for the murder of her father."

The library fell silent, measured more than broken by the ticking of the clock.

"Madame, I share your disgust and revulsion. Since the death of Herr Drescher, a man I admired and loved, I have nothing left but my life. If it be your wish, I will join you in whatever revenge you choose to exact."

Arabella could no longer keep her secret.

"Monsieur Trudaine, I had already decided, weeks ago, to go to France to rescue the Vicomte and Vicomtesse de Vervins. Now the Vicomte is dead. With the situation even worse than before I intend to leave Herzberg for Paris as quickly as possible, to secure the freedom of the Vicomtesse. The thought of her in La Force along with beggars and prostitutes is inconceivable. That is my decision and nothing will dissuade me from my course of action."

"But, Madame, Paris is a vipers' nest. It would not be safe for you. I will go in your stead."

"No, Monsieur Trudaine, you will not. I must go."

"Then I will come with you and I insist that you permit me to do so. If you try to leave without me, I will only follow you," he said.

"Monsieur Trudaine, so be it. To be honest, I would greatly welcome your companionship. But my plan is secret and must not be disclosed to my family until we are on our way."

For the next hour or so Arabella and Trudaine discussed and refined her plan. They decided to leave on the morning of Thursday the 23rd of August, on horseback. As speed was of the essence they would not go as far south as the Rhine and cross there, but travel due west towards Hanover and then Cologne.

From there they would turn south-west towards Lorraine and Metz, and thereafter south-west towards her mother's family estate at Rozac, in order to see whether the château was still intact, before turning north to Paris.

"Monsieur Trudaine, I will travel dressed as a man. It will be easier and afford less chance of me being molested. I still have in my possession some clothes I last used many years ago. With some adjustment they will fit. I will need a sword, which I hope you can find for me. I will make a tricolour cockade, similar to the one you must have worn in France."

Trudaine was astonished by the proposal, but even more astonished by the audacity of the elegant, beautiful woman sitting beside him. He looked at her, still in doubt her scheme would work.

"Monsieur Trudaine, there is no going back. This is what I have decided to do and I am ready to stake my life on its success. Once we get to Paris, Monsieur, I will become dependent on you for the execution of my plan. We will need somewhere safe to stay."

"Madame, I may have an answer to that. Paris is full of spies, informers and money-grubbers. Nowhere is truly safe, but from my travels I know of a room in a small house belonging to a family I believe to be honourable. The husband is dead but as his widow, a well-mannered woman, seemed trustworthy I stayed there several nights. She shares the house with her elderly mother and an aunt. They come and go. One night, while talking about the shortage of food and the struggle to survive, she recalled the days when she had worked at one of the grand residences in the Rue St Louis. When the revolution came the family she served moved to the Palace of Versailles and then with the royal family to the Tuileries. There contact had been lost, but she spoke with great nostalgia of her happiness in the Rue St Louis and expressed sincere regret at the misfortune of the family, as she understood it from the gossip she had heard. I asked the name of the family but she was reluctant to reveal it for fear of retribution."

"Monsieur Trudaine, what was the woman's name?"

"She said it was Sybille."

Suddenly, Arabella recalled that name. It was that of Maria Louisa's young personal maid, who had helped to care for her following her escape to Paris in December 1765.

"Monsieur Trudaine, I believe that Sybille with whom you stayed in safety may be the Sybille who was the Vicomtesse's personal maid. She cared for me. On our arrival in Paris, can you take me to her? She may well be our safe house."

Again, Trudaine voiced his fears.

"Madame la Comtesse, what you plan is dangerous. To carry it out will place your life at great risk. What will your son and daughter say? And indeed what would Sir Charles say, for that matter? Please, stay at Herzberg in safety. Let me go alone."

"No, Monsieur Trudaine, I am going to Paris – with or without you. Yes, I am full of terror at what lies ahead and, yes, my judgement may be clouded. But that is no matter. My grief is full of venom. I must go to Paris and avenge what has happened. My revenge will be to free the Vicomtesse and bring her to safety at Herzberg to be with her daughter. If necessary, I will kill to achieve her freedom. That is an end to the debate, Monsieur Trudaine. Whether you come with me or not, I will resolve this matter whatever may be the outcome."

"Countess, I will come with you. As you avenge so will I – the death of the man I loved."

Three days later, on Thursday the 23rd of August – the day after, unknown to them, royalist riots had begun in France – Arabella von Deppe left the house on horseback, wearing a simple dress and riding coat, ostensibly to inspect the estate. She took with her a leather saddlebag containing the uniform in which she had escaped from London. She had secretly altered it to a revolutionary fashion and pinned to the jacket a tricolour cockade. She left a note with Weisser to hand to her daughter, due to arrive a few days later. Fortunately the Comte and Comtesse de Puyraveau were in Potsdam. After giving instructions to the land agent, Maximilian's successor, Herr Bauer, and changing into her uniform at Robert Trudaine's house, Arabella and her companion began their journey to France. She travelled under the pseudonym of Aristide Badeau, the same she had used long ago on her fateful journey with the disguised Waldemar Drescher in pursuit of the man she loved. By nightfall they had put many miles between themselves and Herzberg. The route they took westwards past Magdeburg further revived the memory of that long-ago journey, made by coach eastwards on the same route.

On Saturday Elise Catherine arrived alone at Herzberg. She read her mother's letter. Its contents caused her consternation.

My dearest Elise,

Three days ago Monsieur Trudaine brought the terrible news that the Vicomte de Vervins had been massacred along with other valiant soldiers defending the Tuileries from an attack by the Paris Commune, and that the Vicomtesse had been removed to La Force prison. The prospects for the King, the Queen and those around them who survived the massacre are now bleak.

Etienne's death has almost broken my heart. To lose Maria Louisa would break it altogether. I can no longer stand idly by at Herzberg to see his death unavenged and my beloved sister-in-law condemned to life or even death in prison. I have therefore left for Paris in the company of Monsieur Trudaine with the intention of securing Maria Louisa's freedom by one means or another. I accept the mission is dangerous and I have embarked on my journey with a fearful heart. But it must be done. I have trust in Monsieur Trudaine, who has his own bitter score to settle. The route we will take is secret.

I intend to return to Herzberg by the end of October – alive and with Maria Louisa. Please take care of Herzberg in my absence. The land agent, Herr Bauer, has his instructions. Your task is to break the news to Marie-Aurore of her father's death. But you must not disclose my full intentions to her husband in case he compromises what I plan to do. Use your discretion as to the excuse you give him. Nor must you disclose my intentions to Joseph or Frederick Daniel or indeed to Sir Charles Gray if he comes unexpectedly to Herzberg. If my plans are revealed I will not succeed. Please pray for me.

If I fail to return by the end of October I wish you to know that in all probability I will never see Herzberg again. If that happens, I will have laid down my life for a noble cause and out of love for you, Frederick Daniel, Joseph and Jacqueline. Herzberg will be left in the safe hands of my children, whom I have cherished throughout my life.

Au revoir.

With my deep affection,

Mama
Herzberg, Thursday the 23rd of August, 1792

"My dearest mama, what have you done? In God's name, what have you done?" cried Elise Catherine.

* * * * *

Almost two weeks later, in the late afternoon of Tuesday the 4th of September, a weary Arabella von Deppe and Robert Trudaine reached Château de Rozac south of Paris. They had barely slept en route, deciding that, apart from stopping to change horses, they should get to the French capital as soon as possible. But Arabella was insistent it was necessary to divert to the estate of her mother's family.

The sight that confronted Arabella as she and Trudaine crested the hill filled her with sorrow and then rage. The house had been destroyed by fire. Only the shell of the once proud and beautiful château remained. The garden had been ravaged and was now a grazing ground for cattle. They went to the side of the house towards the chapel. Asking Trudaine to keep watch she went inside. The tombs in the crypt had been vandalised. Her mother's, nearest the door, had suffered particular damage. Arabella picked up a fragment of its stone carving from the floor and then another and another after that. She placed them together. They formed the letters T-H-E-R, part of her mother's name, Thérèse. Putting the fragments in her pocket, she knelt down beside the shattered tomb.

"Dearest Mama, I pledge to you that I will wreak vengeance on this accursed revolution for the shame and destruction it has brought to the innocent."

Still kneeling she prayed to the Mother of God to conduct her and Trudaine in safety to Paris in order to rescue Maria Louisa de Vervins from the madness now engulfing France.

As she rose to her feet in the deepening dusk she heard Trudaine's voice calling her. She walked quickly outside to see two men gathered around her companion. A boy was with them.

"What are you doing here?" demanded a middle-aged, pot-bellied man with vile breath and wearing a prominent cockade.

"I ask what you are doing here. This is the estate of the de

Miron family," said Arabella sharply.

"They've gone to their maker. We put them to death for profiteering and resistance to the revolution. We burnt the house as a symbol to all of the retribution we will deliver to anyone who supports the old and corrupt regime. Now the house belongs to the people," the man snarled in reply.

"On what grounds did you disturb the dead?"

"All relics of those bastards who support the Bourbon king must be destroyed. Now stop asking questions and get off this land."

"It's not your land. It belongs to the descendants of the de Miron family. It is you who should leave."

"I don't know who you are but you should clear out now before we arrest you and your friend."

As he spoke the pot-bellied man drew his sword; the second man, younger, half drunk and mean-looking, did likewise. They moved towards Trudaine and Arabella.

"Unless you go, we will slice you up."

Trudaine and Arabella stood their ground. The pot-bellied man swore and lunged at Trudaine who in a flash ran his sword into the man's side. As his accomplice fell back, the younger man rushed at Arabella with his blade. She swiftly side-stepped the thrust and in a countermove ran her sword through his stomach. He fell forwards onto the gravel of the driveway, his mouth spilling out blood. Trudaine plunged his sword into the pot-bellied man for a second time. It was now almost dark. They looked around but saw no movement, no lights. The boy had fled, no doubt to report what he had seen. Trudaine unpinned the cockade on each victim and repinned them to display the white reverse, the badge of the Bourbons and their supporters.

"Monsieur Aristide, we must go. Let's put some distance between us and our likely pursuers and then find some shelter for the night."

Arabella did not speak. As they galloped away she realised the enormity of what she had done. She had killed a man. He had sought to wound her and her sword stroke had been in self-defence. But the fact remained she had shed someone else's blood. Yet no tears came to her; she felt no regret. She had struck her first blow of vengeance.

* * * * *

The two travellers reached the outskirts of Paris on Saturday the 8th of September. They stopped overnight at an inn. It was full of people in *bonnets rouges* and other revolutionary clothes swapping gossip. Arabella and Trudaine blended well with the clientele in their mud-stained clothes. Sitting in a corner with some scraps of bread and a mug of wine, they listened to those around them. Those nearest spoke of the latest rumours about the fall of Verdun to the Duke of Brunswick's army and speculated whether the enemy would be thrown back or advance on Paris. Another group spoke of reports of National Guardsmen and army volunteers from the provinces, under orders from the city government, entering the Paris prisons and summarily executing many hundreds of prisoners, including Catholic priests and aristocrats as well as common criminals. There was a cry of joy when someone announced that the Princesse de Lamballe, supposed to be the Queen's lover, had been beheaded. Trudaine's face betrayed no emotion. Arabella found it hard to stop her hands from shaking. Were they too late to save Maria Louisa? Had she placed Robert Trudaine and herself in extreme danger? Though she was afraid, there was no going back. She could not return to Herzberg in failure and empty-handed.

After a sleepless night in a dingy, cramped room, Trudaine and Arabella left early to enter Paris on foot. The city was in turmoil: fires were burning on street corners; crowds of people milled around; leaflets with the latest news and allegations against the King and Queen were being handed out and brandished; revolutionary slogans were shouted constantly. There were random document inspections at street junctions, and menacing National Guardsmen and volunteers, the so-called *fédérés*, were marching and singing the *Marseillaise*. The atmosphere was threatening and intimidating. People not wearing the cockade or the *bonnet rouge* got rough treatment, their loyalty to the revolution in doubt. But few paid any attention to Arabella or Trudaine, covered in mud. After passing close to the hideous guillotine rising and falling, Arabella and Trudaine slowly made their way to the Rue des Boucheries in the shadow of the Abbey of Saint Germain des Prés, often pressing their way through crowds of people joining in the cry of "Long live the revolution!" Once in the Rue des Boucheries they walked to the

Rue Saint-Dominique. There in a little side street leading to the Rue de l'Université they found a narrower alleyway, along which on the right was a small terraced house.

"This is it," Trudaine said to Arabella. "Let me go first. You wait here."

Arabella seemed to wait for ever. Then Trudaine beckoned her in. She followed slowly.

In the darkened, shabby room sat a silver-haired lady. She was holding Trudaine's hand, smiling at him.

"Madame Sybille, I have brought someone who remembers your kindness to her long ago."

The old lady stood up, a look of fear in her eyes as Arabella approached in her long military-style coat with its prominent cockade and heavy black badly scuffed boots.

"Madame, have no fear," said Arabella, taking off her hat. "I am Arabella, the young English woman. You helped care for me when I arrived at the Rue St Louis long ago. You remember – I had blisters on my feet from these very boots I am wearing. You helped to bathe me."

Sybille's eyes clouded as though she was peering back through the mists of time. Suddenly, her face lit up.

"But of course, the young lady who was in love with Madame de Vervins' brother! I remember, and you sang so beautifully. You reduced us all to tears. Please sit down. I have nothing to offer, just some water. These are hard times."

For the next two hours Sybille and Arabella spoke about her stay with the de Vervins. They laughed and they cried. Arabella sang to her.

After a while Sybille turned to Trudaine.

"These are terrible times, Monsieur. Why are you here? You should both be far away in safety, not in Paris where the streets run with blood and hatred. They are calling for the execution of the King, poor man."

"Madame Sybille," said Trudaine, "the Vicomte Etienne is dead. He was killed helping to defend the Tuileries. Madame de Vervins is now in La Force. We have come to rescue her, if she still lives. We do not have much time. Madame Arabella and I will go to the prison tomorrow. If she is alive, we will try to release her."

"How will you do that?" asked Sybille.

"We do not know yet. But we will think of a plan."

The tiny room fell silent. Then Sybille spoke again.

"I have a neighbour down the street, Madame Margot, who sometimes goes to the prison with laundry. Like me she does not like the revolution – the way these ruffians push us around. If you agree, I will ask her to go with you. You will need all the help possible to get in and out of that dreadful place."

Trudaine and Arabella looked at each other. They had already disclosed their purpose to Sybille. Now she was going to tell someone else. But they had no choice.

"Madame Sybille, please ask her," said Arabella.

"I will," replied Sybille. "In the meantime you are most welcome to stay here. There is some space in the loft where you can lie down. My mother and aunt have left Paris."

"Thank you, Madame Sybille," said Arabella taking her hand. "You are most gracious."

"That is the least I can do in repayment of the great kindness I received from Madame de Vervins."

That evening, over some meagre food and rough wine that Trudaine had been able to find, he and Arabella devised a plan for the next day. It would depend on Arabella continuing to masquerade as a dispossessed soldier from the area of Rozac, seeking retribution against an inmate of the prison who, with her husband, had gravely wronged him. Before they retired to the loft, Madame Margot, Sybille's near neighbour, came to see them. They agreed a time to leave for the prison in the morning.

* * * * *

The next morning at just before eight o'clock the three gathered at Madame Sybille's house. As Arabella left, Sybille whispered in her ear.

"If Madame is alive and you can free her, bring her here. She will be safe in the loft until you decide on your escape."

"Thank you, Madame Sybille, I will. Please pray for us."

The front of La Petite Force was sombre and forbidding. Its fabric comprised stone bound together by iron bars. La Petite Force housed women prisoners, many of whom were prostitutes; the nearby La Grande Force housed male prisoners. That morning the debris of the recent riot lay strewn everywhere. Gangs of people were picking up the hacked remains of those who had been summarily executed. The building showed the results of forced entry. Madame Margot, carrying a large basket of washing she had brought from the house, led the way in through the open door. The wreckage and damage inside the prison was beyond description. In the distance they could hear crying, wailing and shouting from the few remaining prisoners, some of whom had been pressed into clearing up.

"Who is in charge?" called out Madame Margot. "Hurry up! Who's in charge? There are two officials of the revolution here."

A dishevelled, unshaven, red-eyed man in a dirty uniform hurried to the entrance.

"What do you want?" he said in a surly voice.

"We want the prisoner de Vervins – now, quickly," said Trudaine, pulling from his pocket a crumpled sheet of paper – the forged document that Waldemar Drescher had used to secure the release of the de Puyraveau family two years before.

The jailer was half drunk and waved the paper away.

"Everyone brings me permits and orders. One is just like another."

"Come on, man, hurry!" said Arabella in the deeper voice she had cultivated on her journey.

"She may have been executed already. Let me check," the jailer growled in reply.

"We will come with you," said Trudaine.

They walked along the ground-floor corridor. The stench of death and lack of air were scarcely tolerable. Most of the downstairs cells were empty, the doors hanging off their hinges. In one or two cells, bloodstained bodies still lay on the ground. They climbed the stairs to the first floor. Again they faced the same scene of desolation, and likewise on the third floor. The jailer turned back. Arabella blocked his way and pointed to the narrow winding staircase leading to the cells in the roof. They climbed the steps one behind another. Here some of the doors were locked.

"Jailer, open them up. We want to see who is left."

He opened each cell door. Some were empty. In another a woman was hanging from the rafters. They came to the penultimate cell on the right. The jailer opened the door. There was a figure crouched in the corner, tending to a woman who was quietly sobbing. The crouching figure turned round.

"Leave us alone," the voice called out.

The woman was careworn but her features were refined and, though her hair was grey it still had a lustrous tint. Arabella recognised the face. It was Maria Louisa's.

Arabella turned and nodded to Trudaine.

"We want this prisoner for examination – now," Trudaine barked at the jailer.

"You cannot. I will have to seek the authority of the Minister of Justice. You can go downstairs and wait."

The jailer turned to usher them out. But Trudaine pulled a stone from his pocket and struck him on the side of his head. The jailer dropped to the floor.

"Quick," said Madame Margot, "help me take off his jacket and trousers. I've been meaning to do this for years, the miserable bastard. He didn't even recognise me, even though in the past he could not keep his hands off me."

Together Arabella and Madame Margot stripped him. Madame Margot then took off her blouson and skirt and stuffed herself into the jailer's clothes. She then took some material from her basket and bound the jailer's feet and hands.

"Come, let's get out of here," she said, half dressed.

Maria Louisa looked on open-mouthed.

"Maria Louisa, it's me, Arabella. We've come to take you to safety."

Maria Louisa tried to speak but Arabella put her finger to her lips.

"But I can't leave her," said Maria Louisa, pointing to the body in the corner of the cell.

Trudaine bent over the body.

"She will be dead within an hour or so. We must leave her."

Maria Louisa knelt by the body and put her fingers on the near-blue lips.

"Let the Lord have mercy on you and let your soul rest in peace," she whispered.

"When we leave this building," said Arabella to Maria Louisa, "you must behave as though you were our prisoner, resisting arrest. If we are stopped we will say we are taking you to the

Revolutionary Court for further questioning to do with the Queen. But on the way we will disappear. You must not speak or indicate you know us, do you understand? If you do, all may be lost."

Maria Louisa nodded.

Down on the street Trudaine commandeered a cart into which he bundled Maria Louisa with her hands bound. Madame Margot, still in the jailer's uniform, walked in front with Arabella making a way through the crowds, some of whom spat at Maria Louisa. In due course they reached the Palace of Justice. They entered the courtyard in which there was mayhem. Arabella and Trudaine dragged Maria Louisa from the cart. While Madame Margot diverted attention the three disappeared into the crowd and, in the mêlée, managed to slip out of the courtyard and walk quickly away in the direction of the Rue Saint-Jacques. Arabella steered Maria Louisa by the arm, frequently shoving her in the back to create the impression of being force-marched. Trudaine went ahead, clearing a passage through the masses thronging the streets, while Madame Margot, still in her jailer's uniform, kept watch at the back to ensure they were not being followed by the curious or the malevolent. At last and exhausted, they reached Madame Sybille's house where there was a tender reunion. That night amid tears, fatigue and the frisson of excitement, Arabella, Maria Louisa, Robert Trudaine and Mesdames Sybille and Margot quietly celebrated in whispered voices the Vicomtesse's escape – a further though small blow against the revolution. The next day they would have to commence their escape from France. They decided that instead of going south they should go north-east towards Verdun and seek to filter through the front line. Once on the other side they could seek refuge with the coalition armies. This would be full of renewed risk but they had to get off French soil as quickly as possible.

After an uncomfortable night in the loft of Madame Sybille's house, they prepared to leave. While Madame Sybille declined to come as she had elderly relatives to care for, Madame Margot asked to accompany them as far as the border. She would now be wanted by the authorities for aiding the escape of a prisoner and had no wish to offer her neck to the guillotine. Maria Louisa, exhausted from her recent ordeal, dressed in some old clothes from Madame Margot and wearing the required *bonnet rouge* said farewell to her erstwhile maid. Arabella gave Madame Sybille some money to keep and to use for whichever purpose she wished. At about nine o'clock on the morning of Wednesday the 12th of September, 1792, the four companions left Paris to go north-east.

They made slow progress towards Reims. The roads were full of people coming and going, many of them refugees fleeing from the threat of the Duke of Brunswick's army. Several times along the route and in Reims, where they stayed for two nights so Maria Louisa could regain some strength, they were challenged by small groups of the National Guard and pockets of *fédérés*. As they left in the direction of Verdun and Metz on Friday the 21st they began to hear rumours that Prussian troops commanded by the Duke of Brunswick had been beaten in a decisive battle near the village of Valmy. Despite this news the four pressed on, bypassing Metz, and reaching Thionville, further to the north and closer to the border, on the 27th. By this time all four were exhausted. Arabella and Trudaine had been on the road for over a month. Maria Louisa was still weak from her harsh captivity and grief-stricken by the death of her beloved husband. Madame Margot, as cheerful as ever, was suffering from severe blisters on her feet.

Two days later, on the 29th, after staying in wet and damp conditions in a dilapidated cottage on the edge of the town, they decided to make their way to the border, first in a horse-drawn cart they had commandeered and then on foot through woods. The weather was bad and worsened as they neared their destination. More serious was the increased number of French soldiers who, encouraged by victory at Valmy, were now more aggressive in their approach to civilians and particularly women. Only a few miles from the border Madame Margot's feet became so blistered that she said she could go no further. To attempt to do so would hold up her companions and jeopardise their chances of crossing safely. After spending a last night together in the woods, Arabella, Maria Louisa and Trudaine took their leave of the washerwoman. Arabella gave her almost all of her remaining money; little was now left.

With just half a dozen miles to go in the relentless rain, they encountered a small army patrol. This time they were unable to shake them off, and the sergeant arrested them on suspicion of being spies. He and his three men took them to a house in the last village before the border. After giving them some water to drink, he locked the two men in one room and Maria Louisa in another. Arabella immediately guessed what was about to happen. Maria Louisa was going to be raped. For the first time Arabella had cause to regret her male disguise; it had separated her from Maria Louisa and compromised her ability to protect her. She and Trudaine banged on the door, shouting they wished to confess. The sergeant unlocked the door and marched the two to a table where he sat them down opposite him. Two of his patrol of three stood by his side. As they began to speak Trudaine suddenly overturned the table onto the sergeant who went sprawling on the floor. One of the two soldiers bent down to pull the table off him. As he did so, Trudaine picked up his stool and struck the soldier on the back of his head. The other soldier went to lunge at Arabella but she kicked him hard high between his legs. He fell to the floor in agony. Meanwhile, the third soldier emerged from the room where Maria Louisa had been placed, his trousers half down and his face badly scratched.

"You bastard," said Arabella and meted out the same punishment. "Did he rape you?" she asked Maria Louisa.

"No," she replied. "La Force taught me to kick and scratch."

Trudaine and Arabella bound the hands and legs of the sergeant and his men and seized their pistols.

"Let's leave now for the border," Trudaine urged.

They ripped off their cockades. Outside it was pitch black but after a while their eyes became adjusted to the darkness. Using his pocket compass Trudaine groped the way through more woods towards the border. At first light they stumbled from a copse and went down a hill towards a village in the valley. Trudaine estimated they were now on Prussian soil. As they approached the few houses, soldiers stood up from the side of the road. They were Prussian and obviously in retreat from France.

"You are under arrest as infiltrators."

Though Arabella and Maria Louisa replied in German, it made no difference. Shortly all three were placed in a horse-drawn cart, their hands bound, and taken to the headquarters of the Prince of Hohenlohe. Pulled out of the cart they were placed in a room to await interrogation.

An hour later, Major Joseph Lange von Schellenhorst entered the room with an escort.

"Joseph, it is me, Arabella, the Countess von Deppe. I have returned to Germany, as I promised your wife – my daughter, Elise Catherine – I would, with the Vicomtesse de Vervins."

The Major stood stupefied.

"Maria Louisa, I present to you my son-in-law, Major Joseph Lange von Schellenhorst."

The major slowly recovered his wits.

"Vicomtesse de Vervins, it is an honour and pleasure to meet you. Please forgive me for my discourtesy. I had no idea . . ."

Arabella interrupted his stumbling words.

"Joseph, I hope you will unbind us."

"Corporal, don't just stand there. Release them."

The following day, Monday the 1st of October, in a fast and comfortable coach, Arabella, Maria Louisa and Robert Trudaine reached Wiesbaden where they were able to wash, change and relax for several days before beginning the onward journey to Herzberg. On the 2nd of October Arabella received a special visitor – Sir Charles Gray. They were alone and neither spoke as he held her tightly. That night in the privacy of her bedroom, tired and bruised, she soon fell into a deep sleep, wrapped in his arms.

As he lay beside her, Charles Gray pondered what he should do about this woman who had been so foolhardy. He loved her deeply and believed she loved him as much. But this damn war with France would go on for a long time and his responsibilities to his masters in London made it difficult for him to decide whether he should ask her to marry him. And, if he did, would she accept his hand? She had been born in England but was half French. Her mother's blood ran strongly in her veins as her vivacity, temperament, fierce independence of mind and musical spirit avouched. But now after so many years in Prussia she had become more outspoken in her views and fervent in her loyalty to the country that had been her home for more than two decades. It was unlikely she would ever agree to return to live in England. Why should she? She was the chatelaine of an important Prussian estate, the patron of a renowned chamber orchestra and a much-respected woman in her own right – and would be even more so after what she had just done in France.

As for himself, he was English and had particular views about Prussia that he had shared with no one. Would marriage to

Arabella von Deppe blend with his English subtlety, his diplomatic work, which had to remain undisclosed, and, he had to confess, with his personal freedom – which he cherished, and which over the years had allowed him to enjoy the company of many women and sometimes their physical intimacy? Such a concern was surely not snobbery or selfishness on his part but a reflection of his innate caution. He was not a philanderer but someone who had so far eschewed commitment. Yet in the Countess von Deppe he had encountered a woman of rare intelligence, great beauty and exceptional courage. Perhaps the time had come for him to be honest with himself – to cease hiding behind excuses, to confront his self-indulgence and to decide whether he wished to remain alone or to ask her to marry him. But, he decided, not just now. That was not putting the matter off. The woman beside him was exhausted and needed time to recover her strength and to receive the adulation that she would surely and rightly receive on her return to Prussia. He resolved to make a final decision soon. But first, he had to play his part in the construction of a fresh alliance to oppose the French – now more than ever in the grip of a rapidly tightening revolution following the proclamation of the First French Republic. The new republic and the slide into national terror threatened the very existence of other European monarchies.

Later he got up and, in the candlelight, wrote a despatch about the recent disastrous events on the front. After he had finished, he crept silently to the bedside to gaze once more at the sleeping Countess before leaving her room. The thick, black lashes of her closed eyes, her high cheekbones, now even more evident from lack of nourishment, and the slight flecks of silver in her long dark hair, which loosely framed her pale face – all highlighted her beauty and irresistible attraction. If only he were a Caravaggio he could capture this moment of personal and fragile intimacy.

"My dearest, dearest heart, what a remarkable woman you are," he whispered.

* * * * *

Over two weeks later, at midday on Tuesday the 23rd of October, 1792, Arabella, Maria Louisa and Robert Trudaine returned as conquering heroes to Herzberg, to be greeted by Elise Catherine,

Jacqueline and the Comte and Comtesse de Puyraveau; the welcome each woman received from her daughter was especially heartfelt. Later in the afternoon Frederick Daniel and Joseph Lange arrived, in military uniform, direct from the French front. Though depressed by the Prussian defeat they were more than ever determined to work for significant military reforms and to enlist the diffident Crown Prince in their efforts. Such reforms would take time but the first step was to begin the building of a fresh coalition against France.

Marie-Aurore, the Comtesse de Puyraveau, spent much of the remaining day alone with her mother, while later in the afternoon Robert Trudaine came to tell Arabella that he would shortly leave Herzberg to return to France, to seek with like-minded friends the release of other innocent French citizens destined for execution. She begged him not to leave Herzberg or, if he insisted on doing so, at least not to return to France. There was plenty he could do in Prussia. He had been a valiant companion and, had it not been for him, she and the Vicomtesse de Vervins would certainly have died, two more victims of an unjust and lawless regime of terror. But Trudaine would not be persuaded; he wished to go in order to do more in his country of birth – his *patrie* – to oppose the new tyrants who had replaced an old tyrant. What he had recently done in France with her at his side, and whatever more he might do in the future without her, would be dedicated to the memory of his earlier companion, Herr Drescher. The only concession he made was to agree to travel to Berlin with her and the Vicomtesse de Vervins early the following week in order that the Prussian King could thank him in person for his valour.

Later that evening Elise Catherine came to see her mother resting in her bedroom.

"Mama, why did you leave us? Why did you not tell us what you were planning to do? Why did you cause us so much worry? Why did you put your life in such danger?" she asked.

"Elise Catherine, I did what I believed it was right to do. If I had told you, you and Frederick Daniel would have stopped me from going. I have had a privileged life, which I owe to your father. I learnt from him and even more so from my mother the primacy of justice and the defence of the innocent. But there is no point in talking about it. Sometimes it is necessary to put words into action.

This was the time for me to do so. The Vicomtesse de Vervins and her late husband took me into their house twenty-six years ago and, together with your father, enabled me to begin the fulfilment of my life as I wished it to be, not as others such as my father wanted. I could not bear to think of the Vicomtesse being alone in a Paris prison at the mercy of villains and killers. I had to rescue her. Monsieur Trudaine, whom you must thank many times for my safe return, protected me. He never really knew my fear, my terror, at entering that wretched prison, seeing the human remains and streams of blood on the floor. But I was determined to prevail – even more so after witnessing my mother's desecrated grave – and to return to my children and Herzberg. Too often the rights of women are ignored. Men pay us compliments for how pleasing we look but seldom pay heed to the views we hold. My mother taught me that women should be the equals of men and I will go to my grave with that belief inscribed on my heart. So do not berate me. I am too tired for that. I wish you all to respect my opinions even if you find them difficult to comprehend."

"Dearest Mama, we do not wish to berate you. My questions were a measure of our concern for your safety. Now you are back we will do more than ever to honour and support you."

"My dear Elise, thank you. The first thing you can do is to instruct your brother and your husband not to talk crossly to me about my recent journey. What you have said is enough."

"Of course, Mama. I will speak to them. There is one other matter I wish to tell you about, in strict confidence – Joseph does not yet know. I am expecting his child."

"Dearest Elise, I am so pleased. That is truly wonderful news to give me. I promise you I will say nothing."

And so for the next hour mother and daughter sat in private holding hands and discussing certain personal matters that do not concern men.

For the next few days Herzberg was filled with liveliness, laughter and music.

* * * * *

On Wednesday the 8th of November, 1792, King Frederick William and his wife, Queen Frederika Louisa, received Arabella at the royal palace in Berlin. She was accompanied by her family; by the Vicomtesse de Vervins and her daughter and son-in-law; and by Robert Trudaine. The so-called English countess's exploits were already the subject of public and press acclamation, in contrast to the gloom after the defeat of the Duke of Brunswick's armies at Valmy.

"Her Majesty and I wish to congratulate you, Countess, on your safe return to Prussia, bringing with you the Vicomtesse de Vervins whose freedom you so bravely secured. You bring great credit to Prussia at this difficult time. You deserve much praise."

"Your Majesty," replied Arabella, "I thank you for your most kind words. But I wish to tell you of two people far braver than me. The first is the Vicomtesse, who suffered cruelly at the hands of the revolution and whose husband died valiantly defending His Majesty King Louis. She was subjected to great indignity and ill-treatment but she survived the brutal attack on the prisons in Paris and tended its victims without concern for herself. Thereafter, she showed equal courage in her escape with us, despite her weakened health. The other person is Monsieur Trudaine, who fearlessly accompanied me and, displaying the greatest bravery, protected us all from constant danger. Without him we would not have returned to Prussia to be here today."

"Vicomtesse de Vervins and Monsieur Trudaine, the Queen and I wish to thank you most warmly for your bravery, courage and determination. Like the Countess von Deppe you have set fine examples to all Prussians."

Then, as the audience neared its close, Maria Louisa asked to speak.

"Your Majesty, Monsieur Trudaine and I wish to thank you for your kind words. We are proud to be here. But the greatest praise must go to the Countess von Deppe. I first encountered her some twenty-five years ago when my late brother, Count von Deppe, brought her to Paris after her escape from malevolent pursers in England. It was immediately evident to me that she was a young woman of high principles and boundless courage, who possessed a love of music of an intensity we had not seen before. My late husband and I were delighted that she and my brother married. Their union was one of rare happiness. Notwithstanding her English birth and her mother's French citizenship, the Countess von Deppe has over the years shown unwavering love for and commitment to Prussia. It was that love, and her courage and inspiration, that caused her to risk her life to save mine. I owe my life to her. She brings to you and Her Majesty, and to Prussia, and indeed to her estate at Herzberg, the greatest respect and honour. We all hope that she will long continue to serve Prussia at this difficult time."

"Vicomtesse de Vervins, you have spoken well. We echo your words."

The following week, in continued celebration and to lift the public mood, the Herzberg Camerata performed at the Berlin Hofoper. The orchestra played the *Cello Concerto* by the Bohemian composer Antonín Kraft, to whom Arabella had been introduced by Mozart on her last visit to Vienna; Domenico Cimarosa's *Piano Concerto*; and Johann Christian Bach's *Sinfonia Concertante in C Major*. In conclusion, and in response to the audience's insistent requests, Arabella was obliged to renege on her pledge never again to perform in public and played Johann Sebastian Bach's *Prelude and Fugue No. 15 in G Major* from his second book of *The Well-Tempered Clavier*. Still the audience would not let her retire. They demanded that she sing. Arabella stood and, moving many to tears, sang *Lascia ch'io pianga* from Handel's opera *Rinaldo*. "Again!" shouted the audience. "Again!" Arabella, close to unbearable emotion, was joined by her daughter, Elise Catherine. Together they sang the aria as a duet.

Five weeks later King Louis of France was brought to trial before the National Convention on the 11th and 12th of December. The emerging leader of the revolution, Maximilien de Robespierre, a lawyer and first deputy for Paris to the National Convention, expressed the opinion that the King must die so that France may live. The King was found guilty and sentenced to death.

Against the depressing backdrop of Prussian defeat on the battlefield, terror sweeping through France and ever-diminishing prospects for peace in Europe, Arabella decided that, in keeping with the increasingly sombre national mood, it was best to show discretion and sensitivity in the celebration of Advent at Herzberg. Besides, Maria Louisa was still grieving over the death of her husband, Etienne, and the loss of her personal belongings and her incarceration at La Force had deeply scarred her emotionally. Despite the companionship of her daughter, Marie-Aurore, and grandson, Antoine, her vivacity and joie de vivre appeared to have been extinguished.

For her part, though Arabella continued to disguise her sentiments towards Sir Charles Gray, whom she greatly missed having at her side, they had not escaped the continued attention of her daughter. Elise still chose to say nothing, preferring to wait to see what might eventually happen. Arabella was aware her daughter knew and recalled with amusement how it had always been difficult to hide secrets from her mother; now it was her daughter from whom she was failing to conceal them.

It was against this background of national unease and personal preoccupations and anxieties that the celebration of Christmas at Herzberg was muted, apart from the singing of carols in the *Spiegelsaal*, to which Arabella invited all those who lived and worked on the estate.

PART THREE: ADAGIO
DARKNESS BEFORE DAWN 1795–1813

CHAPTER 11

Lost Love, Music and the Distant Sound of War

Before the end of 1797 Napoleon Bonaparte had emerged as the undisputed leader of France. Late that year, on Wednesday evening the 29th of November, Arabella sat in the royal palace in Berlin listening to a concert played by the Camerata. She had arranged it in order to mark the accession to the Prussian throne of King Frederick William III, aged twenty-seven.

Situated on an island in the River Spree in the centre of the city, the core of the palace had originally been built in the fifteenth century. Though for the last hundred years the principal residence and winter palace of the Hohenzollern kings of Prussia, it had been finally completed only fifty years before. To Arabella's right in the throne room sat the new King's beautiful young wife, Luise, aged twenty-one and already mother of two sons. To the Queen's right was the King. On Arabella's left were her son, Frederick Daniel, and his wife, Jacqueline; and to their left, Arabella's daughter, Elise Catherine, and her husband, Joseph. Further to the left was her late husband's sister, the widowed Vicomtesse Maria Louisa de Vervins.

The orchestra, which she had founded with Herr Bamberger many years before, was performing with her newly established Camerata Chorus. The work was Bach's cantata *Wachet auf, ruft uns die Stimme*, a composition she had specially chosen because of its lyrical and musical sensitivity from the pen of a composer she had admired throughout her life, and because she thought the cantata would appeal to the young religious-minded King. As Arabella listened she recalled some of the happier and sadder events since her escape from France five years before with Maria Louisa and the late Robert Trudaine.

* * * * *

The gloom at the end of 1792 had deepened the following year.

To the shock of many outside France King Louis had been executed in public on the 21st of January. His wife, Queen Marie Antoinette, was impeached in October of the same year and tried for treason. She was executed the day after the guilty verdict. A tragic woman had met a tragic end.

In November of that year Arabella and Maria Louisa de Vervins received the distressing news from Sir Charles Gray that Robert Trudaine had been captured and interrogated as a spy. After a summary trial he had been sent to the guillotine. Arabella placed a stone in the grounds of Herzberg next to that of Waldemar Drescher. It read:

En mémoire de Robert Trudaine
Vrai patriote et bon compagnon
Ne l'oublions jamais

In memory of Robert Trudaine
A true patriot and companion
Never to be forgotten

Though the news about affairs of state was bleak, events closer to home gave reason for hope. Two new generations were born at Herzberg in the spring and summer of 1793: in late May Elise Catherine gave birth to a girl, Elisabeth Mariette Thérèse, while in July, Jacqueline had a boy, Carl Nicolas Frederick. For Arabella it was an emotional moment in her life. The succession of the Herzberg estate was now assured. She had passed yet another milestone in her life.

Later in the year, amidst further national gloom, there was one other happy event – the marriage on the 24th of December of the

Crown Prince Frederick William to the seventeen-year-old Duchess Luise von Mecklenburg-Strelitz. Frederick Daniel and Jacqueline were present at the marriage, as were Elise Catherine and her husband, Joseph.

The newly married Crown Princess – whose father, Charles, Duke of Mecklenburg-Strelitz, was about to become ruler of Hanover on behalf of his brother-in-law King George III of England – was two years younger than her equally attractive sister, Frederica, who had married the Crown Prince's younger brother, Prince Louis Charles, two days after Luise's wedding. Arabella was quick to observe that Luise had no airs or graces. Her mother had died in childbirth when she was six and, after the unexpected death of her father's second wife, Luise and her sister had been brought up by her father's mother-in-law, the Landgravine Marie Louise of Hesse-Darmstadt, who was also Luise's godmother. The two sisters had grown up in great simplicity in the Lutheran faith, making their own clothes as well as being taught to do good works, including visiting the poor and the needy. They had been educated by a Swiss governess who had taught them to be fluent in French – rather to the neglect of their German. Following their marriage, Luise and the Crown Prince preferred to spend as much time as possible at Paretz on the outskirts of Potsdam, enjoying the simplicity of rural life rather than the bustle of life at court. It soon became well known that they often sang together and read Shakespeare.

*****

In the spring of 1794, while the guillotine was hard at work in Paris, the royal couple had come to Herzberg one weekend. Frederick Daniel, Jacqueline, Elise Catherine and her husband, Joseph, joined them. With great informality they walked and rode, enjoyed the well-stocked library, and one evening listened to new young members of the Camerata Herzberg perform in the *Spiegelsaal*; the programme included Mozart's *Clarinet Quintet* and the *arioso* from Bach's *Cantata No. 156*. Encouraged by her royal guests Arabella played Mozart's *Nine Variations*, which she had helped to compose at Herzberg in the spring of 1789, though of course without disclosing to her guests the rude remarks Mozart had made about the present King's music *Meister*, Monsieur Duport. Then with further persuasion Arabella and Elise Catherine – with vocal support from Herr Bamberger – sang *Soave sia il vento* from Mozart's *Così fan tutte.*

As a final encore, Arabella played Bach's *Prelude and Fugue No. 1 in C Major.* She had played it many times privately to the Empress of Russia. Now she was doing so to a new generation – to a young Crown Prince and his even younger wife with her exquisite complexion and large blue eyes, who looked at Arabella with a half smile; to her son and his youthful wife, Jacqueline; and to her beloved daughter, Elise Catherine, now a close friend of the Crown Princess, and her husband, Joseph. Arabella sensed even more keenly than before that her life was quickly slipping past, as inexorably as a ticking clock, and that before long the time would come for her to relinquish completely her responsibilities as chatelaine of Herzberg and step resolutely into the background. She revealed her thoughts later that evening to Maria Louisa, who responded with great frankness.

"Arabella, there is worse to come from this accursed revolution. If we are not careful we will all drown in a tide of blood. In all this bleakness, I agree with you that the Crown Prince and Princess represent the next generation, as do our own flesh and blood. I agree too that we should be ready to stand aside – but not now and certainly not you. Herzberg needs your steady hand, your wisdom and, dare I say it, your élan to guide it through dark and turbulent waters. However fatigued you may be it is not yet time for you to surrender your position and influence. You must stay the course. I beg you, Arabella, do not leave us. Let us all draw strength and knowledge from your example and dedication."

"There are times, Maria Louisa," Arabella replied, "when I feel as though I am lost alone in a thick mist, unsure in which direction to turn. I sometimes see apparent shafts of light but when I walk towards them they prove to be a mirage. I am so tired, Maria Louisa, not tired of life but tired of the daily burden I have to bear. But I will consider what you say. I promise I will."

"There can be only one answer, Arabella," said Maria Louisa. "You must press on. Carl Manfred would expect no less from the woman he loved so much. But to stay at Herzberg does not mean a solitary life. Carl would not wish you to sacrifice your personal happiness for the sake of the estate. If you have the chance to share your life with another, do so. You would be sorely mistaken if you thought you must choose between one or the other. Both are possible."

Arabella attempted to reply but Maria Louisa put her hand gently on Arabella's arm as though to restrain her.

"Arabella, the affairs of the heart are most private. That is where they should stay, until and unless the time comes to reveal them."

Arabella realised that, despite her efforts at concealment, her love for Sir Charles Gray was evident to others, not just her observant daughter. As her mother once said, women have few secrets from another of the same sex.

Before the royal party left, the Crown Princess asked to speak to Arabella alone.

"Countess, I thank you with all the warmth of my heart for allowing us to spend such a private and enjoyable weekend with you. You have been a most gracious and discreet host."

"Your Royal Highness, I am delighted you and the Crown Prince were able to come," replied Arabella. "Your stay was a great pleasure for us all. Though I know how much you enjoy Paretz, I cordially invite you to return to Herzberg at any time."

"Thank you, Countess. My husband and I would greatly welcome that. But I hope you will come sometimes to Paretz. I would like us to walk together there in my garden, to discuss matters of mutual interest."

"Your Royal Highness, I would be honoured to come whenever you so wish. But I fear there is little that I, an ageing lady, can impart that you do not already know."

"Countess, please may I speak in confidence?"

"But of course," replied Arabella. "I learnt long ago the importance of discretion and keeping secrets."

Princess Luise paused, considering carefully what she wished to say, what she might disclose.

"Countess, you came to Prussia from another country in pursuit of happiness. You found love here, as I have done. Though I was schooled well and taught the importance of thrift and respect for others whatever their position in the world, my approach to life is still yet to be fully tested and applied in the circumstances in which I now find myself. One day my husband will be king. He is shy, often nervous and frequently indecisive. It will be my role to support him, even more than I do now, to encourage him to be strong and resolute, and perhaps sometimes to cajole him."

As she uttered these last words, she smiled.

"But," she continued, "as I am still young I do not have, despite being a mother, the experience, wisdom or respect that you have acquired. Nor do I have the immense willpower, determination, courage and bravery that you have shown, combined with your modesty and gentleness of spirit. You are an example to us all, not least in your commitment to the view that women should be treated the equal of men. My mother died when I was only six and since then my sister and I have seen little of our father. I thank my godmother for her love, discipline and support, which I have greatly valued. Now I need someone else to provide the practical advice I will surely need from time to time. Your daughter, Elise Catherine, has become a good friend and it is my intention that she should often be at my side – two young mothers together. But I still seek someone with the experience of life to whom I can turn in privacy from time to time. Countess, I wish you to be that person and to know that you will answer my questions with honesty and in true friendship. I earnestly hope that you will do me the pleasure of agreeing to my request."

Arabella was momentarily lost for words. How should she reply to such an unexpected request? If the Crown Princess was seeking honesty, then she would have to reply with honesty.

"Your Royal Highness, I am greatly touched by your words. There are many years between us. You are at the start of what will be a fulfilling life of service to this country and as a mother. The road of my life, in contrast to yours, is already much travelled. Times and people change, just as the seasons do. I could say I am in my autumn years. You will be familiar with Shakespeare's description of the seven ages of man. Those ages apply in equal measure to a woman such as me – though, bold as I am, I would venture to alter the detail. But, if it is truly your wish, I would be honoured to offer in friendship and with honesty any view you may seek from me provided that it is understood between us that action in any matter must ultimately be for you to decide."

Luise smiled.

"Countess, I agree to your terms. Indeed, that is how it must be.

I am truly delighted that you will be my companion and adviser, ready to help guide me in a confidential manner. And I know that my husband will be pleased too that we are to be friends. I will write to you soon and when the weather is warmer I expect to see you at Paretz. When you come we can walk in my garden and perhaps you might even play for me. You know so much about music."

"It would be my privilege to play for you," replied Arabella, "and to share with you my deep love of music. It was the seventeenth-century English author John Milton who wrote of the 'sweet compulsion' that lies in music, of its ability to fill the senses, soothe and stabilise. His words have certainly proved true for me in my life."

"I wish to experience that compulsion," replied Crown Princess Luise.

So saying, the Crown Princess left with her husband for Paretz. That evening, after Maria Louisa had gone to bed, Arabella sat alone in the library to reflect on what the young Luise had said. If she were asked to offer advice, it would indeed be an honour but it would be a heavy responsibility alongside many others.

Her thoughts then turned to Charles Gray. She had received no news from him for some months – though that was not surprising. The disruption in France and beyond had made the despatch and receipt of letters nigh impossible at times, and he had always proved entirely unpredictable in his comings and goings. He came and he went with little forewarning. She had once teased him, saying he was like a thief who came in the night. But as always she was patient. That said, though she loved him, she did not dote on him to the exclusion of all else in her life.

* * * * *

The national shock of the military defeat at Valmy was hard to overcome. The retreat of the once invincible Prussian army had proved a shattering blow. Despite his many admirable qualities, King Frederick William II appeared inclined to do little personally to find remedies for the military malaise, relying on others to do what they considered necessary. The Crown Prince, meanwhile, spent much time at his country estate. Frederick Daniel and

Joseph, both officers in the cavalry and garrisoned at Potsdam, were frequently invited to Paretz. When there they continued to advocate reform, but they knew there was – as yet – little scope for the introduction of meaningful change to which they were both strongly committed. The Crown Prince was hesitant whenever they raised the matter of the army with him, though the Crown Princess, if present, often spoke of the need for new ideas. In this she was quietly encouraged by Elise Catherine and Jacqueline, both of whom also spent considerable time at Paretz as companions of Princess Luise. But all were obliged to accept that until the present King left the throne there would be no progress.

It was around this time that, while walking in the garden with her son and daughter, Arabella reminded them that eventually the stewardship of Herzberg would fall to them. For the present she would continue to oversee the affairs of the estate, if that were their wish, but before long they would have to look to the future. Frederick Daniel and Elise Catherine urged her not to entertain any idea of withdrawing. Her commitment and dedication to Herzberg had brought great respect and distinction to the von Deppe family. Frederick Daniel insisted that, as long as he and his brother-in-law remained in the army or, perhaps later, attended on the new King at court, it would be difficult for him – or indeed for his wife, still adjusting to her new life in Prussia – to give Schloss Herzberg the time and attention it required. The same circumstances he felt sure would apply for Elise. Moreover, as Frederick Daniel emphasised, the family home had been extended in size and become a musical centre with frequent performances by the Camerata, which their remarkable mother had founded. So long as she remained in good health, she should oversee the estate. Elise echoed his words. Arabella agreed to leave matters as they were but reiterated that eventually the time would come when she would no longer be able to shoulder the responsibility they wished her, for now, to retain.

Their conversation was interrupted by the arrival of Jacqueline. As they returned to the house, Arabella and her daughter continued the earlier conversation in private.

"Elise, I hope that you will continue to sing. You are already accomplished on the keyboard, for which you have earned great respect. Depending, of course, both on Joseph's commitment to the army and on your friendship with the Crown Princess, to which

I know she attaches great importance, I would like you to consider becoming the Camerata's patron in my place. The orchestra continues to flourish but it requires fresh encouragement and direction, and I believe you would be best able to provide it. You would bring great charm, elegance and intelligence to their proceedings. Whilst your brother has a strong musical interest it does not match yours. Besides, he is too preoccupied with his military career. I hope you will consider carefully what I have proposed."

"Mama, you must not talk in such a way. We have already agreed you must remain in charge of Herzberg and that applies in equal measure to the Camerata. It is you who has established the orchestra's reputation and it must be you who continues to guide its music, to widen its repertoire. But I promise you that I will pursue my love of music and help you to improve the Camerata still further. The good name of Herzberg is due to your stewardship since Papa's death and indeed before that. But the Camerata's fame is solely yours and it must remain so."

* * * * *

The year wore on.

The news from France followed the pattern of the year before – ever greater turbulence. Yet more reports reached Herzberg of the revolutionaries turning on one another and those who lost in the struggle being despatched to the guillotine. In June a French army defeated the Austrians at the Battle of Fleurus, yet more evidence of the unstaunchable bloodletting. Against the advice of his wife, Marie-Aurore, and to his mother-in-law's dismay, the Comte de Puyraveau left Herzberg to return to France in secret to join the Companions of Jehu, royalists who attacked and murdered radical Jacobins in retaliation for previous massacres of royalists. As the revolution waged, Prussia for its part stood to one side, the King unwilling to return to the battlefield.

* * * * *

Sir Charles Gray visited Herzberg briefly in early May during the course of yet another undisclosed diplomatic mission to Prussia.

During his short stay he and Arabella rode and talked and again he enjoyed the intimacy of her bed. Before his departure he decided that he would bring his prevarication to an end by the close of the year; he would decide what he should say to her. He returned at the beginning of September, some weeks after the execution of Robespierre and other members of the infamous Committee of Public Safety in France, which thus ended the Reign of Terror that had shed so much innocent blood in the name of revolution.

The day after his arrival, on Friday the 5th of September, and shortly before his departure later that day for further brief business in Vienna, he walked with Arabella in the garden. At his suggestion they paused to rest, and sat together in the afternoon sun. Gray took her hand in his. She looked at him with apprehension, her face softer and more attractive than ever.

"Dearest Arabella, I wish to speak frankly to you. I have missed you greatly in the past months. Though you once accused me of coming to Herzberg like a thief in the night, I want you to know that I have truly longed for you in the times we have not been together. This accursed revolution has made more frequent visits to you impossible. Over the years I have done what I can to advance the interests of peace and stability for my country and to thwart the efforts of others to spread revolutionary disaffection far and wide. The results of my efforts have frequently been indifferent. In my darker moments I have often wished I was with you in the most intimate of ways. Now my work is done. I have received instructions to return to London and to remain there. The prospect of my returning to Herzberg in the foreseeable future is therefore unlikely. The thought of not seeing you again is too painful to contemplate.

"Arabella, I love you deeply. Your beauty, your elegance, your spirit, your courage, your temperament and your musical brilliance captivated me from our first encounter. The reports that I heard of you before we met made me all the more curious to meet such a remarkable woman. Our physical love – if I may speak boldly – in your bed here at Herzberg and in Karlsbad is welcome evidence of the spell you have cast over me. I wish that spell to remain unbroken and to ensure that it does I ask you to marry me, to return with me to London and to my estate as my esteemed and beloved wife. You asked me once as I lay beneath you whether I sought you as my mistress or *une liaison temporaire*. I replied that neither description fitted our situation. That remains the case. I wish you to be Lady Gray, my wife, to take your place beside me in English society, to share your life with my acquaintances, to let others see and hear you and to be my lover in marriage. Your children are now grown-up and married. Herzberg is surely their responsibility, not yours. You are now able to live the rest of your life free of the burden of family. Arabella, please be my wife and let us spend the rest of our lives together."

She looked at him without saying a word and then for a moment looked away. He said nothing. She turned to him again and placed her other hand on his.

"My dearest Charles, I am deeply honoured that you should ask me to marry you. I love you too and have done so since the moment you touched my hand when I played to you that evening. What happened between us reminded me of something one of Bach's sons once said: 'Above all, music must move the heart.' It seemed then that I had moved your heart and you mine. I wished to resist, fearing what might happen in the future, but I could not. I fell without resistance and I have never regretted doing so. How I long to have you in my bed when you are not here. Nothing would please me more than for us to be husband and wife. But, sadly, it cannot happen. You have to return to England to deal with affairs of government in a different way and to care for your estate. I cannot leave here, nor can I expect you to give up England to be with me. Nothing can change the irreconcilable positions in which we are locked. Each of us is a prisoner of our fate. I have always feared that our obligations would cause our ways to part. That moment has now come."

As she uttered those words her eyes moistened.

"Is there no way, Arabella," he implored her, "that you would change your mind? Surely your work here is done? Surely your family would release you from any obligation you may still have to Herzberg?"

"Charles, it goes much deeper than that. Every time you leave, I feel as though I am falling into a black emptiness – an emptiness of fear. The fear of not seeing you again. The fear of receiving news that you may be dead. Then you return. I re-emerge from the blackness, only for you to disappear again. And when you do the fear becomes even deeper."

"Surely that is all the more reason for us to be together in England?"

"What if I were in England, Charles? What if you resumed your travels, disappearing for months at a time? We would become like ships passing each other in the night. In my case I would be a ship full of fear."

"Arabella, that is unlikely to happen. I am unlikely to do again what I do now."

"How can you be sure? But, my silly fears apart, I cannot leave here, don't you understand? I left England long ago, hounded by my father, then came to Prussia in pursuit of a man I loved. My husband gave me the love I sought and here at Herzberg I built a new life. I pledged to him and to his King that I would do all in my power to earn the respect of this land that gave me shelter and happiness. With good fortune I believe I have been able to fulfil my pledge. But now, with war all around us, there is more to do. Moreover, I live in a world of music, which the Camerata has brought to life. The undeniable and painful truth of the matter is that I cannot leave my family, my friends, the Camerata or Prussia at this time. Besides, all my links with the country of my birth are broken. I could not go back now. It would be a strange land."

Again he started to protest against her argument. But she stopped him.

"Charles, in all truth, and disregarding all practical impediments, our love has been killed by its own nourishment. I have thought about this greatly over the past months. We have loved with such intensity that perhaps there is nothing left, only a carcass for us to pick over. If that is true, it would be unedifying to continue. Perhaps, Charles, we have to accept that we were destined from the beginning never to live our lives together." She paused. "However hard we try to ignore the truth, however many words we may utter, I fear all that is left is for us to say goodbye. Our positions, our obligations, are irreconcilable. So we should not prolong this painful moment. Your departure will be truly hard for me to bear. It will break my heart to see you leave. You only realise how much you love someone when you have to let them go. The pain of my loss will be indescribable but I must endure it. Please, you must go. If you stay a moment longer my suffering will be unbearable.

Please understand."

"Of course, I understand," he replied. His face betrayed little emotion.

Arabella lifted his hand and kissed it gently, inwardly overwhelmed. He realised she could not be convinced to change her mind. The woman before him, the only one he had ever really loved, was slipping through his fingers like grains of sand. Yet he made one last effort to persuade her at least to consider what he had said, but she put her finger to his lips. Though her distress was evident, she remained resolute. The end had come; the last grain of sand had fallen. They walked back to the house without uttering a further word, then bid each other farewell in the most formal way. He walked slowly down the steps to his waiting coach. Before stepping inside he turned and once more bowed and doffed his hat. She gave a gentle wave and turned away, unable to bear the sight of his departure down the long drive.

Later, Arabella sat alone in the *Spiegelsaal*. She played the slow movement of Bach's *Keyboard Concerto No. 3 in D Minor*, a solitary lit candle to illuminate the enclosing dusk. The pitter-patter of rain against the windows accompanied each musical note. She paused as a curtain rustled in a sudden breeze and looked at the encroaching darkness. He had asked her to marry him, to go with him to England. She had refused. He had gone, as she had asked. He would not return. Another – the final – link with England had been broken. There would be no going back to the country of her birth – not now. She would never see Gray again; she would never see Meltwater again; she would never again see London. John Donne had once written, "No man is an island, entire of itself; every man is a piece of the continent, a part of the main." Contrary to Donne, she was now an island entire of herself, an older woman alone and without Gray. Life could be so cruel. She would no longer enjoy the intimacy of a man she had come to love; her bed would be cold like a tomb. The rain now beat against the window. She could see the drops, reflected in the candlelight, gently slipping down each pane of glass like tears, just as she had once seen teardrops of rain on the window panes of her room at Chesterfield Street in London, on that first and frightening evening of her masked transformation and descent into the demi-monde. All she had left were the memories of her husband, of his profession of love for her as he died in her arms; and fresher memories of another man who had brought her great pleasure and bathed her in love. All that remained was for her to witness the happiness of others and to bequeath to her children a legacy worthy of her name, Herzberg and her music.

As she sat at the piano Arabella sought to assuage her inner grief. She drew comfort from the way Charles Gray, an accomplished lover, had responded to her physical allure and sexual intimacy, which had often been provocative, indeed even, at times, profane. Though an older woman – and certainly older than him – still she had been able to use much of what she had learnt behind her mask at Mrs Hallam's all those years ago to beguile him, to enjoy her sensuality, to seek and enjoy the pleasure he had given her. She would so miss his intimacy, his attraction, his sharpness of mind and his humour – the ache of his absence was already intense – but she would be able to soften the ache by drawing on the recent memories of sharing her bed. She would seek even greater solace in the pursuit of music. Perhaps the playing of it, the feel of her fingertips on the keys of the piano, might bring her some physical gratification.

Arabella began to play. She sang softly to herself Ruggiero's aria *Verdi prati* from Handel's opera *Alcina.*

Verdant pastures, leafy woodlands,
Soon your beauty will decay;
What I loved and longed to cherish
Is as dust, destined to perish
And return to barren clay.

Though her love for Gray had proved in the end an illusion, the beauty, intimacy and intensity of the illusion would haunt her for the rest of her life.

She was unware her daughter had entered and was watching her silently in the shadows.

"Mama, that was truly beautiful. I've never heard you sing with such emotion and poignancy before."

"Elise, please sing it for me."

And so as Arabella played Elise sang to her mother. At the end they both embraced.

"Has he gone?" Elise asked, taking her mother's hand.

"Yes, he has gone and he will not be back. What he wanted I could not give. What I wanted he could not grant," Arabella replied.

"Might he change his mind or you yours?" said Elise.

"No, the die is cast. There is no going back. I have passed the proverbial fork in the road. I have chosen my path and now I have begun to climb as it winds in a new and unknown direction. But I have you to comfort me."

"I am truly sorry, Mama. It was evident to me long ago how much you loved him."

"Dearest Elise, you should not be sorry. We must accept that life can be cruel, unbounded happiness one moment, depthless sadness the next. And what often destroys happiness is what we love the most. But this particular chapter for me is now ended. You, Elisabeth and Joseph, and Frederick Daniel, Jacqueline and Carl Nicolas will be the focus of my remaining life, which is as it should be. I love you all deeply. What more could I ask?"

With that mother and daughter extinguished the candle and joined the others for supper. Later that evening Arabella drew the curtains tightly around her lonely bed. He was irrevocably gone.

* * * * *

Though Arabella found it hard to put Charles Gray out of her mind – in her quieter moments the house seemed sometimes to echo with the sound of his voice and when it did a strangeness within her twisted and turned – as the weeks passed and she became preoccupied with the frequent comings and goings at Herzberg in the closing months of the year he gradually began to fade from her immediate thoughts.

Her son and daughter and their families came often from Potsdam, mostly at the weekends. Maria Louisa and her daughter, Marie-Aurore, announced they were going with Antoine to Vienna, to spend time with other émigrés dreaming of a return of the Bourbon dynasty in France. They would not return until early the next year. Before their departure, and on the eve of yet another journey westwards by the Comte de Puyraveau to encourage coalition support for royalist forces still seeking revenge on the

Jacobins, Arabella – in one of her spirited outbursts – said a return of the dynasty was a pipe dream. Yet more blood had to be spilt before there would be any prospect of sanity returning and there were already reports of a young soldier, Napoleon Bonaparte, emerging from the shadows to impose a new order on France. The revolution could not be erased, the clock turned back. Everyone had to learn from it, and adapt it to their own ends. That included Prussia.

De Puyraveau not surprisingly disagreed. Maria Louisa shared Arabella's opinion but it carried little weight with her impetuous son-in-law. Marie-Aurore, though she had adjusted to a simpler life at Herzberg, still spoke fondly of her service at Versailles. A few months in imperial circles in Vienna would, Arabella surmised, be a reminder of her previous frivolities.

The only pleasurable distraction for Arabella was several visits to Paretz to spend time with the Crown Princess and her children. She and the Princess talked together in confidence about many matters; they walked arm in arm in the gardens; they read together; and they discussed the interpretation of poetry and other works. Soon others joined them, including Elise Catherine. Literary criticism of this sort was a refreshing experience for Arabella and it brought her enjoyment and considerable satisfaction, particularly observing the harmony and ease with which Elise and Princess Luise treated one another.

These two gentle and beautiful young women, full of laughter and adored by their husbands, had created a close companionship that reminded Arabella of her own friendship with her mother so many years before. In contrast, her own private conversations with Luise reflected a greater emotional depth, with the focus often on the Princess's efforts to encourage her husband to be less reflective, more confident in his approach to life and to his role. Luise said she could never be cross with the Crown Prince. His soft eyes always melted any argument she might deploy against him. But she knew she had to persevere with her efforts to prepare him for his eventual accession to the throne and for the need thereafter to address Prussia's fortunes in a deeply troubled Europe. Arabella, drawing on her experience of life and the intimate discussions she had once enjoyed with the Russian Empress, was able to bring a wider dimension to these personal conversations and so help Luise shape her private intentions. They also discussed Luise's wish to give further help to the poor and needy. While she had to tread with care so long as the present King lived, she and Arabella discussed and planned what might be done in this direction when the time was right.

Christmas 1794 was spent quietly at Herzberg. Between Christmas and the New Year Arabella and her family – now swollen in number by the birth of Elise's second child, a boy, Johannes Matthias Joseph – were joined by the Crown Prince and Princess. On New Year's Eve the Camerata's soloists played in the *Spiegelsaal* a selection of music by Bach and Reichenauer. The high point of the evening was Elise's rendition of Vivaldi's motet *Nulla in mundo pax sincera*, which the redoubtable Herr Bamberger had previously unearthed on his travels in Italy. Her phrasing, timing and intonation were exquisite, convincing Arabella, not that she needed to be convinced, that her daughter should become the Camerata's new patron. The quality of her voice, her dexterity on the keyboard and her joie de vivre, which affected everyone in her company, would inspire the orchestra to new heights of excellence and achievement, and help assuage the mood of gloom that still prevailed in Prussia.

At midnight family and musicians gathered to wish the old year farewell – some with pleasure and others with a measure of sorrow, including Arabella, who saw the immediacy of her friendship with Charles Gray disappear into the more distant annals of the past – and to welcome the new one, though few were under any illusion that there would be significant improvement in the fate of the nations of Europe.

* * * * *

As the struggle for power continued in France and the rest of Europe watched for the outcome, life at Herzberg in 1795 followed a predictable pattern. Arabella remained in charge of the estate. Her family and grandchildren frequently came to stay. Maria Louisa had returned from Vienna alone, leaving her daughter, Marie-Aurore de Puyraveau, and her grandson, Antoine, in Vienna with other émigrés, to be joined later by Marie-Aurore's husband from France. The Comte arrived in the Austrian capital not only chastened by the way Napoleon was beginning to carve his name but also thankful that he had escaped from France with his life following the crushing of the so-called White Terror. But he still remained committed to the eventual restoration of the Bourbons in France.

Meanwhile, under the leadership of Herr Bamberger's son, the Camerata flourished, vying in popularity with the King's own orchestra. It played often in Potsdam and several times at the Hofoper in Berlin. Persuaded by her mother and in equal measure by the Crown Princess, Elise Catherine became a prominent public performer, much to the delight and popular demand of all who heard her sing. Her husband, Joseph, was not always able to attend on account of his military duties, but when present he beamed with pride.

It was after one concert in Berlin that Elise proposed to her mother a startling new step in the Herzberg musical tradition – the creation of an academy for young music students from amongst whom could be chosen the next generation of players and soloists for the orchestra. While it might seem obvious to establish the music school at Herzberg it would, Elise proposed, be more practicable to locate it in either Potsdam or Berlin, so making it easier for young, talented and aspiring students from across Prussia to gain access to the limited number of places that would initially be available each year. Arabella greatly admired Elise's proposal, adding that Elise should justly become the academy's founder and provide the early impetus that it would require. Her daughter sought to resist the suggestion but Arabella insisted that, as Elise was young and already much respected in her own right as a fine musician, she was better able to assume the responsibility she herself had proposed. Despite Elise's protestations that her mother was more suited to the task, Arabella insisted that it was time for the Camerata and all matters associated with it to become the responsibility of younger hands.

Once the proposal gained favour with the Crown Princess, the Herzberg Academy of Music was founded in Berlin on the 8th of September 1795, with twenty pupils – girls and boys – chosen by Elise and the Camerata's leading soloists. Herr Bamberger became the Academy's librarian, responsible for archiving not only the large repertoire of music that he and Arabella had assembled over many years and but also the many years of correspondence between him and the Countess on the one hand, and with composers, musicians, singers and anyone else brushed by the Camerata's history on the other.

In September the following year, 1796, the Academy gave its first concert, which was widely acclaimed. As honorary patron, a role she had been prevailed upon to accept, Arabella listened with immense pride and pleasure. The formation of the Academy and the continuing fame of the Camerata brought even greater respect to Schloss Herzberg and its chatelaine, still referred to by some as the English countess. But it was her daughter who rightly received praise for inspiring and bringing the Academy to fruition. Elise had taken her first steps towards the inheritance of the Camerata from her mother. Arabella was deeply proud that she had done so.

* * * * *

Earlier that year, between May and July, the performer and composer Ludwig van Beethoven came to Berlin with Prince Lichnowsky, who had previously come to the city with Mozart in 1789 and accompanied him to Herzberg. Beethoven knew of King Frederick William's interest in music and had heard of the King's putative contribution of nearly 4,000 florins to Mozart's tour in 1789. He hoped his own visit would be equally profitable. Learning of Lichnowsky's arrival in Berlin Arabella immediately wrote to him, seeking to renew her acquaintance and asking if it would be possible for her and her daughter to meet the young Beethoven. At twenty-five years old he had already established a reputation as a piano virtuoso and improviser, while his compositions, just beginning to be published – including three piano trios, dedicated to Prince Lichnowsky, which the Camerata had added to its repertoire – were meeting with considerable critical and financial success. Within days of writing her letter shc received a warm reply, urging them to come to Berlin at the earliest opportunity. Herr Beethoven was, Lichnowsky wrote, as keen to meet them as they were him, given the reputation of the Camerata as a fine match for the court orchestra. Besides, it was tedious waiting for an audience with the King.

Shortly after their arrival in Berlin, Arabella and Elise Catherine duly received an invitation to attend the premiere of Beethoven's two sonatas for cello and piano, dedicated to the King and performed by Jean-Louis Duport – brother of the royal master of music, Jean-Pierre Duport – with Beethoven himself at the keyboard. Arabella and Elise were spellbound. They had never heard such compositions played before – the slow beginning, followed by the allegro movement repeating themes from the earlier adagio, and then the rondo. While the young composer had clearly drawn early inspiration from Mozart and Josef Haydn, these works had no precedent. What impressed Arabella and Elise was the way Beethoven had divided the music between the two instruments equally, relegating neither to the traditional basso continuo accompanying role. They wished to applaud but were slow to do so since the rest of the audience appeared more inclined to be moved to tears, which plainly annoyed Beethoven who made it clear he sought demonstrable praise.

The following day, on Thursday the 16th of June, Arabella and Elise invited Prince Lichnowsky and the gifted young musician to tea at the villa in Wannsee where they were staying. Beethoven, an intense man not evidently given to small talk, played for the two ladies. Then, while Arabella accepted an invitation to walk with Lichnowsky along the lakeside, Beethoven asked Elise to play for him. She somewhat nervously obliged. She wore a slim-fitting, simple but nonetheless elegant chiffon-style décolleté dress onto which had been sewn some small yellow ribbon bows. Her silk shawl lay loosely across her shoulders. Her long ash-blonde-coloured hair was pinned in a chignon beneath a white broad-brimmed soft hat, decorated with delicate white feathers. As she sat down the shawl slipped (perhaps deliberately dislodged), revealing the almost white complexion of her delicate shoulders and arms. Elise, with her delicate feminine hand movements, had learnt from her mother the art of flirting with men whose attention she wished to capture.

Beethoven placed before her the music of one of his sonatas. Though still nervous, she began to play. At the beginning, he sat on a nearby chair, brooding and contemplative, watching her first notes. He rose to turn the music for her, remaining close as she continued to play. She paused after the end of the *Allegro*, expecting Beethoven to release her from the keyboard. But he beckoned her to continue. As she played the *Adagio*, Elise began to be moved by the notes and gained increasing confidence, interpreting the music with an ease and emotion she had never experienced before. Again she paused but again Beethoven signalled with an upward flourish of his hand for her to play the final rondo.

Upon finishing the sonata Elise sat motionless, waiting for the composer's verdict. He did not speak. She turned to look at him. He was gazing at her intensely, his eyebrows furrowed beneath his shock of dark hair, his lips pursed and no illuminating smile. Elise could bear the silence no longer.

"Herr Beethoven, your music is exceptional, so innovative. Bravo, I say to you!" she said, clapping her hands.

The composer beamed in appreciation.

"Herr Beethoven, perhaps we should join the others in the garden before the Countess and I take our leave. I wish to thank you for allowing me the privilege and pleasure of playing your deeply impressive sonata."

She rose from the piano stool, gathering her shawl around her shoulders as she did so.

"Countess, I believe you are married," he said suddenly.

"Yes," she replied, "my husband is an officer in His Majesty's army. He is garrisoned at Potsdam but at present is on manoeuvres."

"You played with a particular lightness of touch, understanding the music as you did so, allowing it to convey your emotion. Few could do that with a piece they have never seen or played before. If that is your quality then your Academy will produce fine students and the Herzberger Camerata will continue to flourish. The King's orchestra has a fine challenger."

"Thank you, Herr Beethoven, you are most kind and generous in your remarks," replied Elise, "though I am sure you make similar observations of others."

"Countess, do not be defensive. Your musical talent matches your beauty."

Elise, conscious that he might see her blush, attempted to speak but the composer interrupted.

"The compliment I paid you is richly deserved. Do not scorn it."

"Of course, I will not," Elise hastily replied.

"How long will you be in Wannsee?" Beethoven asked.

"For some days yet," Elise answered.

"Then, Countess, perhaps you would do me the honour of sparing time to receive me tomorrow and perhaps the day after so I can hear you play more."

"I would be honoured, Herr Beethoven, but on one condition," said Elise in a smiling and deliberately coquettish way as she began to realise that the composer appeared to be somewhat taken by her.

"And what is your condition?" he responded.

"That you will play for me," she replied with even greater confidence and a growing awareness that she was beginning to melt the composer's gruff exterior.

"I accept your condition," he said with a smile.

And so it was that for the next week Elise and the shy young composer, Ludwig van Beethoven, played music, talked and walked in the fine June weather. For Elise it was a time of great pleasure as she became aware of how much the composer enjoyed her company, despite his many commitments to play at court and in noble houses, showing off his talent for improvisation as well as his cello sonatas. It was an opportunity not only to be coquettish but also to learn music from him in a way she had not considered before. However, it was not yet fully apparent to her that Beethoven had become deeply smitten by the beautiful, elegant young woman whose company he was sharing for several hours each day. When they parted for the last time, the composer said he would not forget the enjoyment of the past week. Before he left Berlin in July they spent a further day together and after his departure she received a short letter, addressed to the Countess Elise, in which he expressed the warmth of his sentiments towards her, despite the fact she was married. Elise sent him a short note in reply, inviting him to Herzberg should he return to Berlin and promising to call on him should she ever visit Vienna.

* * * * *

Throughout this period of time the shadow of war in Europe never receded.

Ever since 1791 the monarchies of Europe had watched with alarm the revolutionary struggle within France – often considering whether to intervene. In that year the Holy Roman Emperor

Leopold II and King Frederick William, in consultation with French noble émigrés, had issued the Pillnitz Declaration, which asserted that the French King's situation was a subject of interest for all the monarchs in Europe, and stated their intention to intervene to help re-establish a monarchical government. But it had all been to no avail. Instead the French had defeated Austria and Prussia decisively at Valmy the following year.

Following further military campaigns and the French victory over Austria at Fleurus in 1794, which led to the French occupation of the Rhineland, King Frederick William decided that Prussia should withdraw from the allied coalition and in April 1795 signed a peace treaty with France, which contained a secret clause ceding to France the west bank of the Rhine and returning to Prussia all territory east of the Rhine that had been captured during the hostilities. The result was that Prussia would no longer fight against France. The treaty was seen by the other great European monarchies as a betrayal and it left Prussia isolated.

To make matters worse, little effort was made to improve the army, much to the frustration of Frederick Daniel and his brother-in-law. They had learnt even as children how the army had been the very foundation of the Prussian state, a fact that the late King Frederick and his father before him had fully recognised and pursued. The army had always been their first preoccupation and they had personally supervised its efficiency. But the present King had no taste for military matters and had delegated his "warlord" responsibilities to the Duke of Brunswick and General von Moellendorf, to whom Frederick Daniel and Joseph had been assigned as staff officers. To the two young officers' chagrin, no decisive action was taken after the defeat at Valmy to begin to repair the army, which, though still large, remained ill-equipped, or to prepare it to defend Prussia from its future enemies. Instead, the army retained outdated tactics and weaponry, in contrast to the French revolutionary armies, which, according to Frederick Daniel and Joseph, were developing new methods of supply, mobility and command. Prussia was in no position to follow suit; though the kingdom had been considerably extended in size as result of further partitions of Poland in 1793 and 1795, the effect was that it had become unhealthily bloated, rather than robustly enhanced, and increasingly indebted. Deeply frustrated, Frederick Daniel and

Joseph only continued at their posts because of their friendship with the Crown Prince, who had taken part in campaigns against the French, and with his young wife, who agreed with them that remedial action had to be taken. They hoped that before long the Crown Prince would accede to the throne, so providing an opportunity to take the steps they passionately advocated.

* * * * *

King Frederick William II died, unlamented by many, in November 1797. Two weeks later, at the special wish of Queen Luise, Arabella had come to the royal palace with her musicians to provide a simple but compelling musical performance to mark the accession of the new King and a new chapter in Prussia's history. The Herzberg Camerata and choir received warm applause.

As they took their leave that evening, it was evident to Arabella, to Frederick Daniel and to Joseph that the new King wished to choose a path to restore morality to the House of Hohenzollern and emphasise his sense of duty. The Queen whispered to Arabella that there was much to do in the provision of advice and encouragement to her husband in his task, a theme she pursued further when they met again soon afterwards. In the months that followed, the new King reduced royal expenses, dismissed his late father's ministers and began other reforms. But he soon began to show a lack of decisive will to fulfil what he wished to achieve.

Before long, in the following year, Arabella found herself increasingly drawn into companionship with the Queen at court, constantly, and discreetly, reassuring Luise in her determination to help her husband put a new public face on the monarchy. Soon the new King undertook a tour of eastern Prussia and insisted that Luise should accompany him so that he could present her to the people. This was a most unusual break from royal tradition and Luise was warmly greeted everywhere. As requested, Arabella accompanied her, though remaining unobtrusively in the background, providing advice and support. She observed how quickly, and with great poise and confidence, the new Queen began to emerge as a person in her own right, occupying a more prominent role than her predecessors – not by holding her own court and pursuing policies of her own but always turning her skill and intelligence to her husband's cause.

As the Queen gained further confidence during 1798, Arabella withdrew from the royal palace and so was able to spend more time at Herzberg, where in June, much to her pleasure, Jacqueline gave birth to her second child, Alexandra Véronique Lorraine. But later in the year there was sadness. Maria Louisa died, never recovering from the cruel events of 1792. She was laid to rest near to her brother at Herzberg.

CHAPTER 12

Defeat and Occupation

It was 1805 and another year at Herzberg.

King Frederick William had been on the throne eight years. His wife, Luise, had become an influential figure commanding wide respect and popular affection. She was well-informed about court business; her husband frequently sought her views on affairs of state. Yet it was evident to all that he remained cautious in his policies and his dislike of war was as visceral as ever. As he had written in 1798:

> *I abhor war and . . . know of nothing greater on earth than the preservation of peace and tranquillity as the only system suited to the happiness of human kind.*

It was therefore not surprising that the King remained neutral in the conflict that had now engulfed Europe, steadfastly resisting pressure to join a new coalition against the Emperor Napoleon. In the years that had passed since the outbreak of revolution in France, this approach appeared to have served Prussia well. While French military power had increased, Prussia had acquired more territory and its influence in the old Imperial Diet had increased following the departure of the smaller German states from its ranks. As the Queen explained to Arabella one afternoon at Paretz, her husband feared that participation in any anti-French alliance would lead to Prussia becoming dependent on Russia for military support. In his view that would be undesirable and go against the grain of the previous Prussian policy of standing on its own feet. She confessed to Arabella that her own opinion on the matter was divided – a matter of the heart versus the head.

Though the King's argument for neutrality had so far prevailed, there were others, including Frederick Daniel and his brother-in-law Joseph, who still sought general reform. They maintained that, while the Prussian system had once been praised and envied by many, it had fallen into disrepute and now required urgent repair. They lamented the lack of will to take action by those preferring to defend vested interests and privileges. Frederick Daniel and Joseph warned that if there were no reform there could be a heavy cost. Their strong opinions, encouraged privately by Arabella, who was becoming increasingly firm in her own views on the matter, brought them closer to one of the prominent advocates of reform, Baron Heinrich vom Stein, who proposed significant changes to the organisation of government.

For Frederick Daniel and Joseph it was not just a question of reforming government. There were military concerns too. Napoleon was becoming ever stronger, ever more decisive and successful. Since coming to power he had begun a counter-revolution, not to restore the Bourbon monarchy but to install a new system of centralised government and, even more importantly, to extend French influence and power in Europe by seeking to build a new wide and definitive sphere of influence for France. Not for him would there be a return to the traditional concept of maintaining a balance of power. He was using force of arms, guile and political realism to achieve what he wanted. As it would never be possible to reach peace with Britain and so have an entirely free hand in the pursuit of his grand design, Napoleon accepted that the only alternative to gain supremacy on continental Europe was an alliance with Russia. With his emerging *Grande Armée* now numbering some 350,000 men, he had begun to win military victories in Europe and, while still building small alliances, he continued to seek a more decisive alliance with Russia. Napoleon seemed increasingly unstoppable.

Against this backdrop of encroaching war, by the summer of

1805 Arabella was less often at the court in Berlin. Now aged sixty-two and still called by some the English countess – though none questioned her loyalty to Prussia – she believed she had less advice to offer the Queen and, given her English background and the current antipathy at court towards an alliance with the British, she thought it wise to spend more time at Herzberg where she was still greatly preoccupied – at the family's request – with maintaining the financial health of the estate.

Arabella, her hair grey but still tied back in the fashion she had pursued since she was young, continued to dress with aesthetic elegance. Her daughter-in-law, Jacqueline, who was often at Schloss Herzberg in the absence of her husband, was tall, slim and, with her rich reddish hair, still very much the attractive and pleasing woman Frederick Daniel had married following her escape from France in 1789 – though it was Arabella's observation that there was sometimes a hint of residual bitterness in her opinions, which was not surprising given the annihilation of her family during the revolution. Arabella's daughter, Elise Catherine, the warm companion of Jacqueline and now aged thirty-seven, was as vivacious as always, the recipient of ever-increasing acclaim for her singing and custodian of the undisputed reputation of the Herzberger Camerata, Chorus and Music Academy, all now under her leadership.

Despite unease about the French Emperor's constantly expanding power and military prestige and its possible eventual implications for Prussian neutrality, a subject of frequent conversation at Herzberg, life on the estate remained light-hearted. Together the women – Arabella, Elise, Jacqueline and the still somewhat imperious Marie-Aurore de Puyraveau, recently returned from Vienna – all had a pleasing and amusing spontaneity and joie de vivre, emphasised by their beauty and sharp minds. Their attractiveness to any visitor was further enhanced when Queen Luise paid occasional visits to the schloss, bringing her own beauty, outspoken opinions, and love of verse and prose. Quick-witted, often flirtatious, particularly when men were present, the women of Herzberg – with or without the presence of the Queen – were regarded as highly pleasurable and intelligent company, an antidote to the rather stiffer ménages that could be found elsewhere in Prussia. Strong and distinctive musical and literary labels had become firmly affixed to Herzberg. In that regard nothing had changed over the years. It was more than ever the general opinion that it was the delight of the conversation, the quality of the music and the beauty of the women that sustained guests at the dinner table rather than the simple but well-presented food.

With summer gone and a golden October turned into a sombre November, the family gathered, on Friday the 8th, for a weekend's rest at Herzberg. Frederick and Jacqueline and a handful of their closest friends from Berlin were joined by Elise Catherine and Joseph, together with some of Elise's equally close musical acquaintances, notably those associated with the Academy. Arabella, the matriarch of the family, presided over dinner, a position she found uncomfortable but which her family insisted she should occupy.

Inevitably discussion turned that day to the latest news of the French Emperor. Although reports had just been received of the French navy's defeat by the British at Cape Trafalgar, it was the opinion of those around the dining table that Napoleon remained invincible on land. Since 1803 he had slowly but cleverly emasculated all opposition, laying the basis for a new continental sphere of influence with France at its heart. Some of the diners mentioned yet more rumours of Napoleon's continuing efforts to enter into an alliance with Russia and of his increasing hostility towards Austria, a country that not only threatened French acquisitions in northern Italy, notably Venice, but also the growing French interference in southern Germany. But, like Prussia, Austria was reluctant to fight. It was public knowledge that Austria was decaying and many knew that the Austrian Emperor's brother had spoken of the army's weakness. The prevailing view around the table was that, the eventual fate of Austria aside, there was now a French noose around Prussia's neck and it was becoming uncomfortably tight. The question was, what could be done to ease the pressure if not remove the French threat.

Frederick Daniel and Joseph painted a sombre picture. The fragile peace between Britain and France, signed in March 1802, had lasted no longer than fourteen months. War had resumed between the two implacable enemies. By the spring of 1805 Britain had signed a new alliance with Russia, which Austria, not wanting to be left out, joined a few months later. This new coalition – the third – was determined to defeat Napoleon and to restore the Bourbon dynasty. Joseph described from his military sources the size of the French imperial army and its recent successes in skirmishes and other manoeuvres against the Russian and Austrian armies. If these military events were anything to go by, Vienna might soon fall to the French. Frederick Daniel and Joseph argued that the time was fast approaching when Prussia would have to declare its hand – for or against Bonaparte. The Emperor wanted Prussia as a compliant ally. If that were not possible, he was likely to attack it. Whether he wished it or not, the King's hand would soon be forced one way or the other.

There was a lively debate amongst the men around the table about what Prussia should do. Some argued that Prussia should continue to wait and see, but Frederick Daniel and Joseph advocated the end of neutrality, even if this meant war, rather than be obliged to accept a treaty dictated by France. Arabella sat silently observing the debate. Just as they were about to rise at the end of the meal, the Comte de Puyraveau, who had recently returned from yet another stay in Austria with the French noble émigrés remaining there, spoke.

"Countess, what is your opinion of the matters we have discussed?" he asked.

Arabella paused, looking around at her family and guests before she replied.

"Comte de Puyraveau, I was once asked – many years ago – by the late King Frederick where my loyalties lay. I replied that King George ruled the land of my birth and while there I was his subject. That King Louis of France ruled the land of my mother's birth and whilst in France for a short while in 1765 I accepted his country's hospitality and therefore behaved accordingly. And that so long as I lived in Prussia with my husband it was to the Hohenzollern throne that I owed heartfelt allegiance. Since then my opinion has not changed. Accordingly, I will support the views and policies of His Majesty, the present king, whatever they may be."

"Spoken like a true diplomat, Countess, and so typically English," said the Comte de Puyraveau.

Arabella bridled at this latter remark.

"But, if I may say so," he continued, "it does not answer the question I put to you. With all your experience and knowledge, do you believe Prussia should accommodate France or oppose it? Indeed, what opinion do you give to Her Majesty the Queen, since you and she are sometimes together?"

Trying to hide her irritation and to avoid expressing a view in front of guests she did not know well, Arabella replied with some care.

"Comte de Puyraveau, it is true that I enjoy the close confidence of Her Majesty, but it would be inappropriate for me to disclose the content of any conversation she and I might have. On the question you have put to me, I leave it to my son and son-in-law, who are far better informed than me, to express an opinion on matters of state. But perhaps I might say this in answer to your question. I oppose destruction, I oppose bloodshed and I oppose cruelty and the loss of human dignity. There is much in what has happened in recent years to appal me. Through tragic conflict I have lost my husband and two dear friends – Herr Drescher and Monsieur Trudaine. They gave their lives heroically for the beliefs that I have always held and still do. However, whether we choose to admit it or not and whether we like it or not, the revolution has brought significant change in France. There has indeed been much shedding of blood, but from that bloodshed have emerged new institutions which, though they may be imperfect, have begun to enunciate the principles of the revolution – liberty, fraternity and equality – principles that many who do not support the revolution yet consider honourable. You only have to look at Napoleon's army, whose loyalty appears to spring from their freedom to hold land of their own."

"Countess, how can you speak in any way positively of the revolution after what it did to my family?" Jacqueline interrupted.

"Jacqueline, I do not hold a candle for the revolution and the blood it has shed. I do not for one moment ignore the great suffering of your family and the grief it has caused you. I was outraged when I saw how it had led to the desecration of my mother's grave at Rozac and equally outraged by the killing of a King and his wife on spurious grounds when really it was naked revenge. The inhuman treatment of the Vicomtesse de Vervins was an unspeakable act. But I hope that out of the human suffering the revolution has inflicted on us all better circumstances will emerge – a greater recognition of the rights of men and women and of human dignity. Surely that is important? Prussia has earned wide respect in the past not just through force of arms but through its ideas, its culture and its tolerance. Yet even Prussia cannot withstand the tide of history. I believe that as the new tide comes in – which seems to me to be the case – we in Prussia will have to be ready to adapt to new ways. If we do not, the incoming tide may wash us all away.

"Let me add one further thought, one that is perhaps self-evident from an ageing woman. If there were to be an invasion of Prussia, whether by a French, Russian or Austrian army, I would not flee from this estate. I promised the late Count von Deppe that I would remain here until my death to protect Herzberg and those who live on its lands, as well as its reputation and its integrity. That is indeed what I will do, even though I am of the weaker sex. My decision to stay will not change. So if there is an invasion, I will stand my ground. I will look to the future and pray that some good will come of the difficult times I might face. If that is what I will do at Herzberg, others can advise His Majesty as to what they think Prussia itself should do in fulfilment of its own destiny. I repeat that I speak not as an English woman, nor as the daughter of a citizen of France whose family sadly lost their lives in the revolution despite the local esteem in which I believe they were held. I speak as a citizen of Prussia, a kingdom for which I have great respect as it gave me shelter and a loving husband and which provided me with the opportunity to have and enjoy a most loving family."

"I thank you for your opinion," replied the Comte de Puyraveau, perceiving it would be indelicate to pursue his questions any further.

"Mama," said Frederick Daniel, "you spoke for all of us. I fear you may be prescient in your view. The fateful moment for Prussia to decide its destiny is fast approaching. If Bonaparte defeats the present coalition, the King will have to decide what Prussia should do – whether to join in alliance with the Emperor or to oppose him. If His Majesty seeks my opinion, I will advocate opposition to alliance with France and, if necessary, opposition of the French in the field, whatever the cost in blood. But I agree with you, Mama, that whatever the military price we may have to pay, let us hope that out of it will come a better Prussia."

"If Britain stands against Bonaparte, so must Prussia. We have compromised long enough," added Joseph.

"And I would support such a decision because we must oppose France and a regime born from one that destroyed my family," said Jacqueline, unable to conceal her bitterness. The other guests nodded their agreement.

"Mama, if war comes to Prussia, I will be at your side at Herzberg whatever happens," Elise Catherine promised.

* * * * *

Arabella von Deppe had indeed been prescient.

On the 2nd of December, 1805, following the earlier occupation of Vienna, the French army crushed a larger combined Russian and Austrian force at Austerlitz. The defeat led immediately to the Treaty of Pressburg, which ended the Third Coalition against France, ceded territory to the French Emperor and, in recognising the royal claims of certain German states, augured the dismantling of the Holy Roman Empire. The presence of the *Grande Armée* in southern Germany; the demolition of the Austrian army; and moves to create a new federated body, compliant to Bonaparte – the Confederation of the Rhine, a collection of German states, not including Prussia, intended as a buffer between France and central Europe – now directly undermined Prussia's historical position as a strong power in central Europe. The policy of compromise had surely reached its end. What to do – and Prussia's future – became a pressing matter at the royal palace and elsewhere in Prussia, not least at Herzberg. Arabella sensed that old ways were coming to an end and, if that were the case, the uncertain future would encompass Herzberg itself and those who worked the land.

Christmas was inevitably overshadowed by further French military victories. The family gathered at the estate as in previous years. On Monday the 23rd of December the Camerata – including some of the original soloists from the orchestra's first public performance at the St Nicholas Church in Potsdam on Sunday the 18th of January, 1767 – played a seasonal repertoire in the *Spiegelsaal*, the highlight of which was Corelli's *Christmas Concerto*. As they listened to the adagio movement, many of those present pondered the prospect of war and, if conflict came to Prussia, what the consequences for Herzberg might be. Over the following days Arabella did her best to maintain the family's spirits and to ensure that her four grandchildren enjoyed the delight of Christmas.

*****

The King remained indecisive in the early months of 1806. The unstoppable expansion of French power along the River Rhine continued. Then the official formation of the Confederation of the Rhine in July, followed in August by – most humiliatingly of all to Austria and the German states – the final dissolution of the centuries-old Holy Roman Empire and with it the throne of the Holy Roman Emperor at last compelled the King to agree with Queen Luise and those around her, including Frederick Daniel and Joseph, that Prussia should join Britain and Russia in a new alliance against Napoleon.

Frederick Daniel and Joseph went immediately to Herzberg to tell Arabella of the royal decision. They warned her that war with France was now inevitable. Frederick Daniel said he and Jacqueline and their two children, Carl Nicolas and Alexandra Véronique, would remain with the King and Queen in Berlin. Joseph informed Arabella that he would now join General Gebhard Leberecht von Blücher, in charge of the Prussian cavalry, and that they would move quickly towards the French army. He had asked Elise Catherine to go to Herzberg with their two children without delay, for their safety.

"Joseph, do you think the Prussian army will prevail?" Arabella asked.

"Countess, I am not confident that it will. As Frederick Daniel and I have said to you many times, the Prussian army is weak and unprepared. We have failed to improve it, much to our shame. Our military tactics are out of date – we use those of King Frederick. Our organisation is outmoded and our equipment poor. The French Emperor has created a *Grande Armée* that far exceeds ours in military philosophy, tactics and equipment. It has quickly gained experience and learnt from its victories and mistakes. And it is an army that loves its leaders. We will go into this war as underdogs because our hierarchy has not pursued reform, has failed to heed the lessons of history. Napoleon will be a formidable enemy. But we will fight hard to defeat the French."

"Joseph is right. The battle ahead will be decisive – for France and Prussia," said Frederick Daniel. "Defeat would be bitter and its consequences lasting for all of us," he added.

Their words brought Arabella little comfort but she had to show resolve.

August and September passed peacefully at Herzberg. Throughout much of her life there, Arabella had travelled infrequently to Berlin. When she had visited the capital it had mostly been to attend performances at the Hofoper or to visit the royal palace. Before her husband's death, she and Carl Manfred had enjoyed some accommodation of their own in the city but Arabella had since relinquished it. It was a decision she now regretted because Berlin was getting larger. It had in recent years developed a strong literary, musical and artistic community whose company Elise Catherine much enjoyed as indeed did Arabella on the few occasions she visited the Herzberg Music Academy. On her journey to Berlin at the end of September for one such visit, the thought crossed Arabella's mind that perhaps the time would soon come when the von Deppe family might have greater need for suitable accommodation nearer to the city as an alternative to Schloss Herzberg. That passing thought caused her to wonder what the estate's future might be after her death. A few days later the thought recurred. While pleased to be returning to the peace of the estate, as the city receded behind her she realised – more than she had done before – how much she now missed Berlin and its artistic milieu. It was no longer the small town of the past.

Once back at Herzberg Arabella decided to address a matter that had been on her mind since her return from France. The estate had thrived over the years. Those who worked on it had been loyal and hard-working. Arabella had sought to recognise their loyalty in practical ways. However, while land owned by the state had been freed for ownership by those who worked on it, little had been done to improve the rights of those who worked on privately owned land. Indeed, there had been considerable resistance from landowners to such a change. The contrast between land tenure at Herzberg and local land ownership at Meltwater was significant. Arabella decided that the time was approaching to grant greater rights to all those who worked and lived on the Herzberg estate – to remove the remaining feudal vestiges she had long considered out of place and which she had largely ignored. She had derived much pleasure from her life at Schloss Herzberg, particularly its inspiration for her pursuit of music – firstly through the Camerata, which had gained much fame over the years, then through the Chorus, and more recently through her support for Elise Catherine's creation of the Herzberg Music Academy in Berlin. But surely something more substantial was required to define the von Deppe legacy to Prussia. Granting right of land ownership to those families who had helped to farm the estate for generations would be a fitting gesture.

She knew it was a significant decision and would likely arouse the disapproval of some of Herzberg's landowning neighbours and perhaps even that of her own family; she could not proceed without the agreement of Frederick Daniel and Elise Catherine. Moreover, though Arabella was convinced the step was necessary, she realised there was a risk it would be perceived by some as her open support for the reformers in government and around the King. This perceived support might win praise but it might also arouse further opposition to what she intended. Throughout her life she had been skilful in avoiding controversy. To grant land rights would possibly lead to criticism of her – for breaking up the von Deppe estate and for interfering in Prussian internal affairs, which she, being of foreign birth, had no right to do. But she had never courted popularity just for the sake of it. If her son and daughter agreed, it would be a decision she believed to be right and in keeping with her lifelong commitment to equality and the achievement of virtue as the ancient Greeks had defined it. She had perhaps lost sight of this commitment in many personal preoccupations since Carl Manfred's death. The more she thought about the matter the more Arabella was resolved to put it to her son and daughter without further delay.

But before she could do so, Arabella received several urgent messages from Frederick Daniel. The first reported that the Prussian armies had been decisively beaten at the Battle of Jena-Auerstedt on Tuesday the 14th of October. Many Prussian soldiers were reported to have been taken prisoner. The King had ordered a withdrawal and would appeal to the citizens of Berlin to remain calm. A subsequent message on the 25th informed her that French troops would soon be entering Berlin. By early November all Prussian resistance was at an end. Amidst this devastating news, to Arabella's alarm and even more so to Elise Catherine's, there was no report of Joseph. Was he dead? They had to wait until the 13th of November to hear that General Blücher, with Colonel Joseph Lange von Schellenhorst at his side, had fought bravely at Auerstedt, repeatedly charging unsuccessfully at the head of the remaining Prussian cavalry. After further fighting, the General had been defeated at the Battle of Lübeck on the 6th of November and obliged finally to surrender, with honour, at Ratekau, near the Danish border, the next day. Slowly he and his surviving junior officers, including Joseph, who had suffered a wound to his shoulder, were making their way back to Berlin. In the meantime, the King and Queen Luise had already left Berlin for Memel in East Prussia, with the intention of seeking sanctuary from the Russian Emperor Alexander. Frederick Daniel had decided not to flee with the royal family but to remain in Berlin.

As the weeks passed Prussia's fate became clear. Apart from loss of territory, it would have to pay a large financial indemnity and meet the cost of French troops occupying important strongpoints within the shattered kingdom, one of which points was only a few miles from the boundaries of Herzberg. The defeat of Prussia was complete and the cutting of all connections, including the letter post with Britain, underlined to Arabella her isolation.

The family gathered for Christmas at Herzberg. Arabella decided that such a coming together was necessary not only to raise downcast spirits but also to make important decisions about the family, Herzberg and the measure of their support for national reform, of which the King had now acknowledged the country was in dire need.

They ate together on Christmas Eve. Though the meal was meagre because of the recent disruption and the growing shortage of food, there was enough good wine from the cellar to celebrate Joseph's safe return. His left arm was more badly wounded than Elise Catherine and Arabella had at first thought. As his recovery would clearly take time, it was agreed that he should rest at Herzberg, particularly as the cavalry regiments had been severely reduced in the fighting. After touring the estate the following day to distribute gifts of money to the estate workers, the family met again that evening before supper. As they sat around the fire, the mood was sombre. Arabella decided this was the moment to plead her case.

"Some are saying that what has happened to Prussia is catastrophic and already fingers are being pointed at His Majesty. It is all too easy to allow despair to feed on despair, to give up and to adopt entrenched positions that will only serve to make matters worse. I am not one to give up, nor I believe are any of you. The von Deppe family must gather strength to pick up the pieces and join with others – the King, the Queen, vom Stein and von Hardenberg – in seeking to make reforms and so create a new Prussia. We should build on the achievements of the past but ensure they reflect the realities of the world that now confronts us. We should draw on the principles of liberty, equality and fraternity as enshrined in the revolution in France, principles that not even the French Emperor can now disavow.

"I believe these are principles that this estate must espouse. We cannot leave matters as they are – people working for us, the privileged, but doing so without enshrined rights. We have to do more. We must show by example. I have given much thought to what I am about to say. Without compromising our commitment to Prussia, I propose that we take a leaf from our occupiers and grant those families who have helped us to cultivate the estate for generations the right to own the land that they have loyally toiled for our benefit and to be free of the services and financial obligations Herzberg has imposed upon them. If it is our wish to see the emergence of a freer, stronger and more modern Prussia after this nightmare is over, then it is necessary to ensure Herzberg is part of such a transformation. Our neighbours may oppose such a decision, but we should ignore them. Our task is to help ensure that those on the estate do not starve from the shortages we will face, and that they will be able to take over the land and feel pride in their ownership, while still perhaps being our allies in economic improvement and contributing to meeting the financial burden Napoleon will place upon Prussia. Our example may encourage the reformers in our midst to be bold. I wish us to do this as soon as practicable.

"This will be a major change to Herzberg's destiny but I consider there to be no alternative. We must do it. I am convinced Schloss Herzberg will survive as a consequence of this reform. But we have to recognise that so long as Prussia is occupied life will be hard. We will have to economise, to live frugally and to share what we have for the common good. And we must not hide here at Herzberg. We should in due course find modest accommodation nearer Berlin so we can not only appreciate the art, culture and history of the city but also show by public example that we are not cowed by occupation. If we spend more time in Berlin we will be better able to avoid the disbandment of the Camerata, Chorus and the Music Academy. We can use them to help bolster morale, while finding new composers to augment their repertoire.

"I regret if my thoughts have taken you by surprise, but we face desperate times and as an ageing chatelaine of Herzberg I consider that our legacy must meet the needs of the present time as well as look to the future."

Arabella sat back. There was absolute silence. If it were not for the crackling fire it would have been possible to hear a pin drop. Faces showed astonishment. Then Frederick Daniel spoke.

"Mama, it must be painful for you who have carried the burden of this estate for so long, who through hard work and virtue have earned profound respect for your achievements, now to advocate the granting of land rights to those who have served us faithfully. What you are proposing is effectively giving away part of the estate for the benefit of others. I love Schloss Herzberg, so does Jacqueline – so I am sure do all of us. But, painful though it might be, you are right. We must do as you suggest, despite the enmity we may incur from our neighbours. The von Deppe family must pursue the changes you have proposed. You have my support."

"Mama," said Elise Catherine, "you have my support too. We should do as you have recommended. And I agree too that we as a family must spend more time in Berlin and that, though times will be hard, we must do whatever is necessary to keep the Camerata and Academy alive."

Joseph and Jacqueline added their own support.

After further discussion, it was agreed that as early as practicable Arabella would go to Berlin to seek legal advice. Even if the granting of rights were legally possible the family recognised it would take time to implement their course of action and their likely detractors would be vociferous in their opposition and might seek to put pressure on them to reverse their resolution. This would not deter them. They had made an irrevocable decision to which they would remain committed regardless of the obstacles that might be placed in their way.

* * * * *

The early months of 1807 were bleak as the French occupation of Prussia became fact. The terms imposed by Napoleon on his vanquished adversary, the King, at Tilsit on the 9th of July, were as harsh as had been feared, despite, at her husband's request, Queen Luise interceding personally with the Emperor. Prussia was forced to recognise Napoleon's brother, Jérôme, as sovereign of the new Kingdom of Westphalia, to which were annexed all of Prussia's lands west of the River Elbe. An indemnity of 120 million francs was levied on the depleted country as well as the financial obligation to meet the cost of an occupying force of 150,000 troops. Yet even as these punitive terms began to bite, the reformers, led by Heinrich Friedrich vom Stein and Karl August von Hardenberg, began to press for the urgent implementation of their proposals. They welcomed Arabella's intended land reform but warned her of the difficulties ahead. Arabella said she and the family would not be deterred. Shortly afterwards she received a personal letter from the Queen in exile in Königsberg, praising her for her stand.

* * * * *

Frederick Daniel remained firm in his decision not to join the King in exile but to work with the reformers. Joseph slowly recovered from his wound and joined von Hardenberg, concentrating on reforms to the emasculated army in the hope that in due course their implementation might contribute to the defeat of the occupiers. Elise Catherine stayed in Berlin, devoting her energies to the Camerata and the Academy. Jacqueline von Deppe spent more time with Arabella at Schloss Herzberg, helping to remove the picture collection from the walls of the gallery and putting it into a secret store on the estate; other valuables, including books and the most personal of belongings, were also hidden. It was necessary not only to emphasise the new regime of hardship on the estate as Prussia struggled with paying the war indemnity to France, but also to deter any looting by the nearby French garrison. Other items, such as jewellery, were sold to raise money. Arabella, Elise and Jacqueline made new dresses from spare material and wore the iron jewellery widely adopted by women in solidarity with the national cause. Simple and modest amounts of food replaced the rich menus of the past; what little was surplus, Arabella and Jacqueline shared with the families on the estate, where there was greater hardship. Fewer candles were burnt, with the result that after dark the Schloss resembled a ghost house. Towards the end of 1807 life at Herzberg had become truly bleak.

The celebration of Christmas was unadorned and restrained. The family joined Arabella for the last days of December, reconfirming their decision to press ahead with the intended granting of land rights, despite the predicted early signs of disapproval from neighbouring estates and from amongst the nobility, before returning to Berlin.

*****

At the start of 1808, Lieutenant Dufour, the new commander of the nearby French garrison, sent a note asking to call on Arabella. She agreed, though fearing what he might want. Could it be a request to billet troops at the house? If that were the case she would resist.

Dufour was young, good-looking and with pleasing manners. But he looked tired and it soon became apparent he was finding his command hard to bear, isolated as he was with his stronghold of some fifty men. Jacqueline was with her when he arrived. He was accompanied by a scruffy, mean-looking older man, called Leroux, with the rank of sergeant. Dufour ordered him to wait outside.

"Madame la Comtesse, I have come to introduce myself and to ask whether you might be able to provide additional food for the garrison. It is a cold winter and we are finding it hard to keep warm. My commanding officer, Colonel Lucas, suggested you may be able to assist."

"Lieutenant Dufour," replied Arabella, "you will know from observation that there are many on this estate who are hungry and in desperate straits as a result of your army's occupation of Prussia. What little food and fuel we have we share with the families of our workers and tenants. If we strip the land any more there will be nothing to grow in the spring. And if there is nothing to grow in the spring we will have nothing to sell in the summer, and from an even more meagre profit the estate will be unable to contribute to the heavy financial burden the Emperor has imposed upon us. But I will see if there is anything we can do, such as find blankets to help your men keep warm at night."

"Madame la Comtesse, I am most grateful. If I may ask, where did you learn to speak such excellent French?"

"My mother was French. She married an Englishman. Until I left England to come to Prussia to marry my late husband, she and I always spoke French."

"Where did your mother come from in France?" asked Dufour.

"She came from Rozac," answered Arabella.

"I come from the same district. Where did your mother live in Rozac?"

"Her parents lived in Château de Rozac. I have good information that they were killed in the revolution, the house destroyed and the chapel where my mother and her ancestors were buried desecrated," said Arabella.

The young lieutenant was chilled by the look on her face, made all the colder by her darkened, menacing, unforgiving eyes, similar to the eyes of the unknown rider who had once stared down at him in hatred at Rozac when he was a boy and whom he had seen kill a man.

"Countess, I am so sorry. I was once in the district of Château de Rozac as a child. I remember those who lived there. They were most kind and gentle. So many innocent people like them died unnecessarily."

"They did indeed," replied Arabella, "including the parents of my daughter in law, the Comtesse von Deppe, who were summarily executed for seeking to escape the madness that engulfed France at that time."

Dufour found it hard to reply.

"Lieutenant, the Comtesse and I do not hold you personally

responsible for the sins of the past. But it is necessary for you, your men and the army of France and indeed for all of us to bring the killing and the vengeance to an end, to apply the true principles of the revolution."

"I agree, Comtesse," he said.

Reiterating her promise to find blankets she asked the Lieutenant to return within three days. He did so, along with Leroux and another soldier, bringing a cart. Arabella and Jacqueline, assisted by their land agent, Herr Bauer, provided what they could, including a little food.

* * * * *

On the evening of Friday the 5th of February, 1808, Arabella, Jacqueline and the two children, Carl Nicolas and Alexandra Véronique, ate a small, plain supper in the library. After the children had gone to bed, the women talked for a while, huddled round the fire. As it was bitterly cold and wood for the fire in the library was limited, they decided to go to bed early to keep warm.

After checking the doors and windows carefully on the advice of Herr Bauer – who said he had seen some suspicious movement after dark on the estate, which he thought might be poachers, possibly from the French garrison – Arabella kissed Jacqueline goodnight and retired to the master bedroom. She found it difficult to get to sleep, so read for a while. Then, as the bedside candle was nearing its end, she extinguished it. Wrapped in a thick shawl she lay propped against the pillows, looking into the dwindling fire across the room. As she pulled the covers even more tightly around her, she heard what she thought was a muffled cry. She listened intently. The sound did not repeat. She lay back. After two or three minutes she again heard a cry, this time unmistakable. Something was afoot along the corridor. Arabella quickly got out of bed, drawing the shawl around her. She used the embers in the hearth to relight the candle end and after picking up the long, iron poker beside the fire she unlocked her bedroom door. As she entered the corridor, again she heard a cry, louder now and more desperate. She realised the noises were coming from Jacqueline's room and ran down the corridor, her shawl slipping from her shoulders as she did so.

As she stood by the door to Jacqueline's bedroom, Arabella heard a man's slurred voice speaking foul French.

"Come here, you bitch! You are one of those damn aristocrats who escaped the guillotine. Now you are living in this fancy house, you and the old woman, making us believe you are poor. I am going to have you. You are mine, you stupid bitch! I haven't enjoyed a woman for months."

Arabella heard the sound of matcrial being ripped.

"No! No! Get off me. You will not have me!"

"Oh yes I will!"

Arabella threw open the door.

Jacqueline uttered a cry of pain as her assailant used brute force to pin her down and wrench up her nightgown, despite her struggle to repel him and scratch his face.

In the dim, flickering candlelight Arabella could see a bulky figure on the bed, looming over a desperately struggling shape below. The figure on top suddenly turned to look at her. It was Leroux, half undressed and his breeches open. He stank of alcohol and sweat. As Arabella neared the bed, he released his grip on Jacqueline to lunge at her. With Leroux almost upon her, Arabella struck him a severe blow across his face with the poker.

"You filthy bastard!" she cried.

Again Arabella struck him.

"You hag, I will get you for that."

He started to lurch off the bed but in the light of the almost extinguished candle, Arabella struck him again and again. He slumped off the bed onto the floor, semi-conscious. Meanwhile, Jacqueline, screaming, her nightgown ripped to shreds, grabbed Arabella's candle to light her own. Suddenly, she called out.

"Look out behind you!"

As Arabella turned, a figure in a shabby French uniform struck the side of her head with his fist. She fell to the floor. The figure flung itself at Jacqueline, who pushed the lighted candle with its molten wax into his eyes. The figure collapsed back on the bed, howling in agony. With the room now in darkness apart from the remains of the embers in the fireplace, Arabella pulled herself up from the floor and finding the poker hit the writhing figure on the bed several times, until there was no more movement. Jacqueline seized the knife from the soldier's belt and groped on the floor for

Leroux's body.

"In the name of God, you must die for what you have done."

Shaking violently, she raised the blade to plunge it into Leroux's chest.

Arabella, her head still spinning from the blow she had received, threw herself at Jacqueline, grabbing her daughter-in-law's arm and prising the knife from her grip.

"Jacqueline, no, he's not worth it. We cannot afford to be rash with our vengeance. Our endurance of this occupation requires a measure of pragmatism. If you had killed him, you would have risked your own life – a possible French execution. Think of your children. Let others see what he has done to you. Let others punish him."

Jacqueline sat down sobbing, her head in her hands.

"Did he penetrate you?" asked Arabella.

"No," replied Jacqueline, "but I reek of his disgusting smell."

Arabella pulled a blanket from the bed and wrapped it tightly round Jacqueline's shaking body. As she held her, Arabella heard running footsteps and voices calling out. In the doorway appeared Herr Bauer, closely followed by Arabella's faithful maid Hanne. After ensuring Arabella and Jacqueline were not fatally injured, and instructing Hanne to assist her mistress, Herr Bauer dragged the two bodies from the bedroom.

The next morning Lieutenant Dufour, summoned by Bauer, arrived at Herzberg with three soldiers.

Arabella and Jacqueline were in the library. Jacqueline was badly bruised about the face and her wrists bore red marks from Leroux's grip. She was still trembling and her eyes were tear-stained. Arabella had a bruise to one side of her forehead but was composed, her eyes full of menace. She spoke quietly and deliberately.

"Lieutenant Dufour, what happened last night was an abomination. Two soldiers from your garrison broke into this house with the purpose of raping the Countess. Sergeant Leroux's violent attempt to force himself on her would have succeeded had I not intervened, only to be attacked myself. We have sought at Herzberg to hold out a hand of friendship in the difficult circumstances in which we find ourselves. That friendship has been betrayed. Is that what the Emperor and his famed *Grand Armée* stand for – violating defenceless women for drunken physical gratification? We wish never to see a French soldier in this house again. Nor do I wish ever to receive further reports of trespass on the estate. To poach from the estate does not steal from us but from the people who work this land and who like so many others have to go without in order to help to pay for the wicked indemnity the Emperor has imposed upon us. If there is any business to conduct with me or others in my family, it is only you or your commanding officer who may come here. No one else may come. Do you understand?"

Dufour saw before him a resemblance to the chatelaine of Rozac, whom he remembered standing with composure and speaking with eloquence as she and her husband were sentenced to confiscation of their château and to death – a sentence pronounced by his father. As a young boy, he had been shocked by the severity of his father's words. He remembered the calm with which the old woman had stood waiting for her execution. He also recalled the hatred her eyes had conveyed to those around her as her hands were bound. Now, looking into the Countess's soft face, he could see in her eyes the same burning hatred – a hatred of injustice and man's abomination towards women. He had the chance to atone for what his father had done in the market square at Rozac and for what he, as a young boy, had done, with others, to desecrate the tombs in the chapel beside the burnt-out château. But he still did not recognise the woman before him, who had in disguise killed a man at Rozac.

Dufour gave a full and sincere apology to Arabella and Jacqueline. He could not imagine the suffering they had endured. What had happened was a most serious breach of military discipline. It would never happen again. Leroux and his accomplice, whose name was Girard, still both tightly bound and bloodstained, were bundled into a cart. The next day, after a summary trial presided over by Dufour's superior, Colonel Lucas, the two men were shot in front of the garrison. Lucas agreed that a small unarmed Prussian military detachment, provided by Colonel Joseph Lange von Schellenhorst, who had received promotion for having fought with great distinction alongside General Blücher, would be allowed to provide a permanent guard to protect the Countess von Deppe and her family at Schloss Herzberg.

It took several weeks for Arabella and Jacqueline, who immediately returned to Berlin with her children, to recover from their ordeal. For Arabella, who insisted on remaining at Herzberg even though she was in the house alone, it reinforced her determination to press forward with the demarcation of the estate as a prelude to the granting of land rights. Moreover, the attempted rape had brought her and Jacqueline closer together. When they were together in Berlin, or on the occasions when Jacqueline and Frederick Daniel came to Herzberg with their children, the two women became ever firmer companions in their shared commitment to helping their adopted country regain its independence and dignity.

The months passed. As they did so the hardship of the occupation worsened. Food became even more scarce; further personal belongings from Herzberg were sold. Arabella's iron necklace, worn daily, became a badge of honour. The demarcation of the estate into smaller farms progressed slowly and work began on drawing up the legal documents to implement the grant of rights. Arabella, Frederick Daniel and Elise Catherine received representations from other landowners, begging them not to proceed with their plans, but the family remained resolute, believing it was paramount to set an example more widely as the pace of government reform quickened. Besides, it was essential to establish the family's future on a more durable basis. The representations of disapproval were outnumbered by the expressions of support from those on the estate, who talked of their intention to work with the von Deppe family to maximise the economic benefits of land division.

Despite straitened finances, Elise Catherine was able to ensure the Herzberg Music Academy in Berlin flourished, nurturing new talent for the Camerata, which now had its home in the city. The orchestra played often, to large audiences, the programme frequently including works by Haydn, Mozart and Beethoven, who continued to write from Vienna to his dear Elise, sometimes enquiring into her husband's health. Elise enjoyed the correspondence and in her occasional replies flirted with the composer, who, she understood from her musical acquaintances, was now losing his hearing. Arabella and Elise Catherine decided that for Christmas that year they would offer Handel's *Messiah* at the Catholic Cathedral. Not a seat was left unfilled at its performance.

* * * * *

The next year, 1809, was equally difficult but, despite continued austerity and Schloss Herzberg being visibly stripped of most of its treasures, which were either hidden or sold, national reform in Prussia quickened. No one knew how much longer Napoleon would be in power but there was a widespread determination to ensure that Prussia would be ready to reassume its sovereign identity. Frederick Daniel spent nearly all of his time in Berlin, involved in government business. Jacqueline continued slowly to recover from the assault, but it was clear she would never be reconciled with her country of birth. The emotional scars from the loss of her family and the attempted rape were too deep. Yet they seemed to enhance her natural beauty. Many men enjoyed her company and the wit and intelligence she displayed. Apart from her love for her husband, she still found great joy in Arabella's companionship. Arabella's son-in-law, Joseph, also remained in Berlin, working with Gerhard von Scharnhorst and August Neidhardt von Gneisenau on plans for a new Prussian army. Elise Catherine, ever captivating and feminine, remained tireless in her pursuit of music. By the end of the year the legal documents for the granting of land rights at Herzberg were nearing completion. All that remained was to set the date for the award of entitlements to the different families. Yet still the von Deppe family received representations from other landowners and aristocratic families urging them not to proceed with their intentions. Still they refused to comply. The family was unanimous: their decision was irrevocable.

As for Arabella, the years since 1806 had proved hard for her. Her hair was now grey with strong streaks of white, and she began to feel more often the aches and pains of increasing age. She occasionally looked at the painting of her younger self and the late Czarina Catherine. Though she was now an ageing woman, her body still remained slim and alert. She was determined that this would remain the case. She rode regularly on the estate and continued to do whatever was necessary to ensure it maintained its level of productivity, even if a significant proportion was used to feed several French garrisons.

Near the end of the year Arabella heard news that the King and Queen had returned to Berlin after an exile of three years. A few days later a messenger delivered a personal note from the Queen asking her to call on her at Charlottenburg Palace.

Queen Luise received Arabella on Tuesday morning the 21st November, 1809. Arabella had not visited the palace since 1767. Napoleon had stripped it of its treasures, its paintings, statues, manuscripts and other valuable antiquities. As she entered, Arabella remembered how, long ago, by royal invitation, she and her late husband had stayed the night in the bedroom belonging to the wife of Frederick the Great.

Though still young – she was only thirty-three – and still beautiful, with large, penetrating, doe-like eyes, Queen Luise had also visibly aged, even allowing for the birth of her ninth child, Prince Frederick Heinrich Albrecht, the month before.

"Countess Arabella, I am overjoyed to see you. I have thought of you so often. It was always my intention to write to you but circumstances invariably intervened and the moment when I might have put pen to paper passed. Please forgive me. How are you?"

"Your Majesty, it is such a delight to see you after so long. I too have often thought of you, locked away in your exile. Conditions at Herzberg are basic, but they do not compare with what I have heard you and the King were obliged to endure."

"Arabella, times have indeed been desolate and the King has found the present circumstances hard to bear. This empty palace underlines the depth of the fate that has befallen us all. I and others have done our best to comfort him, to advise him and to cheer him. It was not easy when he and I first married and it is no easier now. If only that accursed man Bonaparte would go away. But I have encouraged von Hardenberg and those around him to prepare for the moment when Prussia will no longer be occupied. Yet making progress with the French breathing down our necks is hard and tiring, and there is still much opposition from those who do not wish to change. It is all so wearing. But your son continues to be most helpful, as indeed does your son-in-law. Please thank them again on my behalf. And how is Herzberg?"

"Herzberg still exists," replied Arabella, "but as with all estates it is financially hard to make ends meet. We have surrendered many belongings, as you and His Majesty have done, to help Prussia fulfil its financial obligations to the Emperor. Like others we make do and mend, and eat frugally. If Prussia has to suffer, so must Herzberg. But my daughter, Elise Catherine, continues to do all she can to see that the Music Academy and the Camerata continue. We have held many concerts to satisfy the demand for music to raise spirits. Last but not least, the family has decided to award rights to a proportion of the Herzberg estate to the families who have served us well for several generations. As you would expect, many of our neighbours disapprove and some have tried hard to persuade us not to take this step. They continue to claim with great fuss and noise that they best know the country and what it needs because they are Prussia's backbone. For them no change is better than change. Leave things as they are. Do not disturb the balance. But it was the French philosopher Montaigne who said, 'He who establishes his argument by noise and command shows that his reason is weak.' I believe that what we are doing is right and, moreover, that such a step would be in keeping with the spirit of the reforms begun long ago by the late King Frederick and by his father before him. It is my opinion that if we do not change we will repeat the mistake that led to our loss of freedom. We must reward service and loyalty with liberty on the land. So it is our intention to grant the rights early next year. The result will be that the extent of the land at Herzberg owned by the von Deppes will be significantly reduced. The rest will be owned by farmers who have said they wish afterwards to work with us to improve the amount the land produces and so increase income for all."

"Arabella, I much admire what you intend and support your decision. I will tell the King."

The two women sat together for nearly two hours talking about reform, motherhood, the King and making ends meet. As Arabella took her leave Luise promised to come to Herzberg before long for some fresh air and to see a house she had long admired. But that visit never took place. The Queen died unexpectedly in the arms of her husband in July of the following year. Arabella was deeply saddened by the news. She had greatly respected the Queen for her simple and unadorned style of living, which had endeared her to so many in Prussia, and for her outspoken views to the King on his country's future. Though the disparity between their ages had been significant, the two women had enjoyed a warm companionship on the occasions they were together. Their intimacy had not perhaps been as close as that Arabella had enjoyed with the late Empress Catherine, but the bond of trust between Arabella and Luise had been greater.

Five months after the Queen's death, on Sunday the 11th of November – St Martin's Day – 1810, serfdom throughout Prussia was finally abolished. On the same day, the von Deppe family gathered at Herzberg and formally granted land title to a significant portion of the estate to those who had loyally worked it for them for generations. It was a day of great celebration. The new landholders were now free to cultivate the plots granted to them, relieved of the dues and other obligations they had borne for so long. They all pledged of their free will to continue to work in association with the family for the greater economic good. For the von Deppes, they were now freed from the burden of administering a large estate where all those who worked on it were their servants. They had the chance to look not to the land for their well-being and livelihood but to other activities such as in government, the army, art and music. The financial impact of the change would be noticeable and Herzberg would perhaps not have the same measure of splendour it had enjoyed in the past, particularly since Arabella's marriage to Carl Manfred. But the change of fortune would open new opportunities. Preparations for them would continue – ready for the day when Prussia would be rid of its occupiers.

That Christmas the family once again came together at Herzberg. Though times remained hard there was an expectation in the air that perhaps before too long the tide might finally begin to turn against the French Emperor. As for Arabella, she became adept at dealing with the French occupiers, understanding their mentality and manipulating it to her and Herzberg's advantage.

* * * * *

Two years later, 1812, as the von Deppe family gathered once again at Herzberg for Christmas, they heard the news, as soon did all of Prussia, that the French Emperor had failed to defeat the Russian army on Russian soil in his campaign of that year. Though he had reached Moscow, Napoleon had failed to inflict defeat on the forces of Czar Alexander. Losing over 300,000 men in the bitter winter, Napoleon had been forced to abandon his *Grande Armée* and escape to Paris by carriage. The Emperor was no longer invincible.

* * * * *

It was not until October 1813 that news finally reached Berlin that the French army had been decisively defeated at the Battle of Leipzig, one of the bloodiest battles of the Napoleonic Wars. The army commanded by General Blücher, who still had Colonel Joseph Lange von Schellenhorst at his side, lost 12,000 men. Joseph was wounded but survived. The defeat ended Napoleon's presence east of the River Rhine, with the result that the German states previously under French domination now joined the victorious coalition of Russia, Prussia, Austria and Sweden. Early in 1814 the coalition armies invaded France and before the year was out Napoleon Bonaparte was forced to abdicate.

The defeat of the French army and its allies brought great joy to all of Prussia but especially to the von Deppe family and most of all to Arabella. The years of hardship, struggle and fear had finally come to an end. It was now time to seek to restore Herzberg to some of its previous glory and for the family to turn a new leaf – on the estate and in Berlin. Arabella was proud that her son had become an ever closer and most trusted companion of the King and that her son-in-law, promoted to General, had become a hero of the Prussian cavalry alongside Count Blücher. Jacqueline von Deppe was radiant as she witnessed the parade in Berlin of captured French flags and regimental eagles. Elise Catherine felt privileged to be commissioned to bring the Camerata and the Royal Orchestra together for a musical celebration of Prussian victory in the spring of 1814 and to mark the restoration of national honour. In her preoccupation she overlooked on her escritoire another letter from Beethoven and that it was accompanied by a somewhat crumpled piano composition apparently dated four years previously and dedicated "*Für Elise*". Reading the letter later and playing the composition on the piano at Herzberg, she could not say whether she was the Elise to whom the composition had been dedicated but never delivered or whether the composer had composed it for another and sent it to her by mistake. Whatever the explanation, she was flattered to have in her possession Beethoven's music dedicated to Elise.

As for Arabella, she was at last able to buy some new clothes and to spend more time in Berlin amongst old friends now she was freed of the responsibility of a large estate.

PART FOUR: FINALE (PRESTO)
ANOTHER DAWN 1814–1816

CHAPTER 13

Reflections in a Pool

In the spring of 1814 Arabella received a letter from Herr Anton Kiefer, with a Potsdam address, asking if he might call at her convenience to deliver a much-delayed letter from Mr Elisha De Hague, a lawyer in England. While she immediately recalled the lawyer's name, she did not recollect Kiefer's. She read the letter several times. Then she remembered. Anton Kiefer was the young, well-spoken and well-manicured companion of Waldemar Drescher; the Kiefer who had boarded the boat at Calais with her brother George, following the latter's release from the Bastille in Paris. Hanne, Arabella's faithful maid, reminded her that a messenger was waiting to know if there would be a reply. Though she was planning to leave for Berlin shortly to join Elise Catherine, Arabella decided that as the contents of the letter doubtless concerned Meltwater it would be better to delay her departure in order to see Herr Kiefer at Herzberg. Besides, she could show Kiefer Drescher's grave if he were so inclined.

In response to her reply, Kiefer arrived at Herzberg early on the afternoon of Wednesday the 13th of April. Though appearing significantly older than Arabella had imagined him to be, his hair almost completely grey, he was still fine-featured and well-dressed. She had greeted him in German but he replied in impeccable English, without any trace of a foreign accent. His manners were exquisite, as so often exemplified by the succession of British ambassadors to the Prussian kingdom that Arabella had seen come and go over the years.

"Countess, I regret troubling you but Mr Elisha De Hague, who succeeded his father some years ago as an attorney in Norwich and whose father I believe served your family for many years, contacted me in London. He and I became acquainted some time ago. When he learned I was travelling to Berlin he asked if I would convey this letter to you concerning your brother, Sir George Whitfield."

The mention of the name Whitfield caused a slight shiver in Arabella which she did her best to conceal.

"I am sorry you had to come this far, Herr Kiefer. I am deeply grateful. The least I can do in return is to offer you tea. That is one English tradition I have clung to throughout my years in Prussia."

"Countess, I would be delighted to accept your invitation."

After tea they walked in the garden for a short while.

"Would you like to see the place where I have remembered Herr Drescher?"

"I would indeed," replied Kiefer.

They stood in front of the stone bearing the inscription Arabella had given it.

"When Herr Drescher died, I lost a true friend," said Arabella. "He taught me the necessity in life for eternal vigilance, how easily trust can be misplaced. He also saved my life in circumstances it is still painful to recall after all this time."

"And you once saved his life," Kiefer replied. "He was a singular man, full of secrets, much maligned and much misjudged, and he was lonely for most of his life. His first love was never returned in the way he would have wished. But within him, beneath a shield of flint-hard stone, there beat a warm heart. I did not know him for long but during the time I did he was a source of great kindness and humility. He taught me much about human nature and the importance of true love. Like you, Countess, I miss him greatly."

Kiefer and Arabella walked back to the house.

"Will you give me the pleasure of your company at supper? You can tell me the latest gossip of London."

"Countess, of course I will."

Over supper, they talked about many matters, past and present, and of the prospects for peace in Europe, which still appeared unresolved, with continued fighting between Napoleon's army and those of the allies.

"He may not be quite done for yet," Kiefer said, "but God willing he will soon be dispatched once and for all."

As he prepared to take his leave, Kiefer revealed that he was intending to travel shortly to Spain to be reunited with friends of his in Andalusia, whom he had met some years before. One of them was a painter, Don Alfonso Ordóñez.

"One day, Countess, you should travel to Spain. Leave Herzberg in the hands of others and enjoy the warmth and colour of the south. Thankfully, Napoleon did not ruin everything there."

"I would so much like to do so," replied Arabella. "The last years have been difficult. Now that the kingdom is free of the French it would be refreshing and revitalising to go somewhere new – and warm."

"Countess, I challenge you. In a week's time I leave Berlin. Why don't you come with me, let me be your guide? What about it? Enjoy the sun of Spain, walk in the mountains and be dazzled by the Mediterranean Sea. Indeed, I could introduce you to Don Alfonso. He so enjoys the company of beautiful women."

Arabella smiled.

"Your suggestion is enticing, Herr Kiefer, but I have become an aged lady set in her ways. You are still a young man. You don't want me as a travelling companion."

"Age is no bar to the enticement of travel. I'm sure that if Herr Drescher were here he would have no hesitation in his advice. He would say, despite the years, why not do something new? Any age will accommodate that which has to be done," Kiefer teased her.

"I will think about it, Herr Kiefer," replied Arabella with a smile.

With that Kiefer disappeared into the night.

* * * * *

Later that evening she opened the letter from Elisha De Hague.

Dear Countess,

I have entrusted Herr Anton Kiefer to deliver this letter as

I understand he is known to you and from my acquaintance of him I consider him dependable.

I write to convey the sad news that your brother, Sir George Whitfield, died at Meltwater Hall on the 29th of November, 1813, of tuberculosis. He had been unwell for some time and as a consequence found it difficult to oversee the estate's affairs, particularly following the departure of his esteemed land agent. The estate has fallen into some disrepair and accumulated considerable debts. His widow, Lady Sophie Whitfield, and her two children – Robert Stephen, her son by Sir George, and Alice, her daughter by her first marriage – have decided, in the circumstances, to surrender their rights or any rights of occupation or otherwise they may have to Meltwater and to retire to her father's lands, where they will be looked after by her brother.

As to the future of Meltwater, Mr George Robert Whitfield, son of your late father by his second wife, Lady Barbara Whitfield, has the necessary financial means to purchase the estate to the value of the large debts outstanding. Unless you or more particularly your son, Count von Deppe, intend to return to Norfolk to assume responsibility for Meltwater and settle all liabilities, I recommend that you and he instruct me to draw up the necessary legal documents to bring about the transfer of the estate to Mr George Robert Whitfield, and any heirs he may have, on the financial basis I have outlined. If this matter is not resolved by either of the means I have set out, there is a risk that the estate will have to be sold in order to settle with the creditors, who are seeking repayment. The existing stay of execution will expire on the 30th of June this year at the latest.

I deeply regret that I have to convey this news and hope that it will prove possible for you to send me word of your decision.

I am your most obedient servant,
Elisha De Hague
Norwich, Monday the 31st of January, 1814

Before going to bed that night, Arabella wrote two letters for immediate despatch the following morning.

Dear Mr De Hague,

Thank you for your letter of the 31st of January, which Herr Kiefer delivered to me earlier today, concerning the death of my brother, Sir George Whitfield. I also thank you for the efforts to which you have gone to write to me.

After most careful thought I am writing on behalf of my son, Count Carl Frederick Daniel von Deppe, and to the extent that I may have any interest in the Meltwater estate, to instruct you to proceed with the disposal of the estate into the hands of Mr George Robert Whitfield, and any heirs he may have, in the way you have proposed. My son concurs with this decision. By so doing he and I surrender any legal right we may have to my late brother's estate.

I have asked the British Ambassador to add his signature to this letter, along with that of my son, and kindly to convey it to you by means of the Foreign Office in London.

Yours most sincerely,
Arabella
Countess von Deppe
Herzberg, Wednesday the 13th of April, 1814

As she signed her name, Arabella felt complete indifference. Whereas before she had vehemently opposed the intention of her late father to transfer the right of occupation of Meltwater Hall to his second wife and the descendants of that union, now she had no care for that part of her past. By renouncing her entailment she had cut her very last legal tie with her country of birth.

Her second letter was to Anton Kiefer.

Dear Herr Kiefer,

I wish to thank you again for so kindly delivering Mr De Hague's letter to me earlier today. I much appreciated the journey you made to Herzberg in order to do so. I also thank you for your charming company.

Since you left I have pondered the matter of Spain you and I discussed light-heartedly. It has been my opinion for some while that my contribution to the estate is at an end and that it is time for my son, Count von Deppe, and my daughter, Elise Catherine, to become the true arbiters of its future. That being so, I had already decided that in the remainder of my life I would like to undertake new ventures.

Accordingly, if you are still of the same mind as this evening and would be happy to have an elderly lady as a companion, I should indeed like to travel with you to Spain, where I might spend some time – alone or with others – reflecting on life and enjoying a new landscape.

I would quite understand if you have had a change of mind and would prefer me not to travel with you.

Yours most sincerely,
Arabella
Countess von Deppe
Herzberg, Wednesday the 13th of April, 1814

She left for Berlin soon after breakfast on the 14th, her letter to Anton Kiefer already on its way to Potsdam by messenger. The following day Frederick Daniel agreed with his mother – as she had been certain he would – that he had no wish to become responsible for substantial debts in Britain. Accordingly, he and the British Ambassador, the Honourable Sir Charles Stewart, countersigned her letter to Elisha De Hague. The Ambassador kindly undertook to send it to the Foreign Office with his next despatch for onward transmission.

On learning that Arabella proposed to visit Spain, the Ambassador warned her of the risk of travel at what was still an unsettled time in Europe, but his advice did not convince her. She replied that, if she could go to Paris at the height of the revolution, she could manage Spain and any bandits she might encounter en route. So a week later, after saying farewell to her family, who, like the Ambassador, were deeply reluctant to see her go, Arabella, attended by her maid Hanne, left for Spain in the company of Herr Anton Kiefer. As they left they heard the news that, following a battle in Paris between French forces and those of Russia, Prussia and Austria, Napoleon Bonaparte had agreed to abdicate and go into exile on the island of Elba.

*****

The journey to Andalusia through southern France and across the

Pyrenees was long, at times tiring, sometimes eventful and occasionally put the travellers at no slight risk. But once in Spain Arabella knew she had made the right decision. Moreover, Herr Kiefer proved to be an amusing companion. The scars of the recent peninsular wars were frequently visible but the further south they travelled the more beautiful and rugged became the terrain, the more isolated the towns and villages.

After many weeks of travel in the hands of a trusted guide, Arabella, Kiefer and Hanne reached the Sierra de Almijara, a mountainous area of Andalusia, set between Granada to the north and Malaga and the Mediterranean to the south. Remote, with steep mountainsides of weathered limestone in hues of grey and white, out of which time had scoured a landscape riddled with plunging cliff faces and ravines, it nonetheless displayed a rich and varied flora. Arabella was struck by the contrast, by the majestic birds, constantly circling in search of prey, and by the settlements with architecture dating back to Moorish times. She was transfixed by what she saw, so different from the Prussian plain and the gentle undulation of her childhood Norfolk. But they could not stop, for fear of bandits, and eventually they arrived at an attractive and well-proportioned village.

The inn where they lodged for several days was simple, clean and decorated in white and brown. The floors were stone and the furniture made from roughly hewn wood, similar to that which she had once seen long ago in Magdeburg. The only sounds came from a nearby stream, the clang of goats' bells and from some thin strips of metal, hanging from the veranda roof, which jingled in the hot daily breeze. Kiefer disappeared for several days to explore the nearby mountains on a mule. Each day Arabella sat alone in the shade of the veranda. She had been taught as a young girl to sew, to dance, to play the harpsichord and to sing. But she had also learnt to draw, not large works but thumbnail sketches to illustrate her music book. At Herzberg there had been little time for drawing but now, in Spain, she at last had the leisure to capture people, animals and snatches of landscape.

Almost a week later Kiefer returned – not the elegant man of their earlier acquaintance but a suntanned, unshaven wanderer of the mountains, his face half hidden beneath a wide-brimmed straw hat. That evening as they ate supper on the veranda he appeared different – quieter, more reflective, but more at ease. Two days later the three set out for Granada. After a few days of leisurely but rugged travel they eventually arrived in the dusty town, which still bore scars of the presence of Napoleon's army. They stayed at a pleasant tavern close to the royal chapel in which were buried the remains of Isabella and Ferdinand, who had forged Spain's unity in the late fifteenth century. On the second day Kiefer invited Arabella to accompany him to a *finca* not far beyond the outskirts of Granada, owned by Don Alfonso Ordóñez, a distinguished and handsome widowed Spanish nobleman, now whiling his time away as a painter. Their host greeted them with great enthusiasm and charm.

Don Alfonso's villa was an extensive two-storey building with white stucco walls and a red tile roof. Its main entrance comprised a large wooden door, wide enough to accommodate the passage of a horse and carriage, with a smaller door set into it. Above the door was a stone pediment and above that was another, smaller wooden doorway leading out onto a balcony with a curved-iron balustrade. The upper doorway was surmounted by a second stone pediment, triangular, protruding and elaborately carved. The whole portal was flanked on each side by two impressive carved pillars resting on high square footings. Arabella would come to know and cherish each detail from portraying the villa in her drawings.

The main door opened inwards to reveal a cobbled square with white walls and small doors and windows, the latter behind ornate shutters. In the centre of the courtyard was a large tree, its foliage providing cover from the hot sun. Beyond the courtyard was a smaller one, where the stables were to be found.

Inside, the house comprised several spacious rooms, darkened by the closed shutters. The floors of each room were stone, but covered in an assortment of scattered carpets of Moorish design. On the walls of the hallway and large dining room hung paintings of ancestors but in the even bigger sitting room were more-contemporary pictures – of attractive women who, Don Alfonso said, in response to Arabella's persistent questioning, had modelled for him. The women, of different ages, all had dark hair and strong Andalusian features. Some were clothed, others were half undressed, while two women had been painted in the nude, side profile.

"Doña Arabella, perhaps you will allow me to paint you?" he asked with a broad grin.

"That is most gracious of you, Don Alfonso. But I would be no match for your models."

"Ah! I disagree, Doña Arabella. Such a beautiful woman cannot go unpainted. Let us discuss the matter later."

They ate on the veranda looking out across the valley below and with the ruins of the Alhambra high up in the distance behind them. There was much laughter. Before Arabella and Kiefer took their leave it was agreed that they should come to stay at *El Paraiso.*

The next morning Hanne unpacked her mistress's clothes in a large bedroom with a balcony overlooking the valley. The room was breathtaking. The four-poster bed was of grand scale, its rich, red silk curtains drawn back. The coverlet was Moorish and of intricate design, the pillows similarly so. The furniture in the bedroom was heavy but not out of proportion to the size of the room. At one end was a large and ornate fireplace, above which was a beautiful picture of the ascending Madonna in the style of Murillo. The picture reminded Arabella of her Catholic faith, which in Lutheran Prussia had far too often taken second place in her life. Next to the bedroom was an elaborately decorated bathroom and beyond that Hanne's room, almost as comfortable as Arabella's. Late that night, after supper, Arabella sat alone in her bedroom, gazing into the strongly burning fire. Prussia seemed so far away.

Two days later, early on Sunday morning, Don Alfonso took Arabella and Kiefer by carriage to see the Alhambra palace, the last Moorish stronghold to fall to Isabella and Ferdinand, and largely unscathed by Napoleon's troops. They wandered through the ruined buildings and somewhat untended gardens, still watered by small streams from the hill above. After a while they sat down on a stone bench at one end of a long, narrow, marble-edged pool of watcr, sparkling in the sunshine. At the other end was a tall and fluted Moorish arch with colourful, symmetrical tiling, leading into an elaborate domed room; the dome was reflected in the water. Kiefer got up to examine the Arabic characters above the arch. He beckoned Don Alfonso to join him. While the two men attempted to decipher the meaning of the script, Arabella gazed into the sunlit pool, its surface disturbed by slight ripples from the occasional breeze that created fleeting mosaic patterns in the water.

Arabella felt at ease. She had shed her burden – a lifetime's accumulation – of hopes, fears, anxieties and sorrows. In the fractured ripples she saw momentary glimpses and images of her past life – her childhood at Meltwater and the smiling face of her mother; the teared eyes of the staff when she said goodbye to her family home; her arrival at Chesterfield Street on a grey winter's day; the gilded mask she wore to hide her identity in the months that followed; the hideous, suffocating box in which she had escaped to France. She looked up. The two men were still talking. Don Alfonso acknowledged her with a scarcely perceptible wave. She responded. Another breeze came. Arabella looked into the water once more. She saw the façade of the grand house in the Rue St Louis in Paris, where the de Vervins had given her refuge; Carl Manfred's face; Versailles; and King Frederick in his simple blue uniform. A cloud passed over the sun. The water still rippled but with less sunlight the images were darker: the half-masked features of the man who had tried to kill her on her way to Prussia; her husband dying in her arms; the engraved stones of Drescher and Trudaine. The sun reappeared and in a sudden stronger ripple she saw the laughing faces of her young children. She smiled. She thought she saw the form of Charles Gray. What had happened to him? Then she heard Don Alfonso's voice.

"Doña Arabella, it is time for us to leave. It will be dark before too long."

A day or two later Kiefer announced he wished to continue his travels but promised to be back. Arabella said it would be best for her to leave too but Don Alfonso insisted that she stay longer.

* * * * *

For Arabella it was a pleasure to enjoy the company of a man of exquisite manners, a man knowledgeable about music and art, and a man who flattered her with great charm, reawakening that warm coquettish smile that had been absent for so long. Over the ensuing weeks the two spent much time together. He listened to her play the harpsichord, sometimes accompanying her on the guitar or sketching her. They had lively discussions about books; they walked together; they rode together. He encouraged her to dress in the Spanish style, in clothes that he asked a celebrated local dressmaker to make for her.

One evening as they strolled in the garden, her arm in his, he stopped. Without a word, he turned and kissed her gently on her cheek, and then carried on walking, saying nothing. Later she played to him.

"Don Alfonso, why did you kiss me?"

"I kissed you because I have fallen in love with you. There is nothing more to say."

Arabella smiled. She considered how she should answer.

He read her thoughts.

"Doña Arabella, there is no need for you to reply. But I will say that I wish you to stay here as long as you can. I enjoy your company. I like to see you bathed in sunlight. And I wish to paint your portrait many times over. Please consider my suggestion and I pray to Our Lady you will say yes. It is many years since I last asked the Mother of God for a favour," he said, laughing.

She continued to play while he continued to sketch her.

A few minutes later she paused.

"Don Alfonso, I am old, not the young woman I once was. My life has reached the point of sunset. I cannot be what you wish to paint."

"Doña Arabella, you are a woman of many parts. Some are obvious, such as your elegance, your ease of movement and your refined beauty. Some are less obvious, such as your intellect and love of art, which flash like a diamond when you express a strong opinion. And some are hidden, but can be felt by anyone close to you, such as the warmth of your heart. You say you are at the point of sunset in your life. Even if that were true, which I do not believe to be the case, sunsets can be rich in colour and promise for the next day. I should like to paint you tomorrow to illustrate how I see you. My portrait will not be formal or traditional but simple, rustic and golden. As my guest you will not, I hope, refuse me. Please allow me to paint you. Please, Doña Arabella."

"I do, Don Alfonso. I do," she responded.

Over the next three months Arabella remained with Don Alfonso at *El Paraiso*. He painted many pictures of her – with her hair down, her hair pinned up, fully clothed, half clothed, and once in a side profile without a chemise. When he was not painting her portrait – none of which he would allow her to see until he had finished all of them – they laughed together; he taught her to play the guitar; they walked hand in hand; they frequently lay together in her bed. Herzberg soon began to fade from her memory.

It was a time of great happiness for Arabella, of being physically close to an attentive man at a time of reflection on her journey through life – from a high-spirited and opinionated young woman; through the discovery of her sensuality in the dark demi-monde of London, in her marriage to a much older man whom she had loved deeply, and in her subsequent relationship with Charles Gray; through her love of music, leading to musical encounters with five monarchs and expressed in an orchestra that enjoyed fame and respect; and finally to her role as a mother and chatelaine of Herzberg. Hers had been a remarkable journey. When Don Alfonso played to her, she was without a care, sitting in the warmth of the sun high in its azure blue sky, or held in his arms in her bed. Her happiness was evident in the dozen or so pictures he finally allowed her to see. She was deeply touched by the way he had portrayed her.

It was on the morning of Tuesday the 4th of October that Don Alfonso told his Doña – his muse, as he called her – that she had a visitor. It was her daughter.

"Mama, I have found you at last."

"Elise, I was never lost. Don Alfonso has been such a good companion."

For the next week mother and daughter sat and talked as Don Alfonso continued to paint – not just his muse but Elise Catherine too. Then one morning when Don Alfonso was absent, Elise took her mother's hand.

"Mama, it is time to go home, both of us, together. We have missed you greatly – Herzberg has missed you, the orchestra has missed your inspiration – and I think His Majesty the King wishes to honour you."

"Darling Elise, I am glad to see you and to hear your news and that of Joseph, Frederick Daniel and Jacqueline, and indeed of my grandchilden. But I am happy here with Don Alfonso. I would like to stay."

"I can see how happy you are, Mama, and I am delighted that Don Alfonso has treated you with such kindness and affection. But we wish you to be home with us, not far away in Spain."

"Elise, this is now my home – in the sunlight, adored by a man with whom I believe I have fallen in love. Fancy that, an old woman like me, falling in love again. How silly is that. So can't you see? I would prefer to stay."

"Mama, Prussia is your home, the country you came to so long ago as a brave young woman, pursuing a man you loved. Prussia has survived the tragedy of war. Now it needs to rebuild. You are one of a mere few who can help to provide the inspiration it requires. Please, Mama. Please come home."

"Let me think, Elise. Let me think."

The next day Arabella said nothing, neither did Elise. The day after, following breakfast, Arabella asked Don Alfonso to walk with her in the garden.

"My dearest Alfonso, I have to leave. You have made me unsurpassably happy here in paradise. But it is time for me to return to Prussia to be with my family and those to whom I owe so much for giving me the privileged life I have led. Please do not ask me to stay, because if you did I would find my decision to leave here even harder to bear."

"Dearest Arabella, I knew as soon as your daughter arrived that this moment would come. I will find our parting cruel but I know I have no choice in the matter. Your mind is made up. So I will not beg you to stay, much as I wish you to."

They continued to walk in the garden, arm in arm, without speaking.

On Friday the 14th of October Arabella, her daughter and Hanne left Don Alfonso's villa for Malaga, to board a vessel to take them to Marseilles and thence travel by road to Prussia. Arabella found the parting with Don Alfonso unbearable, but by mutual agreement they gave one another only a cursory farewell, each aware they would never meet again. During the following days, Arabella found it hard to speak. Her face was drawn into a tight mask to hide her emotional turmoil. Her life had been enriched and full of good fortune in very many ways, but in the affairs of the heart ill fate had too often intervened – with the early death of her husband, the sad end of her affair with Charles Gray, and now her farewell to Don Alfonso, her last true love. All she had in remembrance of him were two pictures.

The first was his favourite painting of her – a full-length side portrait, with her face turned to the viewer. She is wearing a light-blue skirt, its triangular sweep dominating the foreground, giving the painter the opportunity to explore the effects of light and shade on the rich folds of pale fabric; above the skirt she wears a white, unbuttoned blouse, revealing the top of her breasts. In her hands she holds an almost-read book. One side of her face, framed by dark-grey, white-streaked hair in a chignon style, is in shadow, while the other is in sunlight, revealing large, deep-green eyes, attractive lips and a delicate half smile. The portrait shows a relaxed and beautiful older woman at ease with herself. The other picture is of her daughter, again half turned to the viewer, her arms resting on a large silver vessel, beside which is a freshly opened book. She wears a rich red skirt and a tight white chemise shirt that reveals the outline of her bust; her hair is ash blonde in colour, her face soft and smiling, full of confidence and purpose. The first picture is of a life almost filled, while the other portrays a life with still much to achieve.

As the boat left Malaga and in due course turned north-east, Arabella knew she had already taken the first of her few remaining steps in life. She would take them without Don Alfonso Ordóñez at her side, a man she had come to love deeply in the short time they had been together. Now she had lost him because once again fate had intervened – once again Fortuna's whim had prevailed. Whereas her affair with Charles Gray had been physical and a duel of intellects, Don Alfonso had touched her soul – a relationship of true equals, a union of two still brightly burning human spirits. But those two spirits had been sundered by the need for Arabella to fulfil an external obligation of her own making – to return to Germany. What a cruel world it was.

CHAPTER 14

La Réjouissance

Arabella and her daughter returned to Herzberg in early December, 1814. Forewarned by messenger, Frederick Daniel, Jacqueline, and Elise's husband, Joseph, were already there to greet them, together with their children. Exhausted by the journey, and in order to prepare herself for Christmas on the estate, Arabella decided to rest at the small family villa in Wannsee, near Berlin. Her instinct to purchase accommodation close to the capital had been a sound one; the lakeside setting made the villa a peaceful haven that nonetheless brought the teeming culture of the capital within easy reach. But in truth there was little time for repose. Many letters arrived, welcoming her return to Prussia, including one from the King in which he expressed the hope to see her soon at the palace. When not answering letters, she was receiving callers at the house. In what spare hours she had, she read and sometimes played the piano. But all the while her heart was still far away in Andalusia.

On Friday morning the 23rd of December Arabella left Wannsee for Herzberg, accompanied by Elise Catherine; the rest of the family would already have arrived. It was a cold but sunlit day. The journey did not take long, thanks to the much-improved road. As her coach approached the house, those to whom she had granted rights of land ownership lined the driveway to greet the woman they regarded as a heroine. She asked the coachman to stop so she could thank them for their kindness. Husbands, wives and children gathered around her to shake her hand. Arabella found it difficult to restrain her emotions at this spontaneous display of unalloyed affection for her. Disregarding her daughter's advice, she decided to walk the remaining distance to the house, accompanied by those who had come to greet her. The staff of the house – some new faces amongst the familiar – stood inside to welcome her home. Arabella spoke to each one.

After a warming drink Arabella asked to see the garden, to which, over the years, she had devoted so much time. There had been some fresh landscaping, one or two aspects of which did not entirely please her, but she kept her observations to herself. Later, following dinner, the family took Arabella to see the gallery. Now hung on the wall was Don Alfonso's portrait of her and next to it his portrait of Elise. The pictures were striking in their informality and vividness, compared to the more formal and traditional portraits nearby. In due course they would become much-admired and famous paintings. When she went to bed that night Arabella found on a table near the blazing log fire a small framed self-portrait of Don Alfonso. Beside it was a letter. She opened it.

To my Doña Arabella, to my love,

This is a small and most personal gift to you in remembrance of me. What an unforgettable time we had!

Please, Doña Arabella, should you ever tire of Herzberg, come back to me. You are the sunlight in my life, far brighter and warmer than the sun of Andalusia can ever be.

Your devoted admirer and companion,
Alfonso
El Paraiso, Friday the 14th of October, 1814

Arabella held the picture tightly against her heart, emotions welling inside her.

As she lay in bed, she thought of him. Alfonso had been closest to Carl Manfred in giving her the love, respect and understanding she had needed ever since her childhood. Though the picture on the table beside her was a fresh reminder of how much she missed him, she knew, just as she had known on the boat leaving Malaga, that she could not have stayed in Spain. She had not asked him to come with her because she knew that, however painful their parting, he would not wish to leave the homeland from which he drew his artistic inspiration. They were condemned to separation in the remaining years of their lives – lost spirits. Once again she and Alfonso were prisoners of fate, just as she and Charles Gray had been.

Christmas at Herzberg was lively, reviving much of the fun and vivacity of the years before the French occupation. And there was an abundance of music, including a concert of Christmas music on the 26th.

In contrast, the early months of 1815 were quiet and cold. Now frailer, Arabella divided her time between Wannsee and Herzberg, where Frederick Daniel and Jacqueline were spending more time. In late February came the news that Napoleon had escaped from Elba and a month later the report that he was in Paris raising a fresh army. Joseph rejoined General Blücher to prepare for a final allied battle with Napoleon, while Frederick Daniel was almost daily with the King in Berlin. In the ensuing weeks Elise Catherine encouraged her mother to spend time with her at the Music Academy, which was slowly regaining strength after the constraints of the war years. The Camerata still played, but it too needed fresh inspiration and new blood. It was a task Arabella enjoyed as it enabled her to revisit some of the music she had enjoyed and indeed had helped to discover over the years. But Elise noticed that her mother was soon physically tired and needed increasing rest. On Tuesday the 20th of June came the news that Napoleon had been defeated at Waterloo by the forces of the Duke of Wellington and General Blücher. The Bourbon King Louis XVIII had once again been restored to the throne, attended, amongst others, by the Comte de Puyraveau, back in Paris with his wife, Marie-Aurore. For his services to the army and his valour on the field, Joseph became Count von Schellenhorst, much to the delight of his wife and Arabella.

By the summer it was becoming clear that Arabella's health was declining. With Napoleon finally beaten, life in Prussia recovered momentum. At the end of August Arabella, feeling somewhat refreshed after a long stay at Herzberg, received a letter from her son, informing her that His Majesty the King wished to invest her with the Order of Luise, which he had established the year before, in memory of his late wife, to honour women of Prussia of all social classes who had given service to the nation. Like Luise herself, the King had written, Arabella had been a mother, a patriot and an example to many. It was right that she should be an early recipient. Arabella was deeply touched that she, of foreign birth, should receive such a personal award, but questioned whether she had indeed lived up to the ideals of the late Queen.

Though often proud of her achievements, she found the prospect of the award daunting. Moreover, acceptance would finally define her as a citizen of Prussia. Over the years she had severed link after link with her country of birth. To her this would be the final, formal cut; public recognition that she was Prussian. Her family encouraged her to accept. She was a woman not only of great status but also of renown for her bravery and commitment to Prussia. To decline would be to disappoint many who had admired her, including the King. Arabella decided to consult the British Ambassador, George Rose. He called on her at Wannsee. He confirmed there would be no bar to her accepting such an honour. Arabella had always made clear to his predecessors her prior loyalty to Prussia, the Ambassador acknowledged, and she had demonstrated this particularly during the years of the French occupation. Acceptance of the honour would be in keeping with her lifelong approach. Moreover, the honour would be endorsed by the British government; indeed they would welcome it. Her steadfastness during difficult times had helped Prussia in the end to join others in defeating Bonaparte.

The next day Arabella wrote to Frederick Daniel to say that she would be deeply honoured to receive the Order of Luise. Two weeks later, on Thursday the 21st of September, 1815, in front of her family, Arabella received from the King a small, black, enamelled cross with a sky-blue centre panel bearing the letter “L”, surrounded by a wreath of seven stars.

The next day, at the Berlin Hofoper in the presence of the King, there was a concert, performed by the Herzberger Camerata and Chorus and students from the Music Academy, to honour Arabella. The programme, which Elise Catherine had drawn from her mother’s treasured music book, illustrated the music she had come to love.

Rondeau and aria, *Forêts paisibles*, from Act Four, *Les Sauvages*, of *Les Indes galantes* by Jean-Philippe Rameau, sung by Elise Catherine and Herr Bamberger's grandson, Heinrich
Overture to *Il trionfo del fato* by Agostino Steffani
A chaconne by Nicola Matteis
Tristes apprêts from *Castor and Pollux* by Jean-Philippe Rameau, sung by Elise Catherine
Vedrò con mio diletto from the opera *Giustino* by Antonio Vivaldi, sung by a new soprano at the Herzberger Music Academy, Christina Schmidt
Nine Piano Variations by Wolfgang Amadeus Mozart
Ode for St Cecilia's Day by George Frederick Handel
Symphony No. 7 by William Boyce
Sinfonia Concertante in C Major by Johann Christian Bach
Brandenburg Concerto No. 1 by Johann Sebastian Bach
Lascia ch'io pianga from the opera *Rinaldo* by George Frederick Handel, sung by Elise Catherine
Christmas Concerto by Arcangelo Corelli

The final item of music was *La Réjouissance* from Handel's *Music for the Royal Fireworks*. At the end the audience rose in wild applause, demanding an encore. Elise Catherine stepped onto the podium.

"Your Majesty, honoured guests, ladies and gentlemen, I would like to dedicate the duet *Pur ti miro, pur ti godo*, from Monteverdi's opera *L'incoronazione di Poppea*, to my dear mother, who has done so much to nurture in me and others a deep love for music."

Elise sang the duet with a young counter-tenor from the Music Academy, Hans Friedmann. Its completion brought even greater applause. Then, to the most enthusiastic ovation yet, Arabella appeared on stage. On the arm of her daughter she walked to the piano. She sat at the keyboard and after a brief pause played Bach's *Prelude No. 1*. Everyone sat wrapt as she played each note with precision and clarity.

As Arabella rose to receive the acclaim of the audience, Elise Catherine presented her mother with a bouquet of flowers, then, with the encouragement of all those present, including the King, she addressed her.

"Your Majesty, distinguished guests, I wish to thank you for your kind and generous presence tonight in the Hofoper to honour my mother.

"Dearest Mama, the Count and Countess von Deppe, General Lange von Schellenhorst and I wish to convey to you on behalf of His Majesty and all present tonight, and those who cannot be here, our deepest gratitude for your service to the nation and for all that you have achieved in music since your arrival in Prussia so many years ago. Your pursuit of virtue, equality and harmony has been an example to us all, particularly during the last most difficult years. Yesterday His Majesty the King honoured you in a most personal way. This evening has provided a more public platform for conveying our admiration. Your commitment to music is exemplified in the Schloss Herzberger Camerata, Chorus and the Herzberg Music Academy. They and your inspiration are synonymous with all that is best in a deeply troubled world. Our applause tonight is a simple but moving expression of our love for you."

Supported by her daughter's arm, Arabella replied.

"Your Majesty, honoured guests, ladies and gentlemen and my beloved family, I never thought, when I travelled across the German plains in the winter of 1766 in pursuit of the man with whom I had fallen in love, the late Count von Deppe, that many years later I would be standing here tonight in the Hofoper, an elderly woman, receiving your applause. It is not the time to make a speech. Instead I wish only to thank His Majesty and all of you for the love and support you have shown me over the years. I do not know how much longer I have to live. Only Almighty God knows the answer to that. But I wish you to know that in my remaining time I will cherish this evening. It was Plato who wrote, 'Rhythm and harmony find their way into the inward places of the soul.' Those words have driven me throughout my life. I hope that long after I have gone they will linger in yours. Thank you again."

* * * * *

For the remaining months of 1815 Arabella continued to divide her time between Wannsee and Herzberg, gradually spending the greater part at the latter, where with the help of Elise Catherine and Jacqueline she began to put her personal papers in order. She still received visitors.

Christmas was once again celebrated at Herzberg, with Arabella watching with pleasure the family at ease. It proved to be a bitterly cold winter but she chose to remain at Herzberg, looked after by the faithful Hanne. She occasionally walked in the garden but mostly spent time in the library with books she had never had time to read.

The following April, after a week at Wannsee and a brief visit to Berlin to hear the Camerata perform at St Hedwig's Cathedral, Arabella once again returned to Herzberg. By now she was very frail. On a warm sunny afternoon she asked Hanne to walk with her in the garden. They sat near the spot where long ago Carl Manfred had asked her to marry him. A short while later Arabella and Hanne returned to the house. After an early light supper the Countess went to her bedroom.

Later that night, when Hanne came to put out her mistress's candle, she found on the bedside table, next to the self-portrait of Don Alfonso Ordóñez, a sheet of paper on which were written Arabella's last words.

> *Of happiness there can be only one source in life and that is to love and to be loved in return. I have been truly blessed in that regard.*
> *I can give no more nor can I ask for more.*
> *It is the end.*
> *May Christ have mercy on me.*

The tearful Hanne carefully placed the sheet of paper in the nearby battered blue music book given to Arabella by Frederick the Great a lifetime ago. It was the last insertion in the book that Arabella had treasured most of all her possessions, together with its predecessor, returned to her mother as a keepsake after her marriage, and the missal she had kept since childhood.

CHAPTER 15

Succession

Arabella Mariette, the Countess von Deppe, died at Herzberg in the evening of Thursday the 25th of April, 1816, at the age of seventy-three. Her death was prominently reported in Potsdam and Berlin, and in due course more widely in Germany. A brief announcement even appeared in the London *Times*, but curiously it omitted to mention her maiden name. The von Deppe family received many tributes. In accordance with her wishes, following a private funeral service in the Garrison Church at Potsdam Arabella von Deppe was laid to rest beside her husband in the grounds of Herzberg, not far from the memorial stones of Waldemar Drescher and Robert Trudaine.

Two months later, on Monday the 24th of June, the family issued invitations to a gathering at St Hedwig's Catholic Cathedral in Berlin to celebrate the Dowager Countess's life. Many prominent people chose to accept, including the British Ambassador, together with members of Berlin's artistic and music communities, and numerous personal friends, amongst whom were Sir Charles Gray and Don Alfonso Ordóñez. The Schloss Herzberger Camerata played Mozart's *Laudate Dominum* with the Herzberg Music Academy choir, the Camerata Chorus and Elise Catherine as soprano. The principal speakers were Frederick Daniel, representing the King; his wife, Jacqueline, the Countess von

Deppe; Elise Catherine; Herr Helmut Schuster, representing those who had been granted land rights at Herzberg; the aged Herr Bamberger, the Dowager Countess's lifelong music companion and founding leader of the Camerata; and Don Alfonso Ordóñez. All spoke with great warmth of the English countess.

Frederick Daniel talked of his mother's deep love of Herzberg and her adopted land. Jacqueline von Deppe recalled the Countess Arabella's courage in going to France in the midst of the revolution to rescue the Comtesse de Vervins from almost certain death, and before that her generosity in offering Jacqueline sanctuary at Herzberg following her own escape from France. Elise referred to her mother's unparalleled passion for music, out of which had been born the Camerata, Chorus and the Music Academy. She also referred to her mother's profound commitment to equality, both of women to men and between all people. This had sometimes led to criticism, particularly over the awarding of land rights at Herzberg, but she had always stuck to her principles, her independence summed up in words she had written when she was much younger: "*Je suis comme je suis.*" Herr Bamberger praised the Countess for her determination to encourage young musicians and to promote music, and Herr Schuster for her decision to grant the right of land ownership, an act for which she would long be remembered. Lastly, Don Alfonso spoke movingly of his short friendship with a remarkable woman late in life, bathed in the light of Andalusia, and which reflected her never-ending pursuit of happiness for mankind.

The celebration ended with Elise Catherine playing Bach's *Prelude No. 1* on the piano. Then those present left the cathedral, passing as they did so the late Countess's Order of Luise.

* * * * *

Early the following month, on Friday the 5th of July, the family gathered at Herzberg to discuss the execution of Arabella's will.

In 1765, before the late Carl Manfred von Deppe had met his future wife, the von Deppe family line appeared to have an uncertain future. The late Count's brother had died some years before in Paris and his sister had eloped with a French army officer, also to Paris, where they had subsequently married. Fifty years later the position was very different. Through Arabella's achievements, and despite the privations of the recent French occupation of Prussia, the von Deppe family had become and remained widely known and much respected – through music, through the prudent stewardship and innovative farming methods of the Herzberg estate, and through the public and military contribution of her two children and their families. One of the most controversial steps in the Countess's later life had been the decision, with her children's support, to grant land rights to those who had worked the expanding estate for many years. That decision had been difficult and had incurred much criticism, though it had not deterred Arabella in the least. A consequence had been to reduce the family's income from the land. But Arabella had spoken of the family's future lying in another direction – namely service to the German state.

It was against this background that the family met to ensure the continued survival of a much-respected family. Frederick Daniel was now a senior official at the royal palace and the King had made it clear that he wished him to remain as a trusted adviser; Frederick Daniel readily agreed to do so, though this decision meant that he and Jacqueline would be obliged to spend much more time in Berlin, a city rapidly expanding. A consequence would be that Jacqueline, stylish and still physically attractive, would bring her personal flair to Berlin's social scene, no longer overshadowed by Arabella's vivacity. General Joseph Lange von Schellenhorst, though retired from active military service, announced that he intended to accept the King's invitation to work with others on further reforms to the army, to ensure that Prussia, and indeed Germany, should never again experience the shame of defeat and occupation by a foreign power. Elise Catherine, as beautiful and energetic as her mother, said it was her intention to improve further the Camerata Herzberg and the Music Academy. For her this would be the best memorial to her mother, whom she greatly missed.

The family decided that Herzberg should remain their home, where successive generations of von Deppes could come to be at ease and to entertain friends and acquaintances. To contribute to its maintenance they decided to re-establish Herzberg as the formal home of the Camerata, making greater use of the *Spiegelsaal* for chamber music and thereby giving the house a new role as a focal point for helping to promote Prussia's cultural legacy. Together with those granted land rights, Herzberg would also remain a place of agricultural innovation. Though Herzberg was the inheritance of both brother and sister it was agreed that Elise Catherine would become the acknowledged chatelaine of the house, a responsibility she accepted with pleasure.

The next day the King and close friends joined the family for a concert in the *Spiegelsaal* to celebrate the fiftieth anniversary of the marriage of the late Count and Countess, a marriage that had helped to chart a new course for Herzberg and the family who had inherited it – a family that would contribute to the evolution of Germany in the decades ahead, and finally, in 1870, into a unified state.

* * * * *

One afternoon a few days later, Elise Catherine was alone in the library at Herzberg. She unlocked the secretaire and removed her mother's precious music book, which Arabella had said, shortly before her death, that she wished only Elise to see and thereafter keep in private. Though the cover was faded it was still a handsome leather book, bearing the crest of Frederick the Great – *Der Alte Fritz*, Old Fritz, as he was nicknamed by the Prussian people.

She undid the ribbon – a new, gold-yellow silk one she herself had provided when she was helping her mother sort out her private papers, to keep the myriad loose leaves secure. Inside the cover of the book was a letter addressed to her. She opened it.

> *My dearest Elise,*
>
> *My love for you knows no bounds and my trust in you has always been complete. It is therefore with profound affection that I bequeath to you my music book, given to me long ago in 1766 by His Majesty King Frederick as a wedding gift. He was such a kind man to me and your father. With it come my secrets.*
>
> *In this book are some of my musical favourites, many of which you will know well; some musical anecdotes; sketches; and random personal reflections on significant events in my life, a few of which are most personal but which I wish to share with you after my death. There are also several personal letters I*

should have destroyed long ago but which I decided to keep. As you read them all, please do not judge me too harshly. For better or for worse they are testimony of my efforts to honour my late husband's achievements and integrity, to protect my children, and to advance respect for Herzberg and all that it has come to represent over the years. Once you have read their contents you are at liberty to destroy them, but if you keep them please regard them as secrets between us and therefore keep them safe.

There is one secret not in this book, however, which I wish to reveal to you.

Since all my father wanted was a male heir to the Meltwater estate, after the birth of my late brother, George, he had little care for me or for the name I should bear, and certainly no care for my mother, whom he sorely neglected and then betrayed by taking a mistress. So, left to her own devices, my mother, with her typical defiance, chose for me at birth the name Cloelia. My namesake, so the story goes, was a young Roman woman, one of a number of hostages taken by Lars Porsenna, the Etruscan king of Clusium; she escaped, on horseback, leading other young Roman girls to safety. As for my second name, she called me, as you already know, Mariette, meaning little rebel, after a feisty mare she once rode at Château de Rozac before her marriage.

When I was ten years old I became entranced by the story of Arabella, a young heroine who had many brave adventures, recorded in the novel The Female Quixote, *written by Charlotte Lennox. I so fell in love with the character of Arabella that I insisted my family call me by that name, as I wanted to be as courageous as her when I grew up. They surrendered to my wishes – my father did not care in the slightest what name I bore as he already had his son – and within a year of my reading the book everyone had begun to call me Arabella. As a consequence, Cloelia was soon forgotten. Since on account of my mother's strong commitment to the Catholic faith, a commitment I shared, my arrival in this world could never legally be recorded in the Meltwater parish church record – unlike my brother's, who was baptised into the Anglican faith at birth as my father insisted – it was easy to achieve this change of name. Years later it was with my mother's support that I gave the name Arabella to the clerk when he recorded my marriage to your father in Berlin.*

Dearest Elise, I wish to remain known to posterity as Arabella and hope that you will agree to this. My great wish is that perhaps one day your daughter, Elisabeth Mariette, will give birth to a daughter whom she might deign to call Arabella in remembrance of me. As for me, I am relieved that I have told you my secret and hope that it will remain safe with you. My reputation and integrity now rest in your hands.

Your loving and most affectionate mother,
Arabella
Herzberg, Sunday the 21st of April, 1816

Beneath the letter lay pages of handwritten and printed music. Amongst the former was the handwritten score of nine piano variations, signed by Wolfgang Amadeus Mozart and dedicated to the Countess von Deppe in gratitude for raising his spirits with her delightful company at Herzberg in the spring of 1789. There were various sheets of paper on which her mother had recorded – randomly indeed – some of her most personal thoughts over the years; what she had written was intimate and sometimes revealing. There was also a crumpled letter from Waldemar Drescher, the scrawled writing stained by what appeared to Elise to be blood. Beneath it was a slip of paper not in her mother's handwriting: a Shakespearean sonnet with the initials *CG* beneath.

"Charles Gray, how romantic," whispered Elise.

Beneath some further pages was more writing in her mother's hand.

Some thoughts:

This afternoon I read a book about ancient Greece and Rome. Though their deities belong to the distant past, I believe they still have much to teach us about the philosophy of life.

What I have read has caused me to recall the night long ago when I slept, my husband beside me, beneath the figure of Fortuna standing in her naked glory above the cupola of the Royal Palace of Charlottenburg. As I lay awake in the early hours I thought I could hear her spinning the wind around her, dispensing gusts of fortune and misfortune indiscriminately, like a farmer throwing seeds hither and thither; or perhaps it was the sound of her wheel dispensing luck and misfortune in random, disproportionate rewards and punishments to those who had pleased or displeased her. It could be said that ever since that night I have been her toy, the object of her caprice, sometimes blown along, like a dried leaf, in her prevailing wind of fancy. Yet I have no cause to levy any complaint against her because she has so often borne me on a sweet wind of good fortune. If I were in Ancient Rome, I would gladly light a votive candle of gratitude in her temple.

My mother taught me that as a woman I should have a passion for life, and moreover that I should not hesitate to seek love even if the tender closeness of skin to skin might sometimes end in heartbreak and harsh recrimination. Nothing, she told me, was ever constant in the human condition: today I might not be the person I was yesterday and yesterday I might not be the person I was the day before. She added that in my daily evolution I should use my power of reason, my ambitions and above all my love of fellow human beings to seek to make the world a more virtuous place in which those of the weaker sex assume their rightful position of equality. Armed with this advice I decided that simply to sew, to be a dutiful wife and a source of fecundity at the whim of a man, only for such virtuous sacrifice to reap the reward of being cast aside by a husband for the satisfaction of a mistress, was not for me. Accordingly – albeit, on reflection, I admit, in a headstrong way – I eschewed this road and set my heart upon another course in search of true love and equal respect, which I pursued despite many obstacles and dangers. I prevailed.

As I would honour Fortuna for her gift to me and my mother of her philosophy of life, so I would burn incense in the temple of Diana, the virgin goddess of women and childbirth. It was she who graciously adorned me with pleasing features and who blessed me with sexual desires and a sensuality that I soon realised men found beguiling. From her I learnt how to use these gifts to fulfil my needs and to satisfy those of a man I would adore and respect. Those intense and sometimes dark desires, which have never left, lurking as they still do deep inside me, brought me the man I married, who gave me the love and respect for which I had yearned. I have never forgotten his qualities. Diana gave me, through childbirth, another gift – my children, to whom I have given my love and who in return have brought me great happiness and solace in my darker moments.

And I must not forget to honour Pallas Athena, not only a shrewd companion of heroes but the patron goddess of heroic endeavour, courage, strength and wisdom – to list only some of her many attributes. I would gladly worship at her shrine in thanksgiving for her protective shield of fortitude and defiance when I left home and when I went to France to secure the freedom of Maria Louisa, and for being at my side as I fought to defend and promote Herzberg in the years following my husband's death.

And there is yet another I would venerate. Accompanying the ancient goddesses, there is a Christian woman to whom I must give immeasurable gratitude – St Cecilia, the patron saint of musical harmony. She has given me throughout my life a boundless love of music and the divine inspiration to share her gift to me with many others. I would offer her many prayers. Nor must I forget Hildegard of Bingen, whose name my daughter bears, for the words that spurred me through darkness, fear and cold to the man I loved. The small white feather still in my music book, which I once found at my feet in St Petersburg, is testament to the power of her words and to her unbreakable religious faith. I would praise the blessed Hildegard.

In the history of the universe my life, like everyone's, has been but a speck of time – too small to be measured; here one moment and gone in another. But the fleetness of our time on earth is no excuse not to do all within our means to flourish and, if possible, to leave a mark of good, despite our vulnerability, selfishness, weakness and fragility. We must make the most of the gift of time each of us is given. My life has been blessed in so many ways, with a loving husband – even if he withheld from me the truth about what happened to my late brother in Paris and, according to Herr Drescher, may have betrayed me in another unknown way – and with the gifts of pleasing fortune, fertility, the ability to love and to fulfil my sexual pleasure and enjoy music. Yet there has been a darker side to my character, which no sweet wind has reached. There was my life in London, where I confess I experienced the seamy side of life, though constantly convincing myself I was not a courtesan; my failure to question my brother's fate; my sometimes misplaced trust in Herr Drescher who, on reflection, may have used me for pursuit of his own ends; my sin of pride; and the frequent relegation of my personal faith in the face of earthly distractions. And I made some unworthy compromises, sometimes abased myself and at times behaved recklessly. I even killed a man at Rozac – in self-defence, but in the blow I struck alongside that of the beloved Monsieur Trudaine there was also deep malice and cold revenge for what had been done to my beloved mother's tomb. That moment has often haunted me.

Yet despite the shedding of blood, my neglect, my many misdemeanours, omissions and commissions, I believe my deep faith has never deserted me. That is surely worth more than all the valiant goddesses of ancient times. I have often sung Almirena's sad aria:

Lascia ch'io pianga mia cruda sorte,
E che sospiri la libertà!

Let me lament my cruel destiny and yearn for liberty!

But if weighed in the balance, my life – in its entirety – has not been cruel. To the contrary, despite some dark episodes, it has been a life of joy and fulfilment. Fortuna has been kind to me.

These are the private thoughts – the testament, shall we say – of a woman who has been driven since childhood by a will to live a full, equal and passionate life, recalling her life as she contemplates what may lie ahead. All that I did was for love and in the pursuit of equality for the weaker sex. In that pursuit it was perhaps wrong of me continually to insist I would do what others wanted but only as I wanted it to be. But that is how it has been and I cannot change what has happened. Soon it will be for others to judge me. I hope they will do so with some understanding and a degree of charity.
Arabella von Deppe
Herzberg, Wednesday the 20th of March, 1816

"Mama," thought Elise as she slowly placed the pages back in the music book, "it can be justly said you led a well-lived life. Whatever your shortcomings might have been – and I for one would not hold them against you – no one can say your life was wasted. It was a life of fulfilment and you gave us unhindered love. Whatever secrets you may not have disclosed, my love for you is undiminished. I sense already that I have been cast in your mould and that pleases me. I will be the keeper of the secrets your music book has revealed, together with secrets of my own. Your past will be secure with me."

She closed the music book, tied the ribbon and locked the book in the secretaire.

Picking up her mother's letter, she read it once more.

"Countess von Deppe," she said out loud, "what a truly remarkable woman you were. It is so sad you are no longer my companion in life. Of course you will have your wish. You were Arabella for most of your life. No one will know otherwise."

Elise put the letter to her lips, then tore it into shreds and threw the pieces into the fire. She picked up the two portrait miniatures – one of her mother and the other of her grandmother, Lady Whitfield. What secrets, what stories, what hidden love, she wondered, still lay locked in those two pictures? Perhaps time would tell.

* * * * *

In the weeks that followed, Elise kept the two miniatures on her dressing table in the bedroom that had once been her mother's. She looked at them often.

The more she examined the portrait of her grandmother the more she was intrigued by it and the dedication on the back. There was something unusual about the image and the inscription.

> *Dans ta face vivent sagesse, la beauté et l'esprit rare qui ni l'age ni froid doivent se désintégrer!*
> *Du fond du coeur que vous avez rechauffé.*
>
> *In thy face live wisdom, beauty and rare spirit, which neither age nor cold shall decay!*
> *From the depth of the heart that you have warmed.*

Her mother had once remarked that she doubted her father, Elise's grandfather, would have been capable of such romantic and tender words, but that she had given him the benefit of the doubt upon receipt of the miniature after Lady Whitfield's death. Yet there was another question in Elise's mind. Who had returned the miniature to Lady Whitfield, and in what circumstances? Had it been after the death of an admirer? And then there was the portrait itself. Painted when Lady Whitfield was young, it portrayed the sitter as captivating, alluring and coquettish – the latter a feature Elise had often seen in her own mother and which she had inherited and sometimes used to good effect with men like Herr Beethoven. But the half smile on Lady Whitfield's face was not just coquettish; it was beguiling, sensual and even imparted a secret she was challenging the viewer to guess. Elise Catherine would even go as far as to say there was an erotic hint about the image, whether added by the artist or present in the sitter and so merely another detail in the artist's faithful representation, who could tell? Elise looked repeatedly but hard though she tried she could see no clue.

Some weeks later Joseph was with her at Herzberg, examining military maps. Elise asked to use his large magnifying glass. Once again she looked at her grandmother's miniature, scrutinising the face, the hair, the background, Lady Whitfield's dress. Then it struck her.

First, she saw the letters *RC* in the bottom right-hand corner. Those might be a clue to the admirer, or the initials of the artist. She continued to inspect the picture. She suddenly saw something else – in the narrow, fine-lace border along the top of the bodice of Lady Whitfield's elegant and stylish dress were the letters *FB*, which on even closer scrutiny seemed to recur along the entire lace border, but skilfully hidden within a holly-leaf pattern. Lady Whitfield's name before her marriage was Thérèse de Miron, so clearly *FB* did not represent that. Might it have been a borrowed dress? This was unlikely as Arabella had told Elise Catherine of the fun she and her mother used to have, going to the finest dressmaker in Norwich to be fitted for new clothes two or three times a year. That would suggest that Lady Whitfield, with a wealthy husband and coming from an equally wealthy family in France, would not have needed to borrow a fine dress to sit for a portrait. If the painter was the admirer, the choice of the lace border would have been deliberate – to flatter both artist and sitter. But the painter could not have been the admirer if the initials in the bottom right-hand corner were the artist's. So, if the initials *FB* were not those of Sir Robert Whitfield, or the artist, or her grandmother, whose were they? Surely the admirer was someone else?

A few days later, in Berlin, Elise Catherine sought advice from the Director of the Royal Prussian Academy of Art. She asked him which artists had been known to paint miniatures of high quality in the early eighteenth century. The Director listed several names but after examining the picture closely suggested that the one which corresponded with the initials on the miniature was probably Rosalba Carriera – unless of course the miniature was a fake, which he doubted. Carriera, who had died in 1757, was an acclaimed Venetian pastellist and miniaturist who painted in Paris, Rome and Vienna, as well as her native Venice. Her work, the Director added, had included snuff boxes for affluent patrons such as young Englishmen undertaking the Grand Tour, and even, sometimes, erotic pictures. In 1705, as confirmation of her reputation among the Italian art establishment, she had been admitted to the prestigious Accademia di San Luca in Rome.

Because of the high quality and style of the miniature, and the coincidence of the initials *RC*, Elise Catherine accepted the Director's opinion that the probable artist was indeed Rosalba Carriera. As there was no evidence that the painter had ever been to England, and since Lady Whitfield had never, according to Arabella, been to Rome or any of the other European cities where she was known to have worked, it would suggest that the portrait, if it were by Carriera, might have been painted in Paris. But Elise remembered her mother saying that Sir Robert had greatly disliked Paris, and to her knowledge had rarely been there apart from at the start of his Grand Tour to Italy. If that were the case, the picture might have been painted before Thérèse de Miron married, commissioned perhaps by an admirer or even a lover. Then again, the miniature might have been painted after her marriage to Sir Robert. If so, where would he have been while his wife sat for the painter? If he had disliked Paris so much, he and Lady Whitfield would not have been in the city together long enough for completion and collection of the miniature. Of course it was conceivable that Lady Whitfield had been alone in Paris to sit for the artist; and if she had been there without her husband, had she been in the company of an admirer, or even a lover – *FB*? And, if so, was *FB* French or English? Elise Catherine could only speculate on these permutations. The original questions still remained unanswered. Who was *FB*? Was *FB* the author of the inscription on the reverse? And what was the nature of his relationship with her grandmother?

These questions continued to intrigue and tease Elise Catherine. But she could provide no answers.

In due course the identity of *FB* would arouse the curiosity of Elise's daughter, Elisabeth Mariette Thérèse von Deppe. Aged twenty-three at the time of her grandmother's death, she was attractive, vivacious and flirtatious, even more so than either of her forebears, it was claimed in some of the salons of Berlin. Pursued by a covey of young men, she had already become a cultivated and deep-thinking woman, moving easily – without her mother's assistance – among sophisticated women, discussing philosophy one moment, Beethoven and Paganini another, and the latest fashion the next. She and her brother, Johannes Matthias Joseph, together with their cousins, Carl Nicolas Frederick and his younger sister, Alexandra Véronique Lorraine, all unattached, represented the new Herzberg generation, successors to the family name and responsible for taking the story of the von Deppes another step forward. Their narrative would unfold under the auspices of a new spirit in Germany, which would become unified in their lifetime. They and their descendants would become involved with the development of the new Prussia and its reforms for the welfare of the Prussian people, laying the foundations for a new modern state.

At the same time, in England, a new generation of the Whitfield family, from a new line, would begin to emerge, not content solely with the restoration of comfortable rural wealth but seeking to create new opportunities closer to power in London.

EPILOGUE

Don Alfonso Ordóñez returned to Spain after the celebration in Berlin of the life of his muse. He died eight years later. His paintings never enjoyed acclaim in his lifetime, but came to public attention after the First World War. A few years later they were forgotten again, until the late 1960s. They are now much sought-after. The two portraits still hanging at Herzberg are considered the finest he ever painted.

* * * * *

Sir Charles Gray, after his parting from the bewitching Countess Arabella von Deppe, had married The Honourable Philomena Barron. They had one child. Three years later Gray and his wife separated, on grounds of incompatibility. They lived apart for the rest of his life, during which time he had several mistresses. His son, William, lived with his mother until he was twenty-one and upon his father's death inherited the Gray estate. Shortly before he died, Gray told William that Arabella von Deppe had been his only true love and that parting from her had been his life's greatest regret.

* * * * *

King Frederick William III reigned until his death in 1840. His eldest son, also Frederick William, reigned for the next twenty-one years; his second son, William, became King of Prussia in 1861 and the first German Emperor and head of state of a united Germany in 1871. William's son, Frederick William, succeeded him in 1888 for 99 days, followed the same year by his grandson, also William, who led Germany into the First World War.

* * * * *

Anton Kiefer stayed in Spain for several years before deciding to return to London, where several years later he was convicted of a homosexual relationship and sent to prison. He died shortly before his release.

* * * * *

Sophie, Lady Whitfield, widow of the late Sir George Whitfield, Arabella's brother, died in London of old age. Their son, Robert Stephen, who failed in adulthood to enjoy good health, never married; her daughter, Alice, by her first husband, did. Alice had no surviving children and died in wealthy obscurity.

* * * * *

Hanne, Arabella's faithful maid, remained at Herzberg, living in a small house on the estate with her memories of her mistress, and sometimes playing with Arabella's grandchildren. She died in her sleep in the spring of 1818.

* * * * *

Several years after the death of her husband, Count Sokolov, the Countess Sokolova remarried into the powerful Razumovsky family. She died two years after Arabella.

* * * * *

Before Robert and Emily Whitfield and their son left Berlin in late 1853 to return to London, Count Joseph von Deppe arranged for them to visit Herzberg briefly.

The house deeply impressed the Whitfields. Though large it had an embracing warmth and intimacy, even more so than their own home, Meltwater Hall in Norfolk, of which Robert was the owner as a result of Arabella's earlier renunciation of her right to it on the death of her brother. Whilst the décor was outwardly German, the furnishings reflected the cosmopolitan background of a previous generation – French furnishings and an underlying trace of English culture and informality. The Whitfields were particularly struck by the beautiful *Spiegelsaal.* It was grand, elegant and ornate, but with a welcoming atmosphere. Emily sat down at the piano and played a few bars of Bach's *Prelude No. 1* from an open music score resting above the keyboard. The sound was perfect. They found the library fascinating with its extensive, varied collection of books and the small, intimate painting of the Countess Arabella arm in arm with the Empress Catherine of Russia, both in military uniform. Then there was the gallery with portraits of many generations of the von Deppe family. Robert and Emily were particularly absorbed by the painting of the young and beautiful Arabella at the time of her marriage to Count Carl Manfred von Deppe and the portrait of her later in life in Spain – still beautiful and elegant but informal. Her smile, as she looked up at the viewer from reading the final pages of a book, appeared almost as though she was about to speak.

As he, Emily and their son returned from the garden and the graves of Arabella and her husband, Robert Whitfield could not begin to understand how Arabella's dispute with her father over her wish to choose whom she should marry had produced such a remarkable outcome. He had already decided that on his return to the Foreign Office in London he would recommend to the Foreign Secretary, Lord Clarendon, who had facilitated and endorsed his journey to Berlin to pursue the story of Arabella Whitfield, that urgent steps be taken to repair the breach between the Whitfields and the von Deppes. The link between the two families might then be used to strengthen the British government's efforts to achieve closer ties and understanding between Germany and Britain in the interests of European peace, and so to avert the prospect of a future war between them. That effort would become of great importance in the years ahead.

APPENDIX 1
Whitfield and von Deppe Family Trees

The Whitfield Family

- Thérèse de Miron m (1) Sir Robert Whitfield m (2) Lady Barbara Ward
  - (by first marriage, to Thérèse de Miron):
    - George Whitfield m Mrs Sophie Charmley
      - Alice Charmley (stepdaughter)
      - Robert Stephen Whitfield
    - Arabella Whitfield m Count Carl Manfred von Deppe
  - (by second marriage, to Lady Barbara Ward):
    - George Robert Whitfield (born illegitimate) m Helen Darnton
      - Robert Emerson Whitfield m Emily Foster
        - Charles Whitfield

The von Deppe Family

- Gottfried Johann von Deppe m Anna Margaret von Nast
  - Frederick Ludwig von Deppe
  - Maria Louisa von Deppe m Vicomte Etienne de Vervins
    - Marie-Aurore de Vervins m Comte Armand de Puyraveau
      - Antoine de Puyraveau
  - Count Carl Manfred von Deppe m Arabella Whitfield
    - Count Frederick Daniel von Deppe m Jacqueline d'Anville
      - Carl Nicolas Frederick von Deppe
      - Alexandra Véronique von Deppe
    - Countess Elise Catherine Hildegard von Deppe m Joseph Lange von Schellenhorst
      - Elisabeth Mariette Thérèse von Schellenhorst
      - Johannes Matthias von Schellenhorst

APPENDIX 2

Composition of the Schloss Herzberger Camerata at its First Public Performance at the St Nicholas Church in Potsdam on Sunday the 18th of January 1767

*****

Arabella, Countess von Deppe
Founder, Harpsichord and Singer

Albrecht Bamberger
Leader and First Violin

Franz Lange
First Violin

Johann Schroeder
First Violin

Ingrid Schneider
Second Violin

Margarethe Dietrich
Second Violin

Anna Peters
Second Violin

Stefan Fuchs
Viola

Dorothea Winkler
Harpsichord, Flute and Singer

Ebert Franke
Oboe

Wilhelm Scholz
Cello

George Pfeiffer
Bassoon

Hans Roth
Bass Viol

Matthias Winkler
Double Bass

APPENDIX 3
List of Musical Pieces

A selection of the music that inspired the book:

Ludwig Abeille
Piano Concerto for Four Hands in D Major

Tommaso Albinoni
Oboe Concerto in D Minor
Sonata in C Major for Two Violins, Two Violas and Basso Continuo

Carl Philip Emmanuel Bach
Concerto for Cello in A Major
Keyboard Concerto in D Minor

Johann Christian Bach
Sinfonia Concertante in C Major
Six Keyboard Sonatas
Symphony for Winds No. 2

Johann Sebastian Bach
Brandenburg Concertos Nos. 1 and 5
Cantata No. 140, Wachet auf, ruft uns die Stimme
Cantata No. 156, Ich steh mit einem Fuß im Grabe
Concerto for Two Violins
Concerto for Violin and Oboe in C Minor
Harpsichord Concertos in D Minor, E Major, F Minor and D Major
Keyboard Concerto No. 3 in D Minor
Partita No. 4
Prelude and Fugue No. 1 in C Major from The Well-Tempered Clavier Book I
Prelude and Fugue No. 15 in G Major from The Well-Tempered Clavier Book II
Sinfonia Concertante in C Major

Ludwig van Beethoven
Bagatelle No. 25 (Für Elise)
Piano Concerto No. 1 in F Minor
Sonata for Cello and Piano No. 9

William Boyce
Symphony No. 7

Domenico Cimarosa
Piano Concerto in B-Flat Major

Arcangelo Corelli
Concerto Grosso in G Minor (Christmas Concerto)

Frederick the Great
Flute Concerto No. 2

George Frederick Handel
Alcina: Verdi prati
Messiah
Music for the Royal Fireworks
Oboe Concerto No. 2
Ode for St Cecelia's Day
Rinaldo: Lascia ch'io pianga
Sarabande
Semele: Where'er you walk
Xerxes: Ombra mai fou

Josef Haydn
Concerto for Keyboard in F Major
Harpsichord Concerto in D Major
Harpsichord Concerto No. 5 in C

Antonín Kraft
Cello Concerto in C Major

Nicola Matteis
Chaconne

Claudio Monteverdi
L'incoronazione di Poppea: Pur ti miro, pur ti godo
Vespers of the Blessed Virgin

Wolfgang Amadeus Mozart
Clarinet Quintet in A Major
Così fan tutte: Soave sia il vento
Flute Concerto
Great Mass in C Minor
Laudate Dominum
Nine Variations in D on a Minuet by Jean-Pierre Duport
Piano Concerto No. 16 in C Major
Quintet for Piano and Winds

Georg Muffat
Florilegium Secundum

Christoph Nichelmann
Concerto for Harpsichord in E Major

Johann Pachelbel
Canon and Gigue

Johann Joachim Quantz
Concerto for Flute, Strings and Basso Continuo in G Major

Jean-Philippe Rameau
Castor and Pollux: Tristes apprêts
Les Indes galantes: Les Sauvages
Les surprises de l'Amour

Agostino Steffani
Il trionfo del fato

Antonio Vivaldi
The Four Seasons
Giustino: Vedrò con mio diletto
Nulla in mundo pax sincera

ABOUT THE AUTHOR

Edward Glover was born in London in 1943. After gaining a history degree followed by an MPhil at Birkbeck College, London University, he embarked on a career in the British diplomatic service, during which his overseas postings included Washington DC, Berlin, Brussels and the Caribbean. He subsequently advised on foreign ministry reform in post-invasion Iraq, Kosovo and Sierra Leone. For seven years he headed a one-million-acre rainforest-conservation project in South America, on behalf of the Commonwealth Secretariat and the Guyana Government.

With an interest in 16th- and 18th-century history, baroque music and 18th-century art, Edward was encouraged by the purchase of two paintings and a passport to try his hand at writing historical fiction.

Edward and his wife, former Foreign & Commonwealth Office lawyer and leading international human rights adviser Dame Audrey Glover, now live in Norfolk, a place that gives him further inspiration for his writing. Edward sits on the board of trustees for Size of Wales and is a director of the Foreign & Commonwealth Office Association, an associate fellow of the University of Warwick's Yesu Persaud Centre for Caribbean Studies and a board member of The King's Lynn Preservation Trust.

When he isn't writing, Edward is an avid tennis player and – at the age of 71 – completed the 2014 London Marathon, raising almost £7,000 for Ambitious about Autism.

Printed in Great Britain
by Amazon

70215841R00265